Bad
Blood

Published by Kensington Publishing Corp.

Bad Blood

MARY MONROE

Dafina
Books

KENSINGTON BOOKS
http://www.kensingtonbooks.com

DAFINA BOOKS are published by

Kensington Publishing Corp.
119 West 40th Street
New York, NY 10018

All Kensington titles, imprints, and distributed lines are available at special quantity discounts for bulk purchases for sales promotion, premiums, fund-raising, educational, or institutional use.

Special book excerpts or customized printings can also be created to fit specific needs. For details, write or phone the office of the Kensington Special Sales Manager: Attn. Special Sales Department. Kensington Publishing Corp., 119 West 40th Street, New York, NY 10018. Phone: 1-800-221-2647.

Dafina and the Dafina logo Reg. U.S. Pat. & TM Off.

ISBN-13: 978-0-7582-7477-9
ISBN-10: 0-7582-7477-7
First Kensington Hardcover Edition: June 2015
First Kensington Trade Edition: May 2016
First Kensington Mass Market Edition: March 2018

eISBN-13: 978-1-61773-974-3
eISBN-10: 1-61773-974-X

10 9 8 7 6 5 4 3 2 1

Printed in the United States of America

This book is dedicated to my beloved aunt,
Mattie Whigham, and my awesome "big sister,"
Alice Curry.

Acknowledgments

I am so blessed to be a member of the Kensington Books family. Selena James is an awesome editor and a great friend. Thank you, Selena! Thanks to Steven Zacharius, Karen Auerbach, Leslie Irish-Underwood, the wonderful crew in the sales department, and everyone else at Kensington for working so hard for me.

Thanks to Lauretta Pierce for maintaining my Web site and sharing so many wonderful stories with me.

Thanks to the fabulous book clubs, the bookstores, my readers, and the magazine and radio interviewers for supporting me for so many years.

I never thought I'd be celebrating the release of my *seventeenth* book, especially when so many people predicted I'd be a one-book wonder. (The same ones ask for a free book each time I release a new one. . . . Ha-ha.)

I have one of the best literary agents on the planet, Andrew Stuart. Thank you, Andrew. Without you I would still be answering phones and running out to get coffee for my bosses at the utility company, instead of writing full-time.

Please continue to e-mail me at Authorauthor5409@aol.com, and visit my Web site at www.Marymonroe.org and my Facebook page.

All the best,

Mary Monroe
June 2015

Prologue

Rachel

*E*ven when I was a teenager, I was attracted to two types of men: the bad boys, whom my mother warned me about, and the Goody Two-shoes type, whom she found acceptable and hoped I would settle down with. I knew that if I ever brought a thug home, I'd never hear the end of it, so marrying one was out of the question. Despite my fairly rigid Christian upbringing, I planned to have as much fun with them on the down low as I could until an "acceptable" guy came along.

As for myself, I was a combination of a good girl trying to be bad and a bad girl trying to be good. I had decided early in life that it would be to my advantage to be a little of both, as long as I kept things in the proper perspective and behaved in an acceptable manner. I had a few problems with my temper in elementary and middle school. But by the time I got to high school, everybody who knew me stayed out of my way. I avoided trouble as much as I could, but there were times when trouble found me, anyway. Most of it was petty and was quickly forgotten by everyone involved. Despite the fact that I had a quick temper and was easily provoked, I was in the church and people wanted to be my friend, because they knew that I was loyal and sincere and could always be counted on in a time of need. Most of the people in my life liked me and treated me with respect. They knew that I could be their best friend, but I could also turn on a dime and be their worst enemy.

Life was still good to me, and I appreciated every day. I had it going on, and I was going to make sure I kept it going on as long as I could. I was a party girl who liked to drink, socialize, and make love—not always in that order. I was also practical and focused on self-improvement. I was willing to work hard to get the things I desired. I wanted what every other woman I knew wanted: security, a nice home, loyal friends, and a good-looking, intelligent, successful husband who would give me good-looking, intelligent, successful children. I didn't think I was asking for too much, but I knew that getting what I wanted was not going to be easy. I was an optimist, and I tried to look on the bright side of everything in every situation. But I was also a realist. I knew that there'd be times when things didn't go the way I wanted, no matter how hard I'd worked. I truly believed that most people eventually got what they deserved.

I didn't have a lot to work with as far as education and money were concerned, but I had the support of my family in most of my endeavors. Unfortunately, my family didn't want me to relocate from our small, sleepy country town in Alabama to the bustling Bay Area in California. But once I got a notion in me to do something, nobody could stop me, not even Mama.

"Girl, you ain't never even been out of the state of Alabama before. Why in the world would you want to move to a wild place like California?"

I looked my mother in the eye that Sunday afternoon, right after we'd spent three hours in church, and told her, "Because I want to." Despite Mama's ongoing protests and colorful descriptions of California—a "jungle" and "a Babylon" were my favorites—shortly after high school I packed up and took off, anyway.

It took a while and a lot of hard work for me to see some success, but the move turned out to be one of the smartest things I'd ever done. I continued my education, landed a dream job, and made some wonderful "big sister" friends, who eagerly took me under their wing, so to speak. With their guidance and support, I was able to experience a fun-filled life—temporarily losing my way a few times, though—continue to grow, and even exceed some of my own expectations.

After I had spent only a few years of living the California lifestyle, everything seemed to be going the way I'd hoped it would—and my family became very supportive. Once I had established myself and had secured my future, the folks back home sat back and waited and prayed for me to get married. I wanted to get married, but I wanted it to happen at the right time and with the right man.

Despite California being the land of plenty, when it came to relationships, finding a good man was not easy. There were a lot of men in my life, though. Unfortunately, most of them were usually the type I wouldn't even consider a future with, so they came and went. The ones I did want a future with didn't want a future with me for a variety of reasons. One thought I was too independent. He even told me to my face that he needed a wife who would *always* let him make the decisions in the relationship. Another one told me he would never marry a woman like me, because I was too much of a challenge. He didn't elaborate, and I didn't ask him to. One man whom I cared about a lot more than any of the others told me on our first, and last, date that he hated kids and that to make sure he never had any, he had already scheduled a vasectomy. The one after him bragged about the six children he had by six different women, children with whom he didn't spend time and to whom he provided financial support only when he "felt like it."

Even with the numerous obstacles I encountered, I still managed to enjoy a lot of fun-filled nights of passion along the way. But I realized that a woman like me could get only so much mileage out of "fun" and that I'd surpassed that limit many times over. I was still in my twenties by then, with a long life ahead of me, but I wanted to be young enough to enjoy an active life with the children I couldn't wait to give birth to. The time had come for me to settle down with the right man and start my real future.

Seth Garrett, the "acceptable" man—according to my standards, as well as those of my hard-to-please mother—came along right on time. My family could not have been happier, and neither could I. . . .

Chapter I

Seth

March 2000 . . .

OUR FLIGHT FROM CALIFORNIA'S BAY AREA TO Mobile, Alabama, landed a little after 11:00 a.m. Even though it was springtime, the heat was sweltering. Rachel and I started sweating right away as we made our way to the baggage claim area, dodging some of the most aggressive flies and gnats I'd ever encountered. I didn't know what to expect next.

Rachel had told me that Coffeeville, Alabama, where she was born and raised, was a one-horse, hick town about an hour's drive from the airport. But because I loved Rachel and couldn't wait to meet her family and marry her, I had agreed to accompany her to a place where I already felt like an alien.

We picked up our rental car and stopped for lunch at an all-you-can-eat buffet a short drive from the airport.

We stuffed ourselves with some of our favorites: collard greens, mac and cheese, corn bread, and yams.

After our feast, we waddled back to our rental car and headed for the freeway. It led us to the tree-lined, gravel-and-tar route that would take us all the way to our destination. For the first twenty minutes, all we saw were four-legged creatures darting across the road and shabbily dressed folks riding bareback on mules, dragging themselves along on tractors, and piled up in old trucks.

"Damn, baby. How could such a sophisticated sister like you have come from such humble beginnings?" I joked. I had to swerve to avoid hitting a deer that had jumped out of nowhere. "Shit!" I hollered.

"Let me drive. I'm used to these roads," Rachel insisted, chuckling.

"Woman, you sit back and relax! I've got everything under control," I said, speaking louder than I meant to.

"All right then. Let me know if you change your mind." A few minutes later Rachel leaned back in her seat and dozed off.

I admired the scenery and listened to a country-western radio station for a while. It didn't take long for me to get tired of all that caterwauling. I turned off the radio and concentrated on the road for the next fifteen or so miles. When Rachel woke up about twenty minutes later, she sat up and rubbed her eyes.

"We're almost there," she said with a yawn.

"Huh?" We were now deep into a semirural area. We had just passed a tipsy shack that had a mule wagon in the front yard. "Your family lives near *here?*"

"Right around the bend," Rachel said proudly. "Baby, you're going to love it down here. You're going to see what the simple life is really all about. Everything down here is so different from things in California. Especially my family . . ."

"This is not what I expected," I admitted. I suddenly got nervous and concerned. Was Rachel not the woman I thought she was, after all? I had fallen in love with an intelligent, sophisticated woman with long black hair, big brown eyes, and cinnamon-brown skin to die for. She was just as beautiful on the inside. She was warm, generous, and caring—everything I wanted in a woman. What about her family? Just how "simple" were they? What if she was the only rose in a garden of thorns? I couldn't imagine my family accepting a bunch of illiterate, backwoods, barefoot in-laws who were still living in the dark ages. My marrying into such a family would kill Mother!

Rachel directed me to pull up and stop in the driveway of a small, green-shingled house with a neat little front lawn and a gray glider on the wraparound porch. My mouth dropped open when a stout woman in a shabby housedress, who looked like a middle-aged version of Rachel, shot out the front door in her ashy bare feet like the house was on fire. I quickly closed my mouth as I parked the car and turned off the motor. Rachel and I piled out at the same time. Birds were circling above, and more flies and gnats were buzzing around our heads, so I moved with caution. I didn't know what to expect now, but nothing would have surprised me. I had to ask myself, *What have I gotten myself into?* With my lips pressed tightly together and my jaw twitching, I took a few steps and stepped into a puddle of brown slime.

"Rachel! My baby's come home!" the woman yelled. She ran off the porch and gave Rachel a bear hug. "Oh, honey, it's so good to have you home again! And just look at you—thin as a rail!"

"Mama, this is Seth Garrett," Rachel said, introducing me as she pulled me toward her by my hand.

Mrs. McNeal shaded her beady eyes and looked at me for a few moments, smiling her approval. Then she wrapped her arms around me and gave me such an aggressive hug, my chest felt like she had sat on it. "My goodness, what a good-looking young man! Just look at you! Your hair is all nice and neat, and you have bright eyes and skin as smooth as brown silk." She reared back and looked me up and down. I was surprised when she slid her hand up the side of my arm. "You just as strapping as them guys on the TV. Ain't no flab on you or nothing!"

"I'm so pleased to finally meet you, Mrs. McNeal," I managed to say when she released me. "Rachel's told me so much about you, I feel like I know you already." That was a big, fat lie. The sweet, charming Southern woman I had pictured in my mind since I'd proposed to Rachel was not the ignorant-sounding, countrified frump standing in front of me now.

"I hope she didn't tell you too much, son. The Lord's still working on me, so don't be surprised if I ain't what you expect." Mrs. McNeal looked from Rachel to me and back. "Y'all, don't just stand here, looking like lost sheep. Get on in the house before them mosquitoes get wind of y'all!"

I retrieved our two suitcases from the backseat of the car, and Mrs. McNeal led us into the house. She held on to Rachel's hand so tightly, you would have thought that she was afraid Rachel was going to run off into the bushes by the side of the house.

The house looked shabby on the outside, but everything inside was neat and orderly. The living room had dark oak furniture and a brown crushed-velvet couch with a matching love seat, and beige draperies covered every window. Colorful area rugs covered most of the linoleum floor; crocheted doilies were on the end tables and the coffee table. One wall contained pictures from top to bottom of Rachel and her family and a large gaudy velvet illustration of Jesus hugging a child. Even though I had never been to this location before in my life, it was so cozy and homey, I immediately felt so comfortable, I didn't want to leave and return to the madness of California. But that feeling didn't last long.

"Where is everybody?" Rachel asked, looking around.

Before her mother could respond, a tall, good-looking dude in his twenties, with Hershey Bar–colored skin, tight black eyes, and fluffy black hair, slunk into the living room. He could not have looked more countrified if he tried. He was barefoot, too, and he wore a plaid flannel shirt with the sleeves missing and blue overalls.

"Ernest!" Rachel hollered. She ran up to him and wrapped her arms around his waist. "Baby," she continued, turning to me, "this is my brother." Ernest looked like he was in a trance. There was absolutely no expression whatsoever on his face.

I set our luggage down and reached out to shake the brother's hand. To my surprise, he just stood there, staring straight ahead. He didn't shake my hand or even acknowledge me.

"Uh, Ernest, this is your future brother-in-law," Mrs. McNeal said in a nervous tone of voice.

Ernest blinked in my direction. Then he shrugged and eased over to the couch and plopped down. He began to look at me with contempt, and that certainly made me uneasy.

"He's a little on the quiet side," Mrs. McNeal explained, giving Ernest a dry look, which he ignored.

"But he's harmless," Rachel whispered in my ear. "You'll get used to him," she added, speaking in her regular tone of voice. Then she turned to her mother. "Where's Janet and Aunt Hattie, Mama?"

"Janet's taking a nap, and your auntie is still at the Piggy Wiggly, getting a few things for dinner," Mrs. McNeal explained, turning to me with a huge smile. "Seth, I am so glad to finally meet you. I always knew Rachel would land a man like you. God sure is good."

"Who's out there making all that noise?" The voice coming from another part of the house was so loud and angry, it made me jump. "I know y'all out there talking trash about me!"

"That's my sister, Janet," Rachel said, whispering again. Then she quickly left the room.

While she was gone, Ernest remained on the couch. He lifted a magazine off the coffee table, flipped it open, and began to stare at a page without moving his eyes.

"Seth, from that blank look on your face, I suspect you can't wait to get some food into your belly. It'll be a little while before dinner's ready. I just put the corn bread in the oven. I started cooking last night, all for you and Rachel. I hope you like deviled duck eggs and poke salad," Rachel's mother told me.

I had never eaten a goddamned duck egg before in my life. And I had no idea what poke salad was. I had a feeling I was not going to enjoy either one. Since I couldn't say what was on my mind, I said what I thought Mrs. McNeal wanted to hear. "Yum-yum . . ."

"Good. I know you must be tired, too. Why don't you sit down and rest your legs?" Mrs. McNeal waved me over to a wing chair facing the couch.

I didn't bother to tell Mrs. McNeal that Rachel and I had eaten a huge lunch, and I certainly didn't want her to know how terrified I was to hear that she had prepared duck eggs and that mysterious poke salad just for us. The last thing I wanted to do was get on my future mother-in-law's shit list. I was still thinking about Ernest's odd behavior and the menacing voice of Janet, but I managed to sit down with a smile on my face.

A few minutes later Rachel returned. Shuffling behind her was a young woman, also in her twenties, in a brown corduroy dress and men's house shoes. She looked a lot like Rachel, too, except she was slightly taller. There was a dazed expression on her face as she looked me up and down.

"Honey, this is my baby sister, Janet," Rachel said, introducing her.

I leaped up and stumbled over to Janet with the biggest smile I could manage, even though all kinds of questions, concerns, and disappointments were bouncing off the walls inside my head. "I'm glad to finally meet you, Janet," I said as I reached out to embrace her.

"Don't you tetch me!" she yelled with a Southern drawl that was so thick, it sounded fake. "I know you the one that's been sneaking into my room in the middle of the night and playing with my titties!"

"Janet, this is my fiancé, Seth. He's never been here before." Rachel didn't even bother to hide her exasperation. She turned to me with an apologetic look on her face. "Honey, my brother and my sister were both born with a, uh, few problems. But they're just fine, as long as they take their medication."

"Okay," was all I could think to say. *Medication? Both of Rachel's siblings have to take medication? For what?* My chest tightened, and my brain felt as if it had frozen. *Uh-oh. What have I gotten myself into?* I wondered.

Chapter 2

Rachel

SETH OFFERED TO TAKE OUR LUGGAGE TO MY OLD BED-room, but Mama insisted on taking it herself. Naturally, I followed behind her, because I could tell from the look on her face that she had something to say to me that she didn't want Seth to hear. I was right. The moment we got inside the neatly organized room, with its roll-away bed, mismatched dressers, and frilly yellow curtains, she set the luggage on the floor, shut the door, and lit into me.

"How come Seth is looking like somebody knocked the wind out of him?"

"What do you mean, Mama?" I asked dumbly.

"What's wrong with you, girl?" Mama snapped, shaking her finger in my face. "Didn't you see the look on his face when Ernest refused to shake his hand?"

"I didn't notice."

"Well, I know you noticed the way he looked when

Janet yelled out and then when she came into the room. You ain't blind."

"Now that you mentioned it, Seth did seem a bit surprised, I guess."

"Surprised? The way that man was looking, you could have knocked him over with a feather. If I didn't know no better, I'd swear you ain't told him about our family."

"I haven't told him everything," I muttered. "I didn't want him to get the wrong impression about Janet and Ernest before he met them. I wanted to wait until we got here."

Mama gasped so hard, she choked on some air. I clapped her on the back, and as soon as she composed herself, she continued. "Oh, my Lord in heaven! All this time he thought we was just a typical American family?"

"Mama, as far as I'm concerned, we are just a typical American family." I began to wring my hands and pace the floor.

"Stand still, because you making me even more upset." I stopped in my tracks, but Mama still seemed just as upset. "There ain't no such thing as a 'typical American family,' unless you count the one on *Leave It to Beaver.* This is a new day. Even Bill Cosby's TV family *and* his real-life family had problems, but they had problems most people can relate to. You can't hide things from Seth before y'all even get married!"

"Mama, you are overreacting. I didn't try to hide anything from Seth."

"Oh, yes you did! You hid something important from him about the family he's going to marry into. By not telling him, that's the same as hiding it! Oh, Lord! How come you didn't tell Seth about your brother and your sister before now?" Mama hissed. She placed her hands on her hips.

"Uh . . . uh . . . it never came up," I said, fumbling.

"What do you mean, 'it never came up'? How could you not *bring* it up? The problems we got ain't the kind you can hide for too long."

"I was waiting for the right time to tell him," I said, sitting down hard on the bed, wringing my hands some more. They had begun to sweat, and so had my armpits. "But I'm sure it won't be a problem. Seth is a very understanding man. And he's in the church."

Mama looked at me and shook her head. "Lord knows how his family is going to react when they hear. All the stuff you told me about how uppity they are . . . lawyers and such. And with him having a mama that don't do nothing but play bridge, suck up daiquiris, and socialize, I can tell you now she ain't going to ease into this."

"Mama, why are you so concerned about what Seth and his family will think about Ernest and Janet? They won't have to deal with them."

"Rachel, I didn't raise you to be no fool. You know how folks around here have always looked at our family like we was *all* crazy," Mama said gently.

"Crazy? Nobody in our family is crazy, Mama," I protested.

"You can call it whatever you want, but when it comes to most of the folks in this town, *crazy* is the first word out of their mouth when they talk about the McNeal family." Mama snorted and shook her head. "Speaking of crazy, how is that baby brother of mine doing out there in California?"

"Uncle Albert is doing just fine." I saw no need to say more, but Mama wanted to know more.

"Is he still fornicating with men?"

"He is still dating men, Mama. He lives with one, and he's very happy. He said that he hopes to get married someday."

Mama looked elated, but not for long. "Say what? Do you mean to tell me the boy is going to come to his senses and marry a woman someday? See there! I knew if I prayed long and hard enough, Albert would straighten hisself out!"

"Uh, yes, he wants to get married. But . . . to a man. The politicians keep talking about making same-sex marriages legal in California, and he's real excited about it."

Mama stared at me with her mouth hanging open, as if I had just turned purple. "I thought I had heard everything, but I never thought I'd hear something as ungodly as men marrying men, and women marrying women. Lord, have mercy! What is this world coming to? Lord knows what my friends will say when and if Albert ups and marries a man!"

I shook my head. "Mama, stop worrying about what people will say. These narrow-minded, ignorant, countrified folks in Coffeeville don't know any better. I'm sure our family is not the only one you know with a few simpleminded people."

Mama shot me a hot look. "There's a lot more to it than a 'few simpleminded people' in this family, girl."

"What I meant was—"

Mama silenced me by waving her finger in my face. "I don't care what you meant. Hush up and let me talk! You can stand here in them white sandals if you want to and act like you don't know no better, but I know you do. The problem in our family goes *waaay* back. I can remember your great-granddaddy doing some of the same outlandish stuff your sister and brother do. I'll never forget how he showed up naked at my high school graduation."

"Oh. I didn't know about that," I mumbled.

"And you didn't know about your late grandmama's late twin sister, who used to eat rocks and live grasshoppers."

"No, I didn't. But those people are deceased, and like I

said, neither Seth nor any of his family will have to mingle with Janet or Ernest."

"It ain't just Ernest and Janet you'll need to tell Seth about. The bad seeds in our family ain't all dead. You got a cousin named Milton. He's just three years younger than me. You was a baby when he was around, so you wouldn't remember him. Anyway, he's over there in the state hospital, wrapped up in a straitjacket, as we speak. He's so bad, he's been locked up in that asylum most of his life."

"What did he do?"

"You name it, he done it. But the man finally took action when Milton busted into a white woman's house and broke a claw hammer over her head. They tried to say he ravaged her, too, but Milton had never had no interest in sex, and they couldn't prove he touched that white woman's tail. And I bet she wasn't even clean."

I looked off into space. "Mama, I know what you're thinking," I muttered. I turned back to face her and gave her a sharp look. "*My* children will be fine. There are all kinds of medication and treatments and therapy available these days. If, and it's a very big *if*, my children have problems, Seth and I will deal with them together."

Mama gave me a pitiful look. "I sure hope you're right, baby. If you ain't, I can tell you right now that you can forget about living happily ever after with Seth. . . ."

Chapter 3

Seth

I WAS SO NERVOUS AND DUMBFOUNDED, I COULD BARELY remain seated. Ernest was still sitting on the couch. No matter how hard I tried to get him to talk, he continued to act like a mute. A few more minutes dragged by.

My stomach was in knots, and my head was throbbing like somebody had attacked it with a paddle. The inside of my mouth was as dry as sandpaper. A belch suddenly flew out my mouth, and I tasted some of the heavy, greasy food we had eaten for lunch, mixed in with the bile that had risen in my throat. I reached into my jacket pocket and pulled out a stick of gum and stuck it in my mouth. As soon as I started chewing, my bladder began to demand attention. It was a one-story house, so I knew that it wouldn't be hard for me to locate the bathroom, but I attempted to get the information from Ernest, anyway.

"Which way is the restroom?" I asked, rising.

He looked at me and blinked a few times and didn't

say a word. He returned his attention to the magazine still in his hand.

I looked at my watch, wondering why Rachel was taking so long to return. I had no idea where Janet was, and I was in no hurry to find out. The last thing I needed was to run into her and have her say something crazy again. My head was spinning. Rachel had some explaining to do! Like, why hadn't she told me that *both* of her only two siblings were mentally challenged?

The bathroom was just as neat and spotless as the living room. Frilly yellow curtains covered the window, and bright yellow towels and a shower curtain made the room look quite impressive. I wondered how Rachel's mother managed to keep such a neat house with Janet and Ernest around. I had a feeling those two didn't do much housecleaning, or anything other than what I'd seen so far.

It was hard for me to contain my frustration and the feeling that I had been duped into a relationship under false pretenses. I let out a few obscene words under my breath and balled my hand into a fist. I wanted to punch the wall as I wondered again what I had gotten myself into! Well, since I couldn't hit the wall, which looked so thin I was sure I'd leave a hole, I just stood there for a moment, shaking my head.

I glanced at my watch and realized I'd been standing there, cussing to myself and shaking my head, for a couple of minutes. I unzipped my fly and stood over the commode and emptied my bladder with a groan. I rubbed the back of my head and chewed frantically on that stick of gum. Even after I had completed my business and had rinsed out my mouth, I still felt like hell. My head was throbbing even more now. This was a major concern for me, because the only time I ever had headaches as bad as this one was when I had to deal with my son's mean-spirited mother.

"Get a grip," I said to myself in a low voice. "Rachel's the woman I love and plan to marry." Somehow I managed to calm myself down, and I prayed I wouldn't encounter anything else that would make me want to punch a wall.

I flushed the toilet and made sure I put the seat back down before I returned to the living room. I was pleased to see that Rachel and her mother had come back and were now seated side by side on the couch with Ernest, I sat down on a bamboo chair, facing them. I was glad that my seat was close to the door, in case something really weird happened and I had to bolt. Ernest was still staring at a page in that magazine.

"How long are you two lovebirds going to stay with us?" Mrs. McNeal wanted to know, looking directly at me. Then she whirled around to face Rachel. "Brother Hamilton is killing a hog next Saturday. I'm sure he'd like to have y'all come to the cookout. He promised to give me the chitlins and hog maws to cook for y'all before you leave to go back to California."

A hog butchering? A cookout with crazy people running around loose? I couldn't think of anything I wanted to attend less. I could not imagine myself eating chitlins. I didn't even know what hog maws were, but I had a feeling they were some part of the hog that was just as gruesome as chitlins, maybe even more so. I had never gnawed on such primitive items in my life, and I was not about to start now! I felt like I had stumbled into *The Twilight Zone,* and I wanted to get my ass out of this place as fast as I could. Did I really love Rachel enough to deal with all the horrors I had encountered so far? I wondered. I shook that thought out of my mind, because I was not ready for the answer.

"Mama, I already told you we can stay only until Sunday," Rachel said, giving me one of her prizewinning smiles. "But if Seth wants to stay longer, I'm sure we can rearrange our schedules."

"Uh . . . no! We have to go back home on Sunday," I said quickly, throwing up my hand for emphasis. "I have several important meetings with clients on Monday."

Mrs. McNeal gave me a disappointed look. "Well, we can all have a real good visit in three days, I guess." She turned to Rachel. "Did I tell you that Maisy Thigpen died last week? That knot on the side of her foot wasn't no bunion, like I told you. It was bone cancer." She tilted her head to the side, then shook it and looked at me again. "Seth, I'm sure your mama done told you before that life is so short. Don't waste no time, because that's the only thing we can't never get back once we done used it. Live each day like it's your last, because one day it will be."

I had no idea where this conversation was going. And since I didn't want to sound as exasperated as I felt, I decided to say something simple. "You are so right, Mrs. McNeal."

"You can call me Essie Mae," she told me. "As far as I'm concerned, you already family."

"Yes . . . ma'am," I managed to say, hoping nobody noticed the uncertainty in my voice. A sharp pain shot through my chest, because my thoughts were all over the place. The inside of my head was ringing like a steel drum. I didn't even want to think about how my opinionated, outspoken friends would behave around Rachel's family when— if—they ever met them. I'd be on defense for the rest of my life if they did.

Janet came back into the room and sat down on the arm of the love seat, staring directly at me. I couldn't even imagine what was going through her mind, because the few times she'd spoken, she hadn't made any sense.

"Grandpa Alex told me you was going to go to the Devil," she said, still looking at me.

"Now, you behave yourself, Janet. You know your granddaddy died when you was a baby," Mrs. McNeal said in a gentle voice.

"I know he died, but he comes to me at night sometimes," Janet said.

With all I had to deal with already, the last thing I wanted to be concerned about was a ghost!

"I'm going to go to my room and . . . *masturbate,*" Janet announced in a voice so loud, it made my ears ring. She leaped up from her seat and sprinted from the room, laughing maniacally.

My jaw dropped. Rachel gave me a helpless look and shrugged. "Don't pay my sister any attention," she told me. "She's confused."

We spent the next half hour or so listening to Mrs. McNeal go on and on about funerals she'd recently attended, who got divorced, who was cheating on their spouse, and her health. About ten minutes later Janet returned to the room in a white nightgown that was so flimsy, it left nothing to the imagination. The naked body of a woman I had just met was the last thing I had expected to see. Janet looked flushed and satisfied, the same way Rachel looked after I made love to her.

"I feel so much better and so relaxed now," Janet swooned as she wiped her face with the back of her hand. Rubbing her crotch, she sat down on a footstool near a small television set in the front part of the room. "Masturbating sure takes the edge off me."

I thought Rachel or her mother would respond to what Janet had just said, or to the fact that I could see her private parts, but they didn't. They resumed their conversation about sick people, funerals, and whatnot. I made a few obligatory comments throughout the conversation, but during that whole time, Ernest continued to stare at his magazine and Janet didn't say another word.

"Uh, Rachel, baby, don't you think we should unpack?" I suggested. I was so uncomfortable by now; my butt was throbbing almost as hard as my head. I couldn't wait to get out of the living room so I could have some space and reorganize my thoughts.

"I already did that. I'm going to help Mama get dinner ready. Why don't you sit here and chat with Ernest?" Rachel said, wobbling up off the couch. She and her mother left the room again.

I took a deep breath, rubbed my forehead, and forced myself to talk again. "So, Ernest, do you play football or fish . . . or anything?" I began, fumbling with my words. Silence. I cleared my throat and looked at Janet. "Janet, what do you like to do?"

She gave me a thoughtful look, and then she scratched the side of her neck and remained silent.

"Okay." I cleared my throat and took a very deep breath. "I guess I'll go outside and admire the scenery." I didn't wait for a response. I went out to the porch and looked around the area. I liked the rustic splendor I saw, but I could not figure out how people could be happy in a place like Coffeeville. Rachel's family had a fairly nice house, but the neighbors on both sides and the one directly across the road lived in double-wide trailers. I couldn't understand such a thing in a region known for its devastating tornadoes. Some of the trailers looked so flimsy, I was surprised that a strong wind had not blown them down already.

Squirrels scurried back and forth in the yard and on the porch. A hoot owl perched on a branch of the pecan tree in the front yard stared at me, and a large, dusty lizard crawled up the porch steps toward my feet. I jumped out of the way in the nick of time. A three-legged dog wandered into the yard and up on the porch and stopped in front of me. When I leaned down to pet it, it growled and ran away.

I noticed the neighbors gazing at me from a window in the trailer across the street, so I went back inside. Janet and Ernest were still sitting in the same spots, looking as inanimate as statues. With a heavy sigh and a groan I didn't even attempt to hide, I sat back down in the same chair I had left a few minutes ago.

I spent the next fifteen minutes staring from Ernest to Janet, and they never said a word.

Dinner was agonizing. Rachel and her mother did most of the talking.

"Is Seth always this quiet?" Mrs. McNeal asked Rachel, giving me a sly look as she dumped more fried okra onto her plate.

"Mama, this man talks a blue streak! He's just tired," Rachel answered.

"Cat got his tongue," Janet finally said. That made everybody at the table laugh, even me. But I had nothing to laugh about.

When Rachel and I finally excused ourselves and went into her old bedroom, I closed the door and turned to her. "Woman, you've got some explaining to do," I told her, shaking a finger in her face.

"Oh." She let out a heavy sigh and started undressing. "You mean about my brother and my sister?"

"Yes!"

"Well, Ernest is autistic, and Janet is a paranoid schizophrenic. I think she's bipolar, too. They were born that way," she said. And in the most casual voice I'd ever heard her use, she told me, "They have their good days and their bad days." That was all she said. From the way she sat down on the bed and removed her shoes and started massaging her toes, I had a feeling she had nothing else to say on this subject. But I had more to say.

"Why in the world did you let me find out this way and *after* I asked you to marry me?"

She looked up at me with a surprised expression on her face. "I probably should have said something sooner, but I didn't think it was that big of a deal. I mean, no family is perfect."

"Is there anything else you haven't told me?" I sat down on the bed next to her with my hand on her knee.

"Like what?" she asked with an indifferent look and a shrug.

"Do you have any more family secrets?" It was a loaded question, but I couldn't think of a more politically correct way to ask it.

"My uncle Albert is gay," she said.

"What . . . I knew that already. That's nothing to me! I have a lot of gay associates," I said. "I don't have a problem with homosexuality."

"Then you won't have a problem with Ernest and Janet, right?"

I honestly didn't know what to say, so I said the first thing that came to my mind. "I'll try not . . . uh . . ." I paused and gave Rachel a guarded look. "I don't know."

Chapter 4

Seth

I DIDN'T SLEEP MORE THAN THREE HOURS THAT FIRST night. THERE was enough on my mind to keep me awake, but outside the bedroom window, crickets and all kinds of other night creatures were making enough noise to wake the dead people in the cemetery a few yards down the road.

I finally drifted off to sleep around 2:00 a.m., but a rooster started crowing at the crack of dawn and woke me up. In addition to that, one of the neighbors was cutting wood using a chain saw. The second day was even more difficult to get through. I was in desperate need of some very strong drinks. The only way I was going to be able to survive this visit was if I got drunk and stayed drunk until we left. Unfortunately, the strongest beverage Rachel's mother had in the house was buttermilk.

Rachel got up before me and went to help her mother prepare breakfast. By the time I took a shower around seven thirty, dressed in some casual clothes, and entered the kitchen, everybody was already seated at the table. By now, I didn't even care if anybody noticed the tight look on my face. I had a feeling it was going to get much tighter before the visit was over.

"Morning, all," I grunted, barely moving my lips. I plopped down hard on a chair with wobbly legs between Rachel and Ernest. He looked at me and blinked. Janet had already begun to eat. Her mouth was full of food, but she muttered some gibberish under her breath and gave me a blank stare.

"You look well rested," Essie Mae told me. "I know you ain't used to all this clean country air, but it'll do more good for your health than anything y'all got in California. All that smog and them earthquakes would drive me crazy!"

"Seth, Mama sprinkled the bacon with a little sugar, the way you like it," Rachel said, placing a hand on my shoulder. "Eat up, because today is going to be real busy. The phone's been ringing off the hook with folks calling who want to meet you."

"Yeah," I muttered. I managed to eat a couple of scrambled duck eggs, half a slice of toast, and a spoonful of grits.

Around 9:00 a.m., I joined the family at the kitchen table again. A few other relatives, neighbors, and friends started coming in through the front and back doors like nobody's business. They all entered the kitchen. Aunt Hattie snatched a biscuit off the table and the rest of them just stood around talking. It seemed like the main thing each one was concerned about was the "cute and smart" children Rachel and I were going to have.

Irene Price, the elderly, beady-eyed woman who lived in the trailer across the street, said something that sent the conversation in a totally different direction. "Rachel, I just hope none of your young'ns turn out the way poor Albert did." After shaking her head a few times, she turned to me and said in a low voice, "I guess you know about Albert's mental condition. He likes men, and everybody knows that is not normal."

Not normal? I couldn't believe my ears. I couldn't ignore Irene's comment. "I'm sorry, but I'm going to disagree with you on that, ma'am. Where Rachel and I live, being gay is almost as 'normal' as being straight," I defended, speaking in a deeper and firmer tone of voice than usual. One thing I didn't want any of these people to think was that I was a wimp who was too meek to speak my mind. However, I had to bite my tongue to keep from saying what I thought a real "mental condition" was. So far, not a single person had mentioned that Janet and Ernest had been sitting on the living room couch, staring off into space for the past hour, and that neither one had said a word the whole time.

"Harrumph! Ain't nothing going on in a nutcase city like Berkeley—or should I call it Berserk-eley?—that would surprise me," hollered a middle-aged cousin whose name I couldn't remember.

I knew that if I remained at the table any longer, I'd say something I'd regret. I forced a smile and excused myself to go use the bathroom. As soon as I got inside, I took a few deep breaths to compose myself. I made sure the door was shut before I pulled my cell phone out of my pocket and called my brother Josh in Berkeley. I was happy when he answered on the first ring, but he was not happy that I had disturbed him so early in the morning.

"Do you know what time it is?" he growled.

"I'm sorry. I forgot about the time difference, and I couldn't wait any longer to talk to you. Man, you are not going to believe the mess I've stumbled into down here in these damn woods!"

"Oh, shit! Are you all right? Please don't tell me you've already had a run-in with one of those racist peckerwood cops! I told you not to leave here with all those expensive clothes and shoes! They'll make you out to be a criminal for sure—"

"Shut up and let me talk," I ordered as I rubbed the back of my head and breathed through my mouth. "We haven't had any trouble like that. This is much worse." I had not shed any tears in years and didn't want to now, so I blinked hard to hold back the ones that had just pooled in my eyes.

"What's the matter? Is Rachel all right?"

"Rachel's fine. Look, bro, this is a serious situation. Her . . . Rachel's family is not what I expected. There's some issues with, um, their bloodline."

"Oh really? Hmm. That doesn't surprise me. I didn't want to bring up the subject, but some of those small-town Southern folks are like rabbits. They are known for *inbreeding!* When I was in the navy, I met all kinds of dudes from the South. Half of them had married first cousins, and one dude had the nerve to tell me that his own sister had been his first lover! Now tell me this. What are we talking about here? Clubfeet, harelips, cone heads, crossed eyes?"

"I don't know about any of them having any of those afflictions. I've met only Rachel's sister and brother and a few of her other relatives so far. Her brother looks like he's in a continuous daze, and her sister acts like she's been sipping on a strange potion that makes her say shit you wouldn't believe. An old dude in a wheelchair named Cousin Woodie mumbled at a picture on the wall for thirty minutes straight a little while ago. He's in his late eighties, so that could be his age. Aunt Hattie is a real piece of work, too. She's so nosy, bossy, and crude, it would make your head spin. I'm telling you, man, this family is *off the chart!*"

"Oh. So we're talking about some mental issues here, right?"

"Exactly."

"Mental illness is quite common, you know."

"Well, I don't want to have anything to do with a bunch of crazy people!" I said in a low voice.

"Calm down, baby brother. You just met Rachel's people. Do you think you're being fair to them, Rachel, and yourself by dismissing them so soon?"

"Marrying into a family with problems this serious could be the biggest mistake I ever made. You know how hard I've been working these past few years to get my life in order. I don't think I can deal with a load this heavy!"

"You've got a point there. I'd probably react the same way as you if I faced the same situation. What baffles me is that Rachel is so open and up front about everything. Two minutes after I met her, she told me her uncle Albert was gay. Didn't she tell you any of this other shit about her family beforehand?"

"Not a word. All these years we've been together and she has not told me a damn thing about her family being full of nutcases. And guess what? It's not just on her mama's side! The mumbling old dude in the wheelchair I mentioned, that's her daddy's mother's brother."

"His problem could be related to his age. You just said that."

"True. But it gets worse." I paused long enough to catch my breath. "Rachel's aunt Hattie told me that Rachel's father's brother died in a mental institution. So this shit *is* coming at me from both sides of her family tree! Marrying Rachel would be like moving into a burning house."

"That's not too cool. I still don't think you should dismiss Rachel so fast. Uh, you haven't noticed anything weird about *her* behavior, have you? Now, if she drooled and rubbed shit in her hair or something worse, I'd say you have something to be concerned about."

"Rachel is practically perfect. You've been around her often enough to know that. That's beside the point. These are her *blood* relatives we're talking about. I don't know how I'm going to deal with this issue in the future."

"I advise you not to let any of those people know how you feel. You don't want to set one off and end up coming back to California in a body bag."

"I'll tell you more when I get back home, and I don't want you to mention this call to Mother. I called her last night to let her and Father know that we had made it to our destination all right, but I didn't tell her anything about all this insanity that I've stumbled into."

"I can understand that. I do want you to know that I'm in your corner. Once you marry Rachel—"

"Stop right there!" I exclaimed, cutting in.

"Huh?"

"What's wrong with you, Josh? I can't marry this woman with all these crazy-ass people in her family and risk having nutty children! And it's not just because of the mental issues. Rachel's family would never fit in with ours. They're almost *primitive.* I didn't know black folks in the South still lived like it was the dark ages."

"That's a pretty potent statement, and it's a matter of opinion," Josh said quickly.

"So what? It is what it is. Neither Mother and Father nor any of our family and friends would tolerate Rachel's people."

"That's for sure. But keep in mind, Rachel's family lives thousands of miles away. We would rarely interact with them."

"I know that, but at some point things could change. What if Rachel's mother decides to move to California? She'd have to bring those two nutcases with her! The thing is, I've already let Mother and Father down enough. You know how long it took me to get my life back on track, so I can't fuck up again."

"I understand everything you're saying." Josh paused and cleared his throat. "But Rachel is a wonderful woman. She's been very good to you, so please let her down gently."

"Listen, uh, I'm not going to break it off with her anytime soon. I did a whole lot of thinking last night. I couldn't sleep, so there was nothing else for me to do but think. After running everything back and forth in my mind, looking at it from several points of view, I've decided that I'll stay in the relationship for a while. . . ."

"I think the sooner you break it off with her, the better. Don't lead that woman on and let her think everything is hunky-dory. She doesn't deserve that. Besides, she could, uh, retaliate."

"Josh, men break up with women all the time. There's nothing unusual about me dropping Rachel. Do you think she'd do something violent or criminal to me?"

"I've prosecuted a lot of cases where one party in a breakup situation ended up injured, stalked, or killed by the other. I'm sure you remember the case last year, when that doctor's wife shot and killed him when she found out he was planning to divorce her and marry his mistress."

"Pffft! I'm not worried. I know Rachel would never do anything that extreme. She's got way too much class. But just to be on the safe side, I'm going to let her think everything is fine for a while."

"Why? From what you've told me so far, I assumed you wanted to dump her as soon as possible."

"Uh, I want to, but I can't. I still need her financial assistance, that's why! As soon as I'm out of the woods with my creditors, she's history. Now let me get back into that . . . that madhouse so I can figure out the best way to survive this mess until I can get up out of here." I paused and sucked in some air. I turned around and noticed that the door was now slightly ajar. . . .

Chapter 5

Rachel

I FELT SO SORRY FOR SETH. I KNEW THAT THIS TRIP HAD turned out to be a real culture shock to him. We were all seated at the kitchen table when Aunt Hattie came to the house that evening for dinner with a covered casserole dish. When she set it on the table and lifted the lid, Seth's eyes looked like they were about to pop out of his head. The dish contained a baked possum with its head still attached, garnished with yam wedges. I thought Seth was going to bolt out the back door and keep running all the way back to the airport. He looked just that scared.

"Why you looking so surprised, Seth? You ain't never seen no possum before?" Aunt Hattie asked, smacking her greasy lips. She looked like a blimp in the gray housedress she wore.

"No, I can't say that I have," Seth mouthed.

"Harrumph! I'm surprised a man like you, who grew up with folks eating raw fish and seaweed and whatever

else mess they eat in California, gets squeamish just looking at a baked possum. This is real food," Aunt Hattie
said. "What piece you want? Breast? Thigh? The tail?"

"I think I'll pass," Seth whimpered with a grimace on
his face. "I don't eat much meat."

"Aw, sugar, one itty-bitty piece won't hurt," Mama told
him, already sawing at one of the creature's hind legs with
her Ginsu knife.

Seth shook his head. "I'm not that hungry."

"I'll pass on it this time," I said without hesitation.
One thing I'd promised myself when I left Alabama was
that I would never eat possum meat again.

"Y'all don't eat none, then. That means more for us,"
Janet said, speaking for the first time since the night before.

Ernest speared the other hind leg. He didn't talk much,
but he had been smiling a lot in the past couple of days.
Mainly because Seth had made so many attempts to include him in the various conversations.

Seth and I left the table first. We had to leave for the
airport soon after breakfast tomorrow morning, so we had
a good excuse to turn in shortly after dinner.

Right after I entered my bedroom, my cell phone rang.
It was Uncle Albert calling from Berkeley.

"I meant to call you sooner," I told him. "But we've
been so busy since we got here."

"Did Seth freak out when he met Ernest and Janet?"

"Not at all."

"You sound mighty odd. Is he nearby?"

"That's right."

"Then let me do most of the talking. He seemed all
right with them, huh?"

"Oh yes."

"Neither one of them did anything strange in front of
Seth?"

"No, and I'm sure they won't. Now I have to go so I can get some more of my packing done." I didn't give Uncle Albert time to say anything else before I hung up.

"Who was that?" Seth asked.

"Uncle Albert. He just wanted to say hello." I shut the door before I continued. "Uh, he doesn't speak to Mama or anybody else down here, except every now and then. I don't think him and Mama have spoken since last year, when he called to wish her a Merry Christmas. It's a damn shame. He's the only brother she has left. I guess you noticed that his name didn't come up much."

"No, I didn't notice. Why does he not get along with the family?"

"Honey, my folks are so old school, they can't deal with gay people. They don't think being gay is normal."

Seth let out such a profound gasp, it sounded like somebody was strangling him. As soon as he composed himself, he looked at me and shook his head. "They can't deal with gay people? But what about . . . I mean, uh, your sister and brother are not exactly normal, either."

"That's true. They can't help the way they are, but my family is convinced that Uncle Albert chose to be gay."

"I don't think Albert chose to be gay. And the same goes for Janet and Ernest. They didn't choose to be, uh, the way they are, either."

"Honey, I'm glad you and I are on the same page. Thank you for being so nice to my family and for not freaking out over Ernest's and Janet's behavior." I gave Seth a quick kiss on his cheek.

"I have to say that this has been an interesting experience," he said, raking his fingers though his hair. "It's almost like being in a foreign country."

"I know what you mean. I felt that way about California until I got used to it. But I hope we'll visit Alabama at least once a year after we get married. That'll help you get used to the lifestyle. You just might want to move down here for good when we get old and retire."

The next morning, around eight, we all gathered at the kitchen table for our last breakfast together. A few minutes later, Aunt Hattie arrived so she could spend a little more time with Seth and me. Janet ate in silence and scowled at Seth across the table every few minutes.

"Janet, it's not nice to give folks dirty looks," Aunt Hattie said, shaking a finger at my sister. But Janet ignored her and continued to stare at Seth with that unpleasant look on her face. I could tell it was making him very uncomfortable by the way he kept shifting in his seat and clearing his throat. "Seth is going to be part of the family soon."

"Uh-uh! No, he ain't! He ain't going to be no part of this family!" Janet shrieked.

"Janet, if you can't behave, you can take your plate and go finish eating in your bedroom or out on that porch, with them gnats buzzing over your plate," Mama said. Then she turned to Seth. "Son, she's on a new medication, and it makes her talk crazy sometimes. Don't pay her no mind, you hear?"

Seth gave me a helpless look, but he managed to nod and smile.

Our flight was leaving at 12:30 p.m., and we had about an hour's drive back to the airport, so we left the breakfast table to get ready. It was raining out, so Seth insisted that we leave a half hour earlier than planned. "In case we have car trouble or run into heavy traffic because of the weather," he said as we finished our packing. What he said next stunned me. "This whole experience of coming down here to these backwoods and being around people who eat possums and duck eggs has been too strange for me. At first, it was like visiting a foreign country, but now it feels like I'm on another planet. I . . . I can't wait to get up out of this place."

"Oh. I didn't know you thought it was that bad," I said, folding my arms and moving toward the bed. His comments were harsh but honest, and that made me sad. Apparently, the culture shock he had been experiencing was more severe than I'd thought. "If you had said something before now, we could have left a day earlier. I guess we won't be moving here when we retire, huh?" I sat down, and Seth quickly sat next to me.

"I'm sorry if I hurt your feelings, baby. I didn't mean to. It's just that, well, I'm a city boy."

I nodded. "I know you are, Seth. And I don't want you to change. I want you to stay just the way you are." When I put my arms around him and kissed his lips, his body stiffened like a piece of wood.

Chapter 6

Seth

*I*T HAD BEEN ALMOST A MONTH SINCE RACHEL AND I HAD returned from Alabama.

I waited until the second day in April to tell her we should not set a definite date for our wedding. Just as I had expected, she agreed with me. I had used "I want my fledgling ad agency business to be a little more secure first" as an excuse. It pleased me to know that I still had Rachel in the palm of my hand and that I was still very much in control.

"You have a point, honey. Starting a marriage and a business too close together could cause some problems," she said. "Don't worry. We'll know when the time is right for us to get married."

While everything appeared to be normal, that could not have been further from the truth. I had decided to end my relationship with Rachel, and I knew it was going to be hard. But I had convinced myself that one way to make things easier was for me to focus my attention on another woman. A brand-new relationship would ease my pain. It didn't take me long to find a replacement for Rachel. My new woman literally landed in my lap.

I rarely used public transportation, but on this particular day I had a breakfast date with an old friend from school who worked in downtown Frisco. I knew from experience that driving across the Bay Bridge during the commute hours, then having to find a decent place to park, was not a pleasant experience. Since my buddy worked in the financial district, one block from a rapid transit station, I decided to take the Bay Area Rapid Transit train, better known as BART, into the city. I boarded at the North Berkeley station.

At the very next stop, a petite young woman with skin the color of honey got on, and I noticed her right away. She wore a navy blue suit with a white silk blouse, and she had a briefcase in her hand. Her short auburn hair was in a cute pixie style, complete with bangs, which made her heart-shaped face look almost angelic. After a couple more station stops, the train got so crowded, people were pushing and shoving like nobody's business. When the train stopped suddenly, the lovely woman I had been admiring stumbled backward and landed in my lap!

"Oh, I'm so sorry," she said, immediately rising. She was not the only thing "rising." I got an immediate hard-on.

"I'm not," I told her, smiling as I looked into her big brown eyes. "I'm getting off at the next stop, so you can stay right where you are."

"I don't think so," she said, giving me the kind of look my mother used to give me when I said something inappropriate.

"Then why don't you sit? I'll stand the rest of the way," I said, already on my feet.

"Thank you." She sat down and immediately began to read a newspaper, which was what almost every other person was doing. For the next few minutes, I was so engrossed in the sports section of the *San Francisco Chronicle* newspaper, I didn't realize that the train had reached my destination.

"Isn't this your stop?"

I turned to see that it was the beautiful young woman who was talking to me. "Oh! Thank you." We both got off the train and began to walk toward the same escalator. "Um, I hope I didn't sound too forward back there."

"You did, but that's all right." She chuckled. "I'm Darla Woodson."

"I'm Seth Garrett. Do you work nearby?"

She nodded. "The savings and loan a block from here."

"Are you a bank teller?"

"I'm a loan manager. Well, it was nice talking to you." I was surprised when she grabbed my hand and shook it. "Maybe I'll see you around again."

"I'm having breakfast with a friend, but I sure would like to see you again. Maybe we could meet somewhere for coffee someday? Do you live in Berkeley?"

"I live on Alcatraz Avenue, and yes, I would like to meet for coffee someday."

Darla and I exchanged phone numbers, and I called her the next day. One of the first things she told me was that she was not involved with anyone.

"I wish I could say that," I began. "You see, there is someone, but I'm going to end the relationship very soon. She's . . . she's got some emotional problems, so I have to ease out of the relationship very slowly and very gently."

"I see. The guy I just broke up with had some emotional issues, too, so I can relate. It took me a whole year to break it off with him. And it is one thing I hope I never have to go through again."

"I feel you. My lady friend is so fragile, I'm afraid she might try something desperate if I don't handle things right. But life goes on."

Life did go on for me. And in a way that I had never expected.

Within a month, I was madly in love with Darla. Unfortunately, the first time we made love it was a letdown, because I couldn't remain erect long enough to please her, or myself. I knew it was the guilt I was feeling. Each time Rachel said or did something I didn't like, I didn't feel as guilty. By the end of the third month, I was so into Darla, I knew that *she* was the woman I wanted to spend the rest of my life with. I had told her about Rachel's nutty family and about how Rachel had kept that information from me for so long. Darla understood my concerns completely. Was it possible that she was just as docile and as willing to please me as Rachel? I wondered. If so, I had hit the jackpot twice.

It had been four months since the trip to Alabama, and not once had Rachel or I brought up the subject of her family's problems. She was so busy planning our future that she hadn't noticed how my demeanor had changed.

Other people had noticed that I had begun to act differently. Last night, when Rachel's uncle Albert came to the apartment, he'd made some disturbing comments.

"Seth, what's up, dude? You haven't cracked a smile since I came in that door two hours ago. With that long face and those bags under your eyes, you look like dog shit! Running a business must really be hard on you."

"Yeah, running a business is not easy," I'd replied, wishing he'd leave or mind his own business. "We're still smoothing out some rough edges."

"He's just working too hard," Rachel had said, caressing my neck. Albert was so brazen, he always made himself at home when he made one of his unexpected visits, which were too frequent and too long for me. He had just poured himself his third double shot of vodka and had flopped down on the love seat, facing Rachel and me on the couch. She'd refilled my wineglass. "But don't worry about my boo, Uncle Albert. I'm taking real good care of him."

"Well, excuse me," Albert said with a neck roll. This man went out of his way to let the world know he was gay. On this particular night he wore a black cape over a skintight red jumpsuit. With his big brown eyes, high cheekbones, and bow-shaped lips, he was just as "pretty" as Rachel. He smoothed back his wavy brown hair and took a long drink. After he let out a mild belch, he continued. "Dude, I have a friend who works for a real estate company on Shattuck. They have been listing some fantastic properties lately. One in particular has a two-car garage and a huge backyard for the future kiddies to roam around in!"

"We can wait," Rachel said. "Things are really heating up at my job, so I'm not sure I want to start a family too soon. I just got a promotion, and it wouldn't do me much good if I had to take off on maternity leave too soon." Rachel turned to me when she heard me gasp. "What's wrong, baby? You look like you just saw a ghost."

"I'm fine. Just a little heartburn," I lied, rubbing my chest for emphasis. I coughed to clear my throat, which was so dry and inflamed, it felt like I had just swallowed a ball of fire. "Thanks for the information, Albert. Rachel's right. There is no need for us to start our family too soon."

"Well, y'all know what's best, but when you do get ready to look for a big enough place, just let me know," Albert said. He stood up and let out another belch and glanced at his watch. "I hate to run, but I have to meet my baby at the country club, and y'all know how Kingston complains when I'm late."

Two minutes after Albert rushed out the door, I raised my arms and yawned. Then, very casually, I said to Rachel, "Sweetheart, I'm glad you feel the way you do."

"About what?"

"About us slowing things down a bit. Us having kids especially . . ."

She nodded. "We're both still very young. Even if we wait five more years after we get married to become parents, we'll still be fairly young by the time our kids are ready for college."

"Uh, yeah. I don't have a problem with that. But I've been thinking about something else, too. Now that we both agree that waiting to have children is a smart thing to do, why not hold off a little while on the wedding, too?"

Maybe it was my imagination, but as soon as I said that, Rachel looked somewhat relieved.

She still gave me a surprised and glassy-eyed look, though. "How long?" she asked.

"Not too long. Now that you've been promoted to head bookkeeper, you'll probably have to spend more time at work, and that can put a lot of stress on you and our relationship. And you know how busy things are with me at work right now. I'm wooing some serious clients, and I need to be able to give them my undivided attention."

Rachel stood up, positioned herself in front of me, and eased down into my lap. "Don't take this the wrong way, but you took a load off my mind by suggesting we delay the wedding."

"Huh?"

"Honey, I didn't know how to bring up the subject of us delaying the wedding for a little while longer. But you're right. I am going to be very busy for a while and stressed out for sure. The girl they hired to do my old job and be my assistant is not too bright, so it's going to take some time for me to train her properly. Besides that, I'd like to lose a couple of dress sizes before the wedding." After Rachel planted a quick kiss on my cheek, she added, "What if we wait until next year? Even a little longer, if we have to. You know I love you from the bottom of my heart and I'm not going anywhere. And I know you're not, either."

I nodded. "Next year sounds wonderful, honey." I wanted to kiss Rachel's feet, but I settled for her lips. I gave her the most passionate French kiss I could manage. She had no idea how easy she had made things for me!

Chapter 7

Rachel

*T*HE MONTHS SLID BY, AND THINGS WERE LOOKING BETter and better for Seth and me. By the time 2001 rolled around, I had received two hefty salary increases since my promotion at the prestigious private middle school I worked for as a bookkeeper. Seth had twice as many clients as the year before, so the ad agency that he had started on a shoestring budget was doing very well. Even though we were more financially secure than ever, our marriage was still on hold. We didn't mention setting a date that often anymore, and there was really no need to. We had pretty much decided that we'd do it sometime toward the end of the year or early the next year, but no later.

In February, on a Thursday a few days after Valentine's Day, Uncle Albert called me up around 7:00 p.m. I had just come home from the market and still had the grocery bag in my hand. I smiled when I saw my uncle's name on the caller ID. That smile didn't stay on my face long. What he had to say made my heart skip several beats.

"Baby girl, I'm in trouble, and I need your help real bad," he whimpered. The tone of his voice gave me enough reason to be concerned.

"I just got home. Let me put the groceries away and take off my sweater," I said. "I'll call you back in a few minutes—"

"Please don't hang up on me, baby!" Uncle Albert interrupted. "I need your help!"

"Calm down, Unc. Hold on for a few seconds." My heart was already leaping around in my tightening chest like a rabbit on crack. Uncle Albert had never asked me for help before. I set the grocery bag on the coffee table and removed my sweater with my other hand. Then I sat down hard on the couch and crossed my legs. "What kind of trouble are you in?" I was sorry that the telephone cord was not long enough for me to get up and walk across the room to the liquor cabinet so I could pour myself a drink. I had a feeling I was going to need one.

"Kingston found out I spent Valentine's Day night with somebody else, and he went off on me this evening. He accused me of cheating on him."

"Were you?"

"Girl, you know me. I can't help myself when it comes to cute young things."

"Excuse me for saying this, but if you were cheating and Kingston found out, why are *you* so upset? Since he's footing most of the bills, I think he should be the one who's upset."

"Oh, he is upset, too! But that's beside the point! To make a long story short, he got all up in my face and sucker punched me. I sucker punched him back. Next thing I know, that wild-ass Jap comes at me with some of his kung fu moves. His foot felt like a sledgehammer when he slammed it against my face. I freaked out and ran out the door. Well, I tripped on the steps and fell and broke my leg in two places. Shit! I'm at the hospital, with my leg in a cast!" Uncle Albert started screaming like a banshee. "Aaarrggh! Aaarrggh!"

"Uncle Albert, please stop crying! I know you don't want me to come over there and give you something else to cry about. Everything is going to be all right."

Uncle Albert sniffed and blew his nose. "I don't know what to do! This is the first time a man has ever hit me!"

"Where is Kingston now?"

"I don't know where that fool is! He rode to the hospital with me and hung around until they patched me up, but before he left, he told me he wanted my black ass out of his life. That yellow motherfucker got some nerve calling me out my name! So, once they release me, I don't have anyplace to go. And, with my leg in a cast, I'm going to have to take time off from work, so I can't go out and look for another place to move into for a while. I'm going to be on crutches, so can I please stay with you and Seth?"

As much as I wanted to hesitate and give this unexpected and intrusive request more consideration, I didn't. There was no way I was going to turn my back on my uncle. There were times, like this one, when he made me so angry I wanted to slap him around myself. But he was probably the last person in the world I'd ever get violent with, no matter what he did or said.

"You know you can stay with us. I'm sure Seth won't mind. What about your stuff?"

"That's another thing. I need for you and Seth to go get every bit of my shit out of Kingston's apartment and put it in storage for me. I know I'm asking for a lot, but I didn't have anybody else to turn to. Can you come right away and pick me up?"

"You can count on me and Seth. I'll call you back as soon as I catch my breath. What hospital are you in?"

After Uncle Albert gave me the name of the hospital, I hung up and called Seth at his office.

"We've got a little problem," I told him as soon as he answered.

He hesitated for a few moments before he asked me, "What problem is that?"

"Uncle Albert and his boyfriend got into a serious confrontation. Kingston got violent with my uncle and kicked him out of the apartment."

"And how is that a problem for us?"

"Uncle Albert fell during the fight and broke his leg."

"Your uncle is over six feet tall and weighs close to two hundred pounds. He let that hundred-and-twenty-pound Japanese dude whup his ass?"

"That hundred-and-twenty-pound Japanese dude is into all kinds of martial arts. Anyway, Uncle Albert is going to need a place to recuperate until he can find another place to live. Is it okay if he stays with us?" One thing I had managed to do since I'd met Seth was to keep my volatile temper in check. I prayed that I would never show him, or anybody else, the side of myself that I had been hiding so well. If he disagreed with what I'd just said, I might lose it, and then he and I would have a serious confrontation of our own.

Seth responded immediately and favorably, even though it was with a heavy, worried tone of voice. "Well, if Albert needs a place to stay, we have to help him. You do know that a broken leg can take several weeks to heal, right? Maybe even a couple of months."

"I know. And he wants us to go to the apartment and pack up his stuff and put it in storage. He gave away his furniture when he moved in with Kingston, so all he has is clothes, books, and his computer. We can put everything in our spare bedroom."

"You mean the room we have set up as an office?"

"I can move my computer into our bedroom or into the kitchen, so I don't have a problem with that. But I know that with all your files and other things, you really need the space. So, uh, could you use your old bedroom in your mama's house as an office for a while?"

"I suppose I could," Seth said dryly. "What about his expenses? He drinks like a fish, so his alcohol bill must be mighty high. He eats like a mule, and I know he'll be using a lot of utilities and whatnot."

"I'll make sure he pays his way. I don't know how much he'll be getting from disability, but I'm sure he'll get enough to cover his food and other expenses."

"What about his car note?"

"Oh. I forgot about that new SUV he just bought."

"I'm sure he'll want to pay that and his insurance before he thinks about paying a light bill."

"I'll take care of his car note and insurance myself if I have to," I said. "He's family, Seth."

"And another thing. Albert is a party animal. I'm sure he'll be having a lot of company running in and out."

"I know. We'll set some rules, which he'll have to follow," I said firmly. "I just don't want to let him down after all he did for me when I moved out here. And if it gets too crowded, or if his presence gets to be too much for you, well, I'll think of something else."

"Let's finish this conversation when I get home. I'll be leaving in about half an hour."

"I'm going to change clothes and go to the hospital where they took Uncle Albert and bring him here. I'll get one of my neighbors to drive me over to get his SUV and park it over here. Do you want me to wait until you get home so you can go with me?"

Seth didn't waste any time answering my question. "No!" he boomed. "Excuse me for hollering. . . ."

"To tell you the truth, I feel like doing some hollering myself. I know it's not going to be easy having Uncle Albert under the same roof, following our house rules and such, but I can't turn him away."

"I know you can't, Rachel."

"Is there anything you want me to tell him before I bring him here? I don't want the first day to be too awkward for him, or you."

"Tell him we've got his back," Seth said gently.

"Thanks, baby. I knew you'd understand. I promise you that this will be a very temporary arrangement, and I'll make sure it's as painless as possible."

Chapter 8

Rachel

I ALREADY KNEW THAT MAMA THOUGHT I HAD MADE A lot of stupid decisions, so when she told me what a fool I was for moving Uncle Albert in with me and Seth, I was not surprised.

"Girl, you are a straight-up fool! Do you want to lose Seth? How long do you think he's going tolerate having Albert in that apartment with you and him?" Mama yelled. I had waited until Uncle Albert had been with us for two weeks before I'd even told her about his dilemma. "As long as he's been out there, don't he have friends he could move in with?"

"Mama, he's got a lot of friends, and I'm sure he'll probably go stay with one of them as soon as he can. He just needs a place to stay in the meantime."

"What if one of his friends don't take him in? What if he's still there when you and Seth get married?"

"Mama, I am not sure when Seth and I are going to get married. Uh, we've changed the date twice."

"Uh-huh. And with Albert in the mix, you might have to change it again."

"If we change the date again, I'm sure it won't be because of Uncle Albert, Mama. Uncle Albert has already been here a couple of weeks, and Seth has not complained about him one time."

"Well, like I been telling you all your life, you sure make a lot of dumb decisions."

"I know I do, Mama."

Unfortunately, my meddlesome girlfriends felt the same way. Right after my conversation with Mama last night, I called up Lucille "Lucy" Foster, my best friend and coworker, and told her about my new living arrangement.

"What's wrong with you, girl? And what's wrong with Seth for letting you move Albert in?"

"In case you forgot, it's *my* apartment. My name is the only one on the lease. Seth has no right to tell me who I can move in here and who I can't," I snapped. "And for your information, Seth agreed to this arrangement."

"I'm just afraid you bit off more than you can chew. You have enough stress in your life. I mean, you're busier than ever at work. You have a wedding coming up. Now you've moved your hard-partying, hard-drinking gay uncle into your apartment. I honestly don't see how it's going to work out."

"Uncle Albert is going to stay only a little while, and Seth and I will be at work during the day, every day."

"All right now. You know I'm here for you, so if you need somebody to talk to, just give me a call."

"Thanks, Lucy."

An hour after my conversation with Lucy, my other

two close friends, Paulette and Patrice, stormed my apartment. I was glad I had dropped Uncle Albert off at the salon around the corner to get his nails done.

"Girl, Lucy told us you've moved Albert in with you and Seth. Have you lost your mind?" Patrice hollered before I could even close the door behind them.

"You are not responsible for your uncle. He's a grown man," Paulette added, already heading for the portable bar.

Since neither one allowed me enough time to respond, I just stood in the middle of the floor with my arms folded.

"How long do you think Seth is going to put up with Albert's antics?" Patrice asked, joining Paulette at the bar.

"It's going to be for only a few more weeks," I finally said.

"Then what?" they asked at the same time.

"Then Uncle Albert will move out."

"Baby girl, once he's able to get around without those crutches, he'll have to go out and look for another place. That could take some time. It took me almost three months to find the place I just moved into," Paulette said, rubbing the side of her cute heart-shaped face. A knitted cap covered her thick brown hair.

"I'm going to start looking for a new place for him myself tomorrow. That way he'll already have a place to go to when his leg heals," I replied.

"Who is going to be responsible for his moving expenses?" Patrice asked.

"I will take care of that if I have to. I've already agreed to keep up his car payment and insurance."

My two friends gulped at the same time.

"You can both stop looking so stunned. It's no big

deal. Seth doesn't have a problem with me doing that. It's all coming out of *my* savings. Besides, I know my uncle would do the same for me."

"Seth must be a saint," Patrice continued. "Speaking of the saint, I noticed he's not with you as much lately. You must be slacking up on your job. . . ."

"What's that supposed to mean?" I asked.

Patrice often made remarks that made me bristle. She was the least attractive of the four of us, and she had the hardest time attracting and keeping men. She blamed it on the fact that she was almost six feet tall. She also had plain features and a head full of coarse black hair, which she usually wore in braids. But when the four of us got together, her bitterness always seemed to be aimed at me.

"What it means is you're probably not as hot as you think, after all. The last three times I called over here and the last five times I visited, Seth was nowhere around. Is everything all right? I can never tell when you're stressed, because you always look so calm. Giving up your privacy and your quality time alone with Seth must be taking a toll on you."

Paulette always came to my rescue in a tense situation. "Honey, Rachel is so on top of her game, she could teach classes on it. If anything is wrong, it's with Seth," she said, giving me a conspiratorial nod.

"Everything is fine. Seth's just spending more time at his parents' house these days. His mother has had some minor health issues, so he needs to help look after her. And he's using his old bedroom as an off-site office," I reported.

I didn't like the fact that I saw less of Seth now. As a matter of fact, he had spent the last two nights at his parents' house, to get some extra work done, he had claimed. I had noticed the exasperated looks on his face when he saw my uncle stretched out on our couch, with a drink in his hand, for hours at a time. In a way I was glad Seth spent a lot of time away so he wouldn't have to look at Uncle Albert and I wouldn't have to look at him. I kept telling myself that since he and I would be spending the next forty or fifty years together, a little time apart wouldn't hurt us.

I found out the following week that Seth felt the same way.

We always had our discussions about my uncle in our bedroom if he was somewhere close enough to overhear us. We had left him in the living room, with a drink in his hand, his feet propped up on the hassock, watching a *Cheers* rerun.

"I think I'm going to move back home for a while," Seth told me less than a minute after we'd entered the bedroom.

I whirled around to face him with my mouth hanging open. "What? For how long?"

"Uh, maybe just until Albert leaves. I think it would be easier on everybody involved." This was the second time in two days that Seth had come home and discovered that Uncle Albert had drunk up the last of his scotch. A few days ago, he had come home and found Uncle Albert in his favorite bathrobe.

"My uncle will be back on his own soon," I defended with a whisper. Having to whisper in our own bedroom was another thing that bothered Seth.

This time he didn't care, I guessed, because he spoke in a very loud voice. "I can't spend another week living with that man!" he roared.

My jaw dropped. I ran to the door and cracked it open. I waited for a few seconds, and when I heard my uncle snoring in the living room, I knew he had not heard Seth's outburst.

"Are you trying to tell me something?" I demanded.

"Baby, all I'm trying to tell you is that I can't spend much more time with your uncle in this apartment." Seth pulled me into his arms and planted a kiss on my lips. "My feelings for you are still the same, so everything else will remain the same."

I blinked. "Seth, your mama called me at work today and asked me when I was going to send out the wedding announcements. I told her we'd moved the date back again."

"Uh, let me think a little more about setting a date."

"Okay. If we don't do it this year, how about early January? That'll give us several more months to complete our plans."

"That might work. I'll let you know when I make up my mind. Give me a few more weeks. . . ."

"If we wait until January, that'll give me enough time to get rid of all the weight I've gained since Uncle Albert's started cooking all that fattening food." I gave Seth a thoughtful look. "I'm going to join a gym and start working out in the evenings, after work. You want me to be in good shape when we take the plunge, don't you?"

"Uh-huh."

"Then November or early January it is. And it's about time! I was beginning to think you didn't really want to marry me at all." I laughed. Seth didn't.

Chapter 9

Seth

I HATED LIVING UNDER THE SAME ROOF WITH ALBERT! I had known before he moved in that the arrangement was not going to be a walk in the park, but since it was Rachel's apartment, I really had had no say in her decision, even though she'd asked for my approval.

The arrangement had begun to get on my last nerve after Darla complained one time too many about not being able to see me more often.

"I know you still have feelings for that woman and you don't want to move out of her place, because she might hurt herself, but seeing you every now and then is not working for me," Darla told me one night, as we lay in bed in her cute loft on Alcatraz Avenue.

I didn't want to lose her, so it was time for me to bring out the "big gun" and move to the next level. "Baby, let's get married," I said, sitting up in bed.

She gasped, and I felt her body stiffen. And I was not surprised. We had known each other only since last April. "What? Do you mean it?"

"I know we haven't known each other that long, but I know what I want, and I hope you do, too."

"I . . . I didn't expect you to . . . I mean . . . what about that woman you still live with?"

"Rachel is still depressed about me wanting to end our relationship, but she's seeing a therapist now, so she's doing somewhat better. I'm sure it won't upset her too much when I tell her I'm moving back home. I'll stay there until you and I can get married. The house I want to buy won't be vacant for a while, anyway."

"Do you think it's all right to leave her alone? You don't think she'll attempt suicide or something?"

"Uh, her gay uncle is living with us right now. He's a real pain in the ass, let me tell you! His Japanese boyfriend whupped his ass and broke his leg and kicked him out of his apartment. He's also depressed, so he and his niece are in the same boat. Since they have a similar problem, they can console each other. He loves her, and I know he'll make sure she doesn't do anything to hurt herself. When I see she's over me, I'll tell her the wedding is off."

I was not sure when I was going to break up with Rachel. I needed more time to give my plan a little more thought. In the meantime, I used Albert's intrusion to my advantage. He was the perfect excuse for me to move back in with my parents. When I told Mother and Father how disruptive Albert's presence was, they insisted that I move back home until Rachel and I got married. And Rachel fell for it, too, hook, line, and sinker.

"I love you to death, baby, and I think it's a good idea for you to move back home for a while," she said. "My apartment is kind of small, and Uncle Albert needs a whole lot of space. But even before he moved in, I felt cramped. We'll have so much more room after we get married and move into our dream house."

I was so relieved! It looked like my plan was going to work better than I had thought it would. All I had to worry about now was the excuse I was going to use to call off the wedding. "You're right. And I've decided that I'll arrange to meet with Albert's real estate friend and tell him that we want to look at some properties just before we get married."

"Thank you, honey. I really don't want you to move back home, but under the circumstances, it's not such a bad idea. Besides, once we get married, we'll be stuck with one another for the rest of our lives."

We both laughed.

Albert stayed in Rachel's apartment several more *months*. In August he finally moved back in with the same lover who had kicked his ass and evicted him. Rather than having me move back into her apartment, Rachel and I agreed that I should stay on at my parents' house until we got married. One of the reasons was that our being apart made us want to see one another that much more when we found the time. Another reason was that her uncle might get his ass kicked again and might need to come back, which, I told her, I would not be so amenable to the next time.

Rachel called me at work on Monday afternoon during the first week in August. I could tell from the meek tone of her voice that something was very wrong. I braced myself and waited.

"What's the matter now?" I asked, forcing myself not to sound too annoyed.

"My aunt Hattie just called me," Rachel began. The pause told me that there was something bad coming.

"Don't tell me *she* needs a place to stay now," I said hotly, meaning it more as a joke than a concern.

"No, that's not why she called. Mama is sick. She's in the hospital. They're going to remove her gallbladder."

"Oh? That's too bad. I'm sorry to hear that. What hospital is she in? I'll call her and send some flowers."

"I'm going to go check on her. Aunt Hattie told me not to worry, but I still think I should go home and make sure everything is all right."

"I'm sure everything will be all right," I said firmly. "Your mama is a tough old broad."

"Well, she is that for sure, but she won't be a tough old broad forever."

I was not sure where this conversation was going, but I knew it was going in a direction I didn't want to go in. It was worse than I thought. If there was ever any doubt in my mind that what I was doing to Rachel was wrong, that doubt was removed when she dropped another bombshell: her taking in her mentally challenged siblings, and me moving back in with her to look after them.

"I know it'll be a big adjustment, but if Mama could take care of them all those years, we can, too."

Just the thought of that made me cringe. I felt like I had become the victim of the worst kind of entrapment. It was a day that would haunt me for the rest of my life, because I knew I had to move forward with my plan to end my relationship with Rachel sooner than I had thought I would.

"You want us to take in two adults with special needs?" The words rang in my ears, giving me an instant headache.

"Seth, I promised Mama and all my other relatives that I would take care of my siblings if . . . uh . . . when she could no longer do it." She told me in such a casual, nonchalant way, I choked on some air.

I thought my heart was going to stop right then and

there. Being the father of kids with mental problems would be bad enough, but that wasn't going to happen. Being responsible for two adults with mental problems would be even worse!

"Rachel, that is a major responsibility." I gulped.

"Honey, we've already agreed that we would move into a house with at least four bedrooms, so we'll have more than enough room to accommodate them. You and I make good money, so we'll be able to support them, too. Besides, they both receive financial and medical aid from Social Security. I am not going to let my brother or sister end up in one of those state homes, because that would kill Mama. Besides that, I just read some hellish news reports about those places—the staff neglecting and beating the patients, the orderlies raping the females, and so on. And if it comes to them having to move in with us, I'll make sure it won't be permanent, per se. One of the teachers I work with has a bipolar son who just moved into a closely supervised group home in Sacramento. That's something we can look into for the future."

"What's wrong with them moving into one of those 'closely supervised group homes' now?"

"For one thing, it's not that simple. Those places have long waiting lists, and in some cases, a doctor has to refer the patient. That could take some time. In the meantime, I need to step up to the plate. It's my responsibility, and I did promise my mama that I'd do it if I had to."

"Uh, that's mighty noble of you, baby, but taking care of two mentally challenged adults could take a major toll on you and our relationship," I warned.

"Seth, if it was your family in a crisis like this, I'd go out of my way to accommodate them."

"I know you would, sweetie, and I appreciate you saying that. You go home to visit your family and do whatever you need to do. I . . . I'm with you one hundred percent." This would have been the perfect opportunity for me to break up with Rachel. But I couldn't do that yet, because I still needed just a little more financial assistance from her. . . .

"Hmmm. I didn't know it was going to be this easy. After having to deal with Albert in the apartment all those months, I didn't think you would even consider having Ernest and Janet underfoot on a short-term basis, a long-term basis, or any other basis. Are you sure you don't have a problem with this? I mean, Mama could be back on her feet in no time, and we won't have to worry about taking care of my siblings. Hell, Mama just might outlive me and you both."

I didn't hesitate to respond. "I don't have a problem with it, baby. Now, you do whatever you have to do."

"I'll make my travel arrangements as soon as I get off the phone. Now, changing the subject, my folks and everybody else keep asking me about our wedding plans. . . ."

"Like I already told you, this coming November or January should be just fine."

"Okay, baby. I love you."

"I love you, too. I have to go now."

I couldn't wait to get off the telephone. I had to make one of the most important telephone calls I would ever make. I breathed a sigh of relief when I heard the sweet voice on the other end of the line.

"Darla, it's me, baby. I don't want to wait. Let's get married in September," I said. "This coming September."

"Huh? That's *next* month! We haven't been together a year and a half, and I haven't even met your family yet! And what about that crazy ex of yours? Has she calmed down enough so we won't have to worry about her?"

"I'm taking you to meet my family next Sunday. And, yes, my crazy ex has calmed down enough for me to move forward with my life."

"I hope she . . . Rachel's her name, right?"

"Uh-huh."

"I hope I never run into her, and I hope you're right about her finally getting the message that you're through with her. I had no idea it would take this long, though. I've never been involved with an unmarried man *and* had to sneak around to be with him."

"I know, sweetheart. I'm just glad you hung in there. I promise you won't regret it."

"I'm sure I won't, either. And I can assure you that if you break up with me, I won't cause you the same problems she has caused you."

"I know you won't, baby."

"Did she honestly think you were still going to marry her and have children with her after you found out about her crazy family?"

"Apparently she did. Darla, I have to get off the phone. I don't think I can stand any more stress, so I need to let my family know what's going on. And I need to let them know *today*."

Chapter 10

Seth

"MENTAL ILLNESS RUNS IN RACHEL'S FAMILY? Aiyeee!" I couldn't remember the last time I had heard my mother scream. "Son, please tell us you're joking! She didn't even tell you before you asked her to marry you? How could Rachel be so deceitful? That girl ought to be ashamed of herself! I knew she was too good to be true!" Mother hollered.

It was a hell of a subject for me to bring up in the middle of our dinner table conversation that evening during the first week of August. But I had to do it. The sooner my folks found out about Rachel, the easier it would be for me to get them to see everything from my perspective and dismiss Rachel for the fraud she was. I was glad that I was alone with Mother and Father.

"Do you mean to tell us that she didn't even bother to tell you about these nutcases until you met them last year?" Father boomed. The look of horror on his face was even more profound than the look on Mother's. "Mercy me! I've always thought in the back of my mind that that girl had something to hide."

"What made you think that?" I asked him.

"Uh, I can't really put my finger on anything specific, other than her shifty eyes. . . ."

"I never noticed her shifty eyes, but I saw only what I wanted to see, I guess," I said.

"How come you're just now telling us about Rachel's family?" Mother asked.

"I wanted to tell you sooner, but I honestly thought that I'd be okay with it over time. But I'm not." I sniffed. "On top of the mental illness issue, her folks are about as countrified and ignorant as can be! I was terrified the whole time I was in Alabama. You would think that those people just arrived in this country on a boat! They even eat possums."

"They sound like a bunch of savages, and Rachel was the ringleader," Father snarled. "Our family has worked too long and hard to get where we are to end up letting Rachel bring us down. I'm glad you're going to get rid of her."

"Seth, you poor thing you. You've been carrying this heavy load all by yourself!" Mother began to shake so hard, I ran to her and put my arms around her shoulders.

"Mother, calm down. We don't want you to have another heart attack!" I yelled.

Father was about to rise and come to Mother's aid, too, but she waved him back to his seat and me back to mine. "I'm all right," she assured us, fanning her face with her napkin. She grabbed the wineglass next to her plate and put it up to her lips. She drank until she had drained every drop. As soon as I returned to my seat, she asked, "Is that the real reason you moved back home, baby?"

"Yes. But I'm going to ease out of the relationship

slowly and gently. She's about to go back to Alabama to check on her sick mother. When she returns . . . well, I'll decide how to break it off with her completely."

"Son, don't you worry. We know how anxious you are to get married and to start your family. With all you've got going for you, you'll meet someone else soon," Father assured me.

"Uh . . . that's the other thing I wanted to share." I cleared my throat and glanced from my mother to my father. "I have met someone else. I'm going to marry her next month."

"*What?*" my parents yelled at the same time.

"You've met another woman, and you've already decided you want to marry her?" Mother hollered. "You can't be serious, son!"

"Seth, do you think it's wise for you to even be thinking about marrying another woman while you're still with Rachel? Isn't this kind of sudden?" Father boomed.

"And we haven't even met her yet!" Mother shouted. Words could not describe the look on her face. "What's wrong with you, boy? Are you sure some of Rachel's family's mental condition didn't rub off on you when you went to Alabama?"

"It's not as bad as it sounds," I protested. "This is not that sudden. Actually, I met Darla last year, in April, and we've been seeing one another on the sly since then. We, uh, thought it best if we kept our relationship a secret until I got out of this mess with Rachel. I couldn't risk having Rachel find out and do something real crazy to me or my new girl. And, believe you me, this one has no skeletons in her closet," I said, holding my hands up in the air for emphasis. "I did a full background check on her myself. I checked all the way back to her great-grandparents on both sides. She's from a fine family, and not a single one has ever had any mental issues. As a matter of fact, I've invited her to have dinner with us next Sunday."

"Does Rachel know about this girl? And what's her name again?" Mother asked.

"No, Rachel does not know about her, and her name is Darla Woodson. I know Rachel does not call or come over here much anymore, but if and when she does contact you again, don't tell her about Darla until I say it's okay." I sniffed and gave Mother a pleading look.

"Ha! After the charlatan Rachel turned out to be, I don't even want to see that hussy's face anytime soon— let alone talk to her! I'm not going to tell her about you and this new girl," Mother wailed.

"I know you won't, Mother. But please promise me you won't tell anybody at church or any of your friends. Uh, this could turn into a very embarrassing situation for me and the whole family." I turned to my father. "Right, Father?" I said with a wink. I had never confronted my father about his mistress, but he was no fool. I had a feeling he knew that I knew. Had he asked me, I would have told him so. Out of respect for him, and to save my mother the heartache, I had no intention of snitching on him.

"That's right," Father agreed, giving me a sheepish look. As soon as Mother left the table to go check on dessert, he continued. "You don't have to worry about me. I've done a few things I don't want anybody to know about—things that could hurt a lot of people. If you know what I mean . . ."

"I do know what you mean," I said with a conspiratorial nod and a thumbs-up.

I felt so relieved. But I rushed to finish my dinner, anyway. I was aware of the way my parents kept staring at me when they didn't think I was looking. I was also glad that I couldn't read minds, because I didn't want to know everything they were thinking. I was also glad that my brothers and their families were not present. I would tell them all as soon as I could, which had to be within the next couple of weeks. I was running out of time. Rachel had begun to look at wedding dresses again.

Chapter II

Rachel

I JOINED A 24 HOUR FITNESS GYM THE FOLLOWING MONday, a couple of weeks after I'd told Seth I would. I was so determined to get in shape that after working out on the treadmill for an hour each day and riding the stationary bike for another eight miles, I lost four pounds the first week.

I had resisted joining a gym for years. I hated exercising with a bunch of other folks, especially if the females had firm, well-tended bodies. However, that was not the case. Most of the women who came to the gym when I was present were in horrible shape. One attractive but slightly flabby woman around my age, whom I'd seen several times already, started up a conversation with me one Friday evening, after I had just stumbled off the treadmill.

"I don't know how you manage to spend an hour on the treadmill. I'm lucky if I can do twenty minutes," she said, sitting down next to me on one of the leather couches in the waiting area.

"I don't know how I do it, either. But I am determined to stick it out at least until I lose enough weight before my wedding," I told her. "I'm Rachel McNeal," I said.

"It's nice to meet you, Rachel. I'm Darla Woodson. When is your wedding?"

"We haven't set the date yet." I paused. "We have, but then we've changed it a few times. My fiancé wants to wait until he feels more secure with the business he started."

"What a coincidence! I'm engaged, too. And my fiancé has his own business, too."

"That's interesting. I guess you and I have something in common." Darla seemed so warm and friendly. I was glad she'd finally initiated a conversation with me. "When is your big day?"

A look of ecstasy appeared on Darla's face. "A lot sooner than I'd expected. I just met his family last Sunday. They are a wonderful group of people. They made me feel so welcome. Anyway, he wants to get married next month. We've been very discreet since we met last year because of his ex, a nutcase to the bone. He had to cut her loose because she was so weird and she kept badgering him to marry her. That cow tried to lure him back with money." Darla leaned closer to me and, lowering her voice, added with a grimace on her face, "She even tried to hold on to him with sex—which he said was lousy to begin with. She's about as vile as they come, a real enema bag. She's gruesome! He told me she's the worst girl-friend he's ever had."

I had to let Darla's words sink in. "She sounds beastly. Why did your fiancé get involved with a woman like that in the first place? There had to be something he liked about her."

"He said she was okay when he first met her. All nice

and sweet. You know the type. My honey was at a low point in his life. His mother was having some health issues, so he was vulnerable at the time. Anyway, his ex took advantage of that. She played a role and hounded the hell out of him until she got him interested in her enough to propose. She spent money on him and was at his beck and call. Most men can't resist all that. But he finally came to his senses and realized he deserved something better."

"That's a damn shame. Some women don't know when to quit," I said, shaking my head.

"It gets worse. She's threatened suicide several times. Being the man he is, my man remained friends with her, which she misinterpreted, of course. He does not have sex with her anymore. At least that's what he keeps telling me."

"Do you believe him?"

"To be honest with you, I don't know. I mean, I wasn't born yesterday. I have four brothers, and . . . they've all done some shitty stuff to their women. If, and I do mean *if,* my man is still screwing that woman, it doesn't mean a thing to him. I hate women like her! They are the reason our men are so spoiled and expect too much in a relationship!"

"I hear you, girl. They make it hard for the rest of us."

"Tell me about it. Well, good luck." Darla rose from her seat. "I'll see you around, Rachel. I'm going to be in the Bahamas with my fiancé next week, but I'm sure I'll see you here again when I get back."

"You're going to the Bahamas *before* you get married?"

Darla rolled her eyes. "He'd already made the arrangements before he decided he wanted to get married next month. I guess you could say we're going on the honeymoon before the wedding. He's so thoughtful, and not

just with me. Since he'd already made the travel arrangements, he didn't want to disappointment his travel agent
by changing our itinerary."

"I'm sure you'll have a wonderful time. Have fun!
And don't let that dude get away!" I yelled.

"Oh, he won't. I've got him right where I want him."

"Are your blind? That's a size six dress you're holding," Paulette snickered. She had invited herself to join
me at Marie's Bridal Shoppe in downtown Berkeley, a
couple of blocks from Dino's, where we had just had dinner Saturday evening. "I think we need to be checking
out dresses in the plus-size section."

"Speak for yourself. This is the one I'm going to purchase. I'll be a size six by the time I get married." Paulette
followed as I wandered over to another rack and glanced
at a few more dresses.

"By the way, I hardly see Seth anymore these days. I
haven't seen him in church in months."

"I haven't seen that much of him myself. He left for
Sacramento this morning."

"Oh? What for? His brother Damon lives up there, but
they don't get along."

"I don't think he's going to visit Damon. He said
something about attending some kind of retreat he found
out about from one of his colleagues."

"What do you mean by 'some kind of retreat'? Is that
all he told you?"

"Yeah. Why? I don't ask for details for something like
that. But he did say that he and several other businessmen
would be attending workshops that will help them hone
their management skills, which sounds pretty boring to me.
Poor Seth. He's still getting used to being in business, so
I'm sure this retreat will help him relax more in his new

role. Being your own boss is not as easy as we think it is, I guess. Poor Seth. He's been working so hard, but it's really paying off. And I'm glad. Me paying most of our living expenses is really shrinking my funds."

"I hope it pays off."

"Meaning what?"

"You should watch *Judge Judy* more. She's always handling cases with women who foot most of the bills in their relationships and end up regretting it. Men love to take advantage of women when it comes to finances. I thought you were smarter than that. . . ."

"Come on, Paulette. Get off my case. Patrice rides my back enough. I don't need you doing it, too. I am not going to regret anything. Seth is not taking advantage of me."

"For his sake, I hope not. You're kind of scary when you get mad."

I didn't purchase a dress, after all. Since I still didn't know the date of my wedding, I decided it would make more sense to wait a few more weeks.

Chapter 12

Rachel

I DIDN'T HEAR FROM SETH THE WHOLE TIME HE WAS AT his retreat. I thought he'd be gone only five days. He didn't return the following Thursday, like he had told me he would, so naturally I got worried.

I didn't like to call up his family, and I didn't like to bother the people at his office by asking nosy questions about him, but in this case I felt I had to. Something could have happened to him, for all I knew.

When I hadn't heard from him by Friday, I decided to call his parents' house. I felt more at ease with his father, and I hoped he'd be the one to answer the phone. I was disappointed when Seth's mother answered on the first ring.

"Hello, Vivian. This is Rachel. I'm sorry to bother you, but I was wondering if you'd heard from Seth?" Vivian had answered the telephone with a cheerful, upbeat greeting. When she realized it was me calling, her tone changed immediately.

"No. I have not heard from my son," she snapped.

"Is he still at the retreat in Sacramento?"

"I don't know." I could almost feel the chill in her voice.

"I thought he'd be back yesterday. At least that's what he told me," I sniffed. "Maybe I misunderstood him."

"Maybe you did."

"Anyway, I'm worried about him."

"I'm not."

It seemed like the more I prolonged this conversation, the more abrupt and indifferent Vivian sounded. I was just as anxious to end this call as she was. "Well, if you hear from Seth, will you tell him to call me? I'll let you go now."

"Yeah." Vivian wasted no time hanging up.

Since early August, almost a whole month ago, I had noticed that Seth's mother, as well as almost everybody else he knew, had begun to treat me differently when I talked to them on the phone and when I saw them in person, which was not nearly as frequently as it used to be. September was just around the corner, and Seth's parents had not invited me to the house in two weeks, whereas before, they used to invite me two or three times in the same week.

I knew that Seth still had a few issues with various folks, whom he didn't like to talk about, including his parents. Had I done or said something to upset all these people? I wondered. I had tried on more than one occasion to get Seth to open up to me, but that had been like trying to pull teeth with a set of tweezers. Each time he'd given me an evasive response about his parents having marital problems. That didn't explain why other people in his circle had begun to treat me in such a mysterious manner. I had even asked him if I had done or said something to his associates that had offended them, and he had assured me that I had not.

Two more days went by before I heard from Seth. He didn't call to let me know he had returned, so when he showed up at my door the following Sunday night, I was surprised but happy to see that he was all right.

"I was getting real worried," I yelled at him when he entered my living room, with a tan, I noticed. I wrapped my arms around his waist and kissed him. It was like kissing a piece of wood, but I kept my arms around him, anyway. "Like I just said, I was worried. Especially when your mama told me she hadn't heard from you. And I couldn't get any information from your secretary or your business partner when I called your office."

"One of the workshop facilitators had to cancel, and I was asked to take his place," he told me, squirming in my embrace. "It was so busy and hectic, I just didn't get around to letting anybody but Howard know that I'd be gone longer than I'd expected."

"I think I annoyed your mother when I called and tried to get information from her. She's the last person I want to upset. So far, she and I have had a wonderful relationship, and I want it to continue. After we get married, I plan to spend a lot of time with her. After all, she'll be my 'other' mother, so I want to stay on her good side."

"Mother's getting on in age. She was probably having a bad day when you talked to her. You know how women get when that menopause thing kicks in."

"You're right. I don't know why I hadn't considered that. I guess those other people I called were just having a bad day, too, huh?"

"I guess."

"I didn't realize Sacramento got that hot."

"What do you mean?"

I removed my arms from around Seth's waist and grabbed his hand and held it up. "You got a lot of sun. We were the same shade when you left here. . . ."

"Oh, yeah, I got a little darker. After each session, a couple of the other participants and I hung out by the hotel pool for a couple of hours each day. The last day, the temperature was in the nineties."

"Anyway, I'm glad you're back, and I'll show you how glad I am before you leave here tonight. But before we get too, uh, cozy, I wanted to run a couple of things by you."

He gently removed his hand from mine. "Can you fix me a drink first?"

"Sure, baby."

I scurried into the kitchen and poured him a glass of Chianti and myself a glass of mineral water. By the time I got back to the living room, Seth had sat down on the couch, removed his shoes, and propped his feet up on the coffee table. His hand was trembling when I handed him his drink. I sat down next to him.

"I'm allowing myself only one glass of wine a week these days." I took a sip of my water and touched his knee. He still had not drunk any of his wine. "I've been walking my ass off on that treadmill, literally! I've lost an inch and a half off my butt since I joined the gym. I would like to be closer to my goal weight when I buy the dress I'm going to be married in. Now, about the wedding announcements, everybody knows we're getting married, so I don't think we should send out announcements again until we set the date. And when we do, I hope it's the *final* date. I don't want people to think we're not sure we want to get married. What do you think?"

"You're right." Seth took a long drink.

"Baby, you sound kind of distant."

He sounded more than "kind of distant." The tone of his voice was so weak and indifferent, it was almost like I was talking to a stranger.

"Huh? I just have a lot on my mind."

"You've been working too hard, for one thing. Oh! Uncle Albert told me to tell you to give him a call so he can get you in touch with his friend at that real estate agency. We can look at some of the properties when you're available." Lately it seemed like whenever Seth and I were alone together, I did most of the talking. Just as I was about to ask him again if something was bothering him, he spoke.

"That's fine, honey."

"Seth, you need to talk to me. I can tell that something is bothering you, and whatever it is, I need to know."

"Rachel, I'm fine."

He silenced me with a firm kiss. A few seconds later, he lifted me off the couch and carried me to the bedroom, where we made love like we'd never made love before. I forgot all about the mysterious behavior of all the people I'd called, trying to get information about Seth. Being in his arms had an amazing effect on me.

I had no idea that Seth and I were making love for the last time.

Chapter 13

Seth

I STILL HAD FEELINGS FOR RACHEL, EVEN THOUGH I KNEW we had no future together. And I knew she loved me more than ever now. Making love to her one last time was as much for my pleasure as hers.

I knew she would be disappointed if I didn't spend the night. That was why I encouraged her to drink three glasses of wine. Shortly after she drained the third glass, she was snoozing like a baby. I eased out of bed, got dressed in the dark, and left.

I decided to call Darla as soon as I got back to my parents' house. I had taken her to the Bahamas to celebrate her twenty-ninth birthday. We had just returned the day before yesterday. I had told everybody the same bogus story about a retreat in Sacramento that I had signed up to attend. But I'd got busted, anyway.

My father had taken me aside yesterday and had told me, "Boy, I have a lot of friends, and they all travel extensively. Robert Strauss, my former law partner, called me when he returned from Nassau yesterday. He told me he saw you dancing up a storm in the nightclub at the same hotel that he and his, uh, lady friend were at. You and Darla . . ."

"Oh." I had given my father a sheepish look and had told him, "Please don't tell Mother or anybody else. I . . . I . . . I'm sure you know how it is." My father was still involved with his mistress, so he knew that it was best for him to keep his mouth shut.

"Pffft! You know I won't do that. You just better watch your step and hope that somebody who knows Rachel doesn't spill the beans about you and Darla. Rachel is going to be upset enough when you break up with her."

"I know, Father. Don't worry about her. I have everything under control."

"When are you going to get rid of her?"

"Real soon, Father. As soon as I feel she's stable enough to deal with it."

On one hand, I felt like a low-down dog. On the other hand, *I* felt like the victim, not Rachel. I just could not get over her not telling me about her family! She had betrayed and deceived me. A woman had to be evil to do that! Her deception and betrayal were more than enough for me to maintain my level of anger and not feel guilty about using her for her money. In some strange way, I *wanted* to hurt her. I wanted a family of my own, and since that was not going to happen with her, I had been forced to go out and find somebody else.

I now loved Darla almost as much as I had once loved Rachel. I was very eager to marry Darla and start my family. And I wanted to do it fast so I could get over my feelings for Rachel sooner and more completely. Darla was not nearly as good in bed as Rachel. I told myself that if I could put up with a woman who had hurt me as much as Rachel had, I could put up with Darla's mediocre bedroom performance.

I was glad that I'd ended my relationship with Rachel with one last bedroom romp. . . .

Both my parents had already turned in for the night by the time I got home, and the house was eerily quiet. Despite the privacy I would have had, I felt safer using the telephone in my bedroom instead of one of the extensions. For some reason, my hand was shaking as I dialed Darla's number.

"It's me, baby," I said in a low voice when she answered on the third ring.

"Honey, I'm so glad you called. I got the sample wedding invitations, and I want you to take a look at them before I send them out. I know it's late, but can you come over?"

"Now?"

"Yes, now. I'm so anxious to see you, I don't think I can get to sleep until I do."

"Well, I am a little tired, so . . ."

"So you need to stay only for a few minutes. Please, come over here, honey. I'll make it worth your while," Darla said, prodding.

"I'll be there in a few minutes. Leave the door unlocked."

Darla met me in front of the elevator across the hall from the front door of her loft. She was naked to the world. I had no choice but to scoop her up in my arms and carry her to the sofa bed in the middle of the huge room that was her loft, which she had decorated so lavishly with antique furniture and brightly colored pictures on every wall. I didn't know how I managed, but I made love to her for hours, too.

* * *

I ignored Rachel's phone calls over the next few days, but the messages she left each time began to sound kind of frantic. I decided that it was in my best interest to talk to her. The last thing I wanted was for her to show up at my office and make a scene.

I called her back the following Tuesday morning. It was a few minutes before ten. I had chosen this day and time because I knew this was when she had to attend her weekly staff meeting.

"Baby, I'm so glad you called! I've left you so many messages," she said, sounding out of breath. "I really would like to talk to you now, but I'm about to go into our staff meeting in a few minutes. Can I call you back after lunch?"

"Rachel, we really need to talk as soon as possible." I held my breath and mentally began to count to ten. I had made it only up to four when she spoke again.

"Is it about the wedding, Seth?"

"Uh-huh."

"Did your mama talk you into us having a big church wedding?"

"No."

"Is it that you want to delay the wedding a little longer?"

"Something like that," I muttered.

"Hmm. Well, we've delayed it more than once already. I don't have a problem doing it again—as long as we don't push it too far into the future. We're not teenagers, you know." Rachel laughed. "I don't want to qualify for the senior citizen discount rate for our marriage license, if there is such a thing."

"Rachel, shut up!"

"Huh? Baby, what the hell—"

"I can't marry you," I blurted. "I'm so sorry to have to tell you this over the telephone."

It took about ten seconds for her to respond. During

that time, she breathed so loudly, I thought she was having an asthma attack. When she finally spoke again, her voice was low and raspy. "Seth, what the hell is going on? What happened between the last time I saw you, which was just last week, and now for you to decide you don't want to marry me?"

"I just don't think it's the right thing to do right now."

"Right now? Well, like I just asked, do you want to delay the wedding a little longer?"

"Rachel, there won't be a wedding at all."

"And you can't tell me why?"

I heard some muffled voices in the background on her end.

"I have to go now," she told me. Her voice sounded stiff and weak. "Our staff meeting is about to start, and I'm facilitating this one. I . . . I want to talk to you face-to-face. I think I deserve more than a phone call and this vague answer as to why you've changed your mind about us getting married. If you're telling me that marriage is too big of a step for you and that you want only to date me, I can live with that. But I want to hear you say that. I am sure we can work out an arrangement that's agreeable to us both."

"Look, I'll come over this evening around seven and we can talk. All right?"

"All right," she muttered.

I didn't give Rachel time to say anything else. I couldn't end the conversation fast enough. I knew it was going to be a long day for me, and for her, too, for that matter. My chest felt tight, and my head was throbbing, as if somebody had pounded it with a baseball bat. I had been experiencing these symptoms for a while now. As a matter of fact, I had not felt the same since I'd met Rachel's family.

Chapter 14

Seth

LOOKING BACK ON THAT TRIP TO ALABAMA, I THINK that if I had ended my relationship with Rachel shortly after that, it would have been better for everyone involved. Yes, I had stayed on with her for financial reasons mostly, but now I wished I had not done that. Guilt was kicking my ass like nobody's business.

I had all day to come up with a reason, or reasons, to give her as to why I couldn't marry her. One thing was for sure. I couldn't tell her that the main reason was the mental illness issue and that her family's class status was almost as serious a concern.

My obese secretary, Sister Beulah, barged into my office a few minutes after my conversation with Rachel. She took one look at the tortured expression on my face and stopped in her tracks. "Son, I heard you yelling at somebody a few moments ago, and you don't look well. What's the matter?"

I glared at the elderly woman, whom Mother had practically forced me to hire, and slammed my fist down on my desk. "What the fuck! Don't you worry about it! It's none of your damn business!" I blasted. "Don't you have work to do?" I had been snapping at Sister Beulah a lot lately. I was sorry that I had begun to take out my frustrations on her.

Sister Beulah's brows furrowed, and her mouth dropped open. She placed her hands on her ample hips and blinked hard a few times. Next thing I knew, she stomped up closer to my desk. She was glaring at me even harder than I was glaring at her. "Seth Garrett, who do you think you're talking to? I'm old enough to be your mama, boy."

"Boy? How big do boys grow where you come from? I'm a man who happens to be the one who signs your paychecks. Now, if you want to continue working for me, you'd better stay in your place."

In all the years I had known Sister Beulah, I had never seen a more horrified look on her face.

"Why, you mannish, ungrateful scalawag, you!" she yelled, seething with anger. "You can't talk to me like that! I used to change your funky diapers! I used to burp you. I used to—"

"I'll be saying you *used* to work for me if you don't watch your step, lady."

Sister Beulah shook her finger in my face. "Harrumph! I've had just about enough of you sassing me, when all I'm trying to do is help you. I don't have to put up with this mess!"

"No, you don't have to put up with this mess."

"And I won't. I'll be out of here in five minutes."

"What? I was going to suspend you for only a few days," I said, wobbling up out of my seat. "You can't just up and quit."

"You just watch me!" Sister Beulah had already started

moving toward the door, stomping like she was trying to put out a fire, and breathing through her mouth so hard, I was surprised she didn't spit out a few sparks.

I followed her to the reception area. "Let's talk this over after we both cool off. I'm having a bad day, and you know I didn't mean what I just said."

"Well, I meant what I just said!" She stopped by the side of her desk. "Just let me get my pocketbook, my rubber plant, my Tupperware bowl with the red beans and rice you won't be eating for lunch today, and my shawl, and I'll be on my way. You know where to send my last paycheck. And if you know what's good for you, it better not be late or short, or you'll hear from my attorney!" Sister Beulah grabbed her hideous black and yellow polka-dot shawl off the coatrack behind her desk and wrapped it around her shoulders. Had this not been such a serious situation, I would have laughed, because she looked like a gigantic bumblebee.

"Sister Beulah, I'm sorry. I didn't mean to upset you," I said, attempting to put my hands on her shoulders. My face was so close to hers, the stench of her sour breath made my eyes water.

"You've done just that one time too many," she barked, slapping my hands away. She snatched open the top side drawer of her desk and removed her bamboo purse and a few other personal items. She looked at me with so much contempt in her eyes, I flinched. "And let me tell you one more thing, young man. From now on, you'd better watch how you treat people. One of these days, you are going to piss off the wrong person, and they are going to teach your black ass a lesson you'll never forget!"

I couldn't remember the last time I had been insulted so severely, but I was prepared to grovel as much as necessary to keep my secretary. "Sister Beulah, have a heart. I'm begging you not to leave like this! Is it a raise you want? Is that what's really ruffling your tail feathers? I'm sure we can work something out. We still need you!"

"Well, I don't need you or your money. I never did. You knew that from day one. I was helping out as a favor to you and your mama."

"Sister Beulah, I've known you since I was a little boy. I care about you, and I worry about you—"

"You don't need to worry about me. I was just fine before I came to work for you, and I'll be fine after I'm gone."

"Okay. I'm trying to be reasonable."

"Reasonable? Boy, you don't know the meaning of that word. Not to me or anybody else. I am not blind. I know what you've been up to with that gal that you lock yourself up with in your office. . . ." A mysterious look crossed Sister Beulah's face, and that was another concern.

"If you're talking about Darla Woodson, that's none of your business."

"No, it's not. But I will tell you this much. If you think you need to worry about somebody, that somebody should be yourself and . . . Rachel."

"What about Rachel?"

"You think all I do is sit out here and type letters and answer the phone? You think the people who call here for you don't tell me more than they should when I answer your phone? And the same goes for the people who come up in here to see you. Like that Darla woman! Don't you know by now that most secretaries know just about everything there is to know about their bosses? Even their personal life . . ."

"What's that supposed to mean?"

"You ever wonder what Darla and I talk about when she's out here with me, waiting for you to finish a call or come out of a meeting?"

"Anything that Darla discusses with you in this office is confidential. Do I make myself clear?"

"Nigger, please! The only thing 'confidential' to me is my stretch-marked booty! You just better pray I don't get mad enough to blab your 'confidential' business."

"You will not discuss my personal business. Do you understand?"

"I'll discuss whatever I want to. If you don't like it . . . sue me. Now, you have a nice day, if you can, *boy*."

I was so stunned, I couldn't say another word or move a muscle. I stood rooted to the same spot as my angry former secretary offered me a sinister laugh before she angrily marched out the front door.

Chapter 15

Rachel

I SPENT MY WHOLE LUNCH HOUR SITTING IN THE BREAK room, ignoring the ham sandwich on the Styrofoam plate in front of me as I read a few pages of the latest issue of *Black Enterprise*. If somebody had come in and asked me what I'd just read, I could not have told them. My mind was on Seth and why he had changed his mind about marrying me.

I was glad to see my desk telephone message-waiting light blinking when I returned to my office. My hand trembled as I retrieved my messages. The first one was from Mama. I interrupted her rant in mid-sentence because no matter what she was whining about this time, it could wait. The second message was from Lucy. She so sounded frantic, I called her back immediately.

"What's up?" I began. "How come you didn't attend the staff meeting this morning?" Lucy was our head librarian, and she rarely missed a staff meeting.

"I had a doctor's appointment. Do you know that motherfucker I've been dating gave me an STD?"

"That good-looking Greyhound bus driver you've been seeing infected you? With what?"

"Herpes!"

"Oh, my God. I'm so sorry to hear that."

"You're sorry. Honey, the person who is going to be sorry is Gary Franklin!"

"Have you told him yet?"

"I just found out this morning, and he won't be back from his bus run to San Jose until tonight. Oh, when I see that son of a bitch, he's going to regret the day he met me!" Lucy snarled. "I'm not coming in to work at all today. Can you meet me at Dino's Restaurant when you get off work? I'm going to get drunk as hell."

"I can meet you, but I can't stay long. Seth is coming over to talk to me about something this evening."

"Then why don't we get together after you've talked to Seth? I'm going to need a couple of hours to vent. I can round up Paulette and Patrice, if they're available, and we can meet at your place or mine."

"That sounds fine, but I'm not in the mood for any of Patrice's stupid comments to me tonight."

"You don't have to worry about her messing with you tonight. All I have to do is give her one of my 'Don't you go there' looks and that'll shut her shut up."

"Is that why she never says anything stupid to you or about you?"

"She has no reason to. A fat, clumsy ox like me with my plain-Jane self . . . I'm no threat to her. But you're everything she's not—petite, smart, and beautiful. She's always been jealous of you."

"If she's jealous of me, why does she come around me and even call me up from time to time?"

"Now, that's a question I can't answer. She's not a mean person, but I would never let my guard down with her if I wore your shoes. I think . . ." Lucy paused.

"Think what?"

"She used to have the hots for Seth real bad. It took her a long time to realize he wasn't interested in her, so she got over him."

"If she got 'over him,' why do you think she has some resentment toward me?"

"She's a woman, and that's what we do. I got over my ex-husband, but I still can't stand the bitch who took him from me." Lucy laughed.

I laughed too. "Well, I hope Patrice finds herself a man soon. And I hope she has gotten over Seth, because I'm not about to let another woman have him." I laughed again. But it was a hollow laugh. I refused to believe that Seth was not going to marry me, unless he gave me a valid reason as to why he had made that decision. "Anyway, if you want to bring her along, I don't care. I'll call you after Seth leaves my apartment."

Seth arrived at six thirty. He entered my living room, dragging his feet like he was on the way to his own execution.

What he had told me on the telephone earlier had not sunk in yet, so I was still able to be cordial to him. "Baby, you look like hell," I told him. "Can I fix you a drink?"

He held up his hand and shook his head. "Don't bother. I won't be staying but a few minutes." He shuffled slowly across the floor to the couch, where he plopped down with a groan.

"Seth, what's the matter?" I demanded. I stood in front of him with my arms folded. "Were you serious about calling off the wedding?"

"Rachel, I think you need to sit down to hear what I have to say." He patted a spot on the couch next to him. When I attempted to ease down into his lap, he pushed me to the side and put his head in his hands and moaned. "I hate to do this to you."

"I have a feeling I'm going to hate whatever it is you're going to do to me, too."

"I'm not ready for marriage!" I could not believe how blunt he sounded.

"Oh." I let out a heavy sigh and looked at the wall for a few seconds. From the corner of my eye, I could see him staring at me with a blank expression on his face. I turned sharply to look at him. "After all this time, you just now decided that you're not ready for marriage?"

"Well . . . ," he sniffed. Then he nodded. "It's been on my mind for some time now."

"Seth, if it's been on your mind for 'some time,' why didn't you say something before now? Why did you let me go on thinking everything was okay? And here I was, out looking for a dress to get married in!"

"Rachel, I'm sorry." He shook his head. I had never seen such a look of anguish on his face. "I wasn't being fair to myself by keeping you in the dark."

"Fair to yourself? What about you not being fair to *me?*"

"I thought maybe my feelings would change . . . but . . . but they haven't! I can't marry you, and that's final."

I pressed my lips together and rubbed the back of my neck. It felt like every muscle in my body from the chest up was aching, like I'd been run over by a bus. And in a way I guessed I had been thrown under a bus. I wanted to crawl into bed and stay there until this was over. It had to be a nightmare, and I couldn't wait to wake up. But when I looked at Seth again and saw the serious look on his face, I knew it was not a nightmare.

I could feel the blood rushing up to my face, the same way it had that day I caught my ex-boyfriend Jeffrey in bed with another woman before I moved from Alabama. I was not about to bust up one of my cute lamps upside Seth's head the way I had with Jeffrey.

"Seth, I advise you to vacate the premises," I said abruptly. "I need to be alone right now." It did me no good to attempt to maintain my normal tone of voice. I sounded as squeaky as Minnie Mouse.

He stood up so fast, he stumbled. Had he not grabbed on to the back of the easy chair facing the couch, he would have fallen. "I . . . I still care about you . . . uh . . . Rachel," he blubbered, blinking hard.

I shot him a hot look and nodded. "Sure you do. Now, if you don't get up out of my place, I am not going to be responsible for my actions," I warned.

"You're not going to do anything stupid to yourself when I leave, I hope."

"If I do anything stupid, it won't be to myself. If you don't get your ass out of here while you still can, you'll find out."

Seth began to move toward the door, walking backward. I was surprised at how calm he appeared to be while I was falling apart inside a piece at a time. "Rachel, are you going to be all right?"

"Good-bye, Seth," I said, rising. I rushed over to the door and flung it open. "And good luck." As soon as he crossed the threshold, I slammed the door so hard and fast, it hit his butt.

He must have flown down the stairs from my second-floor apartment to his car, because a few seconds later, he started his motor and drove off like a bat out of hell. I sat back down on the couch and stared at the wall until the telephone rang an hour later.

"Hey, girl." It was Lucy.

"I'm glad you called," I croaked.

"You free for company now? Paulette and Patrice told me to pick them up on my way over."

"Come on over," I managed to say. "I'll be here."

Chapter 16

Rachel

*T*WENTY MINUTES LATER PATRICE, LUCY, AND PAULETTE arrived. After we had all sat down in my living room, I poured each of us a glass of wine. We immediately started roasting Lucy's boyfriend for giving her herpes.

The telephone rang again, and I motioned for everybody to get silent. I leaped up and darted across the floor to the end table. I lifted the telephone with a shaky hand. This time it was Mama on the other end of the line.

"Hi, baby," she began.

"Mama, I can't talk right now. I have company."

"I just wanted to know if you and Seth had picked a date for the wedding yet—and one y'all going to stick to this time. Shoot! Your aunt Hattie keeps bugging me about it. Since you and Seth keep fiddling around with the date, she can't determine when to start saving enough money to buy y'all a real nice wedding gift," Mama said.

I had a hard time trying to decide what words I wanted to use. I didn't say anything until Mama finished her last rambling sentence and paused to clear her throat. "Mama, Seth and I won't be getting married." Not only did she let out a piercing yelp, but so did my three friends. "He called it off."

"Say what? Why did Seth call off the wedding? What did you do to him, gal?" Mama hollered.

"I didn't do anything to him, Mama. He came by here a little while ago and told me he was not ready for marriage."

With another loud yelp, Lucy rose but fell back onto the couch a few seconds later, fanning her face with her hand. Patrice and Paulette came over and stood next to me with stunned looks on their faces.

"Is that all he told you?" Mama paused, and I heard her mumbling to somebody on her end. Then she said in a loud voice to whoever that person was, "*Seth said what?*" A few moments passed, and then she cussed under her breath. "Rachel, Janet is standing behind me, eavesdropping on my call, like she always does when somebody uses the phone in this house. She just told me that when y'all was down here last year, she heard Seth on the telephone telling somebody he wasn't going to marry you, because your family had mental problems. Did you know he felt that way?"

What I had just heard made absolutely no sense to me, and I didn't believe it for one second. The man had stayed with me long after he had met Janet and Ernest. "Mama, that's not the reason he broke up with me."

"But Janet just told me she heard—"

"Seth didn't care about our family's mental situation."

"Girl, use your head for something other than a hat rack. Didn't you just hear what I told you that Janet told me?"

"And you believe her? Janet's been hearing voices for

years, Mama. What about the time she told you a demon told her to set your laundry on fire? And what about that time she claims the dog who lives in the trailer across the street from you told her to cut off all her hair?"

"She was having episodes when she said all that."

"What makes you think she's not having an 'episode' this time?"

"But why would she say something like that about Seth?"

"Because right after she heard you say, 'Seth called off the wedding,' a few minutes ago, she took it and ran with it. Seth didn't change his mind about marrying me because of her and Ernest."

"They ain't the only ones in our family with mental afflictions. Even your late daddy must have had some mental problems to fool around with another man's wife."

"I know that, Mama. Now, if you don't mind, I'd like to get back to my company. I'll call you back tomorrow."

By the time I got off the telephone, all three of my friends had surrounded me.

"Girl, you let me go on and on about my problem, when we should have been discussing yours!" Lucy boomed. "How come you didn't tell us Seth broke off the engagement?"

"I was going to," I muttered. I returned to the couch, but everybody else stood in the middle of the floor, looking at me.

"What was your mama trying to say about why Seth broke up with you?" Paulette asked.

"Uh, my brother, Ernest, and my sister, Janet, are mentally challenged," I replied.

"What?" Patrice's eyes bulged out like they were trying to escape.

"Mentally challenged how?" Paulette asked.

"My brother, Ernest, is autistic, and my sister, Janet, is paranoid schizophrenic. We have other relatives with serious problems, too. All mental." You could have heard a feather fall to the floor. "Janet hears voices. She claims she heard Seth on the telephone, telling somebody he couldn't marry me, because of . . . my family's mental problems. But she's always hearing voices."

"Did you ask Seth if that's the reason he dumped you?" Patrice asked. She actually looked like she was enjoying the fact that I was distressed. There was even a hint of a smile on her lips.

"You should ask him," Lucy added.

I shook my head. "I am not going to ask him, because I don't believe that's the reason he broke up with me. He's out of my life, and I'm going to move forward."

"Girl, if I was in your shoes, I'd be moving forward with my fist going upside his head," Paulette hollered.

"You're probably better off without Seth, anyway. But I wouldn't let him get off so easily," Patrice yelled. "If it was me, I'd make him wish he never laid eyes on me."

"The man doesn't want me. That's no crime. And the bottom line is, I don't want to be with somebody who doesn't want to be with me," I insisted.

"Well, you're a better woman than I am. Here I am with herpes for the rest of my life. As soon as I see the bastard that infected me, I'm going to slap the shit out of him, and then I'm going to put the word out about his *nasty, diseased dick* all over town. And you should at least do the same thing to Seth! What he did to you is just as bad as what asshole Gary did to me! Maybe even worse!"

"Seth was good to me. I don't want to hurt him because he fell out of love with me," I said. "I have to give him credit for telling me before we got married."

"So you're not going to do anything about it?" Paulette asked. "I can get one of my thug relatives to whup his ass for you."

Somehow, I managed to laugh. "As long as Seth doesn't bother me, I'm not going to bother him," I declared.

Chapter 17

Seth

I DID A LOT OF THINKING AS I DROVE FROM RACHEL'S apartment. I knew that to some people, it would look like I had betrayed her. I didn't feel that way. I was doing only what any other man in my shoes would do. And I was not doing it just for myself. I had my family to think about. They had very high expectations for me. I cringed when I imagined the remarks that Damon or his snooty wife would probably have come up with if I had married Rachel and produced a mentally ill child. *Seth, you're batting a thousand. Didn't you cause the family enough heartache when you got that ghetto woman pregnant? Now you have two idiot kids to raise!*

And poor Mother. Her not having a good relationship with my first child was enough of a source of misery for her. I could not take a chance on her having to cope with another one. Or several more. Rachel had repeatedly indicated that she wanted at least two or three children. Well, she could have all the children she wanted. But they wouldn't be mine.

Yes, I had disappointed her, and I felt badly about it. As a matter of fact, I felt like a piece of shit. Especially knowing how much she loved me and how anxious she had been to get married.

But I was optimistic. Knowing how strong a woman Rachel was, I was convinced that she'd get over me and move on with her life. With that in mind, my main concern now was my own happiness and my future with Darla. With Rachel out of the picture, I could openly focus on that now.

I should have been elated, but I had another thorn in my side. My mind would not let me rest, the way I thought it would, even though I had dropped Rachel. I could still see the hurt look on her face and the tears in her eyes. Because of that, I got so agitated, I didn't want to go home. And I certainly didn't want to talk to anybody yet about what I'd done.

I glanced at my watch. I decided to stay out until I was sure my folks had gone to bed. I didn't want to face either one of them tonight. I couldn't decide what I was feeling. But whatever it was, it was a strange feeling. It felt like a cross between guilt and elation. Guilt because I had hurt Rachel, and elation because I had climbed out of a deep, dark hole that I had slid down into.

I meandered around for hours, driving around in circles and up and down streets I had never been on before. I even sat in a Walmart parking lot until a security guard gave me a menacing look. I started up my motor and began to drive around some more. I needed a drink, and Father kept our liquor cabinet well stocked with booze, so I'd drink at home tonight. With Father and Mother in bed, I could drink to my heart's delight without their interference. I planned to drink myself into oblivion when I got home. At least if I was passed out, I wouldn't have to think about Rachel.

It was almost midnight by the time I made it home. All the interior lights were out, but the front porch light was on. I let myself in and tiptoed all the way to my room. I wanted to change clothes before I started drinking. I had left my cell phone on the nightstand. I checked it and the landline on the same nightstand for messages. Darla had left one on each phone. "Honey, call me as soon as you get this message. I don't care how late it is," she said, sounding so sweet. I dialed her number immediately.

"Hey," I began when she picked up on the second ring. "I see you called while I was out."

Darla took her time responding.

"Darla, are you still on the phone?"

"Yes, I am. Seth, I've been thinking. We did rush things, and lately, you've been acting somewhat distracted. Now, if you are not ready to get married next month, you need to let me know now. After what you've been through with that woman, you might want to have your space to yourself for a while, and if that's the case, I understand. But if you still want to see me, that's fine, too. We can even just date, if that's all you want."

"Baby, I do want to marry you next month. The sooner I do, the sooner I can get on with my life. I apologize if I've seemed distracted. I had a little business issue that had been bothering me. I resolved it a little while ago. Now I can focus on you and our wedding."

"Are you sure we won't have to worry about that woman now?"

"Rachel is out of my life forever," I said with a lot of confidence, because I really thought that that was the case. I never expected to hear from her again. I had already made up my mind that if I ran into her on the street,

I would be civil, but I would not encourage or even participate in a conversation with her."

"I'm so glad to hear that. She put you through so much, and I hope she's sorry about it."

"What do you mean?"

"I hope she offered you some kind of apology the last time you saw her. Did she?"

"Yes, she did. She even suggested we remain friends, but I told her it was better if we didn't."

"She didn't threaten to kill herself again?"

"Uh, no. She wasn't at all happy the last time we talked, but she wished me well."

"Hmmm. That sounds mighty tame for a woman who had been giving you so much trouble about breaking up with her. Maybe she's already got a new fool."

"She probably has. She's the kind of woman who gets around, if you know what I mean. That's another reason I couldn't marry her. She was a big flirt and had already had numerous lovers before she met me. Some were still calling her, so she couldn't be trusted."

"You won't have that problem with me."

"I know I won't."

"Let's celebrate this weekend."

"I was going to suggest that. I want you to join me and your future in-laws for dinner again this Sunday. They're having a few folks over, and I want them all to meet you. We can tell them all about us getting married next month."

"How do they feel about Rachel? Don't you think your folks will be concerned about you marrying me so soon after you dumped her?"

"Don't you worry your pretty little head about my folks. They all want me to be happy."

* * *

Darla had told me that her mother had told her she was a fool for being my "backstreet woman" for so long. Lucky for me, Darla never paid much attention to anything her mother said. The bottom line was, I had kept Darla in the dark long enough, and that was something that a lot of women would not have put up with. I was eager to show my woman off now because I wanted her to know just how much I loved her. And since I was off the hook with Rachel, I saw no reason to continue seeing Darla on the sly. She was going to be my wife soon and the mother of my children.

My main concern was how Rachel was going to react when she found out there was another woman in my life—and had been for some time. And since we had so many mutual friends, I knew that it was just a matter of time before she found out. I hoped that Darla and I were married by then.

Rachel called me a week after I'd met with her at her apartment.

"I can't talk right now," I told her as soon as I realized she was the person on the other end of the line. "I'm very busy." I was sorry I had to sound so brusque, but I wanted to make sure she knew I was in no mood to talk to her.

"When can we talk?" she asked. "There are a few things I'd like to say to you."

"Rachel, whatever it is, it'll have to wait until I have the time to talk to you again, and the interest in doing so," I said firmly. "Now, if you don't mind, I have to go." I didn't wait for her to respond. I hung up immediately, and then I told my new secretary—a cute, docile young Korean woman who never gave me the headaches Sister Beulah had—not to put any more calls through from Rachel.

Rachel began to make a pest of herself. She left numerous messages for me at the office and on my cellular phone over the next few days, and I ignored them all. She even had the nerve to send me a card with a note in it that she "needed to talk to me in person right away." I had no idea what she wanted to say to me, and whatever it was, it was not going to make any difference.

Chapter 18

Rachel

*U*NFORTUNATELY, I HAD TROUBLE SLEEPING AT NIGHT, thanks to Seth. I had been getting up at around four each morning since he'd broken up with me. Almost every day I went to work a couple of hours early so I could read the morning newspaper with my coffee. This enabled me to be relaxed by the time my coworkers arrived.

I rarely talked about my personal life with anybody at work, except Lucy. Most of my straitlaced, stuffy coworkers seemed interested only in work, so they kept their personal business to themselves, too. I had mentioned to my supervisor and a few others that I was engaged, but since nobody had asked me about that since I'd told them, I assumed they wouldn't care one way or the other about what had happened between Seth and me, so I decided not to mention it unless someone asked. That was one consolation. I planned to take life one day at a time and hope for the best.

Life was too short, and even shorter for some folks, as I was about to find out.

It was 5:45 a.m. on that day during the second week in September when a special news bulletin interrupted the jazz radio program I listened to every morning. I was shocked when the announcer reported that a jet had crashed into one of the World Trade Center Twin Towers in New York City. I finished my coffee and shuffled down the hall to the break room to get another cup. When I returned to my office a few minutes later, the same announcer broke into the radio program again. I was getting annoyed because "Caught Up in the Rapture" by Anita Baker had just come on. But when the man said that another plane had hit the other Twin Tower, I got scared. I didn't find out until an hour later that the plane crashes had been deliberate. By then, some of my coworkers had come in. We all gathered in our conference room to watch the events unfold on a portable TV.

"My sister lives in New York," Donna Handel, one of the teachers, said, choking on a sob.

"My nephew works in one of those buildings," one of the male teachers said.

We all turned to Mrs. Trumble, our birdlike, white-haired principal. "In light of this situation, we'll close for the day and remain closed until further notice," she told us.

People immediately began to scramble out into the hallway, cussing and crying. I turned off my computer, gathered my things, and prepared to leave. The principal and a few other staff members were at the front entrance, sending kids back home. I was in such disbelief, I didn't even remember the short drive home.

Mama had already called me and left three messages, so I called her immediately.

"I know I'll never get on no airplane now," she declared. "You lock your doors and stay inside until we find out what else them terrorist fools done cooked up. In the meantime, you take care of yourself." Mama cleared her throat, which told me she had more to say. "Uh, you and Seth still ain't back together?"

"No," I said sharply. "And we won't be."

"Oh, well. Everything happens for a reason. Maybe it wasn't meant for you and him to be together."

"Maybe it wasn't," I agreed. "But I'll do just fine without him, Mama. Don't worry about me."

"You get on with your life, sugar. Don't let this setback set you back."

Mama's advice was good, but it was too late. The breakup was always on my mind, and the hurt was still as painful as it had been the moment Seth told me our relationship was over. I had been eating like a bird since the last time I saw him. It was so ironic that I had lost another eight pounds because of that.

I did everything I could to keep myself grounded so I wouldn't think about the breakup too much. But I did. I thought about it day and night, every day. I'd even called Seth a few times, trying to get him to talk to me. So far, I had not been able to catch up with him, and so far he hadn't returned any of my calls.

After we returned to work two days after the attack, I began to work overtime. I knew it would help for me to keep myself busy. I spent more time with my friends, I read books that had been sitting on my bookshelf for months, and I continued to go to the gym.

I had seen Darla Woodson at the gym, but we had not spoken since Seth had dumped me. But the following Monday evening, when she climbed onto the treadmill right next to me, she immediately began to walk at a slow pace and talk about her love life.

"Girl, I never thought I could be so happy," she gushed. "I am so in love!"

I was taken aback because Darla didn't seem the least bit concerned about last week's terrorist attacks. That was all everybody at the gym was talking about. "I can tell. How is your boo doing?" I asked, speaking in a dry tone of voice. I assumed she was avoiding the terrorist issue because it was so painful and she didn't want it to interfere with the state of bliss she was in.

"Oh, he's doing just fine. Everything is going so much better than I even expected!"

"You must have had some weekend," I said, smiling to conceal my smoldering envy. "Do you know anybody in New York or D.C.?"

Darla gave me a puzzled look. "No. Why do you ask?"

"Some of my coworkers have relatives in New York and D.C. They're okay, though."

She gave me another puzzled look. Either this woman had just crawled out from under a rock or she had a short memory. Then her eyes suddenly got big. "Oh! Are you talking about the terrorist attacks?"

I nodded.

"I don't know anybody in New York or D.C., but my hairdresser had a sister on the plane that crashed into the North Tower." Darla shook her head and let out a sorrowful sigh, but her sympathetic gesture didn't seem sincere. "Oh, well. We all have to go sometime." That was all she had to say about the biggest tragedy that had ever occurred on American soil in our lifetime. I was stunned and disappointed to know how indifferent she was. With a huge smile, she waved her hand in my face, pointing to the ring on her finger. "Can you believe this? It was his grandmother's ring."

"It's lovely," I mumbled. Seth had not asked me to return the engagement ring he had given to me. An hour after our breakup I had removed it from my finger and put it in a Ziploc bag. I was storing it in the same kitchen drawer where I kept my notions, such as my needles and thread, safety pins, and such. "You're one lucky girl."

"You don't know the half of it. We got married at his parents' house last Saturday afternoon. We had not planned to take the plunge so soon, but last month, all of a sudden, he wanted to do it this month. And that was fine with me." Darla began to walk at a slightly faster pace. "Since it was so sudden and unexpected, I had to rush and find a dress. I had always wanted to have a big wedding, and that's what we had talked about. But, you know, it was real quaint to have a little ceremony at his parents' house, with just family and a few close friends."

"That sounds so nice, Darla. Congratulations," I muttered.

An apologetic look suddenly crossed her face. "I'm sorry to be hogging the conversation and talking about me. What have you been up to since the last time I saw you? You look like you've lost a few pounds. Did you find a dress yet? Have you and your fiancé picked a date yet?"

I shook my head. "I won't be needing a wedding dress." I kept my voice strong and my head held high.

Darla gasped. "Oh? What happened? Did you change your mind about getting married?"

"Something like that." I cleared my throat and blinked hard to hold back my tears. I had shed a lot of tears in the past few days, and I didn't want to shed any more. "He broke the engagement." I reorganized my thoughts and kept my chin up. I was determined to keep my wits about me. I refused to show my pain, especially to a person I hardly knew.

"Oh, shit! Well, I hope you're still going to be friends with him! Maybe he'll change his mind later on."

I offered a weak smile and shook my head. "I don't think so."

"Well, if you don't mind my asking, what the hell happened?"

"He just said he wasn't ready to get married yet." I forced myself to smile. "It was good while it lasted, though. He was so special to me."

"What a shame. How are you handling things?"

"I'm okay, I guess. I still feel a little numb about it, but I'll get over him."

Darla gave me a curious look. "That dude is not telling you something. There has to be a serious reason as to why he called off the wedding, other than him not being ready to get married. How long were you guys together?"

"Four years," I said hoarsely.

"And he suddenly calls it quits? Oomph, oomph, oomph! I feel so sorry for what that asshole did to you!"

"We had a lot of good times, though." My voice had begun to weaken, despite how hard I had tried to keep sounding strong.

"He's still an asshole, and I hope that he regrets what he did to you someday!"

I exhaled and touched Darla's shoulder. "Thanks, Darla. I appreciate your concern."

"Well, I know I don't know you that well, but would you like to get together for a drink or dinner sometime? That way, we can really have a decent conversation about this. I mean, that is if you'd like to discuss this some more. I have a lot of time on my hands these days. I've already resigned from my boring job, which I hated, anyway. We just moved into our new house two days ago, so after we finish getting everything in place, you're welcome to come over. I'm sure Seth would love to meet you. Especially after what you just went through. I swear to God, I don't know why some men do the things they do! Thank God there are still some good ones left. Seth is the most sensitive man I've ever known, so he'd be a good person for you to talk to."

Chapter 19

Rachel

*E*VEN THOUGH MY EYES WERE OPEN, EVERYTHING WENT black for about two seconds. I could still hear Darla talking, but the only word that really jumped out at me now was her new husband's name: *Seth*. "Your husband is named Seth?"

She nodded vigorously. "He's already told me that we'll name our first son Seth Jr. I'm probably already pregnant. We've been busy since we met last April."

"Do you have a picture of your husband?" Had Darla not told me her husband's name was Seth, I would not have been interested in seeing what he looked like.

"Oh, I've got lots of pictures of him and me together." Darla paused her treadmill and leaned down to lift her gym bag. She rooted around in it for a few seconds and pulled out a wallet and flipped it open. "Here's one we took when we went to the Bahamas. We won't get our wedding pictures until next week."

The picture in front of my burning eyes made my head swim. There was Seth in a floral shirt and a straw hat, standing in front of a palm tree, with his arm around Darla. There was a tall glass in his hand with a pineapple wedge and one of those cute little umbrellas hanging over the lip. The date at the bottom of the photo was one of the dates on which, he had told me, he had attended that retreat in Sacramento.

"Have you ever seen a more handsome man?" Darla asked, sliding her tongue across her bottom lip.

"Yes," I mumbled. "I have. My ex was just as handsome as your new husband . . ." My head felt like it was going to explode. I ended my session on the treadmill and retrieved my gym bag off the floor, my hand shaking so hard, I almost dropped the bag. I sniffed and gave Darla a guarded look. "It's been nice talking to you. Good luck."

"I wish you didn't have to rush off. I was going to invite you to join Seth and me for drinks this evening. He's working late, so it'll be a couple of hours from now. I'm sure he would love to meet you. He's got a few single friends he could introduce you to."

"Thanks, Darla, but I'll have to decline your invitation. I already have plans for this evening."

"Well, can I get your telephone number so we can keep in touch? If I am pregnant, I don't know how much longer I'll be coming to the gym."

I pretended not to hear Darla's request for my telephone number. I couldn't get out of that gym fast enough. I didn't care if I had to drive fifty miles to another gym, I'd never work out in this one again! I sprinted to the nearest exit, and I didn't stop until I had made it outside and to the end of the block.

I was in such a daze, I couldn't even recall where I had parked. It took me fifteen minutes to locate my car at a meter two blocks from the gym.

With my hands shaking and tears streaming down both sides of my face, I drove to Seth's office. I knew that without an appointment, and with business hours over, the security guard would not allow me to enter the building, so I didn't even try. That didn't stop me from going into the underground parking garage.

There were four parking levels. It took me an hour to locate his BMW. I spat a dollop of saliva smack-dab in the center of the front windshield. Then I keyed the front, the back, and both sides. Just as I was about to leave and go to a hardware store to purchase something that I could use to slash his tires and bust our every single one of his windows, a man in a gray suit appeared. He didn't see me, so I crouched down until I heard him drive away. I decided then to forget the hardware store and instead hang around until Seth showed up so I could give him a piece of my mind and a punch in the nose if he provoked me.

I couldn't remain in the garage too long before somebody saw me and got suspicious enough to call security, so I left ten minutes later. Catching up with Seth so I could tell him to his face what I thought of him was not going to be easy. Especially with the way he had already been avoiding my phone calls and not returning any of my voice mail messages. Accepting an invitation from Darla to "meet" him so I could bust him in front of her— in the house that should have been my new residence— didn't appeal to me. There was no telling what I would do to him if I confronted him at the new house he'd just purchased. And there was no telling what he would do to me.

I couldn't imagine what he was going to say or do when he found out I knew how he had played me. I cringed when I recalled all the nasty things Darla had told me he had said about me. The part about me being lousy in bed was especially hurtful. For all I knew, Darla was in that new house right now, stretched out on an expensive couch, with a tall drink in her hand, telling him about the poor woman she'd met at the gym whose fiancé had just dumped her. All she had to do was mention my name and a few specific details about me, and he would put two and two together and realize I was the "poor woman" who'd been dumped!

Since it was going to cost Seth a pretty penny to get his car repaired, I had caused him some pain, anyway. Even though he had no idea who the culprit was. That was the only satisfaction I expected to get out of hurting him.

It was enough to suit me for the time being. . . .

Chapter 20

Seth

*H*AD I CAUGHT THE BASTARD WHO KEYED MY CAR, I would have beaten the dog shit out of him. Whoever he was, he really took his time and did as much damage as he could. And for what? What kind of satisfaction did people get out of doing something as asinine as keying a car? I tortured my brain, trying to recall if I had cut some dude off in traffic. If so, maybe he had seen me enter the parking garage and had decided to follow me. Back in the day when I was a mischievous kid, my crew and I had keyed a lot of cars. Each time it had been for a reason. Once I'd done it because some old white bitch had rear-ended me and had not even bothered to stop. I'd followed her to a mall. As soon as she had parked in front of Macy's and piled out of her shiny new Cadillac, I'd snuck over and done my business. And I hadn't used just the keys to my old Mustang. I'd done some damage with the blade of the pocketknife I used to carry.

I was no longer that boy who committed petty crimes on a regular basis. I was a respected businessman with a fine reputation in my community. I was determined to find out who had vandalized my car and to hold him responsible. Unfortunately, it didn't look like that was going to happen. I found out that the security cameras in the garage had been out of order and no one had witnessed the crime.

"You were lucky. You got off real easy, my man. One of the lawyers on the second floor had a window in his Porsche broken. The thief, or thieves—these creeps usually work in pairs—stole his CD player and a couple of loose hundred-dollar bills the dude was stupid enough to leave in his glove compartment," the parking attendant told me. "We have a lot of break-ins in this area. I guess the criminals figured out it would be more profitable for them to target the upscale areas than the projects and other low-income neighborhoods." He sounded so indifferent, I wondered if he had been in on the vandalism and other crimes.

It was an inconvenience and a costly setback for me to get my car repaired, but I got over it within a few days. I had too many things to be thankful for.

I was feeling on top of the world, even more so now. Getting rid of Rachel had given me a whole new outlook on life. It felt like a huge weight had been lifted off my shoulders. Everything was now going just the way I wanted it. Well, almost everything. My son's obnoxious mother, Caroline, called me up from L.A. at least once every two weeks to complain about how expensive everything was these days. Caroline had caused me a lot of grief over the years, but it had had little impact on the way I felt— and I felt better and better with each new day. With all the positive things in my life now, I didn't even let a major thorn in my side like Caroline bother me too much. My ad agency was doing better than ever, and a potential new client had invited me to have drinks with him this week. And as long as I had a good, supportive woman like Darla, I was certain that I could continue to move forward.

However, other people had begun to say things that got on my nerves. My brother Josh, who had always had my back, was one. I met up with him at a bar downtown after work one day a week after that asshole keyed my car. As usual, he was decked out in an Armani suit. Every strand of his close-cropped black hair was in place. For him to be one of the scariest pit-bull prosecutors in town, he had a very friendly-looking face. With his big brown eyes and warm smile, he looked more like a banker. I had decided not to mention the keying incident to Josh. After a few comments about work, politics, the economy, and what our family members were up to, all I could talk about was Darla. One reason was that the more I focused on her, the easier it was to keep Rachel off my mind.

"You keep going on and on about what a good woman Darla is," Josh pointed out. He shifted on his bar stool and swirled the cognac around in his shot glass. Then he cleared his throat and gave me a sheepish look. "You used to say the same things about Rachel."

"Rachel was a good woman! But like I keep telling you, she was not the woman I thought she was."

"Nor was her family. . . ."

"That's right. I was not going to burden myself with that woman and her crazy family." It was one thing when I referred to Rachel as "that woman" when Darla and I talked about her. But when I referred to her that way in front of Josh, knowing how much he liked her, a sharp pain shot through my chest.

"Crazy family? Isn't that a bit extreme? Rachel doesn't have any mental problems, and from what you've told me, neither does her mother or most of her other relatives."

"Man, let me remind you, the woman has only two

siblings, and both of them are nutcases! And there are even more in her extended family! That means the tainted blood in that family is pretty potent. I never got the whole story as to just how many nuts that family has, but even one more is one too many! Now, would you want to marry a woman with that many nutcases in her background? Would you want to raise mentally challenged children?"

"To be honest with you, now that I've given your situation more thought, I don't know if I would or not. I love my wife, and we were lucky enough to have a healthy child. But had Chrissie been born with a problem, either physical or mental, I wouldn't love her any less. And the same goes for any future children Faith and I might have." I didn't like the way my brother was looking at me. There was a puzzled expression on his face. His next question caught me completely off guard. "Does Rachel know you decided not to marry her because of her family?"

"Uh, I didn't tell her that. It probably would have caused her a lot of pain," I said, with my chest tightening.

"Little brother, I can assure you that the breakup alone caused her a lot of pain. Look at the facts. Rachel devoted several years of her life to you. Now you have left her and have already met and married another woman—one you didn't know half as long as you knew Rachel before you decided you wanted to marry her. How do you think that's going to make Rachel feel when she finds that out *and* the real reason you broke up with her?"

"I don't see her or talk to her, so I'll probably never know," I said with confidence.

"I sure hope you don't."

Josh's last comment remained on my mind until I got home.

"You look beat. Let me fix you a drink," Darla said when I entered the front door of our sprawling Spanish-style house at the end of a tree-lined cul-de-sac. Our neighbors included doctors, businessmen, and a few retirees. Even though I had a long way to go to reach the lifestyle I wanted, I still felt blessed.

I plopped down onto the plush blue velvet couch with a groan and watched Darla fix my drink at the bar facing me. I enjoyed looking at my wife. However, I had noticed that shortly after we got married, she stopped devoting a lot of attention to her appearance. I blinked at her as she waltzed across the floor toward me. Her hair was askew, her make-up was smeared, and the jeans she wore were the same ones she'd worn the past couple of days. But there were much more important things for me to be concerned about than my wife's sloppy appearance. As long as she looked nice and smelled good when we went out or when my parents came to visit, that was all that really mattered to me.

"Thank you, sweetie," I said when she handed me the drink. I immediately took a sip and then set the glass on the coffee table. "Sit down and let me talk to you." I patted the spot next to me on the couch.

"What do you want to talk about?" Darla sat down, but not as close to me as I expected.

"I just want you to know how much I love you. I've never known a woman as sweet and fine as you, and I promise I will be a good husband."

Darla scooted a few inches away from me. "What's going on, Seth?"

"I had a conversation with Josh today. He brought up Rachel's name, and it disturbed me a little."

Darla frowned. "Her again? Well, what did Josh say about that heifer that was so disturbing?"

"Oh, the fact that she had so many problems. I don't want to go into a lot of detail, but he's glad I'm with you and not her. I'm done with Rachel McNeal forever."

Darla's face froze. She let out a yelp and leaped up like a jackrabbit. "Rachel *McNeal?* Is that the last name of the woman you've been telling me about?"

"Yes. Why?"

"She's of medium height and build, bronze-colored complexion? Wears a ratty hair weave that looks like it was attached to her head with a staple gun?"

"That's a fairly decent description of Rachel, except she doesn't wear a hair weave."

Darla's eyes got big, her lips began to tremble, and then she began to shift her weight from one foot to the other. She couldn't take her eyes off my face. "Oh, my God! It's—it's *her!* I know that woman!"

There was a lot of pressure on my chest, as if somebody had squeezed the air out of me. I felt like a deflated balloon. "You what? When . . . Where did you meet her?"

"At the gym I used to go to! She and I chatted a few times, and she told me she was engaged. The last day I saw her at the gym, which was a few days after we got married, she told me her fiancé had suddenly dumped her. I tried to get her to come with me that day so she could have a drink with us! I even told her I'd get you to introduce her to some of your single friends! All that time . . . all that time I was talking to the same lunatic who had made your life so miserable!"

"Oh, my God!"

"Do you have a picture of her?"

"Not anymore. What makes you so sure we're talking about the same woman?"

"What's the matter with you, Seth? I'm sure it's her. What are the odds of us both knowing a Rachel McNeal in Berkeley and it being two different people?"

Darla sat down hard on the couch arm. By now most of her body was trembling, and sweat had formed in the armpits of her blouse. "When I showed her a picture of you, she got this strange look on her face. Now I know why. Seth, that wild woman could have stalked and killed me. Why haven't you told me everything about her?"

"I told you everything you needed to know. If she knows who you are, and she has not followed you home or stalked you or done anything stupid to you by now, I wouldn't worry about her if I were you. I'm sure she's over me by now."

"Well, I am worried about her. What if she backslides and decides she wants to get back into your life?"

"Sweetheart, please calm down. You don't have to worry about Rachel. I don't. I can assure you that if I run into her, or if she calls me for whatever reason, I will have nothing to do with her."

"It's a good thing I started going to a gym closer to home. There is just no telling what that maniac might have eventually done to me now that she knows I'm the woman you married."

"You dodged a bullet, baby."

"A cannonball would be more like it." Darla let out a sharp laugh, and I was glad to know she found the situation amusing. To me, it meant that she was no more concerned about Rachel than I was. "I don't think you need to waste any time worrying about that woman. I'm sure she's forgotten about you by now."

Darla was right, and I was not really worried about that woman. Despite Rachel's bloodline, I had no reason to believe that she'd do something "crazy" to me or Darla. Rachel was a levelheaded woman with a lot going for her. If she tried to get back at me in some way for breaking up with her, I would not hesitate to take whatever action was necessary to ensure my peace of mind and safety. Even if it meant having her arrested. Worst-case scenario was me having to kick her ass. Hopefully, it would not come to that, because I didn't believe in hitting women or children. With my two brothers being high-powered attorneys, I knew it would be easy for one of them to help me build a strong case against Rachel if she did retaliate. Such a scandal could cost her her job, as well as her freedom. And from what I knew about Rachel, she was not *that* crazy.

"How you managed to stay in a relationship with that woman for as long as you did is a mystery to me. Well, you can forget about her. She's part of your past," Darla assured me.

Yes, Rachel was part of my past. I had a wonderful future ahead of me.

Chapter 21

Rachel

Four years earlier . . .

I WOKE UP AROUND 8:00 A.M. THAT SUNDAY MORNING IN late August with one of the worst hangovers I'd ever had in my life. My head was throbbing, my stomach was doing flip-flops, and there were no words to describe what the inside of my mouth tasted like.

I sat up, opened my eyes, and looked around my bedroom. I was glad to see that the man who had kept me up for hours the night before had put his clothes back on and had left.

If I had stayed in bed on this day, things would have turned out a lot differently for me and everyone else involved. I was not even that eager to crawl out of bed and go church—or anyplace else—to meet Seth Garrett, a potential new boyfriend. But I had agreed to do so. I had no idea that it would be one of the biggest mistakes I had ever made in my life. . . . I sucked in some air and almost puked.

Lucy answered her telephone on the second ring. "My time is your time," she chirped.

"It's me," I said. "You don't have to pick me up for church this morning. I'll catch a ride with Uncle Albert. He's at the nail salon around the corner, getting a manicure. I just got off the phone with him."

"No, I'll pick you up! The last time you told me you had a ride, you didn't show up, and I didn't see or hear from you for two days. Today is too important, so I can't take a chance on that happening again."

I laughed. "I told you I'd be there. I just don't think it makes any sense for you to drive across town, out of your way, to pick me up when my uncle is so close by."

A heavy sigh was Lucy's response before she replied, "Look, I went out of my way to get you and Seth Garrett in the same place at the same time. I want to make up for that disaster you went through with Paulette's brother."

Paulette Ramsey was a mutual friend of ours. She was in her late twenties and was married to a chef who looked as good as he cooked. They had eight-year-old twin sons. Paulette had a younger brother named Walter, but everybody called him Skirt. What Lucy and Paulette hadn't told me when they threw a party last December to celebrate Skirt's twenty-sixth birthday and lured me to it so Skirt could meet "a decent woman" was why people called the brother Skirt. It hadn't taken long for me to find out. The man chased skirts the way dogs chased cats. Skirt was addicted to women and women were addicted to him and it was no wonder. He had the looks and the body of a male model, and he used both to his advantage. He worked as a valet at a hotel parking lot that his grandfather managed. He worked only a few days a month because he had to devote so much time to his love life and other shady activities.

If all that was not enough for me to end my relationship with him when I found it out, which was only a couple of weeks after our first date, what I learned subsequently was more than enough: he had a police record that included carjackings, armed robbery, assaults, breaking and entering, and other crimes. I had endured a somewhat rigid upbringing and had been strongly advised by the old folks to stay away from men who didn't walk the straight and narrow. Since I had more than a few faults of my own, a wild streak in a man intrigued me. But I drew the line when it came to a man with a serious criminal history.

Lucy had apologized to me profusely for setting me up with a straight-up thug. "I am so sorry I didn't tell you about Skirt before. He's always been a bad boy, but I thought he had turned his life around. The next time I hook you up with somebody, I'll make sure he's got a cleaner record."

Well, here she was, playing matchmaker again.

What neither Lucy nor anybody else knew was that Skirt and I were still "friends," or whatever people called ex-lovers who still snuck around and slept together. He was fun to be with, and I had always enjoyed his company, especially in bed. When he'd called me up one night a few weeks after our breakup, I'd reluctantly let him come over. One thing had led to another, and we'd ended up in bed. No matter how hard he'd tried to get me to "resume" our relationship so we could go out in public again, I'd resisted.

"We can still get together behind closed doors now and then, but that's all. That private school I work for did a thorough background check on me before they hired me. I'd probably lose my job if they found out I was affiliated with a criminal," I'd told Skirt the first night I allowed him back into my bed.

"Aw, baby, you know me. I don't want to socialize with none of them folks you work with, nohow, but I respect where you coming from. See, I ain't got no problem being a backstreet lover, so if you want to see me only on the down low, that's cool with me." He'd grinned, blinking his big, brown, almond-shaped eyes at me. From that night on, he'd visited me two or three times a month.

Lucy was the only one of my friends whom I told everything. Well, almost everything. After the big fuss I'd made about her hooking me up with Skirt, I hadn't had the nerve to tell her that I was still fooling around with him. I'd decided to keep my renewed interest in him a dirty little secret.

Lucy's voice jolted me back to the present moment.

"I think it's time for you to meet a real man, and if you don't grab Seth now, some other girl will," Lucy said. "Now, are you going to show up at church this morning or not?"

"I told you I'd be there. The way you've been bragging about this Seth brother, I'm just as anxious as you are for me to meet him. Now, like I said, Uncle Albert will give me a ride."

"And like I said, I'm going to pick you up! I'll be there at ten thirty, so be ready." Lucy hung up before I could say another word.

Chapter 22

Rachel

I DIDN'T WANT TO WAIT TOO LONG BEFORE I CALLED UP Uncle Albert at the nail salon. He was the only relative I had in California and my closest male friend. He had always been my favorite relative, but he could be as bitchy as Lucy. If I didn't call him and he showed up at my apartment after I left, I knew I would never hear the end of it.

I couldn't stop thinking about the night before. I'd spent a few hours at the Fox Club with some friends from work. When I'd got home around eight, Skirt was sitting in his mama's Chevy station wagon in front of my apartment building, with a bottle of my favorite wine.

After we had drained the wine bottle, Skirt and I had spent a few of the most passionate hours together ever. But things had not changed between us, and they never would. I was ready to meet a real man, after all. I needed a man who could escort me to my work-related functions and other social events—and not embarrass me by getting arrested. I was glad Lucy was looking out for me. And so was my mother.

Before I could put my telephone back in its cradle, it rang. The caller was the last person in the world I wanted to talk to on a Sunday morning.

"Hello, Mama," I said, rolling my eyes and rolling over in bed at the same time. Since she had retired from her job in a school cafeteria, she had more time on her hands. She spent a lot of it calling me to monitor everything I did, from what I ate for dinner to me finding a husband.

"You sound like you just waking up, Rachel."

"I am just waking up, and I'm still in bed," I said with a sigh, looking around my room again. My apartment on College Avenue had two large bedrooms. My spare bedroom was neat and organized. That was where I kept my computer, two shelves of books, and a few other odds and ends. The room I slept in was usually neat and organized, but today it was cluttered with clothes, magazines, empty wine bottles, and a few sex toys. Had Mama been able to see my room, she would have fussed up a storm.

"I been meaning to tell you, you don't even speak like that simple country gal you used to be. When you answered the phone just now, I thought I had dialed the wrong number. You sound like one of them black newswomen on the TV."

"Thank you, Mama."

"Don't thank me for something like *that!* The way you talk now ain't natural! You done changed, and I don't know if it's for the better." Mama paused and sucked on her teeth. "I'm worried about you, Rachel. You way out there among them West Coast fools, with half of them running around in robes and cutoff britches—or half naked—protesting this and that, eating raw meat, and smoking Lord knows what."

"Mama, I'm not doing any of that."

"And another thing, you ain't so young no more. You twenty-three years old. How do you expect to find a husband, spending half the day in the bed? It's practically noon. How come you ain't in church, girl?"

"It's not noon in California, Mama. I keep telling you there is a time difference between Alabama and the West Coast. I'm just about to get up and get ready for church."

"Good. Running around with that *funny* uncle of yours, you need all the spiritual support you can get."

"We don't call people like Uncle Albert 'funny' out here, Mama. We call them gay."

"Pfffft! I wouldn't call no man who fornicates with other men gay! Gay is what you call a Easter basket or a—"

"How is everybody doing?" I broke in. The heavy sigh on Mama's end told me she had called to deliver unpleasant news. My twenty-year-old brother, Ernest, was autistic. My sister, Janet, who was eighteen, was paranoid schizophrenic. Growing up with them had been a real challenge and still was in some ways. Every time Mama had a problem with one of them, she called me up to vent.

My mother's younger brother Albert had moved in with us after their parents died in a bus accident when he was thirteen. He had moved to California several years ago. A few years after he'd relocated, I'd followed him.

"Well, I'm glad you asked. Uh, your brother ain't doing too good."

"Oh? What's the matter? Did he stop taking his meds again?"

"He don't take his meds the way he's supposed to. Last night he went to the corner store to pick up a few items for me to cook for dinner. He came home with a bloody nose and a knot upside his head. Somebody had jumped on him again, and he couldn't even tell us who it was."

"Mama, I keep telling you not to let Ernest go out at night alone! Why didn't you get somebody in the neighborhood to drive him to the store, like you usually do?"

"The doctor said I need to let him be more independent," Mama told me with another heavy sigh. "Ernest keeps asking when you're coming back home. . . ."

"California is my home now, Mama. I'm never moving back to Coffeeville, Alabama."

The long moment of silence made my chest tighten. This usually meant Mama had *more* unpleasant news to report. I was right.

"Your sister's been hearing voices again."

"What do you mean 'again'? She's always heard voices. Even when she was a baby."

"Them voices she's hearing now ain't so nice. One told her to haul off and slap me last night."

"Oh no. She . . . she's never been violent before, Mama."

"Well, she got violent last night. I just hope them voices don't tell her to pick up a hammer and bash me in the head."

My heart was beating so rapidly, I had trouble breathing. I worried about my mother all the time. She refused to even consider putting my siblings away, so I felt totally helpless.

"Mama, maybe you should really think about getting Ernest and Janet some serious help."

"What do you think I been doing since I birthed them two kids, girl? I got God's help, and that's better than any doctor or hospital or anybody else!"

"God didn't stop Janet from slapping you last night. What if those voices tell her to burn down the house one night, when you and Ernest are asleep?"

"I'm way ahead of you on that one! I put up smoke detectors in every room in this house." Mama laughed.

"Mama, this is not funny. I don't know how you can live the way you do. Don't you want to know what it's like to live like a normal woman?"

"What's wrong with you, girl? I *am* living like a 'normal woman.'"

"I don't think so. Janet seems to be getting worse instead of better. She slapped you for no reason."

"She slapped me because them voices told her to slap me."

Talking to my mother was so exasperating, especially if she was the one who called. That meant I didn't have time to prepare myself. When I called her, I usually drank a shot of tequila or something equally potent first. I sat up and glanced at the clock on my nightstand and swung my legs to the side of the bed. "Did Janet stop taking her meds, too?"

"No, she is taking her meds. She keeps asking me when you coming back home."

"Mama, I'll come for a visit when I get my vacation. Now, let me get up and get ready for church. My friend is going to introduce me to someone, a man from a real nice family that she can't stop talking about. His name is Seth, and I'm real anxious to meet him."

"Well, don't get your hopes up too high. Most men are descended from dogs. You be careful with this Seth boy. I don't want you to get in trouble on account of him. Like you did with that Morgan boy back here."

"I'll call you later in the week and tell you all about Seth, Mama. If he turns out to be a jackass like Jeffrey Morgan was, I'll just kick him to the curb."

"Good. I'd hate for the police to arrest you again. . . ."

Chapter 23

Seth

"*A*LL YOU NEED IS A GOOD WOMAN BEHIND YOU, SON. If that won't straighten you out, nothing will. No man succeeds unless there's a woman guiding him. Look at your father and your brothers!"

"I don't need a woman to 'straighten me out,' Mother," I said, holding my breath to keep from snickering, like I usually did when she brought up this subject. "I'm doing all right on my own so far."

"And that's only because of *me*. What would you do if I didn't look after you the way I do? You'd probably be locked up or dead by now. You are not like your brothers."

One thing my family never let me forget was that I was not like my brothers. I was the baby in the family, and even though they had spoiled me rotten, every time I got into trouble, it was my fault. I was wild and unfocused in elementary school, and the class clown and a prankster in middle school. My grades were always shitty, so it was a wonder I even made it to high school. And I was always attracted to the kids who couldn't stay out of trouble. After I was suspended from school for everything from fighting to mouthing off to my teachers, my folks finally cracked down on me.

My mother and father had been born and raised in California, so they were not into giving "whuppings," the way the parents of some of my friends with Southern ties were. Punishment in our house meant a stern talking-to, back-to-back church events, and no allowance. That straightened me out for a little while, until I got interested in girls. Sex was on my mind day and night, and I couldn't wait to find out what all the fuss was about. I went from girl to girl and was never in a serious relationship in high school, even though I fathered a child with one of my conquests.

Mother was still convinced that all I needed was a good woman—other than her—in my life. And apparently, so were her friends.

"Last Saturday that meddlesome-ass Florence Patterson's last single son married that Brinkley girl. Florence came up to me after the ceremony and had the nerve to ask me if you were gay!" Mama yelled during our latest conversation about my marital status.

Florence Patterson, a retired high school math teacher and a malicious old hag, was one of Mother's closest friends. She stayed all up in everybody's business. She had four sons, and all of them were now married.

"You can tell that old busybody crow that I am not gay and I can't understand why she'd even think something like that," I shot back. "I've dated plenty of girls." I loved women, and I loved being in a relationship, but I was a lot more picky than I had been in high school. Now I wanted a woman who was going to be a partner in more ways than one. For instance, she had to have more to offer me than her body and her time, and she had to be willing to help me achieve my goals.

It was a typical late summer Sunday morning. We were having a steak-and-egg breakfast in the spacious dining room of my parents' house, a gorgeous five-bedroom Spanish-style structure in the heart of the exclusive Berkeley Hills. I still lived at home for more than one reason. One, I didn't have to pay rent or help with any household expenses, even though Sister Patterson kept hinting that I should "volunteer to contribute," the way her sons and my brothers had when they still lived at home. My parents didn't push it, and so I didn't. I had it made, and I was going to milk this cow dry. Another reason I still lived at home was that I loved the way my mother pampered me. The thought of living on my own scared me. For one thing, I was not making the kind of money I needed to live in the kind of place I wanted. Some of my single friends lived in dumps in crime-infested neighborhoods. One even shared a backstreet hovel with four roommates. Well, none of that appealed to me.

As usual, Mother dominated the conversation, while Father looked on, gnawing on the T-bone steak that Clarice, our part-time cook, had put on his plate just a few minutes ago.

"Well, you're twenty-five years old, and you don't have a steady girlfriend *now*. You spend too much time in San Francisco, *gay heaven*. That's why Sister Patterson—and no telling who else—thinks you're gay. Sit up straight, and don't you leave good food on your plate, the way you did at dinner last night. Clarice doesn't cook for her health. We pay her a pretty penny to spend hours at a time in that kitchen, over that hot stove."

I straightened up in my seat, took another bite of my steak, and then took a sip of tea before I responded.

"Mother, I have had numerous girlfriends. I just haven't found the right one yet."

"The boy has a son in L.A. And he went with that child's mama for several months," Father pointed out with a serious frown on his face. "That proves he's not gay."

"There are a lot of gay men who have dated women and who break down long enough to, uh, get close enough to a female to get her pregnant just so they can have children," Mother countered. She drank some tea, covered her mouth with her hand to stifle a belch, and gave me a sharp look. "What about this girl that Lucy—whom I'd encourage you to go after if she wasn't divorced and a little too close to the heavy side—wants to introduce you to at church this morning? I heard she's real cute and has her own car, her own apartment, and no babies. And I'm glad she's in the church. But you can't trust girls from small towns in the South. Most of them come with a lot of baggage."

"Your mother is from Slidell, Louisiana, a small town in the South, Mother," I reminded. I braced myself for another dose of Mother's wrath.

Instead, she ignored my comment and said, "Don't you tease me, boy. What's the girl's name?"

"Rachel . . . um . . . I forget her last name. Lucy showed me a picture of her. She's only twenty-three and has a fairly high-level management job at some fancy private school. She's doing real well for a girl her age that didn't even go to college."

"Hmmm. She sounds too good to be true," Mother said with a skeptical look on her face. "She must look like a nanny goat and be as heavy as a seal."

"Uh-uh. She looked pretty nice in that picture that Lucy showed me," I pointed out.

"Just be careful with this new girl, son," Father said,

piping up. "She might have two or three closets full of skeletons."

"What about her family?" Mother asked.

"She has an uncle out here, but the rest of her folks live in Alabama. According to Lucy, they are all good, hard-working Christians," I said. "I can't wait to meet them. I have a feeling this girl is going to change my life."

Chapter 24

Rachel

I REMAINED IN BED, LYING ON MY BACK, LOOKING UP at the ceiling. A lot of thoughts were on my mind, and my personal life was at the front. I was ready to be in a serious relationship now, but it seemed like every time I thought I'd met the right man, I was wrong. Last month, when I went to the Department of Motor Vehicles to renew my driver's license, I thought I'd met the "right" man again.

"I knew I should have made an appointment." He had a deep, sexy voice.

I turned around to see who was talking to me. I was stunned to see such a tall, dark, and handsome stranger in a navy blue suit behind me. He appeared to be in his late twenties or early thirties. His dark brown hair was short and wavy, and his smile was so radiant that just looking at him brightened my mood.

"Me, too," I muttered, turning back around. He tapped

me on the shoulder, and I whirled around to face him again.

"I'm Matthew," he said. "Matthew Lawrence Bruner, to be exact."

"I'm Rachel McNeal."

"I noticed you as soon as I walked in," he continued.

"I didn't notice you," I said firmly. I didn't like strange men getting too friendly with me in public. Especially a handsome man in a suit who was probably involved with several other women already.

"Well, from the way this line is moving, it looks like we're going to be here for a while. This is what I get for not renewing my car registration by mail." Matthew laughed.

There were at least twenty people ahead of me, and I'd been in line for half an hour already. I hadn't brought anything to read with me, so having a conversation with the handsome stranger seemed like a good way to kill time.

"Do you work around here?" I asked.

Matthew shook his head and cleared his throat. "I'm a parole officer, and my office is downtown."

"Oh? That must be an interesting job. I'm a book-keeper at a private school."

"That must be an interesting job, as well. Sometimes I wish I had chosen a different profession. I used to drive my wife crazy sharing stories with her about some of my more, uh, challenging parolees."

"Does your wife work?"

"My wife died in a house fire two years ago. She was two months pregnant with our first child."

"I'm sorry." The line moved forward, and I turned back around and moved with it. To this day, I didn't know what made me turn back to the man and resume our conversation. "Where was the fire?"

"She was visiting relatives in Long Beach. It was an old house, and the wiring was faulty. It happened in the middle of the night, and everybody inside died—my wife, her sister and her husband and their three kids." Matthew let out a loud breath, and he suddenly looked unbearably sad. "I was supposed to be with them, but I had to cancel and stay behind to appear in court because one of my high-profile parolees had been arrested again."

"How are you doing now?"

"I have my good days and my bad days." He smiled, but I could still see sadness in his eyes. "Today is a good day."

I smiled back. "I'm glad to hear that."

Matthew glanced at his watch. "Would you like to go for a cup of coffee when we get out of this place?"

"I'd like to, but I have to get back to work. If you give me your telephone number, maybe I can call you sometime."

Matthew gave me his business card, and I called him at his office the next morning, when I got to work. He sounded glad to hear from me, and we chatted for several minutes. I was pleased to hear that we shared some interests, such as old black-and-white movies, mystery novels, jazz, and eating out. That Saturday he took me to dinner, but I didn't feel comfortable enough to get more intimate with him until three weeks later. We had been having so much fun together that when he invited me to spend the weekend in Lake Tahoe with him, I eagerly accepted.

I had packed that Thursday night, and when Friday evening rolled around, I rushed home from work to wait for Matthew to pick me up. Somebody knocked on my door a few minutes before seven, and I assumed it was him, even though I didn't expect to see him for another half hour. I looked through the peephole and saw Skirt standing there in jeans and a leather vest, with a stupid grin on his face. I should have ignored him, but I didn't.

"What in the world are you doing here?" I asked with a scowl. "I told you not to come over here without calling me first."

"I was thinking about you, and since we hadn't seen one another in a while and you hadn't called me, I was worried about you," he said, trying to look over my shoulder. "I didn't want you to think I was slacking up on my job."

"Your job?" I guffawed. "That's real funny, Skirt."

A hurt look crossed his face. "You told me yourself I was your maintenance man, sweet thang."

"Well, I no longer need your services, so you can go visit somebody else tonight," I snapped.

"Lord, have mercy! You ain't going to invite me in? I wouldn't mind having a cool glass of something . . . orange juice, Gatorade . . . beer."

"Skirt, please leave."

A puppy dog expression popped up on his face. "You trying to tell me something?"

"Look, Skirt. We had a good thing going for a while, but it's time for us to end it. Uh, I've met somebody, and it's serious."

I was surprised to see a smile on his face now. "Oh, well. It was fun while it lasted. I won't bother you no more." He paused and glanced toward the street; then he looked back at me and opened his arms. "Just one last kiss and I'll be gone."

"All right." I reluctantly went into his arms. We embraced, and his lips came crashing down on mine. It was a long kiss, and it would have been longer had I not pulled away from him. "Now will you please leave?"

"It was nice knowing you, Rachel. Have a nice life," he said with a heavy sigh.

I quickly shut the door and returned to the couch. After seven thirty came and went, I began pacing the floor. An hour later I called Matthew's home telephone number, and it went straight to voice mail.

He didn't show up that night, and he didn't call.

I finally undressed and went to bed a few minutes after eleven. When I got up Saturday morning, I was so angry, I removed Matthew's telephone number from my address book. I couldn't wait to hear his excuse when he called.

A whole week went by, and Matthew still had not called. That night, around ten o'clock, I reluctantly dialed Skirt's number.

"It's Rachel. Uh, you busy tonight?" I said as soon as he picked up the phone.

"What's it to you? I thought you met somebody," he snarled.

"I did, but it didn't work out," I said. I was already mad at myself for showing how weak I was by calling Skirt. "Can you come over for a little while?"

As much as I tried not to think about Matthew, he crossed my mind a lot, even when I was in bed with Skirt. I wanted to get over Matthew as soon as possible, and since my "relationship" with Skirt was a dead end and I was eventually going to "end" it permanently, there was no way I was going to miss out on meeting Seth Garrett.

Chapter 25

Rachel

I ROLLED OUT OF BED, STUMBLED INTO THE BATHROOM, and took a quick shower. When I returned to my bedroom, I turned on the clock radio on my nightstand to check the weather report so I could decide what to wear. But the first thing I heard was a recap of a report that Princess Diana had died in a car crash in Paris a few hours earlier.

"Damn!" I mouthed, sitting down on the side of my unmade bed, staring in disbelief at the radio. This tragedy made me remind myself how short life was. Death could happen in the blink of an eye, and so I wanted to enjoy my life as much as I could, and for as long as I could. I had always worked and played hard, because I wanted to make sure I didn't miss out on too much. I was always eager to have a good time, and last night had been one of the best times. And as a backup plan, I needed to keep

Skirt happy in case a love connection didn't develop between Seth Garrett and me.

After I had drunk two cups of coffee and had swallowed a few aspirin, my hangover had almost disappeared. I got dressed and sat waiting by the door for Lucy. She arrived right on time, but because of an accident on the freeway, we got to church twenty minutes after service started.

"That's Seth sitting with his parents in the second pew from the front," Lucy whispered as we eased down the aisle toward the front, to one of the few remaining empty pews.

Second Baptist was one of the most ornate and prestigious black churches in the Bay Area. An enormous mural of a black Jesus covered the wall behind the pulpit. The maroon carpeting, the gold and red drapes, and everything else looked new and expensive. The ushers wore crisp white uniforms and white gloves.

"Don't stare at Seth like he's something good to eat. I don't want him to think you're too anxious to meet him," Lucy hissed.

"I won't! This was your idea," I reminded, already wondering if I had made another mistake by letting Lucy hook me up with another man. "I can see only the back of his head, anyway," I whispered as we sat down on the end of a pew near the front.

Even though we were whispering, an old sister on the same pew gave us a dirty look. We remained silent until Reverend Mays finished his sermon.

Seth was one of the first people to rise. Other people got up and began to greet other members of the congregation with hugs and handshakes.

"Don't look now, but Seth just turned around," Lucy told me. "He's looking right at you. Come on." She literally took me by the hand and led me down the aisle to one of the most handsome men I'd ever seen. "And don't act too friendly. I don't want him to know you're desperate."

"Desperate?" I gasped. "What makes you think I'm desperate?" I had never before been desperate for a man in my life, and I couldn't understand why a woman who had known me as long as Lucy had would think that. Her divorce had become finalized six months ago, and she had not been in a serious relationship since. She spent more time in the clubs and visiting singles chat rooms on her computer than any other woman I knew. She was a lot closer to being desperate than I was. "What all have you told him about me?"

"Don't worry. I've said only good things about you."

Seth smiled and his eyes lit up as we approached him. I was disappointed to see that he was not as handsome as Matthew Bruner, nor did he have an impressive, stable job. Lucy had told me that Seth worked in a cannery. Right after she introduced me to him, he shook my hand and gave me a big hug.

Seth held on to my hand as he gazed into my eyes. In the back of my mind, I wondered if there was something Lucy hadn't told me about this man. When he began to squeeze and caress my hand, I really got suspicious. But I kept a smile on my face. "I'm glad we finally met," he told me, releasing my hand.

"So am I," said the stout, bronze-colored woman in the wide-brimmed black hat and the pink dress who was standing next to him. "Seth is my baby." She immediately shook my hand as she looked me up and down with a smile on her face. Her smile faded when she saw the length of my black leather skirt. It was about two inches above my knees. "I didn't know women wore leather to church," she commented. I thought that it was inappropriate for the mother of a man I'd just met to make such a comment so soon.

She went on. "You have nice legs for them to be slightly bowed, but I see you like to show them off, anyway. I'm surprised that they are still making some skirts so short these days." The smile returned to Mrs. Garrett's face, but it was the sneer of a woman who didn't even try to hide her catty nature.

"Shorter skirts are in style again. Especially in leather, Sister Garrett," Lucy blurted, moving closer to me. Her skirt was even shorter than mine.

"I guess so. I see a lot of *teenagers* running around, showing their business," Mrs. Garrett pointed out, still displaying her annoying smile. "But I guess if you've got nice legs, you can still get away with it at any age." She tapped her nose with the tip of her finger and sniffed, with her eyes looking directly into mine. "How old are you?" she asked next. "I can't decide if it's all that make-up you got on your face, that long hair on your head and whatnot, but you look kind of young to me."

"Thank you," I said. "I'm twenty-three."

The tall man in the black suit who was standing next to Mrs. Garrett cleared his throat. "It's nice to meet you, Rachel. I'm Seth's father. You can call me Conrad." He grabbed my hand and squeezed it so hard, he made me flinch. He held my gaze even longer than Seth had.

I know this man is not leering at me up in a church! I told myself.

But when he turned his head to the side and winked at me and slid his tongue across his lip in a suggestive manner, I realized that was exactly what he was doing.

"Nice to meet you, Conrad," I said. I smiled and pulled my hand out of his, but I noticed he was still staring at me.

Seth's mother must have noticed her husband's strange behavior, because she cleared her throat and gently pushed him aside. "You can call me Mrs. Garrett. Not because I'm a snob, but because I'm old school. I don't believe young people should refer to an elder by his or her first name until they get better acquainted," she said with an annoying cackle. I didn't know what to make of that. Seth seemed nice enough, but I had a feeling his parents were two odd pieces of work. Then Mrs. Garrett said something that took me completely by surprise. "You sure are a pretty little thing! Look at those big brown eyes and those high cheekbones. I bet you take after your mama."

"Not really. Everybody says I look more like my daddy," I said shyly.

"He sure must be a handsome man. What does your daddy do for a living?" Mrs. Garrett said, with her head tilted to the side and one eyebrow raised.

"Uh, my daddy passed when I was a little girl. But he had worked for the city and had supervised several employees for about ten years." I didn't see any need to tell these people that my daddy had been the head janitor at the courthouse and that he'd died when the husband of one of his lovers shot and killed him. I had not shared that information with any of my new friends in California.

"It's so nice to finally meet you. I hope you can join us for dinner this evening. You being a country girl, I'm sure you'd enjoy some home-cooked red beans and rice and fried chicken," Mrs. Garrett gushed. "Our cook is from Georgia, so she knows her stuff in the kitchen."

"Oh, yes, I would love to join you all for dinner," I gushed back.

Out of the corner of my eye, I could see Seth looking at the side of my head. From everything he'd done and said so far, I assumed he liked what he saw. I liked what I saw. He wasn't as tall as I'd hoped, but that didn't really matter. I was only five feet four, and I usually wore low-heeled shoes, if I wore heels at all. Seth was the same shade of bronze as his mother, and he had her sparkling brown eyes. His father was a reasonably good-looking light-skinned man in his late fifties or early sixties who looked like he had not missed any meals. He had a pot-belly and thin salt-and-pepper hair with a little too much pomade on it for me. I was glad to see that Seth wore his wavy black hair short and combed back the way Billy Dee Williams wore his in *Lady Sings the Blues.*

"What time should we get there?" Lucy asked. Seth and his parents looked at her at the same time.

I could tell from the surprised look on Mrs. Garrett's face that the dinner invitation didn't include Lucy. But Mrs. Garrett handled it well. "Oh! Uh, I'm glad you're coming, too, Lucy. I'm dying to hear about that singles' cruise you took to Alaska last month," she said, looking embarrassed and annoyed at the same time.

"The Martins will be having dinner with us," Seth's fa-ther said quickly, clearing his throat again. He furrowed his brows and shifted his weight from one foot to the other. "Isn't that right, dear?" he asked with a nervous look on his face. From that, I decided Mrs. Garrett was the one who ran the show.

"Yes, the Martins will be joining us for dinner," Mrs. Garrett announced. I couldn't believe how gruff her voice sounded now.

"Oh. They will? Well, in that case, maybe I'll take a rain check," Lucy said, looking disappointed. She had dated the Martins' divorced son, Ronald, for three months before their bitter breakup two months ago because she couldn't get along with his parents. That was the main reason that Lucy had gone on that singles' cruise to Alaska last month and had slept with two different men in seven days. Lucy looked at me and shrugged. "Rachel's car is in the shop for a tune-up, and I've been hauling her around for the past few days. I don't mind dropping her off for dinner." There was a petulant tone in Lucy's voice. But she was the kind of woman who bounced back from disappointment real fast. I already knew that she would probably head straight to a bar or go on a shopping spree on her way home from church.

"Rachel, I can pick you up this evening," Seth said quickly.

"I don't want you to go to any trouble on my account. I can take a cab—"

"You'll do no such thing," Seth interrupted. "You live in the Dover Circle apartment complex on College Avenue, right?"

"My doctor's eldest son lives in that neighborhood. He's already a very successful pediatrician. That's an expensive residence for a girl your age. What do you do for a living?" Mrs. Garrett asked with a guarded look on her face.

"I'm the assistant bookkeeper at Steele-Royce Middle School, a private school," I said proudly.

All three of the Garretts gasped and looked at me in awe.

"That's one of the most exclusive and expensive middle schools in Berkeley! My two older boys went there. They wouldn't allow Seth to enroll, because his grades were not up to their standards. They pay the staff very well at that place," Mr. Garrett said. "Hmmm. Your family must be real proud of you."

"With your looks and shape and everything else you have going for you, how come you're not married yet, Rachel?" Mrs. Garrett asked. "I got married when I was nineteen."

"Mother! That's kind of personal," Seth scolded. Then he turned to me. "Give me your address, Rachel. I'll pick you up around six, if that's all right with you."

"That'll be just fine, Seth." At the same time I asked myself, *What am I getting myself into this time?*

Chapter 26

Seth

*I*T HAD BEEN ONLY TWO WEEKS SINCE I'D MET RACHEL. The more I got to know her, the more she impressed me. She was a great cook and loved to pamper me, so I didn't have to scramble around to borrow money to take her to a bunch of fancy restaurants like I did with the women I usually dated.

Having a woman who saved me money was good enough, but having one who eagerly prepared my favorite meals two or three times a week, did my laundry, and took care of me in bed was just what I needed. Compared to the other women I'd been involved with, Rachel was the Holy Grail. I already knew that she was the one. So did Mother. Rachel had joined us for dinner several times already, and she had even taken Mother to lunch and shopping a few times. However, Mother still had some concerns.

"Rachel is not exactly what I had in mind for you. I

can't believe she didn't go to college and has never even been to Europe, doesn't like to play bridge, and doesn't even drink tea. What is the world coming to? But she is a hard worker, and she's good-looking for a black girl and is respectful of her elders," Mother said.

This particular Sunday afternoon, my two older brothers, Damon and Josh, and their snooty wives, Helene and Faith, had come to have dinner with me and our parents. The way they were all wolfing down the lamb stew that our cook had prepared, you would have thought they had not eaten in days. I had begun to hate family get-togethers like this. I always left the table feeling like I'd been pepper sprayed and dragged through the mud.

Josh and I were very close, even though he was eight years my senior. I enjoyed spending time with him. He always had my back, no matter what I did. When I got arrested for drunk driving last year, he bailed me out of jail and paid my fine, and he didn't tell anybody. A week after that, I got caught with a hooker during a sting operation. Being a very successful attorney, Josh had enough connections to get me out of that mess, too, without any publicity.

My brother Damon was only two years older than Josh, but he and I had never really gotten along that well. He made it no secret that he thought of me as the "family fool," who had very little hope of changing. He and his prim and proper wife, Helene, an ex-model who thought her piss didn't stink, had a ten-year-old son named Anthony, who was spending the night with one of his friends. Josh and Faith were expecting their first child in two months. Both of my brothers practiced law, just as Father had before he retired three years ago.

My brothers' wives had both stopped working as soon as they got married, which was something Mother didn't appreciate. She believed that women needed to pull their load in a marriage. That included contributing to the household income. Mother had worked as a registered nurse until her weak heart forced her to retire two years ago. She tolerated my brothers' wives, but in private she complained about how much she couldn't stand either one. So far, she had not said one negative thing about Rachel. As a matter of fact, she praised that girl so much, it got on my nerves. Well, not really. I was glad that my mother, who had always been my favorite girl, approved of Rachel. And so did her fussy, busybody friends.

I promptly lost interest in church and had been back only a few times since the day I met Rachel. But I was in the company of what Mother called our "church family" on a regular basis. These individuals were meddlesome old farts, if you asked me. There was bald-headed, mole-faced Reverend Mays and his plump, bug-eyed wife, Pearline. They came to my parents' house for dinner every other Sunday. They usually arrived late, after everybody had been seated and served. But they made up for it. This Sunday was no different. Nobody paid much attention to their tardiness. As usual, I was the center of attention. This time I felt like a goose about to be shoved into an oven. Not only were Mother and Damon saying all kinds of shit that made me want to holler, but the preacher and his wife joined in right away.

"Son, you've got to get yourself together. Life is too short, and God will give a person only so many chances to redeem himself. I hope things are working out for you with that nice young woman you met at church a couple of weeks ago," the reverend began. He sniffed and adjusted his horn-rimmed glasses and looked at me with a suspicious look on his homely face.

He was so anxious to dive into the feast on the table, he didn't even bother to wait for his wife. Sister Mays had a bowel disorder, which she made sure everyone knew about, so she spent a lot of time sitting on a commode. She had made a beeline to the restroom as soon as she entered our house. By the time she waddled back into the living room, with a pinched look on her face, and sat down at the table, Reverend Mays had already started shoveling food into his mouth. He glanced across the table at Josh and Damon and then back at me, shaking his head and chewing like a camel at the same time. After he swallowed the lump of food in his jaws, he started up again.

"I know you want to be as successful as your brothers in everything you do, hmmm?"

"He'll have to slow down first," Faith said. For an ordinary-looking, heavyset woman who had a mother who worked for Goodwill and a father who drove the snow-cone truck in their low-rent neighborhood during the summer and cabs the rest of the year, she certainly had a highfalutin' opinion of herself. "And I hope he's being careful with this one. The last thing Seth needs is another baby."

"Or AIDS or some worse nasty sex disease," Sister Mays threw in.

"What could be worse than AIDS?" Damon asked with a raised eyebrow and an exasperated look on his narrow face. Josh and I had inherited Mother's good looks and bronze complexion. Damon had Father's light skin, shifty eyes, and thin lips. But the difference was, Father had a jovial demeanor and he smiled a lot. With a perennial scowl that appeared as if it had been painted on, Damon usually looked angry enough to cuss out the world. "Seth, you just take care of yourself with this new girl. You don't know how many men she's been with."

Mother gave me a thoughtful look, and I knew she had

something to add to Damon's last comment. "I like Rachel, but she's got a thing or two about her that concern me. I have heard from more than one person that she used to be quite close to Paulette's shady, woman-crazy brother Skirt. If that's true, there's just no telling where else she's laid her . . . uh . . . head," Mother said.

"She seemed like a nice enough young lady when I met her, so let's give her some leeway," Reverend Mays said, giving me a sympathetic look.

"I enjoyed Rachel's company when she joined us for dinner a couple of nights ago," Father said, turning to me. "How come she didn't come with you today, son?"

"She wasn't feeling well," I replied. "Cramps."

"She told you *that?*" Mother asked with a gasp.

"Most women don't discuss female-related issues with men," Sister Mays said with an embarrassed look on her moon face.

"Especially something as personal as cramps. You better be careful with a girl who is that loosey-goosey," Mother added.

I was tired of being talked to and treated like a child. From some of the comments I had to listen to on a regular basis, you would have thought that I was just as irresponsible and impulsive as I had been in my early teens. I had had a few encounters with the cops for doing stupid, petty shit with my buddies, such as egging people's cars on Halloween night and knocking over mailboxes. I had never done drugs, not even weed, and everybody knew that. However, as far as my family members were concerned, I had a long way to go to live up to their standards. I still needed my family, so I didn't want to piss them off. That was why I always remained cool and calm when they got on my case. But I was itching to finish my meal and bolt so I could go be with Rachel, a woman who appreciated and respected me. I made a promise to my-self that I would skip the next few dinners if they included such a large audience. I was glad that Damon was in the process of moving his family to Sacramento. He didn't come around that often, anyway, but the less I saw of him and Helene, the better. And from some of the things Mother had shared with me, she felt the same way.

"As I was saying a few minutes ago, before the conversation took a slight detour . . ." Reverend Mays paused and turned to face me again. "I hope things work out for you and that young woman."

"Yes, sir," I muttered, shifting in my seat. I usually enjoyed spending time with my family, even when they roasted me. And the only reason Rachel had not accompanied me today was that she was spending the weekend in Reno with those crazy-ass heifers she called her friends. Me telling everybody she had cramps had stirred up enough mess, but there was no telling what they would have said if I had told them she was in Reno, gambling and drinking. "Things are really looking up for me." I coughed and cleared my throat. "Rachel is the kind of woman I've been looking for all my life. I'm glad I met her. If things continue to go as well between us as they have so far, I'll do whatever I have to do to take our relationship to the next level."

"And it's about time," Sister Mays snapped, waving a fork in my face. I hated that she'd chosen the seat right next to me. Even though she always looked neat and well preserved, she always smelled like Vicks VapoRub to me. The curly black wig on her head, the false eyelashes she wore—other than the hookers I used to hook up with from time to time, I didn't know any women who wore those damn things these days—and her orange lipstick made her look like a clown. "After that mess you got yourself into that time with that shameless hussy from the projects, you should walk a chalk line when it comes to females from now on."

Sister Mays's comment made me recall a very unpleasant time in my life.

The incident with "that shameless hussy from the projects" had happened more than ten years ago, and some people were still talking about it as if had happened last week.

Chapter 27

Seth

YES, I HAD HOOKED UP WITH CAROLINE MITCHELL, A girl whom almost every boy I knew had already been with. Not only was she cute, but she was also the first girl who spread her legs for me. I was fourteen at the time and she was fifteen, and it was my first time having sex. Well, my first time with a partner. I'd started masturbating when I was around twelve. The older I got, the more I needed to release myself. The times I couldn't jack off, I dry-humped any girl who'd let me. The girls my Mother would have approved of were interested only in the boys who wanted to commit. All Caroline wanted was some dick.

When she smiled and winked at me in the cafeteria the day we returned from Christmas vacation that year, I gave her my undivided attention. Being from a low-income family, she usually brought her lunch to school in a greasy brown paper bag that contained Spam or bologna sandwiches and a bruised piece of fruit. That day, I offered her the rest of the lunch on my tray—half of a chicken breast and some salad. She was so grateful, she asked me to escort her home after our last class so we could "listen to some new Prince tunes." I eagerly accepted her invitation. I had second thoughts when some of my buddies teased me about her. But when I met up with her after school, I forgot all about the mean things my friends had said about her.

We had to take a bus and transfer twice to get to her run-down neighborhood on the south side. After we got off the last bus, we had to walk three blocks through a war zone to get to the place Caroline called home. I was stunned, to say the least, because her building looked like it had been condemned. Almost every window on the ground floor had been boarded up with plywood.

"Is this where you live?" I asked with a gulp.

"Yeah. I live on the second floor, where it's safer and looks better."

We took the creaky stairs to the second floor, which didn't look any better than the first floor to me. The hallway smelled like stale cigarettes, and the lighting was so dim, I could barely see in front of me. A few feet from the unit Caroline lived in, a disheveled man in a rumpled trench coat and mismatched shoes lay on the floor, snoring like a moose. There was a large gray cat standing over him, licking his face.

"That's Clyde, the neighborhood wino. He don't bother nobody," Caroline explained. "I don't know whose cat that is."

Caroline's mother, Mrs. Mitchell, a former stripper, wore a filthy flannel housecoat and pink sponge rollers all over her head. She was on the living room couch, passed out drunk. Empty beer cans and wine bottles were scattered all over the scarred coffee table, on top of the TV, and across the floor. Flies and huge roaches were every-where, even on the ceiling. Caroline took my hand and led me to the small, cluttered bedroom she shared with her four siblings. Other than a dresser drawer and a metal chair, two lumpy mattresses with no sheets were the only "furniture" in the room. But I didn't let any of that bother me. I wanted my first piece of pussy, and I didn't care what I had to go through to get it. I had decided a long time ago that I wanted to know what the other boys were making all the fuss about.

When I pulled from my pocket a package of condoms, which Josh had told me to keep with me at all times, Car-oline slapped my hand. "I don't like the slippery way them damn things feel," she told me. "Besides, I'm on the pill."

Since I had never had intercourse, I had no idea how it would feel to stick my dick inside a girl, with or without a condom, so I didn't protest.

From that day on, I escorted Caroline home almost every day for the next three months. Her mother was al-ways drunk and her siblings were always outside, roam-ing the streets, when I visited, so we had all the privacy we needed. No matter how disgusting it was to fuck her on that urine-stained mattress, I kept going over there.

There were only a few other kids I knew in that neigh-borhood, because most of them went to different schools. The only way Caroline got to attend Berkeley High, which was better in every way compared to the schools in the low-income neighborhoods, was by her mother claiming that they lived at the address of the rich white woman she cleaned house for when she was sober. A lot of the par-ents who lived in sleazy neighborhoods did that for their kids, so it was no big deal as long as nobody ratted them out. Caroline's excuse for attending a better school was that she wanted a better education, but I believed then, and even now, that it was so she could meet a better class of potential "baby daddies" for the kids she was destined to have. Not only would it elevate her status among her peers to get pregnant by a boy from a prominent family, but it would also secure her future. Almost every other teenage girl in her hood had at least one baby. It never occurred to me that she had set me up to get her pregnant, but that was exactly what she did.

She called me one evening and told me she was pregnant, and I almost fainted.

"Pregnant? By who?" I asked. I was glad I had answered the extension in my bedroom. I glanced at my door, glad I had locked it so Mother wouldn't barge in before I could end this hellish conversation. My heart had already begun to race.

"By you, that's who," she barked.

"Oh, hell no!"

"Oh, hell yeah!"

"But . . . but I thought you were taking those birth control pills!" I had just finished dinner and couldn't wait to play one of my new video games. But now my stomach was churning, and the last thing I wanted to do was play a video game.

"I was!" she hollered. "But them things don't always work."

"Well, don't worry," I whispered. "We can skip school one day, and I'll go with you to that clinic where they, uh, you know. . . ."

"The abortion clinic? You think I'm going to kill my baby?"

My mouth dropped open. With quivering lips, I hollered, "Do you mean to tell me you want to have it?"

"Why not?"

"What about school? What about your future? What about . . . *my* future?" I had big plans for my future, and they didn't include a baby, especially one with a skank like Caroline for a mother. I had already disappointed my family one time too many with my antics. But me skipping school and pulling a few pranks was nothing compared to me getting a girl pregnant! The last thing I wanted to be at my age was a daddy!

"Fuck the future. You can do whatever else you want to do with yours, but you are going to take care of this baby."

"Oh, shit," I mouthed. "Uh, let me think about this."

"What do you need to think about?"

"Everything! How do I even know it's mine? I wasn't the only boy. . . ."

"I ain't been with nobody since I got with you."

"Uh . . . uh . . . let me have some time to think about this. I . . . I hear my mother calling me, so I have to hang up. We'll talk at school tomorrow." I couldn't get off that telephone fast enough.

I didn't sleep at all that night. I was tempted to play sick so I could stay home from school the next morning, but I knew that I had to face the situation, and the sooner I did, the better. I got to school half an hour ahead of time that day. I cringed every time I saw a girl who looked like Caroline. By third period math class, the only class she and I had together, I still had not seen her.

Caroline was always in some kind of trouble for one reason or another. She had spent time in juvie for shoplifting and fighting, and she skipped a lot of school, anyway. She didn't show up at all that day, and I didn't think much about it. When I got home that evening, she was sitting on our living room couch with her mother. This woman had a face like a mule and the demeanor of a pit bull.

"Seth, I know what you done to my baby! You . . .

you . . . you sex maniac, you! You horny bastard!" she roared. I couldn't believe these words had come from an ex-stripper.

"Huh?" was all I could say.

My mother was pacing the floor, crying, waving her arms, and massaging her chest. I prayed she was not about to have another heart attack. My father stood in the middle of the floor, with his arms folded. He shot me a hot look.

"What the . . . What's going on?" I asked as I dropped my backpack to the floor.

"Get over here, boy!" Father yelled.

I shuddered and remained standing in the same spot. I looked from Caroline to her mother and then to my mother. The moment my eyes met Mother's, she flopped onto the love seat facing the couch, crying even harder. I had no idea what was going on, and before I could ask, Caroline looked at me and pointed.

"You raped me, and now I'm pregnant!" she yelled. "You better marry me, or I'm going to the cops!"

I felt like I'd just fallen into a bottomless pit. And I wished I had. "I didn't rape nobody!" I yelled, looking from one face to another. By now Mother was wailing like a dying animal. "Mother, she's lying!"

"Everybody at school knows how you followed me home all them times and threatened to hurt me if I didn't have sex with you! You even said if I told on you, you'd beat my butt. Well, I'm tired of you controlling my life!" Caroline leaped up and shook her finger in my direction. "You even been bragging to all your friends about what you been doing to me!"

I looked to Caroline's mother, hoping to see some sympathy on her face. I had no idea what made me think that. She was just as much of a skank as her daughter. She looked as angry as Caroline. "I ain't going to let you get away with what you done to my baby!" Mrs. Mitchell screeched. Her voice was so shrill, it made me shudder some more. And even though I was several feet away from her, I could still smell the alcohol on her breath.

"Mother, I didn't rape this girl! If anything, she raped me!" I insisted.

"Yes you did! My girl don't lie! If I wasn't such a lady, I'd beat the dog shit out of you with my bare hands!" Mrs. Mitchell hollered. "You can stand your uppity self on your head and deny what you done all you want. We can let a jury decide if we have to." I could not believe the smug look on this woman's face. They had me by the balls, and they knew it.

"Mother, Father, I'm so sorry. But you have to help me out of this mess, please," I whimpered, still standing in the same spot like a lamppost.

My parents assured Caroline and her vicious mother that the baby would be well taken care of. As a gesture of good faith, and to prevent them from making a bigger fuss, Father whipped out his checkbook and wrote them a check for three thousand dollars. That sent them on their merry way, with big smiles on their conniving faces, but my parents looked like somebody had sucked some of the life out of them.

"Seth, I'm so disappointed in you," Mother managed to say. She was still massaging her chest with one hand and fanning her face with the other.

"So am I," I mumbled.

I would never forget that day and how hopeless I'd felt. Just thinking about it now almost made me sick.

Chapter 28

Seth

THE LAST THING I WANTED TO DO BEFORE I EVEN FIN-
ished high school was get married, but I had offered to
marry Caroline before and again after she gave birth to
Darnell. When I told Mother I was willing to marry Caroline, she almost had a heart attack. She had had one several years ago, when I got hit by a car. That was how
sensitive she was.

"You want to marry that low-life, ignorant jezebel?
Bah! You will do no such thing until we get that DNA test
done," she informed me. There was a grimace on her face
as she massaged her heaving chest and stomped back and
forth in our living room. "I'd rather see you go to jail. My
poor heart can't take this! Are you trying to finish killing
me?"

"I'm trying to do the right thing, Mother," was all I
said. And I meant it.

The year was 1985. DNA testing had not been around

long, so my test proved only that there was an 85 percent chance that I was the father of Caroline's baby boy. That and the fact that he looked just like me were good enough for me. That was why I'd offered to marry her again. But by that time, she had no interest in being my wife. However, she still wanted to get as much money from me as she could. Since my parents had made it clear that they were not going to support my son, I got a job working behind the counter at a deli after school and on weekends. That chump change they paid me didn't go too far.

I loved my son and wanted to be in his life, but Caroline was determined to make that as difficult as possible. Almost every time I went to her place to see him and take her some money, she was either not home or on her way out the door to "go run some errands," so my visits were brief. I was concerned about what she was spending the money on, because my son usually had on the same cheap outfits every time I visited. The only new things I noticed were things she had purchased for herself, such as new outfits, the latest CDs, and elaborate hair weaves. Raising a son by a ghetto princess was not going to be easy if I didn't have much say in his upbringing. Caroline was even reluctant to let me take the boy around my family.

"I don't want my child to grow up thinking he's better than anybody else, the way your mama and daddy and them brothers of yours do! The only way I'll let you take him around them is if I go, too," Caroline told me.

Well, taking Caroline around my family was like pouring gasoline onto a bonfire. Sparks flew every time I did.

"I love my grandson to death, but I don't think I can stand to spend another hour around that mama of his," Mother had said the last time I brought Caroline and Darnell to the house. "She's raising him to be a thug already, like she is!"

Mother had almost fainted when she'd seen the corn-rows on my two-year-old son's head and his pierced ears that day. Father had shaken his head as he'd stood in front of the portable bar near the fireplace, with an exasperated look on his face. Caroline had had a smirk on her face, which had almost made me sick to my stomach. What she'd revealed later that afternoon had made me sick to my stomach.

"I think y'all should know that I've met somebody and we're moving to L.A.," she'd announced fifteen minutes after she had entered my parents' house.

"That's hundreds of miles away," Mother had said, al-most choking on her words.

"So what? Y'all got three cars and deep pockets. And don't y'all fanny around in L.A. a few times a year, any-way, shopping and eating at them same fancy Beverly Hills restaurants that the stars go to? Well, now y'all will have something else to do when you come to L.A." Caroline had not mentioned relocating to me before. "Seth, you just better make sure them support checks ain't late, or I'll teach you a lesson you'll never forget," she'd hissed.

Caroline and Darnell left Berkeley two weeks later. As soon as she got settled in L.A., she started calling me, de-manding more money. She was relentless. Some days she would call me in the morning and whine about an unex-pected emergency that she needed money for, and I'd wire her the money immediately. Then she'd call me a few hours later on the same day to tell me she needed more money for another "unexpected emergency." To keep up with Caroline's demands, I had to drop out of school in the eleventh grade and take a full-time job doing backbreaking work on the loading dock of a can-nery. Even though my parents had money and could have helped me support my son, they still refused to do so. This was their way of forcing me to "man up" and take care of my responsibilities. However, they usually purchased new clothes and other items for Darnell from the same high-end stores where they'd bought clothes for me and my brothers. When one of Caroline's loose-lipped relatives told me that she was selling those expensive items that my parents sent, they stopped being so generous.

My money was so tight, I couldn't even afford my own place or a car on my own. My brother Josh gave me a two-year-old Mustang to get around in. He also slipped me a few dollars for spending money every now and then. But I was still miserable. I was too gun-shy to get involved with another girl, so when I needed some female attention, I started picking up hookers. When I lost control of that, I had to start borrowing money to pay what I thought of as my "pussy cat" bill. With that and my other expenses, I had to rob Peter to pay Paul almost every month. I felt like I was trapped on a sinking ship.

I had created a no-win situation.

"Seth, you look so sad," Sister Mays said, bringing me back into the conversation.

I shook my head to get that dark period in my life and the image of Caroline and her mother out of my mind and resumed eating my dinner. I didn't want the pastor and the first lady to know how upset I was. "Um, things are really looking up for me, Sister Mays," I mumbled.

"He's attending some business classes after work," Mother threw in, with a tentative look on her face.

"Which he wouldn't have to do if he had stayed in school in the first place," Damon reminded. "Nobody in this family has ever dropped out of high school!"

"I had to quit school and go to work so I could take care of Caroline and my son," I yelled.

"And a fine job you're doing, baby brother. You did the right thing by that girl, even though she was one of the biggest tramps in town," Josh said, giving me a wink. "We all make bad choices when we're young."

"Too bad *you* were the one who got her pregnant, Seth," Damon's wife, Helene, said with a sniff. "You could have done a lot better, but I'm sure she couldn't. The fact that she's had *four* more babies by four different men since she trapped you proves that."

"If that girl is so loose, how does she even know who gets her pregnant?" Sister Mays asked, looking puzzled.

"That's a good question, dear. I'm glad you brought it up," Reverend Mays said, looking at his wife like she had just solved the mysteries of the world. "This girl could be a trickster, for all we know."

"I don't know about the rest of Caroline's babies, but Seth is the father of the first one. We had a DNA test done," Father said with a hint of disgust in his voice.

"Hmmm. Well, tell me this, Seth. Does Rachel know you're already a daddy?" Reverend Mays asked with a frown.

"It was one of the first things I told her." I was proud of myself for not keeping that information from Rachel. I knew that if we stayed together, she'd eventually hear about Darnell. I'd wanted her to hear it from me, so I'd told her on our second date. "She doesn't have a problem with it."

Yes, I had told Rachel about Caroline and my son. I wanted this relationship to work, and the way things had been going, I had a feeling it would.

Rachel was going to change my life in ways I never imagined.

Chapter 29

Rachel

I HAD BEEN SO BUSY LATELY, I HAD NOT HAD A CHANCE TO talk to Uncle Albert. We had been playing phone tag since the day I met Seth.

"Baby girl, call me back so you can tell me about Seth," one of Uncle Albert's messages said. "You know I worry about you, so I just want to make sure everything is going all right."

I felt bad about not being around when Uncle Albert called. He was one of the last people I wanted to worry. He was the only relative I had in California. He was just four years older than me, and we had always been very close. The rest of our family had pretty much written him off because he was gay, and as far as they were concerned, that condition was totally unacceptable.

When I was growing up, I had always suspected that Uncle Albert was gay. Even though he didn't look it or act it, a lot of other people suspected the same thing, because he had no interest in dating females or in other things associated with boys, like sports, fishing, and fooling around with cars and other masculine things. Uncle Albert liked to do hair, shop, and cook. He was six feet tall by the time he was sixteen, and with his wavy black hair, smooth caramel-colored skin, and baby face, the girls were attracted to him like flies to honey. But when he partied, it was always with me and other boys. People whispered about him and prayed that he would "grow out of it" before it was too late.

When Uncle Albert escorted a male classmate to their senior prom, all hell broke loose. People were outraged. Other kids teased and picked on him, and Mama reminded him that "God created Adam and Eve, not Adam and Steve," but it did no good.

Albert began to parade his male lovers all over town and even brought a few to the house. Mama was furious.

"What you do out there in the streets is your business. But you ain't going to spread all that unnatural mess in my house!" she told him.

Shortly after that confrontation, Uncle Albert moved in with his new boyfriend, a plain-looking white man in his late thirties named Raymond Starks. Uncle Albert called his lover Sugar Dick. That made Mama cringe, and me, too, for that matter. I refused to call a grown man by such a ridiculous nickname. Even though Raymond was approaching middle age and was homely, his trust fund and a bad heart made up for that. Uncle Albert was an opportunist, so he took advantage of his sugar dick. Raymond treated my uncle like a prince and showered him with gifts. Uncle Albert was eighteen at the time and was working as a part-time nanny for a wealthy family that Raymond had introduced him to.

"A nanny! That's a job only a woman should be doing," Mama said.

A few months after they moved in together, Raymond took Uncle Albert on a lavish two-week vacation to San Francisco. Not only did they fly first class, but they also stayed in a suite at the elegant Mark Hopkins Hotel.

When they returned to Alabama, Uncle Albert couldn't stop talking about how much he had enjoyed that trip and about how open and free-spirited the gay people were in California.

"Girl, I never saw so many sweet-looking boys in my life. You can do just about anything you want out there, and nobody will bother you. I even saw people making love on the ground, in plain view, during the Gay Pride Parade," Uncle Albert told me. He was so giddy, it was contagious.

"That sounds like the kind of place I'd like to live in someday," I said.

"Rachel, California *is* the kind of place I'm going to live in someday."

Not long after that conversation, Uncle Albert packed up and boarded a plane to California. He fled while Raymond was visiting relatives in Birmingham. As much as I loved my uncle and wanted him to be happy, I thought it was a shitty thing for him to do to the man who had taken him in and had treated him so well. As if his leaving wasn't bad enough, he paid for some new clothes and his one-way, first-class plane ticket using his ex's credit card.

Raymond told anybody who would listen that he was thinking about suing my uncle to make him pay back some of the money he had spent on him. He even came to the house and demanded Uncle Albert's new address. He ranted and raved so much, Janet and Ernest scurried out of the living room like scared rabbits. I couldn't decide what upset Mama more: the disgruntled, bald-headed, fat white man in her house, cussing up a storm, or the way his outburst upset Ernest and Janet.

"I don't have Albert's new address to give to you, Raymond. And to tell you the truth, I don't want to get involved in y'all's mess," Mama said. "Now, if you don't mind, I need to finish cooking dinner so I can feed my kids." Mama left the room immediately.

Raymond turned to me. I stood in the doorway, trying to look concerned. I was, but not for Raymond. I was not about to tell him how to locate my uncle.

"Rachel, you and Albert were thick as thieves. I know you must know how to get in touch with him. You seem like a sensible girl. Don't you think he needs to pay for what he did to me?"

"Uh-huh," I said, nodding. And as strange as it was, I did. I didn't think it was right for a person to use somebody, then go on their merry way and not look back. "I wouldn't let somebody treat me like that and get away with it, either. I would make their life a living hell." I had no idea how prophetic my words were at the time. "But I can't give you my uncle's address or phone number, because he made me promise not to."

"When you do talk to that gold-digging scalawag, you tell him he can go to hell! And make sure you tell him I said his dick was too small for me anyhow! I still might sue his ass!" Raymond hollered. When he left a few seconds later, he slammed our front door so hard, the large family portrait of me, Mama, Uncle Albert, Janet, and Ernest fell off the wall.

Mama galloped back into the living room with a rolling

pin in her hand. I knew she would have used it on Raymond if he had not already left.

"Raymond sure is mad, Mama," I said. I squatted down
and picked up the picture, wiping dust off the edges. "I
hope he doesn't sue Uncle Albert."

"Well, if he do, Albert deserves just what he gets. He
brought this mess on hisself. See, that's what happens
when you piss somebody off. They can drag you into a
legal situation. You remember that with that boyfriend of
yours," Mama warned.

Uncle Albert rarely wrote or called, and when he did, I
was usually the only one he communicated with.

Two years after he had left Alabama, and after several
dead-end jobs, Uncle Albert called home and told me that
he'd been hired to work as a secretary for an engineering
company with offices all over the world.

I was reluctant to share the news with everybody, but I
did so a few days later, during dinner.

"Secretary? Him being a nanny wasn't bad enough, I
guess," Mama shrieked. "I declare, I should have known
he'd go all the way to California and get another sissified
job."

"If you thought the boy was one of them thangs before, him living out there in fag heaven is going to doom
him to hell for sure," Aunt Hattie mumbled. My aunt was
my mother's older sister. Her only child had died at birth
forty years ago. When her husband died ten years ago,
Aunt Hattie began to spend so much time at our house
that people thought she actually lived with us.

"I might move to California myself one of these days,"
I chirped. "I can stay with Uncle Albert." I had just graduated from high school a few weeks ago. Mama and Aunt
Hattie looked at me at the same time. I couldn't decide
which one gasped the loudest.

"Stop talking crazy, girl," Mama advised. "Ain't nothing out there in California for you. You got a nice boyfriend here. That should be enough for you."

Jeffrey Morgan and I had been going together since eleventh grade. My jet-black hair was thick and long, a feature that every boy I knew liked. I had a pretty good shape, and my face was attractive, even without my make-up. However, my brown eyes were not big enough for me, my nose was too sharp, and I didn't have the luscious, full lips like some of the black females I knew. But that didn't stop people from telling me I was pretty, so I ran with it. I had a lot of confidence, and I carried myself in a way that made me stand out. Despite my looks, I still had to work hard to get and keep a cute boyfriend. Jeffrey was the cream of the crop, and a lot of girls were just waiting to get their paws on him.

Everything was beautiful between Jeffrey and me. We had eyes only for each other, or so I thought. A month after we had received our diplomas, I started hearing rumors that he was sneaking around with a girl named Rita Wallace. She had just moved to Coffeeville from Barbados. All the girls I knew, even the white ones, were concerned about Rita. Not only was she too beautiful and exotic for words, and not only did she have a shape like a movie star's, but she also had no shame. Mama told me that the girl's mama had sent her to live with her daddy in Alabama because she had slept with her own sister's husband. I had no respect for girls who would stoop that low. So, like every other girl, I avoided Rita.

I needed to focus on more important things than Rita. One was money. Income was tight in our house, so I wanted to do something to help lighten Mama's load. Two days after my graduation, I began to look for a job.

I had to put college on hold, but Jeffrey, his daddy

being the manager of a huge restaurant, was going to go off to Morehouse in the fall, and it would be months before I saw him again. With that in mind, I wanted to spend as much time with him as possible.

One Saturday afternoon in the middle of July, I decided to go to Jeffrey's house to make sure he was okay. I hadn't heard from him in a week, and he had not returned any of my calls. I knew his parents and two younger siblings were on vacation at Disney World. Since he had the house to himself, I assumed he'd want to get jiggy. When I got to his house and knocked on the front door for at least two minutes, he didn't answer. I knew he was home, because his old jalopy was in the driveway and that boy never walked anywhere. For all I knew, he could have been injured and was unable to get help, so I knew what I had to do next.

I was as familiar with the Morgans' residence as I was with my own. I knew that the lock on the side door was broken. That was how I entered the house. It didn't take me long to figure out what Jeffrey was up to. I followed the moans and groans to his bedroom in the back of the house. I realized he had wanted to get jiggy, but not with me. I kicked open his bedroom door, and there he was, humping that island girl like it was going out of style.

"Rita, turn over, baby! I want to hit it from behind!" he panted.

"You son of a bitch," I said through clenched teeth. He was so into what he was doing, he didn't even hear me! But Rita did. She whipped her head around, and when she saw me, she pushed Jeffrey so hard, he fell to the floor. He wobbled up to his feet, with a stunned look on his face.

"What the hell—" Jeffrey didn't even have time to finish his sentence. I shot across the floor, grabbed the lamp off his nightstand, and started swinging it at him. I pummeled Jeffrey until I got tired. I left him curled up on the floor in a fetal position, with his tears, snot, and blood all over his naked body.

I ignored Rita, who was cowering on the bed, looking like she'd seen a ghost. Apparently, she was too frightened to even get up and run or to scream. I casually left the room, but when I got outside, I took off running. I ran the six blocks to my house, with Jeffrey's blood on me from head to toe. When I got home, I snuck in through the kitchen door. Before I could make it to my room, Mama came out of nowhere and accosted me in the hallway leading from the kitchen.

She threw her hands up and screamed, "Rachel, what in the world happened to you? Did you kill somebody?"

"I don't know, Mama."

"What do you mean by that? Whose blood is that all over your clothes?"

Before I could respond, Ernest entered the hallway. He swallowed hard and looked from me to Mama. He spoke for the first time in three weeks. "Two cops just walked in the door. They come for you, Rachel."

Jeffrey had called the cops, and they had come to arrest me for breaking and entering and aggravated assault.

Mama begged and pleaded with the cops not to take me to jail, but they handcuffed me and took me in, anyway. I waited in a cell for seven hours, while Mama scrambled around to borrow enough money to bail me out.

The next day she visited Jeffrey in the hospital and begged and pleaded with him to drop the charges against me. To my surprise, he did. However, his meddlesome mama made him take out a restraining order against me, and he did just that as soon as the hospital released him.

I was not allowed to go within five hundred feet of him for the next three years. That was all right by me, because I never wanted to see his cheating face again, anyway.

Chapter 30

Rachel

COFFEEVILLE WAS SUCH A SMALL TOWN, THERE WAS NO way I could go on about my business and not run into Jeffrey from time to time. It seemed like everywhere I went, there he was. From a distance, I watched as he brazenly romanced the same girl whom I'd caught him in bed with. Each time I saw them together, I got mad as hell. I was afraid that sooner or later I'd snap and commit violence against Jeffrey again.

What bothered me the most was the way Jeffrey had started bashing me to our mutual friends. People told me he was going around saying things like "I had to drop that ignorant bitch" and "She ain't got nothing to offer me, nohow." I recalled how he used to tell me that it didn't bother him that I lived in a low-rent neighborhood and that my family had so little, but now he was singing a different tune, and that bothered me. I was proud of my family, and it didn't bother me that we didn't live in the upscale neighborhood he lived in. I knew I had a lot to offer in a relationship, and I knew that someday the right man would realize that.

In the meantime, I got a job on the day shift, waiting tables at Jimmie's Soul Food Restaurant. Since it was one of the few black-owned restaurants in town, and they served excellent food, Jeffrey eventually showed up for lunch with Rita. It had been three weeks since I'd attacked him.

"You need to take the next table," I told Vernell, the other waitress on my shift. "I don't want to go to jail today."

Vernell knew about my situation with Jeffrey, as did almost everybody else in town, so she didn't ask any questions. She was from my neighborhood, and we'd been friends since elementary school.

"That punk has some nerve stepping up in here with that island monkey! You want to spit in his order before I serve it to him?" Vernell asked, giving me a mischievous wink.

"No, I don't think so. The best thing I can do is stay away from that two-timing bastard. He'll be leaving for college soon," I replied.

But Jeffrey didn't leave for college that fall. I never found out the reason he didn't, but he started working as a cashier at the same grocery store I shopped in. I didn't want to violate the restraining order, so I had to plan my movements around his. I couldn't go grocery shopping at the market during the hours he worked. I changed churches, and I stopped going every other place I knew he went. Finally, I decided that Coffeeville was not big enough for him and me.

That was the real reason I decided to leave Alabama and move to California to live with Uncle Albert. I quit my job and got another one at a catering company, making a little more money. From the get-go I made it clear to my folks that I was saving my money to move to California, but nobody supported my decision.

"You must be crazy to want to leave this nice home and that good job you got to move to a jungle like California," my aunt Hattie said.

"And it's a lot more expensive to live out there than it is here," Mama pointed out.

"I'll have enough money to live on for a while, so I think I'll be just fine until I get a job. Besides, Uncle Albert said I could stay with him for as long as I want to," I assured them.

I missed Uncle Albert and couldn't wait to see him again. He had always been like a big brother to me, and it had been nice to have a "normal" brother to look up to, one who didn't have mental issues, like my real brother, Ernest. Just thinking about Ernest's condition was painful, and I thought about it all the time.

We had always known that something was wrong with Ernest. He didn't talk until he was three years old. And the first thing he said was that a flying pig had come into his bedroom the night before. He would sit for hours at a time, just staring at the wall. Mama didn't take him to a doctor until he started running through the house, yelling that invisible creatures were chasing him. When the doctor told Mama that Ernest was autistic, it was a word that she had never heard before. Instead of trying to find out more about the condition, she and everybody else in my family just lumped my brother into the same category as retarded people, or people they called "slow." Ernest was not retarded.

Despite my brother's condition, he was very gifted in some ways. He attended regular school until Mama got tired of trying to get the school staff to stop the other kids from taunting him. Then she began to homeschool him. By the time he was seven, he could read as well as I could. He loved animals, and without any formal training, he trained almost every dog on our block.

Even though Daddy had loved Ernest and had treated him well, after a while he couldn't cope with him the way Mama could. We never knew from one day to the next what Ernest was going to do or say. At the time, my sister, Janet, was in preschool, but she had begun to act strangely, too. But her mood swings, outbursts, and blank stares didn't seem as serious as Ernest's problems, so she didn't get the attention she needed until it was too late. By then she was what some people referred to as "mad as a hatter." After a while, Daddy couldn't hide his frustration. The burden of having two mentally challenged children was too much for him. He began to spend most of his time at work cleaning the courthouse or with one of the women he had started fooling around with.

When Janet turned five, things got really bad. It didn't take long for us to realize her problems were just as serious as the ones Ernest had, maybe even more so. She was as cute as a button, but other kids avoided her because she did things that frightened them. She would stare off into space for hours at a time, and she would carry on conversations with animals. When Janet was six, she began to complain about invisible people whispering in her ear. Mama didn't wait as long to take her to a doctor as she had done with Ernest. The first doctor she went to told her that Janet was bipolar and paranoid schizophrenic, more words that my mother had never heard before. When the doctor told Mama what to expect Janet to do, hallucinate and maybe even get violent, my mother got her tubes tied a month later because she didn't want to take a chance on having another child with special needs. But that was like locking the barn door after the horse had been stolen. Daddy's married lover's husband shot and killed him the same evening Mama came home from the hospital.

A few days after Daddy's funeral, Aunt Hattie barged into our house, clucking and complaining like a wet hen. She vented for over an hour. She had always "known" that some old gal's husband was going to kill Daddy, and if she had ever gotten "proof" that her long-suffering husband, Marty, had cheated on her before he died, she would have killed him herself.

On this particular day, Mama and Aunt Hattie sat talking like fishwives, totally ignoring me as I sat at the kitchen table, helping them make a quilt for Ernest's bed.

"I'm glad I got myself fixed. If I ever get married again, I don't want to bring no more kids into this world that'll have to be looked after as long as they live," Mama stated.

Aunt Hattie took the conversation and ran with it. "Harrumph! That's why I'm glad I couldn't get pregnant again after my baby died all them years ago. Our family is cursed with all kinds of brain disorders. I know you ain't forgot how Daddy used to get naked and run up and down the street when we was kids. And what about Cousin Nadine's boy, Rollo? Last time I went to visit him in that military institution they put him in years ago, he told me he couldn't wait to get out so he could go to a mall and kill a few folks and go down in history."

That was how I found out that various forms of mental illness ran in our family. I didn't even bother to ask any questions. What I had already heard was painful enough. Ironically, I still wanted to have children someday. I remained quiet as we continued to work on the quilt.

"Well, I'm glad I did have children, anyway. Ernest is a good boy when he's medicated, and I know that with God's help and the right meds, Janet will be just fine," Mama said. "And look at how well Rachel turned out."

"Harrumph!" Aunt Hattie said again. "Rachel's weak

and naive. I bet she's going to marry some knucklehead who'll make a fool out of her, like Marcus done to you."

That was when I finally spoke up. "Y'all don't have to worry about me. I'm not going to let a man make a fool out of me," I vowed. I made up my mind that day that I would not let a man cheat on me and get away with it. "And if I do have children with special needs, I don't care. There is not one perfect person on this planet right now, and there won't be until Jesus comes back." My last statement shut Mama and Aunt Hattie up. We finished making the quilt in silence.

I really didn't care if I had children with special needs. As far as I was concerned, *everybody* had special needs. Some more than others. My siblings just happened to be among the "others." I didn't love them any less, though.

After a while, Mama began to refer to Ernest and Janet as "still being worked on by God," and I felt the same way. I didn't balk when she asked me to stay home and babysit them when she needed to leave the house, or when she asked me to take one or both of them out for a walk. I didn't even protest the day Ernest got hysterical and took off running down the street because some jackass had tossed a firecracker in front of us. It took me, Mama, a small army of neighborhood do-gooders, and Aunt Hattie several hours to track him down and bring him back home. A few hours later, I took a baseball bat and hunted down the boy who had tossed that firecracker. I had every intention of laying his head open with that baseball bat. But when he started crying and apologizing, I let him off the hook.

"Mama, I think you need to start thinking about putting Ernest in some kind of home," I said after we had calmed Ernest down and had put him to bed.

"The boy is 'in some kind of home,'" Mama defended.

"This house is his home just as much as it is yours. If you don't like what goes on in my house, you can either lump it or move out. And, in case you done forgot, Ernest ain't the only 'boy' in this family with special needs. There is no telling what all Albert is into out there in that Babylon they call California with all them sissies."

What I was never able to understand was why some folks, especially my family, thought that mental problems were acceptable but being gay was such a blight. It made no sense to me.

"I'm going to pray for Albert and for you, too," Mama told me. "If you do move to California, don't you eat nothing Albert or one of his boyfriends cook. You don't know where their hands been."

The day I boarded the plane was one of the most exciting days of my life. Uncle Albert had already arranged to take the day off from work so he could pick me up at the airport in San Francisco and drive me to his apartment in Berkeley.

The moment I set foot on California soil, I felt like I had been reborn.

Chapter 31

Rachel

*A*s soon as I got settled into my new location, Uncle Albert taught me how to use a lot of different software, so I had no trouble landing temp office jobs. I made a lot of new friends right away, and before long I was enjoying my life again.

I didn't do much socializing. I joined my new friends for drinks after work every once in a while, but my main focus was on my future. I dated a few guys along the way, but I made sure they all knew I was not interested in anything too serious at the time. Most of the men didn't have a problem with that as long as they got what they wanted, which was a little company that included sex now and then. That was the extent of my "love life."

I took a twelve-week business course at a community college in nearby Oakland, and a week after I completed it, I landed a permanent job as the assistant bookkeeper at Steele-Royce, a private school in one of Berkeley's most prestigious areas. It was a job to die for. The midsize white stucco building had all the luxuries that money could buy, and these included state-of-the-art furniture and electronic equipment, and an indoor swimming pool. I even had an office all to myself. There were only two hundred seventh- and eighth-grade students, all from prominent families, including those of a few local celebrities. Some of the kids came to school in chauffeur-driven limousines. My salary and benefits were incredible, so I counted my blessings every day.

Lucy had been the head librarian at the school for a couple of years and the only black employee, other than one of the janitors. We were both in our twenties, so we hit it off immediately and quickly became best friends.

I was still living with Uncle Albert at the time, and even though he kept telling me I could stay as long as I wanted, I was anxious to move into a place of my own. For one thing, my uncle partied too much for me. Every other night he had company. Sometimes up to a dozen men at a time, including a drag queen who performed in one of the clubs in San Francisco that Uncle Albert often went to.

Lucy had a friend who managed a couple of apartment buildings, so she was able to help me move into the two-bedroom, second-floor apartment with a balcony on College Avenue. As soon as I got settled in, with cute furniture and trendy knickknacks that I'd picked up at secondhand stores and flea markets, Lucy and some of her friends began to try to hook me up with their single male friends. Even though it had been more than two years since my fiasco with Jeffrey, I was still somewhat gun-shy. I had told my friends about Jeffrey and what he had done to me. I'd even told them what I'd done to him.

"Too bad you didn't hit him where it would have hurt the most—his crotch." Lucy laughed.

Lucy, Paulette Ramsey, who was one of her closest friends, and I were having drinks at a bar in downtown Oakland, where Paulette worked as a personnel manager for a small insurance company.

"My cousin Bobby just got a divorce, and he likes to party. If I was still single, I'd go after him myself," Paulette said.

"Thanks, but no thanks." I chuckled.

"Girl, you need to forget about dude back in Alabama and get on with your life and get you some new meat," Lucy scolded.

"I am over him," I insisted. "And I do want to meet somebody special. But I'm in no hurry to taste any new meat." It had been several weeks since I'd met and lost Matthew Bruner, the parole officer I'd had such high hopes for.

Lucy was the kind of woman who didn't take no for an answer. She continued to try to set me up with men she knew. And I began to weaken. When Lucy finally told me about Seth Garrett, I was only slightly interested in meeting him, and I didn't get my hopes up. But the more she talked about him, the better he sounded.

"Not only is he fine, but he's from a fine family, too. And I don't just mean in the looks department. His daddy, his brothers, and one of his aunts are lawyers. They live in this huge house in the hills," she gushed.

"Oh? Why would a man with all that going for him want to meet a little old country girl like *me?*"

"I have to be up front and let you know that Seth has a little bit of baggage. He has a son by some hoochie mama who moved to L.A. a while back. She's about as wretched as they come. That heifer has such a long reach, she's still making his life a living hell, so he spends a lot of time down in the dumps. Especially lately. He's a real cutie-pie, but he's not as smart or ambitious as his brothers. He didn't even finish high school, but he eventually got his GED and is supposedly taking some kind of business class and working a pooh-butt job in a cannery, of all places. "

"The dude is a high school dropout who works in a cannery," I mused. "And you want to dump this loser off on me?" I couldn't stop myself from laughing.

"Seth is going to run his own ad agency someday. He's working toward a real future. He goes to church occasionally, and he's good to his mama. A man who treats his mama well usually treats his women well. Besides all that, I've already told him about you. If you don't agree to meet him, it'll make me look bad. I think he really needs a strong, smart, hardworking, sensible woman like you to help him stay afloat. . . ."

"Help him stay afloat? That doesn't sound too appealing to me. I hope you didn't make him think I was looking for a man to take care of. The last thing I need is a man who needs a mama, or a nursemaid, more than he needs a lover."

"Girl, please! Do you want to meet the man or not?"

"I'll meet him, but I'm letting you know now, I am not going to jump into anything with him anytime soon. Especially bed . . ."

"That's good enough for me. Now, how about this Sunday? He'll be attending church with his parents. I've already checked with him."

"I guess that's as good a time as any. But I'm telling you right now that if this Seth Garrett turns out to be another criminal like Skirt or looks like Godzilla, I'm holding you responsible." I laughed again.

I didn't laugh when I met Seth and his parents that Sunday in church. There was something about him that made me tingle all over.

After our first date, we immediately began to spend

several nights a week together. I got so attached to him, I didn't want him out of my sight.

A year into our relationship, I asked Seth to move in with me.

Uncle Albert adored Seth, and the feeling was mutual. Seth had even accompanied me to a few parties at Uncle Albert's new residence. Uncle Albert had recently moved in with Kingston Takahashi, a small-framed, baby-faced Japanese American man in his early thirties, with shoulder-length black hair and lots of attitude. Kingston's family owned several upscale restaurants in Japan, Singapore, and San Francisco. Once again my greedy, free-spirited uncle was being showered with gifts and treated like a prince by a man of means.

One Saturday night a few weeks after Seth moved in with me, he and I had dinner with my uncle and his new lover. While Seth was in the living room with Kingston, admiring some of the artwork he had picked up on his last trip to Japan, Uncle Albert and I were in the elaborate master bedroom in their three-bedroom apartment a few blocks from UC Berkeley, where Kingston was a professor of political science.

"Girl, you've struck black gold," Uncle Albert whispered. "I used to read in the newspaper about Seth's daddy and all the high-profile cases he'd won over the years before he retired. The Garretts might not be as rich as some of the other families in their neighborhood, but they've got more than me and you. Get what you can while the getting is good," Uncle Albert advised me. "Milk that cash cow dry."

I gave my uncle a dismissive wave. "I don't want to 'milk that cash cow' or any other cow. I can take care of myself without a man footing my bills," I said firmly.

"What's wrong with you, girl? These days, you have to take somebody before they take you. This is America, the land of opportunity, where any and everybody is out for all they can get. How do you think I got where I am today?"

"Yeah, but that man who was taking care of you back in Alabama was not too happy with you when you snuck off and left him with a bunch of humongous bills."

"So? He got what he wanted from me. I'm still getting what I want from my men. I've got money in the bank, credit cards I don't even have to pay for, a generous allowance, and I live in a pad that most people would kill for. I couldn't have done all this by myself on my pooh-butt secretary salary."

I shook my head. "I would never take advantage of Seth like that. Or any other man, for that matter. If you'd stop eating steak and lobster three times a week and shopping at Neiman Marcus, you could do all right by yourself."

"Hell's bells, girl! You and your Dollar Tree–shopping, buy-one-get-one-free, coupon-clipping self. You're going to have a miserable life if you don't wake up and smell the bubbly, girl. You straight people sure have some warped ideas when it comes to love, romance, and finances."

I had already decided that I would never let my uncle know that I was the one footing most of the bills for me and Seth. I didn't mind being generous with my money, because I truly believed that Seth was a good investment in my future.

Chapter 32

Seth

*I*T WAS BECAUSE OF RACHEL THAT I HAD BECOME A CHANGED man, and everybody could see that. Some of the same people who had lost faith in me were now helping me make improvements in my life, some with apprehension, though. A couple of weeks ago, the only time in *years* that my stingy, smug brother Damon had loaned me money, he'd made me sign a promissory note! I'd been flabbergasted, but I'd signed it, anyway. When I didn't repay the loan when I'd said I would, he'd threatened to take me to *The People's Court*. I had had to scramble around to borrow the money from several of my friends. Then they had all hounded me until I'd paid them back.

My parents had reluctantly loaned me money a couple of times in the past few months, and then they'd stayed on my case until I'd paid them back. That well dried up real fast. Last week they turned me down when I asked for another loan, even though I offered to pay them back with interest.

"We've already spent thousands of dollars on your behalf, son. It's time for you to be more self-sufficient, and you'll never get to that point as long as somebody keeps coming to your rescue," Mother told me.

I sulked, even though I knew they were right. They had fed and clothed me, and they had put spending money in my pocket long enough. And even though I had a job, they had allowed me to live at home rent free for years.

I was on my own now, and even with Rachel's financial assistance, I was still struggling. The main reason I was struggling so hard was that my son's mother was so greedy and extravagant. I continued to send her as much money as I could to keep her off my back. But I also had some pretty expensive tastes of my own. I liked fine wine, expensive clothes, and regular excursions to the casinos.

I wished that Rachel had *never* told me about the generous paychecks she brought home every other week, not to mention the numerous high-limit credit cards she had but rarely used. The minute she revealed that information to me, and knowing how sweet she was, I immediately heard the *ka-ching* of a cash register. Now I had somebody else I could borrow money from! I didn't want to get too greedy with her too soon. She was already doing more for me than anybody else. So I still got what I could from other sources.

Josh was one of the most intelligent and sensible men I knew. But my brother was quite soft and gullible when it came to me. He had always been my ace in the hole. However, I didn't like to fall back on him unless I really had to. He owned a town house a few miles from our parents' house, but I didn't like to go there often. For one thing, his wife, Faith, and I didn't really get along that well. A few years ago, I had briefly dated one of her cousins. When I broke up with her, she and Faith joined forces and trashed me for weeks to their whole family. That was the reason I went to Josh's posh office on University Avenue this particular Thursday afternoon.

"What do you need the money for this time?" he asked, adjusting his red tie and brushing off the sleeve of his expensive navy blue suit jacket. He must have owned more suits than Armani. I couldn't remember the last time I'd seen him wear the same suit more than once. He had already pulled out his checkbook.

"Uh, Caroline called me up and told me that Darnell needs some dental work done," I lied. Well, that was only half a lie. I did need to help Caroline pay for Darnell's dental work, but I also had some gambling debts that I needed to pay off. As generous and sympathetic as Josh was in my case, he probably would have given me the money no matter what I told him it was for. But I didn't want to take that chance. And I didn't want him to know just how frivolous and irresponsible I still was.

"I have to say that I am proud of you, baby bro. You've really stepped up to the plate with your son. It's a damn shame Caroline won't let us see more of Darnell. I would like for my daughter to get to know him someday."

"I'm working on that, Josh."

"Well, you keep working on that and your goals." Not only did Josh give me the grand I'd asked for, but he also threw in an extra five hundred, which I didn't have to pay back. "As long as you are trying to do something with your life now, I will help you," he told me, looking me straight in the eye, like he was trying to see through me. His penetrating gaze didn't bother me, because I was used to it. "Now we need to do something about that half-assed job of yours at that damn cannery! I know you don't have much of an education, but I know you can do a lot better than that. You need a job with a better salary, medical benefits, profit sharing, and all the other benefits!"

I hated it when Josh talked to me like I was still a child. But it was a small price to pay to keep him happy enough so he'd continue to help me out. "I've been going on interviews. I expect a callback from Charles Schwab any day. I really am looking for a better job," I said in the most humble tone of voice I could manage.

"You need to look harder. My goodness. It was bad enough you dropped out of high school and had to get a GED, and then you fiddled around in a community college."

"I had planned to take advantage of some military opportunities—"

Josh threw up his hands and gave me an incredulous look. "Boy, puh-leeze! You told me about that, but you never followed through on it."

"I did talk to a recruiter, but the military didn't want me, because I have flat feet," I whined.

"You'd better trot those flat feet to a few employment agencies and get your act together. There are decent jobs out there if you know where to look. Immigrants come here from all over the world and get jobs left and right. Americans have every advantage in the world."

"I know that." I didn't expect Charles Schwab to call me back for a job in their mail room, nor did I expect to hear from any of the other places I'd sent my résumé to. I didn't really care if they did or not. I had big plans, and each day I got a little closer to fulfilling my dreams. "Josh, as you know, my goal is to have my own advertising business. I think it'd make more sense for me to stay with the cannery until then. Besides, why should I waste my time learning a new job at another place when I'd have to leave as soon as I get my business off the ground?"

"If you change your mind and want me to put in a word for you with some of my contacts so you can get the hell up out of that cannery, just let me know. And, you can pay back the loan whenever you can. . . ."

Rachel was like a mother to me in so many ways. She pampered me to death, and I enjoyed every minute of it. She was spoiling me even more than I already was. After the long, lingering baths I took, she cleaned out the bathtub. After my baths, she liked to give me back rubs and foot massages. Last Saturday, while she cleaned up the mess in the living room that a couple of my buddies and I had made the night before, she allowed me to sleep in. Then she served me breakfast in bed.

"Baby, if you don't watch yourself, you're going to make me marry you," I teased that morning, as I enjoyed the cheese grits, grilled ham, toast, and poached eggs she had just set in front of me on a platter.

She smiled. "Is that a proposal?" she asked with a shy look on her lovely face. Even without make-up, and with her long black hair in two braids, this girl looked like a film star to me.

I sat up straight and gave her a serious look. "It could be. But first I'd have to get myself in better shape so I can be a good provider. I want to be in a position where I can take care of a wife and the children I hope to have."

"I want to be a good wife and mother. But taking care of a family is a lot of hard work. And one thing I want you to know right now is that I don't expect the man I marry to carry the load by himself."

"I thought today's women wanted to live the easy life and let their husbands take care of them."

"I do. But I want to be a partner to my man, not a liability. My husband and I will take care of each other. I want my man to know up front that I am not going to be totally dependent on him. I have a good job, and I'm going to move up even more. I love working, and I plan to do so until I'm old enough to retire."

Like I said, Rachel was spoiling me. I didn't want to marry the kind of woman that my brothers and some of my friends had married. I was pleased to hear that she was so eager to pull her load. I was convinced that she was a superwoman in her own right. She could work full-time, maintain her looks and shape, keep me happy in the bedroom, and raise our children as well as Mother had raised my brothers and me. The idea of marrying her was getting sweeter and sweeter. . . .

"Baby, let's take things slowly," I advised. From the smile on her face, I could tell that she was in agreement with me. What more could I ask for in a woman? This one was *perfect* for a man like me. . . .

Chapter 33

Seth

I KNEW THAT THINGS WERE GOING TOO WELL FOR ME. JUST when I thought I had my life on track and the only direction I could go was up, my son's mother started giving me hell *again*. That brought me back down several notches. I loved my son, but I regretted the day I'd laid eyes on his mother. Caroline was now even more disgusting and mean-spirited than before. At least back in the day, she'd had a nice body and a cute face, but her hard living ways and four more babies had taken a toll on her. The last time I saw her, she looked ten years older than she really was, and her body was sagging in every direction. I was surprised that she was still able to attract men.

"Nigger, how come you don't return my calls?" Caroline shrieked as soon as I answered the phone. Her voice was so loud, I could have set the telephone down and still heard her from across the room. I was glad Rachel was at the market, picking up some steaks for our dinner.

It was the day after the Fourth of July. Rachel and I had been together almost two years. We had just returned a few hours ago from a romantic holiday in Reno.

"I didn't know you'd called," I snarled. I unbuttoned my shirt, kicked off my shoes, and got comfortable on the couch. But I couldn't sit still. I kept crossing and uncrossing my legs and wiping sweat off my face and glancing toward the door, praying that Rachel wouldn't get back before I got Caroline off the phone. "And I don't appreciate you calling me names, God damn it!"

I didn't like to sound mean, but whenever I talked to Caroline these days, she provoked me to do so. Despite the fact that she was such a thorn in my side, she was still my child's mother, and that meant a lot to me, so I decided to soften my demeanor. "I'm sorry I missed your calls, but I went out of town, and I forgot to take my cell phone with me," I explained, speaking in such a gentle tone of voice now, you would have thought I was talking to a child.

"Uh-huh! I heard about your happy ass and how you been gallivanting all over the place with your new whore—"

"Don't call her that! You don't even know the woman," I interrupted.

"I don't need to know her to know that if she's involved with a dick-headed motherfucker like you, she has to be a straight-up whore. Fucking was all you ever cared about when I was with you, and I know you ain't changed."

"I have news for you. Rachel is not a whore. As a matter of fact, she's worth about five of you. How is my son?"

"*My* son is just fine, as if you care."

"Caroline, you know I care about Darnell."

"Yeah, right."

I shuddered when I imagined some of the nasty things

Caroline had probably told Darnell about me and some of the reasons she'd given him for why I didn't see him that often. I kept attempting to see him more, anyway. I called her place on a regular basis, and she would almost always tell me he was "out with his friends." Or she'd say, "He's busy. Call back later." One week I called ten different times and didn't get to talk to him. Finally, when I called on a Saturday morning and he answered the telephone, he cried, as he was so happy and surprised to hear from me. I didn't even bother to tell him how hard I had been trying. One thing I was not going to do was trash his mother. I was sure that he knew what kind of woman she really was by the company she kept and the things she did and said. Every man she got involved with was into some shady activity, and I had heard that from members of her own family who still lived in the Bay Area. One thing was for sure, as soon as I got myself into a comfortable position, I was going to do all I could to get custody of my son.

"What's wrong? Is Darnell in trouble at school again?"

"Is that all you think about? Do you ever *not* think that the boy is acting a fool in school?"

I hated talking to this woman. No matter what the subject was, we would always say something to piss one another off. "You call only when there is a problem with him or when you want more money. Is he all right?"

"He ain't dead, so I guess he's doing all right. I am, too, in case you care." Caroline snorted and coughed to clear her throat. "I called because I need to send him to you for a couple of weeks."

"You what? All this time, my trying to get you to let me see him more has been like pulling teeth. Now you want to let me have him for a whole two weeks?"

"I'm going on a cruise, and I don't have nobody else to leave him with. My other kids will be staying with their daddies," she hissed. "Letting Darnell stay with you is the least you can do since you too busy to come down here to see him, like you should."

"Caroline, the last time I came down there, you didn't answer your fucking door or your phone. The time before that, when I got there after driving for six hours straight in the rain, you told me Darnell had gone camping with his friends—when you knew I was coming to see him."

"What . . . ever!" she huffed. I could picture the neck rolling and finger snapping that went along with that comment.

"I'd love to have Darnell with me for two weeks. As a matter of fact, I'd love to have him with me permanently. That way you can do whatever else you want to do and not have to worry about him."

"Ha! Let you have him? That'll be the day. My mama didn't raise no fool. I know you want to get out of giving me my money every month, but you can forget about that. I will get paid until that boy turns eighteen."

"I know that, Caroline. I've never been late making the support payments, and I've never said no when you asked me for extra money."

"Speaking of extra money, can you wire me an extra grand this month? I'll even pay it back to you . . . if you want me to."

"What do you need an 'extra grand' for? And how is it you're able to afford a two-week cruise?"

"Don't worry about what I need the extra money for. Will you send it to me or not? And for your information, my man is footing the bill for my cruise."

"I don't have an extra thousand to spare right now," I admitted.

"When can you get it?"

"I can't say. I just borrowed more money from Josh, and I have to pay him back before I ask for more."

"What about that woman?"

"What woman?"

"What's her name? Uh, I heard it was Raquel . . . or Rochelle . . . or Rasputin, or some shitty name that starts with an *R*."

"Her name is Rachel," I said flatly.

"Whatever. I heard she's making some pretty sweet money working at that white-ass private school."

I couldn't believe this woman's nerve! But then again, Caroline always had worked both sides of the street. She had shown me that the day she and her mother showed up at my parents' house and claimed that I had *raped* her.

"You know something, Caroline. For you to be several hundred miles away, you sure know a lot about what's going on up here in Berkeley."

"I still have friends and family up there. They tell me what's going on."

"Hmmm. Well, you don't need to have anybody keeping an eye on me or Rachel. What we do is none of your business. And I can't believe you would even think that I'd borrow money from her to give to you! My mama didn't raise no fool, either!"

"Don't worry about it, then. I'll get it from somebody else."

"What do you need the money for, Caroline? Maybe if you tell me that, I'll figure out some way to get it to you."

"I got jumped by a bunch of Mexicans a couple of nights ago. They took everything I had," she sobbed, sniffling to add more emphasis to her words. "If you don't believe me, I can send you the newspaper clipping."

"I believe you. Did they hurt you?"

"I got a few scrapes and bruises. Other than that, I'm fine." Caroline blew her nose and continued. She began to speak in a voice that was so low and weak, I could barely hear her. "It was the money that I was going to use to pay my rent and to get the rest of Darnell's school clothes out of layaway at Kmart. . . ."

My son was the most important thing in the world to me. And even though I was certain Caroline lied more than any woman I knew, she might have been telling the truth this time. But I still didn't want her to think she was dealing with a fool. "If your new honey can afford to take you on a cruise, why can't he help you out with your financial situation?"

"I tell you what. Don't worry about the money. And don't worry about watching Darnell while I'm on vacation. I can leave him with my sister Lorna."

"No!"

"No, what?"

"Your sister lives in one of the most dangerous neighborhoods in L.A., with a *drug dealer.* I don't want my son in that environment!"

"Since when did you care? You ain't trying to put us in a better neighborhood."

"Look, Caroline. I'll get the money for you, and you can still let Darnell spend the two weeks with me. I'll drive down to pick him up, or I'll pay his airfare to come up here."

"You got money for a plane ticket, huh?"

"I'll get the money to help pay your rent, and I'll get the money to pay for Darnell's plane ticket."

"I need it by tomorrow."

"Your rent is due on the fifteenth, and this is not even the middle of the month."

"Didn't I tell you I was going on a cruise? I need to pay my rent before I go away. And I have to get them clothes for Darnell out of layaway before I leave, or I'll lose that money, too."

"I don't know if I can get it by tomorrow. My parents don't like to loan money too often, and I already told you I'm still in the hole with my brother. I owe most of my friends, too, so I can't go to any of them. And my credit cards are all maxed out!"

"Then you'd better find some other way to get that money to me by tomorrow. Do you hear me?"

"I hear you," I muttered. "What about Darnell? Do you want me to drive down to pick him up?"

"My sister Maggie is down here. She'll bring him back up there with her tomorrow. But I tell you what you can do. The money you was going to get to pay for his flight, you can include that with the money you wire to me tomorrow. Do you hear me?"

"I hear you."

"I'd like my money no later than noon."

"I'll send it." I let out a sour breath and rubbed the side of my throbbing head. "Anything else?"

"Just one more thing. If that woman mistreats my child, I'm going to come up there and whup her—"

I didn't let Caroline finish her threat. I hung up and turned the telephone off.

Chapter 34

Rachel

"YOU NEED TO BORROW SIXTEEN HUNDRED DOLLARS from me to get your car fixed? That's a mighty big loan, Seth."

"I know it is, but I hope you'll help me out. I'll pay you back. I don't like to borrow money, but this time I have no choice. I'll sign a promissory note if you want me to."

"Well, I'll let you have it this time, and if you don't pay me back when you're supposed to, I'll sue you," I teased. I didn't like to loan money to anybody, especially friends and lovers. But I decided to help Seth this time. "I know how hard you've been struggling to get out of debt and take care of your son. And if your son is going to spend two weeks with us, you'll need a car that you can depend on to get around in, since you refuse to borrow mine that often." I chuckled. "And you don't have to sign a promissory note."

Had the situation been in reverse, I knew I could have borrowed money from Seth. He had told me that more than once. At the end of the day, I was glad that I was in a position to help my man. But despite my generous nature, I was a very frugal woman. Yes, I spent money on nice things like my friends, but what they didn't know was that the designer clothes I wore and some of the fancy things in my apartment came from upscale consignment shops, flea markets, Goodwill, and estate sales. After I paid my rent and other bills, most of my monthly pay went into my bank accounts. And thanks to Uncle Albert, I had learned how to invest in the stock market, so I made money that way, too.

I didn't share that information with anybody. Mama had told me never to let the right hand know what the left hand was doing. I saw no reason to let my friends, or even Seth, know how shrewd I was and how much money I had in the bank. One thing I had learned about people was that if they knew you had extra money, they suddenly needed a "loan" for some random financial emergency. Lucy and Patrice made good money, but they were always broke, because they were so extravagant. Paulette and her husband lived high on the hog, too, and had recently filed for bankruptcy, so that told me a lot about them. None of my friends had ever asked me for a loan, and I didn't want them to start. But they borrowed money from everybody else they knew. Seth often borrowed money from his family members and a few of his friends. This was the first time he'd asked me for a loan, and I didn't hesitate, because it was for a good cause.

The more I saw Seth, the more I loved him. Our relationship could not have been better. I was convinced that we were going to have a relationship for a very long time.

* * *

I called home on a regular basis. During almost every conversation, Mama and Aunt Hattie made wild predictions about how Uncle Albert was going to catch something from one of his gay boyfriends and end up dead. Then they bombarded me with news about funerals, their health issues, and a few comments about Ernest and Janet, which were usually repeats of their previous conversations. They also wanted me to keep them in the loop about my personal life, and I was happy to oblige them. I was hopelessly in love with Seth, and I couldn't stop thinking about him or talking about him to anybody who was willing to listen.

Every time I mentioned Seth to Mama and Aunt Hattie, I told them a little more about how good he was to me and for me.

"Seth is the best thing that's ever happened to me. He's handsome, funny, and smart. And he's ambitious. He's the kind of man I hope to marry someday," I told Mama, clutching the telephone with both hands. Aunt Hattie was listening on the extension, something she often did when she was present during Mama's telephone conversations with me. Just as I had expected, they put in their two cents' worth—more like two dollars' worth, I should say—and warned me not to act a fool with him, the way I had with Jeffrey.

"Uh-huh. I don't care what this Seth do to you, you better not do nothing that'll make him set the law on you," Mama warned. "Them jails in California is like Hades compared to the ones back here. They always showing that on the Discovery Channel. And I ain't going to beg around to borrow money to bail you out of jail like I done that other time. You got a bad temper, like your daddy's mama had."

"You don't have to worry about me getting arrested again," I insisted. "I haven't lost my temper since I moved out here, and I've had more than one reason to do so! Besides, I love Seth. I'd never do anything to hurt him."

Aunt Hattie jumped in with both feet. "Girl, love ain't nothing but a four-letter word. Women your age don't know menfolk like me and your mama's generation. You see all the headaches men done caused us? We worked hard to keep our men happy, and what did it get us? Your daddy had to have another woman on the side and got hisself killed for doing it. After that *thang* I married died, I heard all kinds of rumors about women he was involved with. Stay single and have just a casual friend every once in a while. Come laundry day, you ain't got to wash nobody's funky, piss-stained drawers but your own. Besides that, you need to be focusing on another four-letter word. W-o-r-k."

"I have a job, Aunt Hattie. A good job," I said with a sigh.

"I ain't talking about *your* job! Didn't you say this new Romeo you done hooked up with is only working in a cannery, lifting boxes of canned goods and whatnot?"

"He is. And he's taking a business course a couple of nights a week."

Aunt Hattie gasped. "Do you mean to tell me you done got involved with a man that ain't even out of school yet?"

I was glad I hadn't mentioned that the class Seth was taking now was a six-week on-line course on his laptop in the comfort of my apartment. "Well, he didn't finish high school when he was supposed to, but he got his GED. He's going to open his own ad agency eventually. He'd already taken a few courses before I met him, and this new one will benefit him even more."

"Bah! Eventually, my foot. That's a word folks use when they don't know which way is up. In the meantime, you better 'eventually' watch your step with this man.

For him to be from such an uptown family like you claim, he don't sound too . . . uh . . . reliable to me."

"Aunt Hattie, don't worry about me and Seth," I said. "When you meet him, you'll see why I'm so crazy about him."

I always expected my mama and my meddlesome aunt to say something off the wall when it involved my love life. But my girls were my support system, and so far all I had received from them was positive feedback when it came to Seth.

Until now.

"Do you think it's a good idea to start lending money to a man you've known for such a short time?" Lucy asked during our latest after-work get-together.

It was casual Friday, and we were all dressed accordingly. I had worn my favorite running shoes and a light green sweat suit to work that day. The booth we occupied was near the front entrance at Dino's, one of our favorite Italian restaurants. It was a small, dimly lit place near downtown Berkeley. The fireplace in the middle of the main floor, the wine bottles dangling from the ceiling, and one of the best menus in town attracted a lot of people. As usual, Dino's was crowded with college students, the business crowd, and families that included cranky babies and cranky elders. My crew and I had finished off a large pepperoni pizza, and we were working on our third bottle of Chianti.

"If I trust him enough to let him move in with me, why wouldn't I lend him money?" I wanted to know. I looked from Lucy's face to Paulette's cute, heart-shaped face. Her dark brown skin was so smooth and flawless, it was hard to believe she was almost thirty. She was the most sensible one of the four of us most of the time. "Paulette, what's wrong with me lending Seth sixteen hundred bucks?"

"Nothing," she replied with a shrug and a skeptical look on her face. "But I can't think of any man who could get sixteen hundred bucks out of *me* unless he stole it. . . ."

"Aww," I said, giving her a dismissive wave. Then I turned to Patrice. As a flight attendant for a major airline, she traveled all over the country and dated all kinds of men. She was more worldly than the rest of us. She was twenty-nine and had never been married, but she had been in several serious relationships. "Patrice, you have more experience with men than me, and you used to live next door to Seth when you were growing up. You probably know him better than the rest of us put together. Would you lend money to him if he were your man?"

Patrice sighed, and a mysterious smile crossed her nut-brown face. "I had a crush on Seth all through my teens, but he was never attracted to tall girls like me."

"You didn't answer my question."

She smiled again. "I've *never* lent money to *any* man before, and I probably never will. It's a recipe for disaster. Does that answer your question?" Patrice replied, emphasizing each word.

I rolled my eyes and turned back to Lucy. "Whatever. Regardless of what you hens think, I'm going to do all I can to make my relationship with Seth work. I can't wait to meet his son. Any man who wants his woman to get to know his son can't be too bad."

Lucy exhaled and ran her fingers though her freshly curled hair. Then she folded her arms and said, "Rachel, all I ask is that you be careful with Seth. I know I introduced him to you, because I thought you two would be good for each other. I don't know about all that now. Maybe I should not have pushed you into meeting him. I didn't twist your arm, though. You could have told me to mind my own business, and I would have left it at that.

But you didn't. At the end of the day, you get what you settle for."

"Meaning what?"

"Seth's daddy and his brother Damon have mistresses," Paulette blurted.

Lucy gasped and whirled around so fast to face Paulette, one of her curls hit her in the eye. She gave Paulette the most threatening look I'd ever seen. "Girl, I told you not to go blabbing everything I tell you! Now I guess everybody you know knows what I told you about the Garrett men."

"I know all about them, but Paulette didn't tell me," Patrice said with a smug look on her face. "I've seen old man Garrett with his girlfriend several times a year on flights to Vegas and Reno that I've worked. The woman Damon is involved with goes to the same beauty shop I go to, and she likes to share her business. I am sure his wife has heard about his affair by now, but she probably doesn't care anymore. Most women married to prominent men want to stay married to them, even if they have to share them with other women."

"So what? What's that got to do with Seth?" I wanted to know. "If one of you busybodies is trying to tell me that Seth is already cheating on me, stay out of my business!"

Everybody got quiet. All I could hear was chatter and the clinking of silverware coming from the tables and booths around us.

"Nobody said anything about Seth running around on you," Lucy said in a tentative tone of voice. "I don't think he's the type to cheat. I think he really loves you." She touched my shoulder and gave me a tender look, and that made me feel somewhat better, because a few moments earlier, I had been thinking about bolting out of that restaurant. "He could hurt you in other ways, girlfriend."

Lucy's last statement sent me back into my defensive

mode. "Well, when and if that happens, that's my business." I snorted. "Now, since you three witches are so deep into my business, y'all can pay the bill!"

"I think we need another bottle of wine," Patrice said, adding a hollow laugh.

Lucy and Paulette laughed, too, but I didn't. To me, Seth was the most serious thing in my life, so I had nothing to laugh about. However, my friends' concerns had settled in the back of my head like a long-term migraine headache, and that worried me.

Had I lost my perspective? Had I become one of those gullible, stupid females that my mama and auntie sat around talking about like dogs? No, I didn't think that I'd slid down that low on the food chain of common sense. I was a lot of things, but I was not a damn fool when it came to men. I was just a woman in love.

One thing I knew for sure was that if Seth ever did anything that made me feel like he was using me or disrespecting me, he would regret it for the rest of his life. . . .

Chapter 35

Seth

*I*T WAS CAROLINE'S BROTHER MICHAEL WHO DROPPED off Darnell that Friday. Rachel took off work early so she could be home when they arrived, because when I took off, I didn't get paid. And we needed all the money we could get our hands on. By the time I got home, my son and Rachel were behaving like old friends.

"Daddy, Miss Rachel said she'd take me to the video arcade tomorrow!" Darnell yelled as soon as I got inside. He was big for thirteen and looked more like me than ever.

"Hey now! Don't I get a hug before we start talking about video arcades?" I scolded. He ran to me and wrapped his arms around my waist. I held my breath and looked into his eyes and then at the rest of him. I tried not to look too closely at the shabby clothes he wore. But what I saw was disturbing, to say the least. First of all, his hair was knotted up on his head like cockleburs. "Darnell, don't you have any combs or brushes in your house?" I asked, struggling to keep the tone of my voice light.

"Yeah," he answered with a shrug. "We got a bunch of combs and brushes. Mama buys them two or three at a time from the Dollar Tree store, but I couldn't find nary a one before I left."

Surprisingly, he wore a pair of new-looking Nikes, but his thin plaid shirt and purple jeans were wrinkled and torn in a few places. Rachel must have read my mind.

"Honey, I told Darnell I'd take him shopping for some new clothes." Rachel walked over to Darnell and gave him an affectionate touch on his shoulder. "We'll get an early start tomorrow so we can take our time."

Darnell looked back at Rachel like he wanted to hug her. He turned back to me and said, "Miss Rachel said she'd take me to the movies tomorrow, too!"

"I said we could go to a movie if we could find one that's rated G," she said, gently shaking a finger in Darnell's face.

"That's nice," I muttered, looking over Darnell's shoulder at Rachel as she stood there, smiling, with her arms folded. "I thought you had plans to do something with your uncle tomorrow."

"I did, but I can see Uncle Albert anytime," she told me. "Now, let me get in the kitchen and get that pizza in the oven."

"What about the collard greens and fried chicken you said you'd cook for me today?" I whined.

"Have I ever let you down? I've already cooked dinner for you, but the pizza is for me and Darnell."

I couldn't remember the last time I'd seen such a huge smile on my son's face, and the one on mine was probably even bigger. I was beaming because the two most important people in my life had already bonded. Not only was Rachel a good mate, an immaculate housekeeper, and a great lover, but she was also going to be an awesome mother, because it seemed to me that all she really cared about was making her loved ones happy.

Darnell gobbled up half of the pizza. And he also had two helpings of the greens and several pieces of fried chicken.

"I wish my mama would cook real food sometime," he said, speaking with his mouth full of food.

"Sweetheart, don't talk and eat at the same time," Rachel said gently.

"Oh. I'm sorry, Miss Rachel—"

"And I told you not to call me Miss Rachel. You can call me Rachel."

Before Darnell could continue, I jumped into the conversation. "What does your mama usually cook for you and your sisters and brother, son?"

"Mama don't cook that much. We mostly eat TV dinners and sandwiches. When she got money, we get Big Macs and Happy Meals, and every once in a while she'll have a pizza delivered," Darnell told us.

"What about her friends?" I asked. Rachel kicked my foot under the table.

"What friends? She got a bunch of boyfriends, and her girlfriends only come around when they want to smoke weed or borrow something."

My heart sank. I knew that my son was not in the best environment, but since he lived in L.A. and I didn't get to see him but a few times a year, there was little I could do about it.

"Uh, Darnell, how would you like to live with us someday?" Rachel said, surprising the hell out of me. "You can have your own room, but you can only eat Big Macs and other fast food every once in a while." I had casually mentioned to her a few times that I was probably going to ask for full custody of my son someday, and she had been very supportive. But the subject had not come up in a while.

"I don't know," Darnell said, speaking slowly. "Mama said . . ." He stopped talking and looked from Rachel to me and back. "Mama said she would put me in a foster home before she would let me live with you and your . . . She called Rachel a bad word." He gave Rachel a sympathetic look.

"Son, you don't have to go there. We get the picture," I said, with my jaw twitching. "I'm going to do everything I can to make life easier for you," I vowed.

We finished our meal in silence and watched a few comedy shows on TV until Darnell fell asleep on the couch in the new pajamas that Rachel had purchased for him without my knowledge. This woman was so thoughtful, it was frightening.

When I got out of bed Saturday morning, Darnell and Rachel were already up and about. He had showered and put on some fresh clothes, another cheap shirt and a pair of jeans that looked as if he had slept in them.

"Daddy, Rachel made me—" Darnell stopped talking and turned to Rachel. "What was that egg thing you cooked for me this morning?"

"An omelet," she said.

"And some grits! I hadn't had no grits since that time Mama took me to Denny's for my birthday a couple of years ago." He turned back to Rachel. "We still going to the video arcade?"

"We sure are."

"You can count me out." I chuckled. I had hung out at the video arcade so much when I was a kid that it was now one of the last places on the planet I wanted to be.

"We didn't invite you to go, anyway! Besides, you've

already told your mama that you would spend some time with her today," Rachel said.

I had planned to go alone to my parents' house that Saturday afternoon. I hadn't told my family that Darnell was spending a couple of weeks with me, and I wasn't going to if I didn't have to. For one thing, my mother still had a difficult time dealing with my son's hard-core inner-city personality. I had scolded him on several occasions about using crude street language in her presence. And I thought he did things on purpose to antagonize her. The last time I'd brought him to the house to spend time with my folks, he had taken a bath and had not even bothered to let the water out of the tub after he'd finished. But the thing that drove Mother up the wall, and Father, too, for that matter, was how he would spray the toilet seat with urine in all three bathrooms and leave without flushing the toilet. Such habits horrified my mother, so it was no wonder she rarely asked about Darnell anymore. To say he was a "black sheep" was putting it mildly. And that saddened me.

I was not concerned about any of the folks I knew seeing Darnell out and about with Rachel. My mother and most of her friends wouldn't be found dead in the places Rachel usually patronized. Mother shopped at high-end establishments in San Francisco and in some of the outer suburbs that didn't attract a lot of black folks. I was pleased to know that she liked Rachel. She had recently advised Rachel to call her by her first name now. Mother had never allowed any of my other girlfriends to do that, not even Darnell's mother.

I waited until Rachel and Darnell left before I called Mother.

"I'm on my way," I told her.

"Is Rachel coming with you?"

"Um, nope. She's going to spend some time with her uncle."

"Well, if she changes her mind, tell her she's more than welcome."

"Yes, ma'am."

"As a matter of fact, I was going to come over there so she can show me how to make hush puppies in time for my next Tupperware party next week. If she's not too busy, of course. I know she works and has to come home and cook dinner."

"Huh?"

"I really want to get to know her even better. I know how serious you are about her, and I want to do all I can to help you make this relationship work."

"Well, uh, let us know what day and what time you want to come over here. And, oh, did I mention that Darnell is with us for a couple of weeks?" Right after I finished my last sentence, I held my breath.

Mother hesitated for a few seconds. "No, you didn't mention that. Will he be coming with you today?" For my mother to be such a warm and caring person, she could be very cold at times. It saddened me to know that it was my son who had her acting like an iceberg this time.

"Well, yes. I was going to ask Rachel to bring him over after they come back from the mall. I hadn't said anything, because I wanted it to be a surprise." I was used to doing damage control with Mother, so she almost never questioned my motivation.

"I see. I hope she comes, and I, uh, can't wait to see my grandson again."

Mother hung up, and I immediately called Rachel on her cellular phone. "Baby, Mother wants us all to come by the house today so she can see Darnell."

"Oh. All right. We're just about to go have foot-long

hot dogs and fries. Darnell and I couldn't find a decent movie, so we'll go over to your parents' house around three or four. Will that time be all right?"

"I think so. I hadn't told her he was coming up here, because I wanted to surprise her. So do me a favor and go along with it, okay?" I had already told Rachel how my mother felt about Darnell.

"Okay, baby. We'll be there. Now, you get up and get on over there. You know how your mother is when you tell her you're coming over. She'll peek out the window every five minutes until you get over there." Rachel laughed, and I laughed along with her.

Chapter 36

Seth

I STILL HAD MY KEY TO MY PARENTS' HOUSE, BUT I ALways knocked now.

"What's wrong with you, boy? Why don't you just let yourself in, like you're supposed to?" Mother asked, swinging open the door. "You know I gave Minnie the day off." Minnie Finch was the woman who came to the house several times a week to "help" Mother with the housekeeping.

"Mother, this is no longer my home, and I don't feel comfortable acting like it is at my age," I said, trying to sound firm. "I keep telling you and Father and everybody else that I want to be more independent."

"Uh-huh. Is that why you moved in with Rachel? How do you expect to become 'more independent' living with her?"

"I thought you liked Rachel."

"I do. I think she's the nicest, sweetest girl you've ever

brought to the house. And it's about time!" Mother brushed off the sleeve of my jacket and patted the top of my head. The same way she used to do when I was a little boy. It was no wonder I still felt like a baby when I was around her. "And judging from that muffin top around your waist, she's cooking up a storm for you!" Mother patted my belly, which had expanded considerably since I'd moved in with Rachel.

I spent the next hour playing bridge with my mother and two of her nosy friends. I had to answer every question in the book regarding my health, my job status, and my love life.

"I am so happy for you, Seth. I loved Rachel the minute I met her," Mrs. Wilson, a plump retired doctor's wife, said in a raspy voice.

"All I want to know is, does she have any grown sisters? I'd love to see my boy Earl settle down with a nice girl with some of the same old-school virtues I hear Rachel has," said Mrs. Carter, my mother's thin, long-faced hairdresser.

"Uh, yeah. She's got one sister around eighteen or nineteen, I think. Her name's Janet, but she lives in Alabama," I responded.

"Is she as nice and as pretty as Rachel?" Mother asked.

"I've seen pictures of Rachel's sister, and she's even prettier than Rachel." I paused when every woman in the room gasped. "I've talked to her on the telephone only once, just to introduce myself. I didn't talk to her long enough to determine anything about her personality. But I'm sure she's just as nice and as sweet as Rachel."

"Does she have any brothers? I've been praying for some nice fellow to come along and take my trifling daughter Francine off my hands," said Willena Morris, Mother's former sorority sister, shaking her head.

"She's got a brother who is a couple of years younger than she is. I don't know much about him, though . . . his education or what kind of work he does. When I asked Rachel to let me introduce myself over the phone, the way I had done with her sister, he wouldn't come to the phone for some strange reason. I haven't been able to get him on the phone yet."

"Maybe he's shy. Anyway, from everything you've told us about Rachel and everything we've witnessed with our own eyes, she's from good stock, so her siblings have to be, too. I'm just surprised she's got a grown sister and brother who are still unmarried and still living at home," Mother said. I didn't know how to interpret the worried look on her face.

"Mother, I'm grown and still unmarried, and I just moved away from home recently," I reminded. "Besides, I am sure that Rachel's sister and her brother are already involved with other people."

When Rachel arrived with Darnell an hour later, I wanted to jump up and kiss her as soon as she entered the living room. I did just that, and not just because I was happy to see her. I had a more important reason. She was a lot more patient than I was, so she could deal with these old hens and shift the focus off me and the fact that my relationship with Darnell was so shaky. Just as I expected, Rachel handled the situation like a pro. By the time we left, she had Mother and everybody else practically eating out of her hand. Especially Darnell, and that pleased me more than anything.

"I'll help you out with Darnell as much as I can," Rachel told me when we got home that night. "As long as it's within reason . . ."

"Thanks, baby. That makes me feel so much better. So far you're the only person who seems to be able to get through to him," I told her. "I appreciate all you do for him—and all you do for me, too. I can't tell you that enough."

When we went to bed, I made love to her for hours.

Rachel was a woman of her word. When she promised to do something, she did it, no matter how much of an inconvenience it was to her. I could see why her friends were so crazy about her.

Rachel went out of her way to please my son. She even rearranged her schedule and canceled a few appointments so she could accommodate him. She quickly realized how much Darnell loved shopping and hanging out at the mall, and she didn't hesitate to take him. However, she made him "earn" those privileges. She came up with all kinds of incentives to make him more proactive. She had him wash our cars, wash dishes, or perform some other chore when he wanted her to take him to the arcade or anywhere else.

"I ain't never in my life done no laundry or vacuumed no floor. But Rachel said she'd pay me or take me anywhere I want to go if I did," he told me one day, when I came home from work.

When Rachel ran out of chores for Darnell to do, she had him earn points by running errands for her neighbors. And not once did he balk. He enjoyed the challenges. He even called up some of his friends in L.A. and bragged about all the "good deeds" Rachel had him performing and his rewards for doing them.

"I can't wait to tell Mama how much fun I had and how much money I made for vacuuming floors and doing other things for Rachel, and for running to the store for old people next door that she hooked me up with," he said, grinning from ear to ear. "Daddy, I hope you and Rachel never break up!"

"I hope we don't, either," I said.

Chapter 37

Rachel

I WAS NERVOUS ABOUT GOING TO SETH'S PARENTS' HOUSE when Darnell and I finished our shopping. I took him back to my apartment first so he could change into some of the cute clothes I had purchased for him. I didn't even want to think about how Seth's mother would react if he showed up in the baggy, shabby clothes he had brought with him from L.A.

"Do I have to go over to my grandparents' house?" Darnell asked with frown.

"Yes, honey. If you behave over there, I'll take you swimming tomorrow. Now go change your clothes and let's get going. The sooner we get over there, the sooner we can leave."

"Cool!" Darnell yelled as he laid out his new clothes so he could decide what to wear.

* * *

Seth's father answered the door when Darnell and I arrived. Before I realized what was happening, he draped his arm around my shoulder and kissed me on the cheek, which was the way he always greeted me. But this time, before I could pull away, his hand brushed the side of my hip. He looked away too fast, so he didn't see the scowl on my face. He gave Darnell a brief hug and walked away, but not before winking at me as I followed him into the living room.

"Rachel, honey, I don't know what you're doing to my son, but whatever it is, please keep doing it. I've never seen him so happy," Seth's mother told me. For a woman of means, she sure looked downright cheap to me most of the time. She wore way too much make-up and too many outlandish outfits. Today she had on a flowered muumuu, and her make-up was so thick, it looked like clay.

"Well, Seth deserves to be treated well. By the way, Vivian, you look as glamorous as ever." It was so easy for me to lie to a woman like Seth's mother. I liked her, but because of some of the things she'd said to me the first day I met her, I didn't trust her and never would.

"Thank you, sweetie. So do you," she squealed. A split second later, she narrowed her eyes and looked me up and down. "How do you breathe in those tight jeans?" Then she made a clucking noise and promptly turned to Darnell and opened her arms. "Come give your granny some sugar!"

Darnell rolled his eyes and reluctantly went up to her and gave her a hug, one of the weakest I'd ever seen.

"I'm so glad to see you in some decent clothes for a change."

"Rachel took me shopping," Darnell announced, looking around the room. I had a feeling he was just as uncomfortable about being around his grandmother and her friends as I was.

"Rachel, we were just talking about you, honey," the retired doctor's wife said with a hiccup. She had very light brown skin, but because her nose was as red as a cherry, I could tell she'd had several daiquiris already. The empty pitcher and empty glasses on the table were an indication that the rest of the old ladies had, too.

Things went downhill from there.

I liked Seth's parents and their friends, but I dreaded spending a Saturday afternoon with them. The first time I excused myself to go to the bathroom, Conrad was standing in front of the door when I came out.

"Can I talk to you for a second?" he asked, nodding toward the end of the hall.

"What about?" I wanted to know, backing away from him.

He took my hand and pulled me down the hall. Since I didn't want to create a scene, I followed in silence.

"Rachel, when can we get together?" he whispered.

"Huh?" I gasped and shook my head. "Get together for what?"

"You don't fool me, girl. I've seen the look in your eyes every time you look at me. I know you want to be with me as much as I want to be with you. I know a place—"

My life had improved so much in the past few years that I was a lot more mellow than I used to be. I had learned how to control my temper and my mouth. The "old" me probably would have slapped Conrad and cussed him out. I didn't want to go back to my old ways, and I didn't want to make myself look like a fool in Seth's parents' home.

"I'm going to pretend this didn't happen. But if it does happen again, I will tell your son and your wife."

Conrad's mouth flew open, and an angry look appeared on his face. "I know you're not threatening me!"

"I don't fool around with other women's men!" I hissed.

"Since when? What about Skirt?"

"Skirt?" I gasped again.

"This is a small town, young lady. Men talk. I know how you used to lay up with Skirt, and all during that time he was involved with several women. Don't you stand here and tell me you don't fool around with other women's men! I'm sure my son would love to know what a slut you really are!"

If Seth's lecherous father didn't deserve to be slapped, I didn't know who did. I was surprised that I was still able to control my temper. But I wasn't sure how long I'd be able to do so. I decided to end this encounter as soon as I could. I leaned closer to Conrad and poked him in the chest with my finger. "If you ever approach me again like this, you will be very sorry." I walked away and went back into the living room.

A few seconds later, Conrad returned, grumbling about an appointment with a friend that he'd just remembered. I was glad when he left the house, but I had a feeling I was going to have another encounter with him. If so, I wouldn't be as nice to him as I'd been a few minutes ago.

Vivian ordered me to sit down and join the bridge game, which was one card game I had never really cared for. Darnell plopped down on the couch, grabbed the remote off the coffee table, and turned the TV on. About ten minutes later, he jumped up and danced a jig to the music of a popular commercial. He accidentally knocked a vase off one of the end tables. It didn't break, but Vivian almost had another heart attack.

"Darnell, you have to act more civilized when you're in this house!" she yelled. "Now, you pick up that vase and put it back where it was, and then sit down and stay still until your daddy takes you home." She turned to one of her guests and said something I never thought a grandmother would say in front of her grandson. "With Caroline for a mother, no wonder this boy is such a savage."

I looked at Seth. He stood behind the chair his mother occupied, with his hands on her shoulders. I had never seen him look so hurt. He blinked and offered me a weak smile, but I knew him so well by now, I could still see the pain in his eyes.

"Daddy, when can we leave?" Darnell asked, totally ignoring his grandmother. "I don't like it over here. It smells like bug spray."

Vivian gasped and gave her guests an apologetic look. "See what I mean?" she said, shaking her head. "My other grandson never behaves like this. . . ."

"Mother, Darnell is not used to being in such a rigid setting," Seth said, using a tone of voice he rarely used with his mother.

"Well, he doesn't have to come to this 'rigid setting,'" Vivian said, something else I had never expected to hear a grandmother say in front of her grandson.

I felt so sorry for Darnell. Even more so for Seth. The poor thing was trying so hard to please his mother, but it seemed like it always backfired.

To add insult to injury, when we prepared to leave a couple of hours later, Darnell stumbled over to Vivian and kissed her on the cheek. "Bye, Grandma. It was good to see you," he said with a grimace on his face. Vivian wiped her cheek with a napkin as soon as Darnell turned away from her.

"Yeah," she muttered. "It was good to see you, too," she added after hesitating for a few moments. She sucked in her gut and turned to me, flipping on her smile as if she'd used a light switch to do so. "I'll see you again soon, I hope, Rachel. It's always a pleasure to see you. Let me know when I can come over this week so you can show me how to make hush puppies."

"Come over this Monday evening, around six thirty, Vivian."

I wanted to show that woman how to make hush puppies as soon as possible and get it over with. Why she had to come to my place for that was a mystery to me. "She just wants to keep tabs on how clean you keep your place," Lucy had told me when I'd mentioned it to her the other day. I knew that I would keep as much distance between myself and my potential future mother-in-law as I could. And because of the way she treated and spoke to Darnell, I shuddered when I thought about how she might treat Seth's children by me if they didn't suit her. . . .

I couldn't take off from work to spend the days with Darnell, so I took him to a child-care center owned by a woman who lived in my neighborhood on my way to work the first Monday of his visit. I wanted to help Seth out as much as I could.

"Baby, I really appreciate what you're doing for me," Seth told me when he called me from his job at around ten that morning.

"Seth, it was no trouble at all for me to take Darnell to the center. And don't worry about the payment. My neighbor is giving me a ten percent discount for braiding her hair last month."

"That's wonderful." His silence told me there was something else on his mind. "In a few weeks, I'll have my business up and running. I'll be able to help out more with our finances."

"Seth, I'm not used to lending money or helping people out financially, but I'll help you when I can, if it's not a hardship, and as long as you agree to pay me back when you say you will." It seemed like every time I uttered words like these, it led to another one of his financial situations. This time was no different.

"That's why I hate to ask you for more," he started,

speaking slowly and in a low voice. "But I swear I'll pay you back when I say I will."

"What else do you need?"

"Could you cover my child support payments for this month and next? I'll pay you back in about three months, when I cash in some bonds my grandmother left me. I'd like to go ahead and get some better transportation now. It makes no sense for me to keep spending money on repairs for that damn jalopy I have now. It broke down on the freeway twice last week, and I'm sick of having to call tow trucks."

"I guess I can," I replied with hesitation. I took a deep breath and smiled to hide my concern. I promised myself that the very *first* time Seth didn't keep his end of a repayment agreement, I'd never help him out financially again. "I'm glad to hear that you've decided to go ahead and get a new car. Not only do you really need one, but you deserve one."

Seth financed most of the things we did to entertain Darnell. We went to every animated movie there was, the video arcade several times, McDonald's, and we went shopping to get him some more new clothes and some school supplies. I was glad Seth didn't ask me for even more financial assistance. I was nervous about the sixteen hundred dollars I'd already lent to him and my agreement to cover his child support payments for a couple of months. My money was a major part of our relationship, but I let that slide because I knew Seth was doing the best he could. If a man couldn't count on his woman when he was in a financial bind, who could he count on?

Chapter 38

Rachel

THE DAY AFTER WE PUT DARNELL ON THE PLANE TO GO back to L.A., I went car shopping with Seth. He had practically driven the gas-guzzling jalopy he owned now into the ground. I had eagerly agreed with him that it was time for him to get something newer and more reliable. We browsed very briefly at several locations. At the last place on our list, he took a lot more time to look around. Since it was a Nissan dealership, I assumed he'd get something reasonable, like an Altima or one of the other cars that he had expressed an interest in. There were a lot of brand-new Nissans to choose from, as well as dozens of used cars of other makes and models. I was stunned when Seth asked the salesman if he could test-drive a year-old BMW with a *sale* price that was more than my mother had paid for her house! He loved it and decided it was the car he wanted.

"If that's what you want, that's what you should get,

honey," I said, beaming at the way he was looking at that shiny black vehicle he had fallen in love with.

"I'm glad you feel that way, sugar," he said, kissing me on the cheek. He turned to the salesman, who was a creepy-looking, brown-skinned man whose ethnicity was so ambiguous, I couldn't tell what it was. But he had shifty eyes, and he smelled like curry. "Let's get the paperwork started, my man."

The salesman grinned, and so did I, but I could feel a rock already forming in my stomach. The one thing I had never done was overextend myself. I felt that since Seth was already having a hard time paying his bills, a BMW car note was the last thing he needed. I wondered how long it would be before he asked me for more financial assistance. I didn't have to wait long to find out.

A few minutes later I found myself in a position that made me very uncomfortable. Seth was going to trade in his Mustang, but the dealer told him he'd need a cosigner, too. Even before he asked, I knew he was going to ask me to do it.

"Uh, Rachel, can you do it for me?"

Normally, I would have asked Seth to give me some time to think about it. For one thing, I didn't want him to get too comfortable asking me for financial assistance. However, I had a feeling it was too late, and I was angry with myself for letting things get to this point. Loaning him a few hundred dollars at a time was one thing, but cosigning for a BMW was a very big leap. I had heard more than enough horror stories from other people who had cosigned for somebody. Patrice was still paying off a car that she had cosigned on for her cousin Richard. He had paid the first month's payment and then had skipped town, leaving the other forty-seven monthly payments for her to pay.

Before I could respond, Seth continued with a pleading look in his eyes. "I didn't know I was going to need a cosigner, and if you won't do it for me, I'll have to scramble around and find somebody who will." We were seated in the salesman's office. The salesman sat behind his desk, tapping a pencil impatiently on his desk and glancing at his watch every few seconds. Seth snorted and returned his attention to the salesman. "What if I came up with another two thousand toward the down payment? Would I still need a cosigner?"

Another two thousand? Who could Seth borrow *another* two thousand bucks from? I answered that question myself. *Me.* I held my breath and prayed it would not come to that. And I made a mental note that I would have to learn how to say no to Seth. . . .

"Well, uh, I'm afraid so." The salesman cleared his throat and lifted a document off his desk. "This a copy of your credit report. Your credit score is in the low four hundreds, Mr. Garrett." He held the report up in the air for a couple of seconds, then abruptly dropped it, as if it had burned his fingers.

Low four hundreds? My body stiffened, and I had to cover my mouth to keep from letting out a gasp. I couldn't believe my ears! I didn't even know that credit scores went that low. Mine was over eight hundred, which meant I had an excellent credit rating.

"I'm working on getting my credit score back up," Seth mumbled.

"That's nice to hear. But in the meantime, with the rating you have now, and for a car in this price range, you'd still need a cosigner no matter how much you put down."

I turned to Seth and blinked. "Honey, do you really need a *BMW?*" I drove a five-year-old Toyota Camry and planned to drive it until it fell apart. When that happened, I would replace it with another economy car.

"No, I don't really need a BMW. I can get by a few

more years with another economy car, I guess," he said, pouting. I breathed a sigh of relief until the next sentence rolled out of his mouth. "Baby, *please* cosign for me."

The salesman cleared his throat again and adjusted his tie. I didn't have to be a mind reader to know what he was thinking. All this man cared about was making a sale. "One thing I'd like to point out is that this is a quality car. I've had my Bimmer for fifteen years and have had nary a problem with it. With all the maintenance, an economy car would set you back, and you'd end up paying for it several times over in the long run and replacing it in five or six years. A BMW makes a statement! And it's a good investment."

A good investment? I couldn't argue with that. I honestly thought that my helping Seth out so much was a good investment, too. I was not trying to buy his love; I was just trying to make things easier for him so that he could get his life together. Because when he was happy, I was happy.

"Can we go home and think about it?" Seth asked the salesman.

"You can do anything you have a mind to. But this sale price ends today, at close of business."

Seth turned to me with a puppy dog look on his face. "It would be nice to have a dependable car for fifteen years," he said slowly. Then in one breath he gave me a tentative look and said, "Go ahead and cosign for me, baby."

I looked at the floor first for a few seconds, and then I looked up at Seth. I guessed what Tina Turner sang about being "a fool in love" was true. I was a fool in love, so my common sense flew out the window. I didn't *want* to cosign, but I agreed to do it, anyway. I had already done a lot of things for Seth that I probably shouldn't have done. What was one more? "Well, if this is the car you really want . . ." I paused and squeezed his knee, and then I gave the salesman a stern look. "Sir, my credit score is over eight hundred. I'll cosign." A wall-to-wall smile suddenly appeared on the salesman's face.

After we signed all the paperwork, the salesman gave Seth the keys, and his face lit up like a lamp. So did the salesman's face. Seth looked at those keys like he wanted to kiss them. "I'll meet you back at the pad," he told me.

"I'm going to meet Paulette at Dino's for lunch," I reminded.

"Oh, yeah! That's right. Thanks for doing me this favor, baby!" After he gave me a sloppy but quick kiss, he rushed out the door and jumped into that BMW and shot off like a bat out of hell.

"What's up with you and Seth?" Paulette asked me when I arrived at Dino's. She occupied a booth near the back. There was a bottle of wine on the table, and half of it was already gone. Knowing she was a little tipsy, I was prepared to be careful about what I said to her. I had not told her, or anybody else, that I'd agreed to pay two months' child support for Seth. I certainly was not about to tell her I'd just cosigned on a BMW for him. Paulette was the kind of woman who would not even be that generous to the man she had been married to for over ten years. She'd purchased his last birthday gift, a pair of house slippers, from a flea market.

"Oh, nothing much," I said, flopping down across from her. I was glad she had requested a wineglass for me. I needed a drink immediately.

"Did your honey get his new car?"

"Uh-huh." It was difficult for me to look Paulette in the eye.

"Well, I hope he's happy now. It was time for him to

replace that piece of shit he's been dragging around town for all these years. You told me he was going to buy an Altima, right? Hmmm. That's a dependable car. And it's reasonably priced. I love mine."

"He got a BMW," I said quickly.

Paulette's jaw dropped, and her eyes got as big as shot glasses. "A BMW? Well, la-di-da. I don't know anybody who owns a luxury car like that. Well, *excuse* me! He bought a used one, I hope. Even if he did, a car like that costs a pretty penny, and those monthly notes have teeth as sharp as a razor, especially if he misses a payment."

I sighed. "He got one that's a year old. But the monthly payments are almost as much as the rent on our apartment."

Paulette turned her head to the side and gave me a strange look. "Why would he go into debt like that? He goes from a rusty old Ford Mustang to a BMW. Don't you think that's a bit extreme for a man who was recently so broke, he almost qualified for food stamps?"

"He got the car he wanted," I said with a shrug. "And if he's going to be courting clients for the business he's about to start, I guess he'll make a better impression by rolling up in a BMW rather than an Altima."

"Oh well." Paulette sniffed and took a long drink. Then she looked at me and blinked a few times. "The thing is, Seth is a Garrett, and that family likes to show and tell. The way things look is very important to them. If you and him ever have kids, you'd better hope they don't come here looking like gremlins or gnomes. If they do, Old Lady Garrett will treat them like shit, like you told me she treated Darnell while he was up here." Paulette ended her statement with a modified neck roll.

"I know how high maintenance and vain Seth's family is. You don't have to remind me. This BMW will keep him happy for a lot of years, I hope."

"A fucking B . . . M . . . W. Honey, you'd better do

more than *hope* it keeps him happy. If it doesn't, he'll be whining to you like a sick puppy. I'm surprised he didn't need a cosigner. You just better hang on to him if you want to go along for the ride."

"I intend to do just that," I said with confidence. And I did. I loved Seth, and whether he became a big success and put us on easy street or not, I was going along with him for the ride. Since his new car was technically part mine, I'd be riding in style.

Chapter 39

Seth

I COULDN'T BELIEVE HOW WELL THINGS WERE GOING! Thanks to another loan from Rachel, one from Josh, and the money I had saved, I was able to quit that backbreaking, bitch-ass job at the cannery and start my ad agency a month after I got my BMW. I beamed when I looked at the business cards for Garrett-Grundy Advertising.

My boy Howard Grundy, one of my closest friends since high school, had agreed to work with me. I let him think he was my business partner. But since this was my baby, I was going to be the main person in charge. I would call most of the shots and make all the critical decisions. However, I would treat Howard as much as I could as an "equal" partner.

Everything was going just the way I wanted it, especially my personal life. My relationship with Rachel got better and better with each new day. I had finally paid off all my credit cards. My vision to run my own ad agency, one that focused on women- and minority-owned businesses, was in place, and it was time for me to get the ball rolling.

"I'm real proud of you," Josh told me when I took him to see the office space near downtown for which I had signed a one-year lease. It was located on the ground floor of an old but well-kept building in the middle of a block near a busy strip mall. All my space consisted of was a couple of small offices and a reception area. We shared a lunchroom and restroom facilities with the other two businesses on the same floor, an insurance company and a deli.

"Thank you," I replied, bursting with pride.

"Uh, this place is all right for a start, I guess." My brother snorted and looked around with an expression on his face that was a cross between a frown and a look of concern. Howard and I had picked up used furniture here and there. Most of it was tacky and didn't match, but I was still proud of what we had. "I always thought this place was just some kind of warehouse."

"This is nowhere near as posh as the office you work in, bro, but I didn't expect to start off at the top," I said, still beaming with pride.

"Good luck, little brother. I'm sure you're going to do well." Josh gave me a big smile and a big hug. "Let me know if you need any more help."

"I will."

I was determined to make the right decisions and keep things in perspective, no matter how difficult it was.

To make sure Howard didn't feel like my flunky, I was going to do as much grunt work as he did to ensure our success. I didn't have a problem being a foot soldier.

I wasn't going to waste my time trying to compete with the big boys by going after some of their clients, such as the national chains and the huge department stores and restaurants. I wanted to focus on the "small" businesspeople. What I planned to do to drum up business was something unique. On a regular basis I would scope out targeted minority- and women-owned companies. With a notepad in my hand and a lot of patience and determination, I would spend hours at a time in their vicinity to monitor their foot traffic. After I had completed my "research," I would then approach the business owners and offer them my services for a reasonable fee, of course, to help them promote their business. I felt that no matter how successful a small establishment already was, they would be interested in even more success. Who wouldn't?

The big companies had started out small, and they would have remained small had they not done whatever they had done to enhance their image and increase their revenue. The story of how Kentucky Fried Chicken got started was my inspiration. A few years ago I had read an article about how Colonel Sanders had roamed around with a portable pressure cooker and a secret recipe for "finger lickin' good" fried chicken. Eventually, he allowed restaurants across the country to prepare chicken using packets of his secret recipe. He made a nickel for each piece he sold. Nobody could deny that KFC was the number one place to buy fried chicken in the country and possibly the world.

Howard was as enthusiastic as I was about our partnership. He was more than an asset; he was a necessity. He worked part-time—at night and on weekends—in the reprographics department of one of the largest engineering companies in Frisco. One of his job responsibilities was to maintain and order office supplies. He was alone most of the time, so he didn't have somebody micromanaging him. With nobody looking over his shoulder, he ordered enough office supplies for our business, as well. Yes, it was sneaky and dishonest, but from what Howard had told me, a lot of the supplies he ordered went to waste, anyway. Besides, what was an extra few thousand dollars a month for supplies to that world-famous, behemoth company? They were probably cheating and overcharging their clients, anyway. Not only that, Howard's supervisor and most of his coworkers asked him to order school supplies for their kids and other things for their personal use.

With all that in mind, I didn't see anything wrong with us taking advantage of the situation, too. Each day that Howard came to our office, he had a backpack and a briefcase full of copy paper, ink for the two used computer printers we had picked up at a flea market, pens and pencils, and everything else we needed, except a high-volume copy machine. Because my plan was to make several hundred photocopies of flyers and whatnot on a daily basis, a copy machine was one of the most important items we needed. Howard had that cornered, too. At his other job, there were numerous state-of-the-art copiers at his disposal. He took care of all our copying, as well. I did find a small, cheap copier, which I used for small jobs.

My office and Howard's were about the same size, but I took the one with the better view across the street from the busy flower shop between the pizza joint and the shoe repair shop. All Howard could see from his office window was the side of the building next door. Howard didn't trip, and he knew not to. I was giving him the opportunity of a lifetime. Like me, he had had some problems in the past. He had married his high school sweetheart. When she ran off with another man two years ago, he'd turned to drugs and alcohol to ease his pain. Because of that, he had lost his job as the office manager at a firm in Oakland and had ended up back at home with his mama. Therefore, I could relate. But Howard was smart, and he had always been there for me, so when I'd offered to make him my "partner," he'd jumped at the chance.

"Seth, you won't regret offering me this wonderful opportunity. I promise I won't let you down." My boy had once been almost as handsome as me, but the excessive drinking and the drugs had wreaked havoc on his looks. He was at least twenty pounds underweight. His once bright brown eyes were now cloudy and droopy, with noticeable bags and lines around them. He had to coat his lips with ChapStick several times a day to keep them from cracking. It was no wonder he had a hard time getting girlfriends now.

"I hope not, bro. This is my last shot at doing something that'll please my folks," I'd told him. He'd stood by the side of my desk that morning, a couple of weeks after we'd started working together.

"And that's another thing. I want to prove to my family that I can make something out of my life, as well. I did it once, and I can do it again."

Howard had given up drugs and drank only in moderation now, so I was glad to help keep him on the straight and narrow. I believed in "giving back," so to speak. My brother Josh and Rachel had helped me a lot, so I felt it was my duty to help someone else in need. Howard needed help more than anybody I knew.

"If we're going to succeed, we need to be more creative in a way that sets us apart from the big agencies," Howard said. "I know we've already agreed on most of the ideas that we've come up with, but let's firm up a few of those things."

"Not only that, let's always try to come up with additional ideas, bro." I turned to my secretary, who happened to be Beulah Peterson, one of Mother's oldest and dearest friends, and a grumpy old lady, if ever there was one.

"Let's get some brainstorming ideas on paper. Take thorough notes, please," I told her in a gentle voice. She was a churchwoman and demanded respect from everybody, including Howard and me. Everybody I knew referred to her as Sister Beulah at all times.

"Let me get my notepad off my desk, sugar pie," Sister Beulah said, wobbling up out of the chair facing my desk, with the tail of her floor-length, flowered dress flapping like a flag during a high wind. Since we were so informal for now, I didn't bother to ask Sister Beulah not to refer to me or Howard as "sugar pie" or any other cute names. She was a feisty old woman with a pit-bull demeanor, which she didn't hesitate to show when provoked. I didn't want to upset her and have her go off on me and quit and leave us in the lurch.

Sister Beulah was a retired schoolteacher and a widow with four grown children who lived in various states. For some reason, her kids rarely visited or even called her, so she was always looking for ways to keep herself busy. Mother had practically begged me to hire Sister Beulah. Since she was so eager to help us out, and since her late husband had left her well provided for, I'd gone for it. The biggest perk was that she was willing to work for minimum wage and no benefits. She was just that anxious to get out of the house every day. I would have been a fool not to hire her. Howard and I agreed that having a secretary like Sister Beulah was a smart move. I wanted my business to be a success, so I needed to be serious at all times, and I wanted to be taken seriously. An older, plain-looking secretary who was at least a hundred pounds overweight would be less of a distraction than a cute young thing swishing around the office, like the ones I had seen in other businesses.

I liked Sister Beulah. She had always been like a second mother to my brothers and me. She had a few quirks associated with old ladies that I didn't really care for, though. One was the way she would walk up to Howard and me and brush lint off our clothes, straighten our ties, and run her thick fingers through our hair if she didn't like the way it looked. Another thing about her that annoyed me was the way she scolded us for eating too much fast food for lunch. But when she started bringing us home-cooked meals in fancy Tupperware containers for lunch, we didn't complain. I looked at that as another way for us to save money. Besides that, we preferred Sister Beulah's smoked turkey necks and black-eyed peas and other scrumptious meals over the burgers and fries that we used to pick up.

Sister Beulah returned with her steno pad, but before she sat back down to take notes, she waddled over to me and straightened my tie and brushed off my sleeves. When she finally sat down, she crossed her thick legs and then honked into a handkerchief that she seemed to produce out of thin air. Then we both looked at Howard. He stood by the side of my wobbly-legged office desk with his hands on his hips.

"We want to keep things plain and simple," Howard began. "I'm pretty good at doing artwork, so I'll create and print up catchy flyers and pass them out to let the local businesses know there are some new kids on the block. Then I'll personally go to every major parking lot within a specified radius and place a flyer on each car. We're talking about hundreds of cars per lot, several lots just in Berkeley. I'll do the same thing in Oakland, Frisco, and other Bay Area cities."

"Hmmm. That sounds like a lot of footwork for one man. You could wear yourself out in no time, sweetie," Sister Beulah said, not even looking up from the notepad she was furiously scribbling on. "You're not a teenager anymore, and after that little problem you had with drugs and drink, your body can't be in the best of shape. . . ."

Howard looked at me and rolled his eyes. "That's true, but I've got that covered, too. My man, remember some of those young boys you used to mentor at church?"

"Uh, yeah."

"I run into some of them from time to time at the basketball court across from the building I just moved into. I've already hooked up a few who are willing to work for peanuts on an as-needed basis. I will do a lot of the running around, the boys will do some, and I hope you will be willing to do some, too. Seth, I know it's grunt work and you are the head man in this venture, but that's my vision. We all have to get our hands dirty if we want to succeed."

"Sounds good to me," I said, giving Howard a nod. "Like I already told you, I'll do as much grunt work as you."

"Yep, you sure did! I just wanted to make sure we were still on the same page. Anyway, that's how we'll advertise our service. With our hands-on approach, I'm sure a lot of folks will come check us out because they are curious. Once we hook up a few work orders, then I'll print up even more flyers, and eventually postcards and posters. Things like that can drum up a lot of business, if they are strategically placed. Not only will I continue to place flyers on car windshields, but I will also place cards and whatnot featuring ads in every club I know—and you know this former barfly knows them all. I will walk the street and pass out promotional items all day if I have to."

"And you boys know I have a lot of contacts at my church," Sister Beulah piped in. "Hundreds! And a lot of them run businesses. Sonny's Rib Joint, my niece's nail shop . . . and my godson still has that radio show that he does three nights a week. I can get us some free air advertising time."

I was so excited, I could hardly contain myself. However, I was still nervous about running my own business. I had always heard that the first six months were the hardest. That was not so true in my case. By the end of the first month, we had three new clients. One had agreed to work with us only on a month-to-month basis, but the other two had each signed a yearlong contract.

The money was good, but not good enough yet. In addition to handling my car payments, new credit card charges, my child support payments, my employees' pay, and other expenses, I had to deal with the financial hole I was still in. I still owed my brother and Rachel, but they had told me to get my business situated first and then worry about paying them back. And that was just what I was going to do. I didn't have to worry about Josh. He was blood and had always had my back—and I knew he would continue to do so. However, I wanted to make sure Rachel stayed on my team, and I could think of only one way to do that: I had to marry her.

I had hinted at matrimony a few times just to feel her out. Each time she had been receptive. I eventually made up my mind that I wanted to spend the rest of my life with this wonderful woman, but I had to be sensible about it, too. I decided to wait another year before I proposed. I needed to be sure that I had all my ducks lined up, that my money was right, and that Rachel continued to please me. . . .

Chapter 40

Rachel

I HAD A VERY DEMANDING JOB. MAINTAINING THE SCHOOL'S financial records, processing payroll checks, and looking at various other numbers all day long, five days a week, was a real challenge. But I loved my work. No matter how busy I got, I never complained. I was good at prioritizing my schedule at work and at home. So when Seth asked me to help him out as much as I could, I did.

"Sister Beulah's not too good with numbers, and the woman we just hired to help her with payroll has her hands full right now. I know you're busy, baby, and this will be a one-time favor. I'm sure I'll be able to hire an accountant in a few months. So if you could do my taxes this year, it would be a great help and a load off my mind," Seth said to me. It was the second week in January 2000.

"You know I'll find the time," I chided. "Just give me all your paperwork and your W-two documents, and I'll get on it right away." Every year, I did some of my coworkers' and friends' taxes to make a little extra money on the side. Some of them had been paying H&R Block and other tax preparers up to five hundred dollars to do what I did for a fraction of that amount. Seth was the only person I didn't charge.

The second Friday of the month, I got home around six. Seth was already in the apartment. He looked frazzled, so I was not surprised to see an empty wine bottle sitting on the coffee table, next to an empty glass. He sat cross-legged on the living room floor, with a small stack of papers in front of him. I squatted down and joined him on the floor.

"Baby, let's get this shit done as soon as we can. I want to get Uncle Sam off my back as soon as possible," he said, wiping sweat off his forehead.

"If you have all the tax forms and everything else, I can get started right after I fix dinner." I wiped some of the sweat off his forehead with the back of my hand. "Stop stressing so much," I scolded, rising from the floor.

"Cool!" Seth wasted no time handing me two sheets of lined yellow paper on which he had listed all his business expenses and deductions. There was something on every single line. I was shocked to see how much he had spent on business lunches, office supplies, and other things last year.

"Do you have all the receipts for your deductions?" I asked.

"Oh, don't worry about receipts," he answered, giving me a dismissive wave. "It's too much trouble to fiddle around with a nuisance like little scraps of paper for months on end, baby."

A sharp pain shot through my chest. I was concerned about Seth's nonchalant attitude regarding something as serious as receipts. "You might need those 'little scraps of paper' someday. What about the office supplies you're claiming? You told me that Howard took office supplies from his other job."

"Yeah, I did tell you that. So?"

"Well . . ." I paused and looked at the sheets of paper in front of me. "According to your notes, you paid several thousand dollars for office supplies. And if Howard is sneaking to use the copy machine at his other office, how can you claim several thousand dollars for photocopying, too?"

"Look, baby. This is the real world. Every business stretches the truth when they do their taxes." Seth laughed.

Stretching the truth was one thing. Telling straight-up lies on tax forms was another. I stared at more outrageous claims on his itemized list. When I saw what Seth had claimed as his total income, I almost fainted. "You . . . you claim you made only twenty thousand dollars last year?" I looked at him with my mouth hanging open. "Honey, you made a lot more than that."

"I thought you were going to help me," he said with a pout.

"I'm trying to, but I am concerned about all these things you want me to put on your tax forms. I don't want you to get in trouble."

"Look, if you want to help me, do that and let me worry about the tax people. My signature will be the only one on the forms."

"All right, Seth." I was more than a little concerned, but I refused to show it. I didn't want him to accuse me of trying to tell him how to run his business, or his life, for that matter.

After I changed clothes and started dinner, I gathered up all of Seth's paperwork. It took me two hours to complete his forms, and because of all his deductions, he did not owe the IRS and the state any money at all. They owed him! He had almost three thousand dollars coming back to him. The one thing I made him promise me was that if it ever came up, he would say that he had done his taxes on his own. I didn't want my name connected to this in any way.

"I'd rather get a whupping than have the tax man come after me," I said. I laughed, but I was dead serious.

"Baby, I wouldn't do anything to put you in jeopardy. If there is a problem, I will take full responsibility." He signed each form with a flourish and a toothy grin.

"Seth, you should make a copy of everything when you get to the office tomorrow. Make an extra copy for me to file with the notes."

"Will do!" He whistled as he folded his tax forms and slid them into his briefcase.

It turned out to be a pleasant evening, in spite of my concerns. After dinner we watched a couple of TV movies, and then we went to bed.

Ten minutes after we made love, Seth was snoring like a moose. I went to sleep and forgot all about his fraudulent tax claims.

Seth rarely called me up at work. When he did, it was usually to complain about something his son's mother had done or said. When I saw his name on the caller ID on my phone that afternoon, the day after I'd done his taxes, I braced myself.

"What's up, baby?" I greeted.

"Rachel, can you take off early today?" Seth sounded like he was out of breath, which was not a good sign. The first thing that came to my mind was that his son's mother had done something really stupid this time. Last month she had called Seth and demanded money to get her car fixed, and Seth had sent it to her right away. The next day he had run into one of her sisters and had been told that she didn't even have a car. "I need to talk to you."

"What did Caroline do this time?" I asked, rubbing my tightening chest.

"Nothing that I know of," he replied with a chuckle.

"Then what do you need to talk to me about? The way you sound, I know something's wrong."

"Nothing's wrong, honey," he chirped. "As a matter of fact, everything is very *right*."

"Did you get that account with the pizza parlor across the street from your office?"

"Yes, we did. I sent the contract over to Josh's office so he can make sure everything is worded right. But that's not what I want to talk to you about."

"Oh. Well, I'm sure I can get off early. Do you want me to meet you somewhere? Or is this something we need to discuss at home?"

"You really like that Dino's place, huh?"

"Yeah . . ."

"Then meet me there."

I didn't know what to say or think next. Seth sounded cheerful, but he could have been having a nervous break-down, for all I knew. And it would not have surprised me. He had been under so much pressure lately.

"Seth, I'm not meeting you anywhere until I know what it is you want to talk to me about," I said firmly. I still got angry when I thought about how my relationship with Jeffrey had ended. If I was going to get dumped again, I didn't want it to be in a public place, because I knew I wouldn't be responsible for my actions. "If you want to end our relationship, that's something you need to do in private. Is that it?"

He snickered. "I am not about to let a good woman like you get away from me." He paused, and I heard him suck in some air. "Since you asked, I'll tell you. Or ask you, I should say. What are you doing for the next forty or fifty years?"

"What the hell kind of question is that?"

"Woman, I'm trying to ask you to be my wife!"

"What?"

"I didn't want to do it over the telephone! But since you don't want to meet me in public, I'll ask you again when I get home this evening."

"Seth, are you serious?" A couple of our teachers were lurking around my desk, giving me some strange looks. "Let me go somewhere so I can call you back on my cell phone," I said, already rising. "I'm going to hang up and go tell my supervisor I need to leave early. What time do you want me to meet you?"

"Right now, if you don't mind, but let's change the location. Meet me at the pad. And just to let you know, I spent two days and a fortune on your engagement ring, so . . . so I hope you won't disappoint me."

"Seth, the answer is yes," I whispered. "I will marry you."

"This is a big step, baby. Don't you want to give me your answer to my face?"

"I will do that as soon as I see you," I squealed. "But I'm telling you now, I will marry you."

Chapter 41

Seth

AFTER I HAD PRESENTED RACHEL WITH A ONE-AND-A-half-carat diamond engagement ring last night, we were so anxious to make love, we didn't even make it to the bedroom. We did it on the living room couch. When I got up to go take a shower, Rachel picked up the telephone and started calling up her friends and coworkers to share her good news.

Two hours later, she was still making telephone calls, talking to each person for ten or fifteen minutes or longer. She had called up Lucy first. After she had spoken to four or five more, she'd called Lucy again. I motioned to the bedroom door and blew her a kiss, and then I went to bed.

We were not going to have a big church affair, much to Mother's dismay. I didn't want to spend all that money for one thing. My business was doing really well, but I had recently racked up a lot of new expenses. The new office furniture, several new suits and shirts, and upgrading our electronic equipment had cost me a pretty penny. Wining and dining potential clients kept me in the hole, something I had been trying to get out of for years. Even though it was a fairly shallow hole now, it was still a hole, and I didn't want to slide into it any deeper. What was even better about not spending money on a big wedding was that Rachel had made it clear to me that she wanted something small and private.

I was one happy man. With the exception of my son's mother being such a pain in the ass, I couldn't imagine my life getting any better, and I wanted everybody to know how I felt. A good job and a good woman were the two things that most of the men I knew bragged about. I had both, and I couldn't stop running my mouth about how lucky I was.

Now that Rachel had accepted my marriage proposal, I had even more to brag about. "I must be the luckiest man alive," I boasted a month after I had proposed to Rachel. I had met Billy McGinnis, one of my occasional poker buddies, for drinks at a bar near the auto body shop he managed.

"Dude, you just happened to be in the right place at the right time. You just better be glad I was not between honeys when Lucy was running around, trying to find somebody to hook Rachel up with," Billy teased. "By the way, how is Lucy-goosey doing these days? Is she available?"

"You'd have to ask Lucy that yourself," I said with a sigh. "But I'd be careful with her. Wear protection, even if you just kiss it. That puppy between her thighs must get more traffic than the Golden Gate Bridge during commute hour. I hear she goes around like a record."

A thoughtful look crossed Billy's face. "Hmmm. And on top of that, last time I saw her, she looked like she'd put on a few pounds, too."

"She's as big as a whale, bro. You can do so much better."

"True that. Now, you look here. I've asked you this before, and I'm asking you again. Does Rachel have a sister?" Billy asked, slurring his words. He had arrived at Kelsey's Bar an hour ahead of me and was on his third martini.

"And I've told you before that she has a younger sister named Janet," I replied. "I saw a picture of her, and she's as fine as Rachel."

Billy was practically drooling. "Is Janet coming out here for the wedding?"

"Huh?" I hesitated for a moment, recalling the strange look on Rachel's face last month, when I had told her how anxious I was to meet her family. Anyway, her verbal response to my mention of her family had been just as odd as the look on her face. "My family? Oh! You'll meet my family soon enough," she had told me. I'd socialized with her uncle Albert a lot over the years. He seemed like an okay dude. However, he was somewhat evasive when I tried to get more information about Rachel's family from him. That bothered me. . . .

"Answer my question, Seth."

"What did you ask me?" I was still thinking about that odd look on Rachel's face.

Billy rolled his eyes and gave me an exasperated look. "I asked if Rachel's fine sister would be coming out here for the wedding."

"I'm not sure. But her uncle Albert, who lives in the Bay Area, will be attending the wedding," I told Billy.

"If the sister, Janet, does decide to come out here, I want to be the first to know. I can't wait to meet her."

"I can't wait to meet Janet myself," I said, finishing my drink.

I planned to ask Rachel more about her family as soon

as I got home. To my surprise, she brought up the subject a few minutes after I walked in the door.

"I just got off the telephone with my mama," she chirped. She gave me a quick kiss.

"She's doing all right, I hope."

"Oh, she's fine, honey." Rachel removed my briefcase from my hand and placed it on the console by the door. Then she took my hands in hers and stood in front of me, grinning like a fool. "She's almost as excited about me getting married as I am. You wouldn't believe how skeptical she once was. After my daddy died, she pretty much gave up on serious romance." Before I could respond, she added, "But now she can't wait to meet you."

"I'm happy to hear that. When is she coming? We'll pay for her flight."

"I doubt if she'll ever come out here. Or go to any other place outside of Alabama."

"What? Why is that?"

"My mama told me that a lady she used to work with was on that Korean airplane that the Russians shot down back in eighty-three. Because of that, she doesn't fly anymore. And she's not too crazy about getting on a bus, because her parents died in a bus accident when they were coming from a church event in Birmingham. She won't even get on a train."

"Does she drive?"

"Nope."

"What about your brother? Do you think he'd be willing to drive your mother and your sister out here? We can help with the gas and other travel expenses."

Rachel sniffed and took her time responding. "Uh . . . I don't think so."

"You don't think he can get the time off from work?"

"My brother, Ernest, doesn't work. He doesn't drive, either. Neither does my sister, Janet."

Now I was real curious. Her brother being unemployed was not so unusual, but since she didn't elaborate, I didn't ask more about that. But I was curious as to why her siblings didn't drive. I didn't know any persons over the age of sixteen who didn't. Driving a car was one of the most basic functions in a person's routine.

"I can understand your mother not driving. My mother doesn't drive, either. She hasn't driven in years. But if you don't mind me asking, why do your brother and sister not drive?"

"They were never interested in learning how, that's all."

"Don't you think that's strange in this day and age?"

Rachel shrugged. "Not really. Wait a minute! Didn't you just tell me that your mother doesn't drive?"

"No, Mother does not drive."

"Why not?"

"She was in a real bad accident many years ago. It traumatized her so badly, she refuses to get behind the wheel again." I paused long enough to clear my throat. "Well, I guess when we want to visit with your family, we'll have to go to them. But if your brother and sister ever want to get on a plane and come out here, just let me know."

"They don't fly, either."

"Do they ride buses or trains?"

"They've never been on either one, but there's a first time for everything." Rachel nodded toward the kitchen. "I'm thawing out some steaks for dinner."

"That's nice, baby," I said, finally moving to the couch and flopping down with a groan. Rachel sat down next to me, and I draped my arm around her shoulder. "Getting back to the subject of your family, since they can't come to us, we'll go to them. I'm dying to meet them. Let's go to Alabama as soon as possible."

Chapter 42

Rachel

"GIRL, I CAN'T THANK YOU ENOUGH FOR INTRODUC-ing me to Seth," I told Lucy over lunch in the employee lunchroom on Monday afternoon, right after our routine fire drill. She sat staring at my engagement ring as if she wanted to snatch it off my finger and run. Seth and I had been engaged for two months. "I hope I can do something as nice for you someday."

"If you ever run into that parole officer you let get away, and if he's still on the loose, you can introduce me to him." Lucy chuckled. "Matthew Bruner. I'll never forget that man."

I would never forget Matthew Bruner, either. Just hearing his name caused my heart to skip a beat. I had not thought about him in a while, and I wondered what had become of him. Had I not met Seth, I probably would have gone to Matthew's office just to get one last look at him, without him seeing me, of course. Getting dumped was certainly nothing new to me, but having a man just not show up for an important date was. Matthew was the first man who had ever stood me up.

"I hope Matthew didn't get attacked by one of his disgruntled parolees or wasn't in a serious accident and hasn't been lying in a hospital, in a coma, all this time. Maybe I should call his office to make sure he's all right," I said.

"You read the newspaper every day. If some thug had kicked Matthew's ass, or if he'd been in an accident and was in a coma, you would know it."

"I don't care what you say. Matthew was a nice dude, and I really liked him. I don't see anything wrong with me calling him just to say hello and . . . to let him know I'm getting married."

"And let him know how desperate you are? What's wrong with you, girl? What the hell would you getting married mean to him? If anything, he'll be even less interested in you, if that's possible. The man doesn't want anything else to do with you, and you need to accept that. There is nothing more pathetic than a woman harassing a man once he's dumped her. I know that from experience," Lucy said. A sad look suddenly appeared on her face. "After my husband took off, I tried my best to get him to talk to me and tell me what I had done wrong. When he finally told me, I was more hurt by that than him just leaving me and filing for divorce."

"Why did he leave you?"

"He fell in love with someone else. I don't think you'll have to worry about that with Seth."

"I sure hope I don't. After losing Matthew so mysteriously, I'd probably never get over it if Seth changed his mind about me, too."

After lunch I returned to my workstation and dialed Mama's telephone number. My heart skipped a beat when my sister, Janet, answered. She was so unpredictable, I never knew what to expect from her.

"Is Mama home?" I asked.

"She's taking a bath," Janet told me, sounding more normal than she had in months.

"Tell Mama I called and I'll call again later this evening. I have something to tell her, and I—" Janet had hung up on me.

I called home again a few hours later, when I got to my apartment. I breathed a sigh of relief when Mama answered the telephone.

"Hi, baby. Janet told me you called," Mama told me.

"She didn't sound too good," I remarked.

"Your sister is doing as well as always." Mama snorted. "And she'll continue to do so as long as she takes her medication."

"How's Ernest been acting?"

"About the same," she told me in a tired voice.

"Mama, do you still believe that he and Janet don't need to be in a facility?"

"They ain't going into no facility as long as there's a breath in my body. I love them just as much as I love you. How would you like it if you was in one of them asylums?"

I closed my eyes and shook my head. It was time to change the subject. "Um, Mama, I know you don't like to travel, but I thought I'd ask you, anyway. How would you like a trip to California for my wedding? Seth and I will cover all your expenses."

"Child, you know I ain't getting on no airplane. It's just a matter of time before them Russians or some other foreign maniacs blow up another one."

"You can come on the train."

"Do you think I'm crazy? When was the last time I got

on a train? Just last year, some folks from my church got all broken up when the train they was on derailed in them mountains when they took that trip to Nevada."

I didn't even bother to suggest that we hire a car and have somebody whom Mama trusted drive her and my siblings to California. "Well, since you won't come to us, I guess we'll have to come to you."

"You guessed right."

"Seth is anxious to meet you and everybody else. We're going to come to Alabama real soon. Isn't that wonderful?"

"That's Jesus. And didn't you tell me you met Seth in church?"

"Yes, ma'am. His whole family is in the church. As soon as I check with him about his schedule, I'll call you back to let you know our travel plans."

"Baby, I'm so happy! I can't wait to see you again!" Mama hollered. "I can't wait to rub this in Velma Carson's face! Her kids are married already and have started families. She told me I should forget about being a grandmother, because Janet and Ernest will never marry, and you probably wouldn't, either. I'll get the last laugh on her, after all!"

"Mama, don't tell anybody but family yet. We haven't even set a date, and you know things do change. . . ."

"Change? What do you mean by that? I thought Seth was a done deal."

"Well, Seth asked me to marry him, and I said yes, but something could happen that would prevent us from getting married."

"You mean like him dropping dead?"

"Nothing that extreme, I hope." Somehow I managed to laugh. "People do change their minds when it comes to things like marriage."

"Yeah, I know. As long as you treat him good, you

shouldn't have to worry about that. Any man would be lucky to get a girl like you."

I smiled. "Thank you, Mama. I think so, too." I looked around my neatly organized living room. "Now, I don't like to rush, but I just got in from work and I need to get dinner started. Seth likes his dinner on time."

"Well, you do whatever it takes to keep Seth happy long enough to get him to the preacher, you hear?"

"I will, Mama. Tell everybody I said hello and that I'll be home soon."

Chapter 43

Seth

*M*Y LIFE HAD CHANGED IN SO MANY WAYS. I WAS DO-
ing things I had never given much thought to before.
Rachel had me reading books by authors I'd never heard
of, watching documentaries that taught me things I
needed to know, and she was still making a positive impact on my son.

When Darnell called, he usually spent more time chat-
ting with Rachel than with me. Sometimes he would call
and would talk only to her, whether I was home or not.

I was in a damn good mood most of the time now, but
despite the change in my everyday demeanor, I had
begun to dread having Sunday dinner with my parents. I
joined them only every once in a while now. I had gotten
so tired of the endless questions about my personal life,
my business, and everything else that I could barely stand
to be around my loved ones too much anymore. It seemed

like no matter what I did, they still scrutinized my movements. I was glad it was only me, Josh, his wife, Faith,
and their two-year-old daughter, Chrissie, at my parents'
latest dinner gathering. Damon had recently moved to
Sacramento and was still getting settled in, so I knew it
would be a while before I saw him again.

We had just seated ourselves at the table. Less than
one minute after Mother got comfortable, she poured herself a glass of merlot, took a few sips, and then got on my
case. "I have a thing or two to say to you, boy."

I held my breath and filled my wineglass. I gulped
down a few sips before I responded. "Such as?"

"Seth, are you sure Rachel is the woman you want to
spend the rest of your life with?" she asked, shaking her
fork in my direction.

"Of course I am. That's why I asked her to marry me,"
I said. I was stunned that Mother would ask me such a
question this late in the game.

Mother gave me a pitiful look. "Son, you've made so
many mistakes in your life, and I'd hate for you to make
another one. Especially one as serious as marrying the
wrong woman. Divorce can have a negative impact on a
person's life for years. Some folks never recover from it."

I couldn't believe my ears! Rachel and I had not even
exchanged vows yet, and Mother was talking about us
getting a divorce! "What are you getting at, Mother?" I
rarely raised my voice to my mother, and I didn't like
doing it now.

"I've been having some strange feelings about Rachel
lately, and I don't know why. Maybe it's my intuition trying to get my attention or my gut telling me everything is
not what it appears to be. The thing is, I think you should
find out more about Rachel's family and their background before you marry her."

"Lord knows you should, Seth. She might not be what you think she is." Sticking her meatball nose into my business was my sister-in-law Faith.

"Aw, come on, people! Leave the boy alone," Josh yelled, coming to my rescue as usual when I found myself in the middle of a dinner table controversy. "Rachel is a wonderful woman! I'm surprised that another man hadn't already claimed her before Seth met her."

"Rachel and I will be going to Alabama so I can meet her family this coming Thursday," I announced. Except for Josh's and the baby's, every other face at the table had a horrified expression on it. The blood had drained from Mother's face so rapidly, it looked like she had turned two shades lighter.

"*Alabama?*" she gasped, fanning her face with her napkin. "Where they lynch black men for sport? How come you haven't said anything about that before now?"

"We finalized our travel arrangements the day before yesterday," I answered.

"I won't sleep a wink until you get back home," Mother wailed. "I never thought I'd live to see the day when one of my sons would even think about going to a place as savage as Alabama."

"We're not talking about Iraq or Rwanda, Mother," Josh said, rolling his eyes. "Alabama is no worse than California."

I could tell from all the shifting in seats and throat clearing that there was a lot of discomfort at the table now. I was the most uncomfortable one of all.

"How long will you and Rachel be in Alabama?" Josh asked, giving me a sympathetic look.

"Aren't they in the middle of tornado season?" Faith asked before I could respond.

"This is March. Other than a little rain, the weather

down there is just fine this time of year," I said, looking around the table some more. "We're going to be down there only a few days, just long enough for me to get somewhat acquainted with Rachel's family."

"I hope the rest of Rachel's family is not as mysterious as that uncle of hers," Josh said with a shudder. "Faith and I ran into him while we were having dinner a couple of months ago, and he seemed very nervous."

"Well, big brother, you are one of the most feared prosecutors in the state. You make me nervous, too," I joked.

"Isn't the uncle homosexual?" Father asked with a raised eyebrow. The subject of homosexuality rarely came up in my parents' house. One of the reasons was that people had once suspected that I was gay, and my family knew how much that had bothered me. Father's question surprised me.

"Yes, Rachel's uncle Albert is gay," I said firmly. "He doesn't try to hide it."

"He couldn't hide it if he tried. I knew he was gay the first time I met him!" Faith exclaimed. "He makes me nervous, but I do like Rachel. She wouldn't fit in with me and my friends, but I'd like to get to know her better."

Mother cleared her throat again and took another sip from her wineglass. I was glad to see that the color had returned to her face. "How come Rachel didn't come to dinner with you today?" she asked.

"She's been busy all day. She had an appointment to get her nails done at four, then she needed to run a few errands for one of our elderly neighbors, and she wanted to spend the evening having dinner and drinks with her girlfriends. Today is her girl Lucy's birthday, and you know how sisters can get when they hit thirty," I explained with a chuckle. The situation was still fairly tense, so I tried to lighten things up with another chuckle, but nobody else was amused.

"Tell me about it. Turning thirty was traumatic for me," Mother said with a mock groan.

"Rachel sends her regrets," I offered. "She wanted to be here."

"Tell her we all missed her, and when you two get back from Alabama, you'd better bring her to the house as soon as you can. She promised to share her Southern-style grits recipe with me!" Mother yelled. "Bless her heart. I really like that little country girl, and I can't wait to spend more time with her. It's been three years since we met her, and I still don't know her as well as I'd like to. Maybe once she gets pregnant, she'll have more time to spend with me."

"Is she . . . uh . . . expecting a little person already?" Father asked with a stiff look on his face. I would never forget how much I had disappointed him when I got Caroline pregnant.

"Not that I know of," I said. Father immediately relaxed. "But we do plan to start our family right after we get married. Rachel wants only two or three children, but I wouldn't mind having a houseful with a woman like her."

"When is the big day?" Faith asked.

"We're still working on that. I don't want to set a date until I meet her family," I said, clearing my throat. "But I'm sure I'll love them, too. . . ."

"Let's just hope they are not hiding a bunch of deep dark secrets," Father threw in. "A lot of those people in the South are caught up in voodoo and other odd behavior."

I gasped so hard, I had to cough to catch my breath. First divorce had come up, and now voodoo. "Oh, this conversation is getting way off track," I yelled, coughing some more. Josh clapped me on the back and handed me my glass of water, but I ignored it and reached for my wineglass again. I took a big gulp and looked around the table. Every eye was on me again. "Rachel tells me everything. If her family has some deep dark secrets, I'm sure she would have said something about it by now," I insisted.

"Not necessarily," Mother said gently. "Then they wouldn't be secrets."

For the second time in less than a few minutes, I raised my voice at my mother. "This conversation is over!" I snapped.

Chapter 44

Rachel

*A*FTER I LEFT LUCY, PAULETTE, AND PATRICE AT DINO'S, I drove to Uncle Albert's new apartment. He and his boyfriend had recently moved a couple of miles from me.

Uncle Albert greeted me wearing a very expensive-looking black and gold bathrobe. There was a tall glass of wine in his hand. Despite the large amounts of marijuana that he and Kingston and their friends smoked, they managed to hide the odor with strongly scented room deodorizers. It smelled like I'd just entered a rose garden. Their new apartment was in a building that stood on a hill that offered a spectacular panoramic view of Berkeley. You could even see the bay and downtown San Francisco from the large living room window.

"Where's your honey?" I asked.

"Which one?"

"Uh, the one you just moved into this cool place with." I laughed. "I see you haven't changed."

"No, and I probably won't. I don't like to eat the same thing every day, and I'm sure you don't, either," he said as he lifted a bottle of wine off the counter and filled another wineglass and offered it to me.

I shook my head. "I've had my limit for today. I just came from Dino's, where Lucy made me drink so much wine, my eyeballs are swimming. I just came by to see your new place and to give you a big hug in case I don't see you before Seth and I leave for Alabama this coming Thursday. This place is very posh. It looks like you and Kingston are going to be together for a while."

Uncle Albert set both glasses on the counter and stood in the middle of the floor, with his arms folded. "My baby and I are still going strong, but I have a few spares to keep me company when Kingston is not around. He went out of town today, which is why I'm having company later on tonight, and why I'm decked out in this new frock. His name is Stefan, and he's perfect. He's young, dumb, full of cum, has blond hair, blue eyes, and is a real feast for a greedy, slightly old queen like me. He's a sailor to boot, and you know how much I love seafood," Uncle Albert said, swooning.

I shook my head. "Do you think you'll ever be happy with just one partner?"

"You mean like you?"

"Well, yeah, I guess. I'm totally happy with just Seth. I don't need anybody else."

"You know me. I can't stand being alone for more than a few hours at a time. Kingston just left for Tokyo a few hours ago, and I'm already climbing the walls. Apparently, his papa-san has been flaunting his young mistress all over the place, and it's been upsetting Mama-san. He had the nerve to bring the mistress with him to the airport when he came to pick us up when we visited last year!

The man is a natural-born cock hound." Uncle Albert shivered and poured himself another drink.

"Listen to the kettle calling the pot black!" I exclaimed.

"Now, you behave yourself, little girl. You ain't too big for me to lay a whupping on. Kingston will be gone two whole weeks, girl. I would ball up and die in this place if I had to go that long all by myself. My pecker is itching so bad, I'm scared it might fall off if it don't get some attention."

"Oh, you are so bad," I scolded. "Anyway, like I said, I just came by to see your new place and give you a hug." I went from room to room, with Uncle Albert right next to me. When we got back to the living room, we stopped in front of the front window and stared out at the area below. There was a kidney-shaped pool, several lounge chairs, and several barbecue grills. I hoped to live in a place this opulent someday. I imagined myself kicking back with Seth and our children, and other family and friends, on our patio.

"Don't you want to take off your jacket and sit for a little while?"

"I have to get back to my place and make sure I packed everything I'll need." I noticed a concerned look on Uncle Albert's face. "Why are you looking at me like that?"

"Rachel, I care more about you than anybody else in the world, except Kingston. You were the only one in the family who never judged me or turned your back on me when I came out of the closet. And I appreciate that."

"I care about you, and all I want is for you to be happy. It wouldn't bother me if you slept with a bull."

"Honey, I love beef, too, so I've been with more than one bull, and a few snakes, if you really want to know. But let's be serious. Romance is a double-edged sword, so it cuts both ways."

"Where is this conversation going?"

"Hush up and let me finish. Now you tell me the truth. Do you really think you're going to be happy being married to Seth?"

"Unc, I know I'm going to be happy being married to Seth. I love the man, and he loves me," I declared.

"What about Ernest and Janet?"

"What about them?" This was a subject that my uncle and I rarely discussed. As far as I was concerned, everything that could be said about my siblings had already been said. But I was only fooling myself. "Are you talking about their conditions?"

"Yeah, I'm talking about their conditions. How does Seth feel about marrying into a mentally challenged family?"

"Mentally challenged *family?* There is nothing mentally challenged about me or Mama or you."

"But you know as well as I do that there are several more folks in our family that . . . uh . . . have a few problems *upstairs.*" With a frown on his face, Uncle Albert stabbed at the side of his head with his finger.

"Like I said, there is nothing mentally wrong with me."

"Then you have told Seth about Ernest and Janet?"

I shook my head.

Uncle Albert's jaw dropped, and he gave me a wild-eyed look. "Girl, do you mean to stand here and tell me to my face that you're about to marry a man who doesn't know you come from a family tree that grows poisonous fruit?"

"That's an ugly thing to say about your own relatives!" I scolded. "You make our family sound like a bunch of sideshow freaks."

"It's true, and sometimes the truth is ugly. Don't you think you should have told him by now?"

"The subject has never come up."

"Bullshit! You don't need to wait for something like

mental illness to 'come up' to let the man know what he's getting into. The man deserves to know about something as serious as this. I'm black. Some well-to-do Asians don't take too kindly to black folks at all. Kingston told his family about me right after he and I hooked up. I would have felt like a fool if I'd gone way over there to Japan to meet his family with them not knowing I was black!"

"I know I should have said something about Janet and Ernest to Seth by now, but—"

"Boo! Girl, I need to scare some sense into you! The longer you put it off, the worse it's going to look when you do tell him. He'll think you were trying to hide it from him, and that's no way to start off a marriage, sweetie. For all you know, Seth might offer you some advice that might help you deal with Ernest and Janet."

"Help me deal with Ernest and Janet?"

"Honey, your mama told me she already made you promise that you would take care of your brother and your sister if something happens to her. And she ain't going to live forever. Eventually, you'll *have* to take over her responsibilities, anyway!"

"I know I promised Mama that I would take care of them when the time comes . . . except . . ."

"Except what?"

"Except I haven't discussed that with Seth yet. But he loves me and has already said he's accepting me for better or worse. I'm sure he'll help me with Ernest and Janet, if and when it comes to that. For all we know, some smart doctor just might come up with medication that will make them as responsible and normal as the rest of us."

"And they might not. Girl, you better get real. Taking care of mentally challenged people, especially adults, ain't no picnic. Why do you think I left Alabama? Even though your mama had pretty much disowned me, I figured that sooner or later she'd come to me and ask me to help out with Janet and Ernest, regardless of how she felt about me. I didn't want to get dragged into a responsibility like that. And while we're on the subject, why do you think I don't have any kids of my own?"

"You don't have any kids, because you only sleep with men."

"Harrumph! You don't know Uncle Albert as well as you think you do, honey. For your information, I have been with a few females."

This time it was my jaw that dropped. "What?"

"Oh, I got me a little bit of pussy before I came out of the closet. Believe you me, it didn't take long for me to figure out that that fishy-smelling shit between a woman's thighs was not what I wanted. And if, for some reason, I ever sleep with a woman again, I don't have to worry about babies. I got myself fixed right after I moved to California. With my luck, I probably would have had kids that were gay *and* mentally challenged. Just thinking about the field day your mama, Hattie, and all their small-minded friends would have had makes my flesh crawl."

What my uncle said saddened me. I could not imagine life without children of my own. "Well, I hope to have at least three or four babies. And if any—or all of them—have special needs, I will love them just as much as my mama loves all her kids."

"You are one brave little woman," Uncle Albert said, giving me a thoughtful look. "And a smart one, too. You've come so far, and I'd hate to see you end up miserable and disappointed. I just think you should tell Seth about problems as serious as this."

"Problems? Ernest and Janet are not my problems."

"Not yet."

"That's not what I mean—"

"I think I know what you mean, baby girl. But the bottom line is, you can't keep information like this from the man you're going to spend the rest of your life with."

"I will tell him as soon as we get to Alabama. I'm sure it won't make any difference at all in our relationship." I turned my head so Uncle Albert couldn't see the worried look on my face.

The trip to Alabama had come and gone, and because of what it had involved, so had Seth. What bothered me so much was not just that he had severed all ties with me, but that he had met and married another woman and gone on his merry way. His betrayal had reignited the aggression that I had been able to keep at bay since my move to California. Now he was going to see the dark side of me, which I had managed to hide so well. I was determined to do anything and everything possible to disrupt his "merry way" for as long as I could.

Chapter 45

Rachel

MAMA HAD BEEN CALLING ME EVERY EVENING SINCE I'd told her about Seth calling off the wedding. She called like clockwork at 7:00 p.m. each day. I had come home from work an hour earlier today, so by the time she called, I had already drunk a few glasses of wine and was feeling slightly tipsy.

"Hello, Mama. How are you doing?" I slurred. I felt a hiccup forming in my throat. I tried to stifle it with my hand, but I was too late. It sounded like something coming from a drunken frog.

"My goodness, Rachel. You sound terrible. You all right, baby?"

"I'm fine, Mama." I slid my tongue back and forth across my chapped lips. "Don't worry about me."

"Well, I *am* worried about you. That's why I called. I don't want you sitting around boo hooing over no man or doing nothing stupid, like drinking or suicide. Why don't you move back home? We'd love to have you back with us."

"Mama, I don't want to move back to Alabama," I insisted. Silence followed for a few seconds. This seemed like the appropriate moment for me to change the subject. "How is everybody?"

"Your aunt Hattie is down with the shingles. Ernest and Janet and everybody else are about the same." More silence. "Remember what I told you Janet told me about why Seth changed his mind about marrying you?"

"What about it?"

"I know you still think she was hearing voices, but whether she was or not, that could be the reason Seth did what he did. Have you even given that notion some serious consideration?"

For the first time, I gave that notion some serious consideration. "If that's the case, why didn't he break up with me sooner? Why did he stay with me as long as he did after he found out about Ernest and Janet?"

"Maybe because you was helping him with his bills, baby. Like Janet said she heard him telling somebody on the telephone that day. Have you even given that some serious consideration, too?"

"Seth didn't need my money. His business was doing really well."

"It is now. He told me how he had struggled for a while before he started making money. Listen, honey, everything happens for a reason. Just think if you had married Seth without him knowing about our family first. Can you imagine how your marriage would have suffered? Be glad he broke up with you before you got into him too deep." Mama let out a loud breath, which was usually an indication that she was about to end her call. "God's got a better man in store for you."

I heard Mama's last comment before she hung up, but

I couldn't focus on that. All I could focus on was the fact that Seth had stayed with me for all that time after he found out about my family, and I had paid most of the bills. I could have lived with the knowledge that I'd been played for a fool for my money. But I couldn't live with the knowledge that I'd been mistreated because of something I had no control over.

I knew right then and there that I had to find out the truth, and the only person who could tell me that was Seth. But getting him to talk to me at all had been so difficult, I wasn't even going to try anymore. If and when he decided to talk to me on his own, I'd confront him point-blank about what Janet claimed she had heard him tell that person on the telephone.

In the meantime, I planned to move forward with my life.

For the next few weeks, I gave the impression to my friends, family, and coworkers that everything was all right with me. But Uncle Albert knew better. He came to my apartment one Saturday night to check up on me. I hadn't talked to him all week or responded to any of the telephone messages he'd left.

"I know you, Rachel. That smile on your face is about as phony as a three-dollar bill," he yelled. "I know you're hurting. I've been in pain before, and it's like having a poisonous snake biting you up and down. Sooner or later, that poison is going to destroy you. The only way to get rid of that snake is to cut off its head."

"Meaning what? Me begging Seth to leave his wife and take me back?"

"Girl, you ain't *that* crazy. If you did something like that, I'd be biting you up and down myself. Now, you know me and Kingston have our problems. One of the reasons he treats me better now is that he knows I can get anybody else I want. Don't let Seth think you sitting around, thinking about him. I know from experience that the minute somebody thinks that another man is interested in you, he'll change his tune. Once he realizes you don't give a damn about him leaving you, he'll be begging you to take him back."

"Unc, I haven't seen or heard from Seth since he dumped me. Even if I wanted to try to make him jealous, I wouldn't know where to find him, and I am not about to start stalking a man who has made it clear he wants nothing more to do with me."

"Well, get over Seth and find yourself another man, anyway. That's the best advice I can give to you. Now pour me a drink so I can be on my way."

When Paulette and Patrice came over later that same evening, they basically told me the same thing.

"Get over Seth and find yourself another man," Paulette told me.

"I will," I promised in a feeble voice.

And I probably would have, had I not run into Sister Beulah at the weekly flea market on Ashby Street on Sunday of the week before Thanksgiving. It was fairly warm for November, but it was threatening to rain. The sky looked like a dark gray blanket.

After Sister Beulah's greeting, one of her extended hugs, and a few obligatory remarks, she started talking fast and loud.

"I'm so glad to see you out and about," she told me, clutching the handle of a canvas bag bulging with various vegetables. "I come here every Sunday, and I've never seen you here before." She wore one of her outlandish shawls. This one was red and black with fringes. Her gray hair was so tightly curled, her head looked like a large pinecone. I prayed that I wouldn't end up like Sister Beulah—fat and alone, with only church and shopping at flea markets to look forward to. "It's good to see that after all Seth did to you, it didn't get you down the way what he done to me did. For days, I wept and wailed and hid out in my house like I had leprosy."

I swallowed hard and gave Sister Beulah a serious look. "What did he do to you?"

"Girl, where have you been? Once he got into the swing of things and moved into that fancy new building, he didn't have any more use for me. I wasn't surprised. The way things were going, I knew it was just a matter of time before he decided I was not good for his image. He hired a man to do artwork for the flyers and cards that he pays young kids to go hand out on the street and leave on folks' car windshield. Then he got a real good deal on a high-volume Xerox machine and an even better one with an office supply store. Now Howard doesn't have to steal office supplies and do Seth's copying at his other job. Matter of fact, Howard quit his other job the day before I left the company."

"You don't work for Seth anymore at all?"

"Nope. Seth and Howard are on a gravy train, and that same train ran over me when Seth up and booted me out."

"You didn't quit? Seth fired you? But why? What did you do wrong?"

"Nothing!"

"What reason did he give for letting you go?"

"He claims it was because I sassed him. Actually, he didn't fire me, per se. He was going to, but I quit just minutes before he got that far. He claimed he was only going to suspend me, but to me that's the same as getting fired. I wouldn't give him the satisfaction of firing me, and that pissed him off, too. You ought to see that big-tittied Asian gal he hired in my place. I saw him and her having lunch the other day at a sushi place, which I'm sure she picked out. Asians eat the damnest things! Raw fish! Eyeew! I know Seth misses all the lip-smacking pig ears, oxtails, black-eyed peas, and whatnot I used to bring to the office. Anyway, I believe he let me go because he wanted to upgrade everything. And from what I've heard, that included you. "

"Yes, he did break off our engagement."

"He's a fool. I mean, it was bad enough he made us all keep certain secrets about his personal life. I can't tell you how many times I wanted to hunt you down and tell you about that other woman coming to the office to see him, staying for hours on end. I paid the company credit card bills, and every month there were three or four hotel charges, always on the same days when that woman came to see Seth. Each time, he'd leave with her and be gone for hours."

"It doesn't matter now. Seth fell in love with another woman, and I have to accept that."

"Is that what he told you?"

"Not exactly. But it's obvious. He fell out of love with me and in love with this other woman."

Sister Beulah set her bag on the ground and placed her hands on her hips. Then she reared back on her legs and looked me in the eye and said, "When my brother was in Vietnam, he got shot up real bad. He came back home with a bullet in his head and some serious mental issues. His fiancée married him, anyway."

"I'm happy for your brother." I shrugged. I couldn't think of anything else to say after hearing such an off-the-wall comment. "Excuse me, but are we still talking about Seth?"

"I am, and you should be, too. I just want to make a point. My brother's wife stayed with him even after he started having blackouts and hallucinations because of all his war injuries. He died in her arms many years later.

That's true love. And if you ask me, love knows nothing about mental illness. For Seth not to marry you because he was scared he'd have children with mental problems, that's a sin and a shame."

The wind was fairly mild. Had it been any stronger, it would have knocked me to the ground after what I'd just heard. "Excuse me? Who told you that?"

"Do you mean to stand here and tell me you didn't know?"

"I didn't know." My ears felt like somebody had come at me with a blowtorch. "Is that what he's telling people?"

"I don't know what he's telling everybody else, but that's what I know. After he returned to work after you and him went to Alabama, he told us all in the office about your brother and sister being, uh, the way they are and how he couldn't accept it. He didn't go into a lot of detail around me, but I know how to put puzzle pieces together. I knew more about his personal life than he thought I did, and I told him that to his face."

"Seth discussed my family with you, and his feelings, but he couldn't talk to me about it?" I felt like I'd been stomped on from head to toe. Every muscle in my body tightened, and for a few seconds I had a difficult time breathing. I was glad Sister Beulah didn't notice me wheezing to catch my breath. The last thing I needed was for her to tell somebody who would tell Seth how pitiful I was, so he could sit back and feel sorry for me. Pity was the last thing I wanted from Seth Garrett!

"Honey, like I said, he didn't discuss all his business with me, per se. But I heard enough out of his own mouth, and I know how to read between the lines. He even laughed about it a few times after he'd had a few glasses of wine with his lunch."

"He thought it was funny?"

"Sure enough. Oh, he thought it was a big old joke the way your brother would sit and stare off into space and all the crazy stuff your sister said. I don't think he meant it to be mean, but it was something he had to share with somebody. His mama, oh, Lord, his mama! She told Sister Brooks, and Sister Brooks told me that Vivian said if Seth had married you and gave her retarded grandchildren, she would either die or leave the country."

I was so stunned and angry, I wanted to scream. "So everybody knew about this except me."

"I won't say everybody. Just the people he works with and a few close friends of his family. Which no longer includes me. Once Seth let me go, his mama and daddy were through with me, too. That Garrett family is a bunch of two-faced, backsliding heathens, if you ask me. And Seth is the ringleader." Sister Beulah swallowed hard and blinked her hooded eyelids a few times. She looked like she wanted to cry as much as I did. She sniffed and abruptly changed the subject, glancing up at the sky, then back to me. "You better hurry up and buy something before this rain starts pouring down. Please get you a bunch of those hothouse mustard greens!"

The last thing I wanted to discuss now was a bunch of hothouse mustard greens. "I really just came out to kill time. I didn't come to buy anything in particular," I muttered. "Thanks for sharing that information with me about Seth, Sister Beulah. I had no idea."

"Be glad he's out of your life. I'm glad he forced me to quit. I didn't like working full-time again, the way I thought I would. I didn't realize how much more I enjoyed sitting at home, just watching *Judge Judy* and *The Price is Right*."

"I think I'd better get going." I glanced at my watch. I couldn't wait to get home so I could organize my thoughts.

I felt like a damn fool! Janet had not been hearing imaginary voices, after all!

"Don't forget to get you some mustard greens. It's the booth right by the exit on Grove Street."

"I will. It was nice seeing you again." I dragged my feet toward the exit. I looked back and smiled and waved at Sister Beulah.

"I'm going to pray for Seth," she hollered, shaking her head. "Otherwise that boy is going to mistreat the wrong person and end up cooking his own goose."

"He already has," I said to myself.

Chapter 46

Seth

DARLA AND I HAD BEEN MARRIED FOR ONLY TWO MONTHS when she told me what I'd been waiting to hear again for years: I was going to be a father.

It was a day that I would never forget, and for more reasons than one. First of all, when Darla came to the office that Friday evening in November to give me the good news, I was so ecstatic, I insisted on taking her out to dinner.

"I am too excited to get any more work done today!" I hollered. "We'll have a wonderful time tonight."

"But, honey, I thought you were going to have dinner with a client," she said. She had never looked more beautiful than she looked at this moment. Her cheeks had a rosy glow, and her eyes sparkled like diamonds.

"Sweetheart, my client can wait another day," I told Darla. I delicately wrapped my arms around her waist. "My baby is having my baby, and there is no way I'm going to put off celebrating a day longer."

I took her to Bridges, one of the most popular restaurants in the Bay Area. We spent two hours enjoying our seafood selections and a bottle of nonalcoholic wine. I wanted a double shot of Jack Daniel's, but since I was driving and Darla couldn't join me in a toast, I didn't have it. When we left the restaurant and got to my car, I wished that I had had that drink, after all. Somebody had slashed the hell out of all four of my tires!

For the rest of the evening, I spewed more profanities than a drunken sailor. The road service representative I called, who had taken over an hour to arrive, blushed every time I opened my mouth. "I'm sick of these low-life, cock-sucking motherfuckers!" I yelled. "Them keying my fucking car was bad enough! Now this!"

"Honey, I just called the police," Darla said in a soft voice.

"Shit! Like those bastards can do anything!" I hollered, glaring at the road service guy. "All they are going to do is write up a fucking report."

And that was all the cops did when they arrived half an hour later. When they asked if I had upset somebody recently, somebody who would take it out on me by vandalizing my vehicle, I told them no. At the same time, I wondered who could have done such a thing. Then it hit me like a sledgehammer: Rachel. She had every reason in the world to be pissed off at me to the point where she'd want to make me suffer. But I kept that thought to myself. For one thing, I had no proof. I thought about calling her and accusing her, but she was the last person I wanted to talk to these days. Besides that, if she was not the person responsible for the vandalism, my accusation would anger her more, and then she might do something even worse than what I'd experienced so far. My main concern was what she was going to do next, if anything. I just prayed that it wouldn't be something too severe. I could

live with a keyed car and even slashed tires. If she didn't
do anything to harm me or my family physically, I would
let everything run its course. I was convinced that as long
as I didn't react, or fuel the flames, so to speak, she'd
eventually get tired and leave me alone. I hoped . . .

My tires had been slashed so severely, repairing them
on the spot was not an option. My car had to be towed. I
couldn't reach any of my family or friends, so Darla and I
had to take a cab home. To my horror, when the driver
stopped in front of our house and I attempted to pay the
fare with my Visa, the transaction was declined.

"What the hell do you mean it got *declined,* sir? Do
you even know how to process a fucking credit card?" I
screamed at the Middle Eastern cabdriver.

Darla scrambled out of the cab. I had vented my frustrations all the way home from the restaurant, making her
flinch. From the look on her face, she was just as upset as
I was. My rage added to her distress.

"That credit card has a zero balance! Run it through
again, sir."

The cabdriver, looking more bored than anything, did
as I instructed. "Meester, dis card is no good. Do you haf
a nudder one?"

I was so enraged, my hands were shaking. I snatched
my credit card out of the cabdriver's hand and slid it back
into my wallet. I had changed wallets earlier that day and
had not transferred everything. My other three credit
cards were still in my other wallet, and I had only a few
bucks on me.

"I got it," Darla said, already handing the driver a wad
of bills through the front passenger window. "Keep the
change," she told him with a smile. That made him smile,
but it only angered me more. I stormed into the house,
still cussing.

I immediately called the credit card's twenty-four-hour customer service telephone number. You could have knocked me over with a Q-tip, because I was not prepared for what the dude on the other end told me. "Sir, this card was reported stolen earlier this evening."

My first thought was that the representative had entered the wrong number into the bank's system. "Bullshit! That can't be true! I paid for dinner with this card this evening, and it was fine then." I gave the man my credit card number again and made him repeat it back to me.

A few moments later he told me, "I'm sorry, sir. This credit card was reported stolen about an hour and a half ago. It's been canceled."

"The hell it was! I did not call and report this card stolen an hour and a half ago! You reactivate my card immediately, or I *will* cancel my account right here and now!"

"Sir, please accept my sincere apology. Apparently, it was an error on our part. But since the card has already been canceled and a new one will be mailed to you within three to five business days, it's not possible to reactivate the card you have in your possession now."

I slammed the telephone down as hard as I could. "That's why I hate all this automated shit!" I yelled, loosening my tie as I paced back and forth like a caged lion.

"Sit down, honey. You don't want to walk a hole in this new carpet. And don't make such a big deal out of a little credit card problem. I'm sure it was an honest mistake. These credit card companies will hire anybody these days," Darla said, leading me to the couch. "Now we have something a lot more important to deal with than your slashed tires and a rejected credit card." She eased down onto the couch, pulling me by the hand to sit next to her. "I can't wait to tell everybody about the baby. We have so much to be thankful for now."

Just hearing those words made all the difference in the world. My heart stopped racing, and a smile formed on my face. "You're right, honey. We do have a lot to be thankful for."

Chapter 47

Rachel

Seth was so cocky, complacent, and self-assured that he hadn't even bothered to change the routine he knew I was familiar with. I assumed he had no reason to think he needed to. He probably thought that I was the last thing he needed to be concerned about. He was dead wrong.

I knew more about that no-good dog than any other person he knew, including his parents. I knew where he got his hair cut, and his favorite bars and restaurants. I even knew his AOL screen name and his password. I was surprised that he had not changed it by now. I could log in to his account from any computer in the world. I planned to utilize his information as much as I could before he changed it, if he ever did.

After I had checked my own e-mail, I signed in to Seth's account. I had access to his e-mail, his on-line cal-

endar, his notes, and everything else. I could even order
merchandise from his Amazon account, and it would au-
tomatically be charged to the credit card he had on file.
But I didn't want to do that. I was more interested in other
things. I was pleased to see that he still posted his daily
schedule and appointments. He updated both on a daily
basis. That was how I had found out his new wife was
pregnant. That jackass had revealed the information in an
e-mail—in one of the boldest fonts in the system—to one
of his friends. The message turned my stomach!

> Dude, my life is finally complete. My beautiful
> bride told me this morning that she is expecting
> our first child! I hope this one is a boy, too. LOL. I
> just reserved the best table at Bridges for this
> evening, seven p.m. sharp. Mother and the rest of
> the family are over the moon. You were right. I
> have such a good life now!
> God *is* good. . . .

I could not believe my burning eyes. The only thing
missing from his message was a smiley face. This motherfucker had betrayed me in the worst way, and here he was,
giving God credit for his "good life."

I was glad that he still had some allegiance to God, because he was going to need Him more than ever by the
time I got through with him!

Seth used to take me to Bridges at least once a month
when we were together. It was one of his favorite restaurants. Because a valet had stolen some CDs out of his car
a couple of years ago, he parked his own car now, instead
of using the valet service, no matter where he went. I had
no trouble locating his car on the street two blocks from
the restaurant a few minutes before 7:00 p.m. As I drove
slowly along, I saw him and Darla strolling toward the

restaurant entrance. I drove around a few minutes more before I parked my car a block from his. Then I casually walked over to where he had parked. I was dressed in dark clothing, and I wore dark glasses and a scarf. My own mother would not have recognized me. It took me just a few minutes to slash all four of the tires with the razor-sharp Ginsu knife I had brought with me.

When I got back to my apartment, I called up the credit card company and reported his card as being stolen. Like I said, Seth was too complacent for his own good, which was a mistake on his part. Since I had paid most of the credit card bills, his and mine, I had copies of his old credit card statements, his pin numbers, his security questions, his Social Security number, and his tax records. I had big plans. I was going to make his life a living hell. I would do it in such a devious, random, and unpredictable way that he would not even suspect me, at least not for a while. Until I was ready for him to know that I was his worst nightmare, I planned to be as subtle as possible. In the meantime, if he mentioned what was happening to him to one of our mutual friends, they wouldn't even suspect me. With that in mind, I decided to wait a reasonably long time before my next attack. I wanted to give Seth just enough time to get comfortable again. His punishment was going to be slow, carefully planned, lengthy, and severe.

A week after I had slashed Seth's tires and canceled his credit card, Lucy called me up. She invited me to go on a double date with the bookstore manager whom she had been dating for a few weeks and some dude he had served military time with in Iraq. "I've told Carl all about you, and he's anxious to meet you. You'll like him," Lucy assured me. "He's just your type."

"And what is my type?" I asked, only slightly interested in dating anybody at this time.

"I know you like your men big and strong. Well, Carl is into bodybuilding. And, like you, he's into watching old movies, relaxing with a glass of wine, and he loves him some Southern-style cooking. Just like S—" Lucy stopped, but I finished her sentence for her.

"Just like Seth," I hissed, spitting out his name like vomit.

"Well, Carl's got a few things in common with . . . your ex. But don't let that stop you."

"If you think I want to get involved with another man like that jackass, you are wrong."

"I think you need to get out more and stop sitting around that apartment, thinking about what Seth did to you."

"What makes you think I'm still sitting around, thinking about Seth? I had a life before I met him, and I still have a life."

"I don't want you to be lonely."

"I'm alone, not lonely." I chuckled. "Since you already told your honey's friend about me, I'll go this time. But don't you make this a habit. Your matchmaking history is not too good."

I went out with Carl Thurman that night, and I saw him a couple of times later in the month. I was not interested in getting back into bed with another man too soon. And when I was ready to sleep with another man, I knew I could always get in touch with Skirt, my old standby. I was not interested in starting up another serious relationship, anyway. Once I made that clear to Carl, he never called me again, and that was fine with me.

In addition to Skirt, I had another option. I went to a housewarming party with my coworker Lonnie Ford. He had been recently hired to replace our boys' phys ed teacher. He was shorter than all the other men I'd dated, but he was in better shape than them all, even Carl the bodybuilder. Lonnie was so health conscious, he inspired me to eat better and get more exercise in no time. We had a great relationship for the next two months and some fairly decent sex.

It would have continued had he not become a pest who thought he could control me. Since we worked at the same place, that made matters worse. Lonnie's office was on the other side of the building, but he came to my area to collect his interoffice mail a couple of times every day. Each time he would poke his head into my office. If somebody was with me, he would wait until they had left so I could give him some attention. One day he strolled into my office while I was on the telephone. He sat and waited ten minutes until I'd hung up, and then he demanded to know who I had been talking to.

"I don't think that's any of your business," I told him with an incredulous look on my face. "And I think it's very rude of you to walk up in here and see me on the phone and not leave."

"I just need to know what my woman is up to," he whined. "I am not going to stand for you keeping any secrets from me and playing me for a fool."

I stood up and stared at Lonnie in slack-jawed amazement. I could feel my anger rising. I didn't want to cuss him out or display my violent nature and lose my job, so I managed to contain myself. "Well, you won't have to, Lonnie."

"Are you trying to tell me something?"

"I'm not trying. I *am* telling you something. I don't want to see you again on a personal level. I advise you to leave my office lickety-split. I have a lot of work to do."

"Oh, you're going to kick me to the curb just like that, huh?"

"You can call it whatever you want, but from now on,

we'll just be friends and coworkers, nothing more," I said firmly and with a smile. "Now, if you don't mind, please leave *now,* or I'll call security."

Lonnie gasped and turned around to leave so fast, he ran into the wall. From that day on, other than exchanging a casual greeting, all he and I ever did was discuss work.

"You sure are hard-hearted these days," Lucy mentioned during lunch, when I told her about my "breakup" with Lonnie. "But at least I'm glad that you're finally over Seth." She sniffed and gave me a guarded look. "I heard his business is booming these days. He's even hired four more people. One is an *Asian* woman. Seth ought to be ashamed of himself, especially with so many black folks out of work!"

"I know his business is booming," I said flatly.

"Oh? How do you know that? Have you been in touch with him lately?"

"No. I ran into Sister Beulah at the flea market on Ashby one day, and she told me," I said, with my jaw twitching. "I haven't spoken to him since the last time I told you about."

"Well, I'm glad to hear that. I hope you don't speak to him anytime soon, or ever again, if you don't mind me saying. It'll just upset you, and you're doing so much better now."

I had "seen" Seth almost every day since the night I slashed his tires. After work and on weekends, I followed him like a shadow. I did it from a distance, and when I had some free time, of course. I wanted my anger to be nice and potent before I made my next move. I planned to wait several months before I went to the next item on my agenda.

Chapter 48

Seth

*T*HE MONTHS SEEMED TO BE FLYING BY. IT WAS JULY, and the weather was so beautiful, I wanted to get naked and run up and down the street like I used to do when I was a child.

I was in such a good mood this particular day, I couldn't wait for it to end so I could pick up a dozen roses for Darla and take her to dinner. Eating out was something she enjoyed tremendously. I didn't find out until after we were married that she didn't like to cook that much. . . .

But no matter how happy I was, there was one thing I couldn't do anymore: waste time thinking about Rachel. It had been so long since I'd seen her, I rarely thought about her anymore, anyway. Besides, I had so many other things on my plate that occupied most of my time. Having lunch with a current or potential client was one of my favorite pastimes. For one thing, he or she usually paid the tab.

Today I had insisted on footing the bill myself.

My lunch companion, a jovial old geezer named Warren McGinnis, and I occupied a table in a corner by the bar in Betty's Creole Cuisine restaurant near city hall. I wanted Warren, the owner of McGinnis's Authentic Soul Food Restaurants, to know how generous and eager I was to work with him, so I had encouraged him to order whatever he wanted, despite this restaurant's extremely high prices. Two of Warren's three sons had been in some of my classes before I dropped out of Berkeley High, and his mother and my father's father were now in the same nursing home. Warren was a light-skinned, ordinary-looking man in his fifties who was about the size of a jockey. I was tempted to ask him how a man who provided some of the most fattening soul food in town managed to stay so thin, but I didn't want to be rude. He had just opened his third Bay Area restaurant. This one was in Oakland, near Mills College.

We had finished our lunch and were working on our third shot of scotch each.

"Seth, I hate to admit it, but whoever they have in the kitchen here, cooking that gumbo we just had, he or she could sure give my chef a run for his money," Warren told me with a chuckle as he picked his teeth with a red toothpick.

"I feel you on that one. They've even got my beautiful mother beat, and her folks come from Louisiana." I covered my mouth with my hand to stifle a belch.

"Speaking of beautiful women, I hear your beautiful bride is going to give birth soon."

"Darla's due any day now," I replied with a proud grin. "This one's a girl," I added, rolling my eyes. "But as long as she's healthy, that's fine with me. We plan to have at least two more, and I'm sure I'll get lucky one of those times and get that boy!"

"One thing about us men is, no matter what our age, race, or economic status is, we all want to duplicate ourselves with a son. I feel so blessed to have three boys, one by my ex and two by my current wife."

"I have one son already," I said with a touch of sadness in my voice. "He lives with his mother in L.A., and I don't get to see him much."

"That's a damn shame. How old is he?"

I cleared my throat first. "Uh, believe it or not, I was fifteen when he was born. He'll be seventeen on his birthday this year."

"My God," Warren gasped. "You and my son Mike are the same age, and he just had his first child!"

"I didn't want to be a father at such a young age, but, you know, things happen. I love my son, and I don't regret having him."

"I know it's none of my business, but are you taking care of him? We black men have such a bad rep when it comes to taking care of our kids."

"That boy does not want for a thing. I've been there for him from day one," I said proudly.

"Then I take it you and his mother get along all right? My ex went out of her way to turn my son against me, and she almost succeeded. When he finally realized she was lying about what a dog I was, he and I developed a wonderful relationship. He works for me now, and he's one of my best workers. I believe in giving back to the community. Most of my staff is black or Hispanic, and when I hire family members, I am only interested in the ones who are *not* looking for a handout or a free ride. I'm a considerate and caring man, but I'm not a damn fool."

"Tell me about it. I—" I stopped talking because our waiter suddenly approached our table.

"Gentlemen, please excuse me. We have a problem," the waiter growled, looking directly at me with a menacing scowl on his face. I had no idea why he was looking at me with so much contempt. I blinked at the Visa in his hand, which I assumed was the one I had given to him a few minutes ago.

"Oh? And what problem might that be?" I asked.

"Your credit card is invalid, sir," the waiter told me with a smirk on his face.

I blinked and shook my head. "There must be some mistake. That credit card is good. Put it through again, please."

"I've already tried twice, sir. Do you have another card?"

I didn't want to make a scene, so I promptly reached into my breast pocket and pulled out my wallet. "Good old American Express," I said with a grin. I took out my gold American Express and handed it to the waiter. He snatched it and swished away immediately.

"As you were saying—" Warren gasped and suddenly stopped speaking. "Have mercy on me!" he exclaimed with a hungry look on his face. "Now, that's a fine specimen of a woman, if I don't say so myself."

I whirled around to see the fine specimen of a woman he was referring to. My heart almost burst out of my chest. Sitting just a few feet from me, at a table for two, was Rachel!

"If I was thirty years younger, I'd ask that sister for her telephone number! With juicy lips like hers, I'm sure she can give a mean blow job." Warren made a slurping noise with his mouth and shook his head. "Oomph, oomph, oomph!"

"I . . . I see what you mean. Uh, she is easy on the eye," I blubbered, clearing my throat as I turned back around. "But I would never cheat on my wife."

"I hope you mean that. I know from experience that

it's not worth it. And I'm paying the hefty alimony payments to my ex to prove it."

I took a drink from my shot glass and mopped sweat off my brow with my napkin. I couldn't stop sweating. I had not seen or heard from Rachel since last year. I had instructed my family and friends not to mention her name to me. Since I had convinced them all that she was a phony who had strung me along for all those years, they had agreed that I should put her out of my mind completely. Rachel was one woman who was very hard to forget. Memories of some of my more pleasant experiences with her were on my mind when the waiter returned. This time he looked twice as angry.

"Sir, this card isn't any good, either!"

I was stunned, and for more reasons than one. One reason was I didn't have any other credit cards with me or enough cash to cover the three-digit lunch tab! The other reason was, I didn't want to look like an irresponsible jackass in front of a potential client.

"That can't be!" I yelled at the waiter. "My card has a zero balance!"

"Then you have a problem that you need to resolve with your bank." The waiter sniffed. "Now, how do you wish to pay this check?"

I could not believe this waiter's nasty attitude. I couldn't wait to get back to my office so I could compose a strongly worded letter of complaint and send it to the restaurant's owner. "I come here all the time. Just put it on my tab, and I will settle with you later today," I said with confidence. I would send my secretary to the restaurant to pay my tab as soon as I made it to an ATM and back to my office. One thing was for sure, I was not going to include a tip!

"That's not acceptable, sir." By now this mean waiter had attracted the attention of every other patron in the restaurant, including Rachel. I could see her out of the corner of my eye, sitting there, sipping on a margarita, with a smug look on her face.

"I got it," Warren said, already pulling out his wallet. He handed his platinum MasterCard to the waiter. "I *know* my card is good. . . ."

"Uh, I don't know what's going on with these credit card companies. But this is not the first time this has happened to me. It happened with another card from a different bank," I said, wiping more sweat off my brow. That was one thing I should not have said. Warren's eyes got big, and he leaned back in his seat.

"Oh, you've experienced this before?" he said. "I'm surprised to hear that coming from you, Seth. I thought your company was doing so well. . . ."

"We are! What I meant was, I've had problems with banks screwing up my accounts."

"Tell me about it. My brother-in-law has the same problem with his bank."

"As soon as I get back to my office, I'll send my secretary to your office with the funds to cover the check." I blinked rapidly a few times and wiped sweat off my face with my napkin. I should have stopped while I was ahead, but I didn't. I chuckled. "This is so embarrassing!"

Warren gave me a stone-faced look, but he didn't seem the least bit amused. "Don't worry about it. It's on me." Warren finished his drink and began to tap his fingers on top of the table. "I have a feeling you have enough to worry about. Well, we've all had our crosses to bear."

Now, what the hell he meant by that, I didn't know. But it didn't sound good for me.

"I am sure I will enjoy working with you. There's nothing I like more than helping another brother succeed.

I can assure you that with our unique method of promoting business, you will see a huge increase in your sales."

Warren cleared his throat and shifted in his seat. I could see that he had become uncomfortable, because he was sweating now, too. Not only that, he wouldn't look directly at me when he spoke. "Uh, let me get back to you on that," he said, looking at the floor.

As far as I was concerned, those words were the kiss of death. Warren had all but said, "I'm not going to trust a deadbeat who doesn't keep up his credit card payments to handle my business."

I was not about to give up so easily. "How about another drink later this evening? Or even dinner? At my house, if you don't mind. I'm sure my wife would love to meet you. We still have to discuss the terms of the contract I proposed."

Warren gave me a long hard look before he responded. "I already have plans for this evening, and I have your contact information," was all he said. The waiter returned, and Warren promptly signed the receipt. With a mildly disgusted look, he told me, "Good luck." And then he got up and left without saying another word.

I didn't turn around to look at Rachel again until I had finished my drink. When I did look in her direction, she was looking at me with an expression on her face that sent a chill up my spine. She looked like she wanted to eat me alive. I got up and rushed out of the restaurant and sprinted all the way to my car two blocks away. I spent the rest of the afternoon in my office, doing some paperwork and screaming on the phone at the credit card representatives, who both told me that the cards I had attempted to use to pay for lunch had been canceled.

Seeing Rachel had upset me more than the credit card fiasco. I was still upset by the time I got home, but then I had another dilemma to deal with.

Darla met me at the door with a frantic look on her face. "I think I'm in labor!" she yelled. Those five words made me forget about everything that had happened a few hours earlier.

When I saw my squalling baby girl for the first time six hours after I'd taken Darla to the hospital, I was so overjoyed, I squalled like a baby myself.

Having a new baby made it easy for me to forget about my chaotic lunch with Warren. I never heard from him again, but because of my new daughter and everything else that was going so well in my life, the next few months were heaven for me, anyway.

Chapter 49

Rachel

I COULDN'T BELIEVE THAT IT HAD BEEN A YEAR SINCE THE night I slashed the tires on Seth's car.

I was glad that fall had arrived. It was my favorite time of the year because the brown leaves on the ground and the mellow weather reminded me so much of Alabama. But every time I thought about my home state, I thought about my family and how much I missed them. Even more so on holidays.

Uncle Albert and Kingston had invited me to their place to eat Thanksgiving dinner with them this year. Even though I was not in the mood to put up with them and their party-boy friends, I had accepted the invitation. As it turned out, this was the first time I attended one of their soirees where I was the only guest. But I was not in a holiday mood.

"You didn't eat much, and I spent all morning standing over that hot stove, preparing this feast," Kingston complained. He sat at the head of their opulent table in their spacious dining room. I occupied the chair directly across from Uncle Albert. My uncle's eyes were glassy, so it was obvious that he was stoned, but he continued to puff on a thick blunt, dropping ashes into a gold-plated ashtray next to his plate.

"I wasn't that hungry," I explained, blinking at the huge turkey leg with all the trimmings on my plate. I lifted my head, which felt like it weighed twenty pounds, and looked around the room. A life-size ceramic bust of Elvis Presley sat on the mantel above the fireplace. A huge mural of some Chippendale strippers covered the whole wall facing the fireplace. "The place looks wonderful," I commented.

"Well, it should. We put enough money into it," Uncle Albert said.

"And we're not done decorating it yet," Kingston added. "Rachel, do you want a slice of that pumpkin pie Al made?"

"Thanks, but I don't want any right now. I'll take a plate home. But I wouldn't mind having another glass of that potent Japanese sake you brought back from Tokyo last month. It gives me a really nice buzz."

After dinner, Uncle Albert left the dining room and went to another part of the apartment. Kingston and I moved to the living room. He eased down onto the plush blue couch, and I plopped down on the hassock, facing him.

"Uh, I know you've been depressed for a while, and I wish I could do or say something to help," Kingston began. "I know what it feels like to be hurt by someone you love."

"You and Uncle Albert are doing all right, I hope."

"We are now." Kingston leaned forward and lowered his voice. "Um, that little incident that happened when Al broke his leg . . . I've been trying to make it up to him ever since. As soon as he came back to me, I took him on an all-day shopping spree at Bloomingdale's, Macy's, and Neiman Marcus and told him to get anything he wanted." Kingston paused and shook his head. "That little excursion set me back thirty thousand bucks. You would not believe how much his new girdle cost—and he doesn't even really need one! I'm going to treat him to a butt lift for his birthday and a week in Aruba. But I've told him, and I'm telling you, if he ever mistreats me again, I'm going to make him suffer."

Kingston paused and looked at his fingers, then back up at me. "I care about you as much as Al does, and I'll do anything for you. I know how you're feeling about what Seth did to you. I can sense your anger. If there is anything I can do to make you feel better, I will." Kingston gave me a mysterious wink.

"Are you trying to tell me something, Kingston?"

"I made Al suffer for hurting me, and you should make Seth suffer in some way for hurting you. I can even teach you some martial arts moves that would do the trick. He'd have to eat and drink everything through a straw for weeks. Either that or I can have some of the Vietnamese goons I know rough him up a bit, break a few bones and whatnot."

I shook my head. "One of my girlfriends already offered to get somebody to beat Seth up. I tried violence with another man who betrayed me. It didn't make me feel any better, and it got me arrested." I laughed for a few seconds, but then I got serious. "I'm not that girl anymore."

"Well, if you change your mind, just let me know."

I didn't feel much better when I got home that evening, and none of my close friends were around for me to talk to. Lucy was on another cruise. Paulette was in San Diego, spending the holiday with relatives, and Patrice had to work the flight to Miami. For a brief moment, I was tempted to call up Skirt. But that thought didn't stay on my mind for long. For one thing, Paulette had already told me that Skirt had just moved in with a new woman. Knowing that and the fact that he and I had not spent any time together since I'd met Seth, I didn't think Skirt would want to start back up with me, anyway.

I was still down in the dumps when December rolled around. I was not looking forward to the two weeks the school was closed down for Christmas. Everybody I knew was, though. Lucy was going to spend that time lying on a beach in Mexico with her new man. Paulette and Patrice planned to spend time with their families. I didn't want to spend Christmas with Uncle Albert and Kingston, which meant attending the party they planned to throw at a restaurant, with over a hundred of their friends in attendance. I was definitely not in the mood for that. I had also turned down dinner and party invitations from a few coworkers and people in my apartment building. But I still didn't want to spend the rest of the year alone.

Apparently, somebody else didn't want me to spend it alone, either. A week before Christmas Seth's father knocked on my door.

"Conrad, what are you doing here?" I asked as I waved him into my living room.

"I came to wish you a Merry Christmas," he replied, already unbuttoning his coat. He paused and looked around my living room. "Are we alone?"

"Yes, we are alone. You didn't answer my question. What are you doing here?" I asked with my arms folded.

He shrugged. "I thought you'd want some company. If you know what I mean . . ."

"You'd better leave," I said.

Before I could go back to the door and open it, he grabbed me and kissed me long and hard. As soon as he released me, I balled up my fist and hauled off and socked him in his right eye with so much force, my knuckles began to throb immediately.

"If you ever come near me again, I'm going to hurt you."

"You just did that, bitch! And don't think I'm going to let you get away with socking me in my eye," he yelled as he rubbed his eye.

"I'm going to call the police first and then your wife," I threatened, walking toward the telephone.

"I'm leaving!" he hollered, holding up his hand. He practically ran to the door and opened it. But before he left, he glared at me and said, "I'm glad my son didn't marry your countrified ass! You belong in a fucking cage in a zoo! You bitch!"

For the first time, I was glad that Seth had called off the wedding. Me having to deal with Seth's snooty mother and a lecherous father-in-law would have caused more problems than I cared to think about. Because of my violent confrontation with Seth's father, I felt more alone than ever now.

The next day I scrambled around until I found an affordable ticket for a flight to Alabama. I couldn't wait to see Mama and my siblings.

I didn't sleep much during the five-hour red-eye flight on Christmas Eve. As a matter of fact, I usually didn't sleep much any other night, either. Not even in the comfort of my own bed. I didn't know who it was who said, "Time heals all wounds," but it was not true in my case. It had been two years since my breakup with Seth, and I was still angry and hurt. I knew that I had already caused him a considerable amount of grief, but I had no intentions of stopping until I was satisfied that he had suffered enough. I had no idea how much suffering he had to endure for me to get to that point.

And until then, I planned to continue my reign of terror. . . .

Chapter 50

Rachel

As soon as I saw my family's house, I burst into tears. Mama stood in the doorway, with a thick black hairnet covering the stocking cap on her head. It was past noon, and she was still in one of her loose-fitting terry-cloth bathrobes. She shaded her eyes to look at me as I parked the rental car in her driveway.

"Rachel, is that you? How come you didn't let us know you were coming?" she hollered.

I got out and ran up to the porch. "I wanted to surprise you all," I managed to say, still crying as I wrapped my arms around her waist.

"Oh, you surprised me, all right!" Mama said, patting my back. "You still as thin as a rail, girl. But I'll take care of that. I just put the turkey in the oven, and I'm fixing to make some dressing."

"That's good, Mama. I haven't had a decent meal since the last time I was down here." We both laughed. I looked over Mama's shoulder and saw Ernest peeping out one window and Janet peeping out another. I let out a sigh and turned back to face Mama. "How is everybody doing?"

"About the same," she replied with a heavy sigh. "Your aunt Hattie just left yesterday on a three-week cruise to Mexico with her bingo club members."

"Oh? That's nice. I'm glad to hear she's getting out more, and I wish you would do things like that from time to time."

"I wish I could. But I can't leave Ernest and Janet for more than a few hours at a time. Lately, they get into all kinds of mischief when I ain't around. I'm scared to death that one day I'm going to come home and see they done burned down the house."

"I'm sorry to hear that, Mama. Why didn't you let me know?"

"For what? If I told you *everything* them two got into, I'd be so frazzled, you'd be trying to put me in one of them homes. Now, you stop fretting about your brother and sister and come on in this house and get comfortable."

I removed my suitcase from the backseat of the rental car and followed Mama into the house.

"You should have seen the look on Bernice Hayes's pig face when I told her about your latest raise." Mama laughed. "You make more money in a week than her daughter makes in a month working at the turpentine mill!"

"Mama, you always told me not to brag," I reminded, setting my suitcase on the living room floor. Despite the December chill, I felt overheated. I sat down on the couch, facing a huge Christmas tree with at least a dozen gift-wrapped boxes under it. "Did you receive the gifts I sent last week?"

Mama nodded. "I had them all up under the tree until last night."

"What happened last night?"

"Janet got a notion in her to open hers. She didn't like that sweater you sent or that perfume. Ernest ain't interested one way or the other in that eel-skin wallet and them socks you sent him." Mama shook her head. "My poor babies. They don't know if they coming or going."

"Mama, I told you they could come to California and stay with me for a while, if you want them to. I have an extra bedroom, and my living room couch lets out into a bed. A change of scenery might do them a world of good."

"Who is going to look after them while you at work? And what about your own life? A young woman like you needs to be trying to find a husband. Especially after what that jackass Seth done to you!"

"Don't mention matrimony to me," I groaned. "You said something about Janet being in love in your last letter. What was that about?"

"Well, the more I thought about it, the more worried I got about telling you the whole story. And I wasn't going to bring it up again unless I had to. Since you just brought it up, I'll get it off my chest and be done with it."

There was a pitiful look on Mama's face as she continued. "Two months ago, Letty Cross from next door came up to me. She's young and foolish, but she means well, or so I thought. Anyway, she offered to treat Janet to a concert in Miami for her birthday. Letty had just got her first car and was anxious to put some mileage on it, so they gassed it up and took off to Miami. Letty's cousin was one of the ushers at the concert hall that night, so he was able to get her and Janet backstage to meet the stars. They was from Atlanta and real popular with the females, I heard." At this point, Mama gave me a serious look. "I read about them musicians in the *Enquirer,* so I know they get girls doped up and pregnant in every city they do a show in."

I narrowed my eyes and looked at Mama with my mouth hanging open. "Please don't tell me some musician took advantage of Janet!"

"I wish that was all that happened. Letty, who ain't the sharpest knife in the drawer, even though she graduated from school with all As, she got caught up with one of them singers. Janet got caught up with one of the others. And, as you know, your sister ain't never even seen a man's pecker before in her life, unless you count that time she walked in the bathroom while your brother was taking a bath."

"Oh, Mama. How did you find out about what happened in Miami?"

"Janet told me out of her own mouth."

"Now, Mama, don't jump the gun. You know you can't believe everything Janet says. She hears voices and has delusions, so she thinks things are happening that are only in her head."

"Girl, you still walking around thinking that she didn't hear Seth telling somebody he couldn't marry you, because he didn't want to have no crazy kids?"

"That was different. I found out she was telling the truth, after all. A woman who used to work for Seth told me the same thing Janet told you."

"Well, then. Give Janet some credit for not being as crazy as people think she is. Anyway, a month after that concert, she told me she had had what she called 'relations' with that musician. I carried her straightaway to Dr. Porter's office and had him check her out. Thank God she wasn't pregnant and didn't have no deadly disease!"

"I'm glad to hear that. There is no telling what kind of trouble Janet could have gotten herself into in Miami. Thank God she's all right . . . this time."

"I ain't finish." Mama snorted. "Last week, when she got her SSI check in the mail, she took off."

"What?"

"I come home from choir practice, and she was gone. Ernest didn't know nothing, so I called the police. Them fools is about as useless as a worm when it comes to locating black people, even ones with mental problems. To make a long story short, Janet had took off on a Greyhound bus. She had hightailed it to Atlanta to look up that nasty buzzard that took advantage of her in Miami. She called me from a pay phone as soon as she got there. I tried to tell her that she didn't mean nothing to that fool, that them devils got a different woman for every day of the month. But she didn't want to hear none of that."

"Did you call the police back and tell them that? With Janet being the way she is, you could probably have that man arrested for statutory rape."

"No, I didn't call the police. I called Reverend Dixon, and he got a prayer chain going that same night. Praise the Lord, God was listening. Janet called me from a pay phone again three days later and told me to come get her. She had spent every night sleeping on a bench in a park. Reverend Dixon and his grandson drove over there to get her. That girl was so glad to get back home, she kissed the living room floor when she got in the house."

"Mama, who was the singer?"

"One of them rappers, just another one of Satan's offspring."

"What was his name?"

"Girl, them cornrow-wearing, gold-toothed fools all look and sound alike to me! I wouldn't know one from the other!"

"I'm going to find out his name, and then I'm going to call the police myself before I leave here," I said, looking toward the door. I was surprised to see Janet standing in the doorway, staring at me with a glazed expression on her face. "Janet, who was the man you were with?" I asked, rising.

"What man?" She shrugged. "I don't know nothing about no man."

"The man you went to see at that concert in Miami," Mama said with a heavy sigh and a serious frown on her face.

"What concert?" Janet glanced from me to Mama and shook her head. "I ain't never been to Miami or no concert before in my life." Then she turned around and went back to her room.

"Drop it, Rachel. Trying to get that man to be held accountable for what he done would be a waste of time and energy, and I ain't got too much of neither one left no more," Mama said. The grim expression on my mother's face suddenly disappeared. She began to speak in a very cheerful tone of voice. "Now, set back down and tell me what you been up to yourself."

I returned to the couch and began to tell my mother about a few of the things that I'd been up to. As I talked, her face went back and forth from frowns to looks of total disbelief. She could not understand why I paid money to go to a gym just to exercise when I could walk or run up and down any street for free. My weight loss didn't impress her. If anything, it gave her something else to worry about, like maybe I had "a cancer" or "a touch of AIDS" or something even worse. She was pleased to hear that I was dating again. So was I, for that matter. It was a distraction, and it helped me pass the time.

However, I had no desire to get involved in a serious relationship with another man as long as Seth was still causing me to lose sleep. . . .

Chapter 51

Seth

ONE OF THE MANY THINGS I LIKED ABOUT THE BAY Area was that I could go for months or years without running into somebody I didn't want to see. After our breakup I had not seen Rachel until that July day in the Creole restaurant last year. But I often ran into some of her associates. So far none of them had given me a hard time. Until today.

It was the first week in January. I'd made a New Year's resolution that I was not going to let too many trivial things upset me, the way they had the previous year. Just before Christmas, Father had been the victim of an attempted robbery on the street. During the chaos, his attacker had given him one of the most horrific black eyes I'd ever seen. I was glad that my father had not been seriously hurt and that the thug had not succeeded in taking his wallet. He had kept Mother from having another heart attack by telling her that he had hit his eye with his car door when he'd opened it too abruptly. I had tried to get my father to file a police report, but he had refused to do so.

"Son, I wouldn't be able to identify the perpetrator, and he didn't get anything from me, so I'm not going to waste my time with the cops. I refuse to let trivial matters bother me, and I don't want you to, either," he had told me.

"I won't. It will be my first New Year's resolution," I had assured him.

That resolution went out the window as soon as I saw Lucy, the nosy, fuck-faced, fat-assed bitch who had introduced me to Rachel. Had I stumbled into the lair of a demon, I could not have been more distressed.

I had just come out of the Babies"R"Us store with two huge bags of new clothes and toys for my daughter when I bumped into Miss Piggy. She was on her way in. It was a Wednesday evening. As usual, she had a smirk on her miserable face. How she managed to attract men was a mystery to me.

"Seth! I thought that was your car I just saw in the parking lot," Lucy squealed, looking me up and down like I was something good to eat. "I haven't been to church in months, so I haven't seen much of you and your family lately. Do you still go?"

"Not that often," I admitted. I had been back to church only three or four times since Lucy had introduced me to Rachel there almost five and a half years ago.

"I've been reading my Bible, though," she said, rolling her eyes.

"So have I." I couldn't remember the last time I'd picked up a Bible.

"I'm glad to see that you're looking well."

"You're looking well, too," I lied. As usual, she was dressed like she was about to attend a fashion show for plus-size women. Why in the world designers made certain outfits, like the tight purple dress she wore today, in her size was a mystery to me. She looked like a giant egg-plant, which was the only vegetable I refused to eat, be-cause when I did, it turned my stomach. Seeing Lucy turned my stomach. I would have continued walking to my car, but her yard-wide hips were blocking my path.

She looked me over some more, as if sizing me up. I was so uncomfortable, I couldn't wait to get away from her. "I heard about your new baby girl!" she hollered. "Congratulations!"

"Thank you, Lucy." I looked her up and down, focus-ing on her belly. "When is your baby due?" I knew she was not pregnant. Had she been, she would have shouted it from a rooftop for everybody in the state to hear. I also knew she was sensitive about her weight. I enjoyed the hurt look on her face.

"I'm . . . I'm not pregnant. I got carried away during the holidays and gained a few pounds. I came here to get something for my godchild, Sharise. I do hope to have children someday, though," she mumbled. "I've spent a fortune on gifts for other folks' babies, and I'd like to spend some of my hard-earned money on a child of my own soon."

"I hope you will do just that one of these days," I said with a snort.

"What's your little girl's name?"

"Gayle Marie. We named her after my mother's late mother."

"That's a nice name. I remember your grandma. I was only eight, but she was my Sunday school teacher until she had that stroke that killed her. She was good looking for a woman her age. Even with all those moles and the hair on her chin. Anyway, I'm sure your daughter is just as beautiful as your grandmama was."

"Actually, Gayle looks more like my wife. She's beau-tiful, too."

"I figured that. As long as I've known you, I never knew you to tolerate an ugly woman."

It took all my strength for me to remain civil to the ugly woman in front of me. "Now, I hate to run, but my wife is waiting for me."

That fat-assed heifer didn't even budge. From the way she shifted her weight from one foot to the other and folded her arms, I got the impression that she was just getting warmed up. I was right.

"I can't wait to tell Rachel I saw you. By the way, she's doing real well. She just bought herself a new car, she's down to a size six, and she's looking better than ever! She's dating up a storm and beating the men off with a stick."

"That's nice to hear. She was a good woman."

"Was?"

"Oh, you know what I mean. When she and I were together, she was a good woman to me." I stopped talking, because even I realized how ridiculous and hypocritical that statement sounded. No man in his right mind let a "good woman" go, unless . . . well, unless he had a damn good reason. Which I still believed I had.

Lucy's face was only a few inches away from mine. When she let out a loud breath, I not only heard it, but felt it and smelled it, too. There was no telling what she had eaten for lunch, because her breath stank like manure. I had to get away from this woman as soon as possible, before she made me sick.

"It was nice to see you again, Lucy," I said in the sweetest voice I could manage. "When you see Rachel, tell her hello for me, please. I hope she enjoyed the holidays."

"She's in Alabama, but when I talk to her again, I'll tell her what you said."

"Oh?" Now, this piece of information piqued my interest. "She's in Alabama? Hmmm. Did she move back home?" I was hoping to hear that she had. I honestly didn't know what I'd say to her if I ran into her again. And I wasn't sure I wanted to hear what she'd say to me. But Rachel being the kind of woman she was, she had probably forgotten all about me. Especially if she was "dating up a storm" and "beating the men off with a stick," like Lucy claimed.

"No, she just went back home for a holiday visit and to check up on her family. She was supposed to be back here right after Christmas, but she decided to stay a few more days. As you know, Rachel's mama is getting on in years, and her brother and sister have some issues. . . ."

"I know. I hope they are doing well, too." I no longer cared about being nice. I rudely walked around Lucy, making her stumble. I heard her gasp, but I didn't even bother to turn around. "Have a nice day," I said, over my shoulder.

"You look flustered," Darla told me when I got home.

"Uh, I ran into somebody I despise," I admitted, dropping my packages onto the couch. I gave Darla a hopeless look and said through clenched teeth, "A bitch from hell."

Darla stood stock-still. The disgusted look on her face told me what she was thinking. "Not that Rachel, I hope."

"Not quite, but just as disgusting. It was her girl Lucy."

"Isn't she the woman who badgered you to go out with Rachel in the first place?"

I nodded. "She's the one."

"Oomph! You ought to be just as mad at her as you are at that Rachel. Had it not been for Lucy, you wouldn't have gone through that trauma with her crazy-ass bitch friend!"

"Well, that crazy-ass bitch is in the past, so I don't have to worry about her anymore. She's in Alabama right now, Lucy claims."

"If she was on the moon, that still wouldn't be far enough away! I hope she stays in Alabama!"

"Unfortunately, she's only visiting. She'll be back here soon."

Darla let out an angry breath and continued with her brow furrowed. "Do you . . . do you ever think about her?"

"Only when somebody else mentions her name," I said. "Lucy also told me that Rachel's dating a lot of guys right now."

"From what you've told me, I'm not surprised. The way she dressed when I saw her at the gym, she looked like she was advertising. How that woman can keep a bunch of men interested in that loathsome pussy you told me she had is a mystery to me. I don't know how in the world you managed to stick your dick into such a sloppy cow for as long as you did!"

"It wasn't easy, honey. But since she was sometimes so nice to me, I did it out of gratitude. Rachel was a sex addict. I couldn't keep her satisfied—which is why I know she was seeing other men behind my back." The more I bashed Rachel, the better I felt. Even though almost every bad thing I said about her was not true, it still helped ease my guilt.

"And as horny as you told me she was all the time, there had to be a hell of a lot of gratitude involved on your part."

"There was. But you've more than made up for that hellish nightmare. Let's hurry up and eat dinner so we can work on getting that baby boy you promised me!"

Chapter 52

Rachel

I HAD ENJOYED EATING CHRISTMAS DINNER WITH MY mother and my siblings. Ernest had not paid much attention to me until we had gathered at the table to eat. Right after Mama had carved the huge turkey and dropped two large slices of dark meat onto his plate, he'd thanked her in the sweetest voice, and then he'd turned to me.

"Rachel, I wish you could stay with us forever," he'd told me. "You'd be happy here."

Mama had gasped. This was the first time my brother had spoken since I'd arrived. I was more surprised by what he'd just said than the fact that he was talking again.

"Thank you for saying that, Ernest." I had to blink hard to hold back my tears. "But I am happy in California."

"No, you ain't," Janet piped in. "Not after what that Seth done to you. Want me to go out there and kill him for you? I could throw some battery acid in his face or beat him over the head with something until he's dead. That's what you should have done in the first place."

"Now, Janet, you behave yourself. We are not a violent family, so ain't nobody going to touch a hair on that man's head," Mama said, turning to me as if she expected me to confirm her statement.

"You're right, Mama. I wouldn't hurt a hair on Seth's head," I said, crossing my legs at the ankles.

"Jesus spoke to me that night I heard him on the telephone. The Lord told me I should have struck him down dead right then and there," Janet said.

"I did not tell you no such thing!" Ernest yelled, waving his fist in the air. "Don't you be lying on *me!*"

Mama looked at me and shook her head. I waited until my siblings calmed down, finished their dinner, and left the room before I spoke again.

"Mama, I thought you told me things were about the same."

"I did. Why?"

"Since when did Ernest start thinking he was Jesus Christ?"

"Oh, that wasn't nothing. One time when he was a teenager he told me he was the Devil. It was that new medication they had him on back then."

"Maybe I should move back home, after all."

"Hush up! You talking nonsense. I know you don't want to move back here no more than I want you to!"

Mama's last statement surprised me and made me feel sad. "You don't want me down here to help out?"

"All I want is for you to be happy. And I know you wouldn't be happy living down here again. Now, you go on back to California and live your life."

I went home that first Sunday into the New Year, but I didn't return to work until the following Wednesday.

Before I could even sit down at my desk, Lucy popped

into my office. "Guess who I ran into while you were in Alabama?" she began, shutting the door with her foot.

"Who?" I sat down and crossed my legs.

"Your ex."

I shrugged. "Skirt? Hmmm. I hope he's behaving himself. I just might give him a call. . . ."

"Girl, don't you play stupid with me. You know I'm talking about Seth."

"Oh." I knew it was going to be a long day for me. I could tell from the tight look on Lucy's face that she was about to tell me something I didn't want to hear.

"I ran into him as I was leaving the baby store in Emeryville. That fool was loaded down with enough toys for *three* babies. By the time that little girl starts preschool, she'll be spoiled rotten to the bone! And you should have seen how smug he looked! I wanted to slap him when he started bragging about his new baby girl. Gayle Marie is her name, and according to him, she's just as beautiful as his wife."

"Was he alone?"

"Uh-huh. I told him how well you're doing. But it didn't even faze him. He looked like he couldn't have cared less. I don't know how you can stand to live in the same town with that man. The way he dogged you was a crying shame! Then for him to up and marry another woman and go on his merry way, like he didn't have a care in the world, added insult to injury. Honey, if I were you, I wouldn't worry about him. God don't like ugly, and sooner or later Seth will get what's coming to him."

"He sure will. . . ." And it was going to be sooner rather than later.

After I had gone through my in-box, my e-mail, and my phone messages, which took most of the morning, I

decided to take my lunch early and go get a manicure.
The shop I went to was a few blocks from Seth's office
building, so when I drove down that street and saw him
strutting out of the building in a navy blue suit, my heart
skipped a beat. I had to pull off to the side for a few minutes and compose myself. Just as I was about to leave, I
saw him barrel out of the parking garage and turn at the
corner. Knowing him, he was probably rushing to get to a
bar.

I followed him to Miguel's, a popular Mexican restaurant near an industrial area that he used to take me to.
After he parked and went inside, I waited in my car
across the street for about ten minutes before I went in.
Once I got inside, what I saw made me want to throw up.
There he was, sitting at the bar, with a huge Cadillac margarita and a bowl of chips and salsa on the counter in
front of him. He was showing pictures of his new baby to
the bartender when I approached and tapped him on the
shoulder.

"Hello, Seth," I said casually. He almost tumbled off
his stool when I sat down next to him. "I hope you and
your family had a nice Christmas and a happy New Year."

"Uh . . . uh, we did." He closed his wallet and shifted
in his seat.

"May I have a margarita, please? And make sure mine
is a Cadillac, too," I told the bartender.

Seth and I remained silent for a few seconds. Then I
turned to face him and looked directly into his eyes,
which looked like they were about to explode. "Seth, you
could have been man enough to tell me the real reason
you didn't want to marry me."

"Look, Rachel. Why are you even going there after all
this time? You and I are over, and it doesn't matter what
the reason was," he snarled.

The bartender placed my drink on the counter and

gave Seth a puzzled look. "Put that on my tab," Seth told him.

"That's mighty generous of you, Seth," I said with a dry laugh. "So, tell me, how is married life treating you?"

"Better than you are." He gave me a hot look and added, "I never thought you'd be the *Fatal Attraction* type."

"Ha! Don't flatter yourself, black boy. I'm not fatally attracted to you."

"Then why are you stalking me?"

I took a sip of my drink first. "I'm not stalking you," I said, purposely not stifling the loud belch that popped out of my mouth.

"Well, what do you call what you're doing to me, Rachel?"

"I call it letting you know you hurt me. I didn't deserve to be treated so badly, Seth."

"What . . . ever," he growled. "It is what it is." Then he rolled his eyes, and for some reason, that made me flinch. I was surprised that I did not jump up and start beating him over the head with the first thing I could get my hands on, like I had done with my ex back in Alabama. I was glad that I was able to remain calm. The last thing I wanted him to do was run out of the place before I had a chance to say everything I wanted to say.

"Do you think you made the right decision by dumping me for that other woman?" I asked.

"For your information, 'that other woman' is the woman I love, and I'm very happy to be with her. Thank you for asking."

"Seth, if you had told me the reason you didn't want to marry me, I would have understood. At least we could have still been friends."

"Rachel, what do you want from me?"

"You don't have anything I want now. Look, it wasn't

what you did to me. It was *how* you did it. You were not even man enough to tell me the real reason you dumped me. I had to hear it from my so-called 'crazy sister,' who overheard you telling it to somebody on the telephone when we were in Alabama. Then I heard it from Sister Beulah after you fired her. From what she told me, everybody else already knew."

"So what do you want me to do about it?"

I looked directly into Seth's eyes. For the first time since I'd met him, I realized how unattractive his eyes were. They seemed empty and false, as if they belonged on a dead man. "Then it is true? You broke up with me because you didn't want to take a chance on having children with mental problems, but you stayed with me until I helped you finish paying off some of your bills."

My accusation caught him off guard. He almost tumbled off his seat. "If you already believe that, why do you need to hear it again?"

"Because I want to hear it from your mouth." I couldn't believe how calmly I was still talking, because I wanted to scream. My long-suffering heart was breaking in two, and I was getting more pissed off by the second.

"All right. If you want to hear it from me, you will. I did not want to have children with you!"

"Because they may have been born with mental problems?"

"Because they may have been born with mental problems!" he confirmed, speaking through clenched teeth, with both of his jaws twitching. "Now that I've said what you wanted to hear, will you leave me the hell alone?"

I finished my drink and set the glass on the counter. Then I slid off the stool and looked at Seth one last time. "Thank you for being honest."

His eyes looked like they belonged on the Devil. Had he given me a more evil gaze, I probably would have melted. "Now, is there anything else you want to know, Rachel?"

I shook my head. "Not at the moment."

When I turned to leave, Seth grabbed my arm. "I don't want anything else to do with your crazy ass," he told me with his teeth clenched and his face covered in sweat. "If you see me on the street or anywhere else, please ignore me, because that's what I'll do if and when I see you again. Get on with your life and leave me the hell alone, woman!"

"I already have, Seth." Then something happened to me that I couldn't explain. My head began to spin, and I felt hot all over. "But there's one more thing I need to say to you. *One* word."

"*What?*" he roared. He slammed his fist down on the counter and glared at me like he wanted to gouge my eyes out.

I spoke the word as slowly and as clearly as I could. *"Karma."*

"What the fuck—"

I nodded. I cocked my head to the side and finished what I had to say. "Karma is a bitch named Rachel."

Seth's jaw dropped, and his eyes got big. "Is that a threat?"

"That's a *promise.*" I took a deep breath and strolled back out to my car.

Chapter 53
Seth

I FINISHED MY DRINK AND LEFT MIGUEL'S TO GO MEET with another potential client. She had invited me to have lunch with her at a restaurant she'd chosen.

I was early, so I took my time driving to Grace's Cove, a place near the marina that the college crowd had made popular over the years. They served only organic items, which I had no use for, and no alcohol. I would never have chosen to have lunch at such a place on my own. None of the items on their menu appealed to me, so I knew it would be a light lunch for me, most likely a cup of soup and a sandwich. I had planned to order a couple of tacos at the Mexican restaurant, until Rachel showed up. I was still shaken because of that encounter, but I was not about to let that damn woman ruin my day.

My business was still doing well, with a few ups and downs along the way. If I managed to land this new account, a string of clothing stores for tall and big-boned women, I'd be on easy street for a very long time.

My lunch date had already arrived at the restaurant when I got there. I joined her in a booth in the back. Less than a minute later, Rachel came through the door! That bitch! I could not believe she had followed me from Miguel's. She sat down in the booth directly across from ours, staring at me like she wanted to kill me. Because of that karma foolishness she had said to me, I had a feeling she did. But I was not going to be intimidated by a woman, especially not this one. The strange thing was, women in general had begun to get on my nerves lately. I loved Darla and wanted to spend the rest of my life with her, but I was slowly seeing another side of her. She was not the docile, well-groomed, sweet-talking woman she had been before we got married. She didn't cater to me the way she used to. She argued with me a lot, and she was hard to please.

Last night, when I'd handed her the glass of water she had asked me to get, she'd said, "I didn't want a full glass." When I'd drunk some of the water and handed the glass back to her, she'd said, "You drank too much." There was no pleasing her, and I had stopped trying so hard, because I had come to realize that with her I couldn't win. It was easier to keep the peace when I allowed her to have her way.

Darla had hired a nanny, so she usually didn't get out of bed until noon. Some days when I got home in the evening, she'd still be in her bathrobe, and her hair would still be in those loathsome sponge rollers she wore all the time. One of the main things that bothered me about Darla was that she and my son, Darnell, didn't get along. When he'd called and asked to come spend his last Christmas vacation with me, Darla had bitched and moaned about it so much, I'd had to tell him at the last minute not to come. Rachel had welcomed my son with open arms, and she had gone out of her way to make him feel loved and appreciated. Of all the lovers in my life whom my son had met, the only one he had ever asked about after the fact was Rachel. I recalled how happy he had been those two weeks he spent with us. She had introduced some serious structure into Darnell's life, the one thing that his mother and I had failed to do. I didn't want to forget the positive influences that she had brought into my son's life, but I told myself I had to. Especially now that I knew what a hothead she had turned into.

"You're looking as lovely as ever," I said to my lunch date across the table as I looked at Rachel out of the corner of my eye.

Sadie West was old enough to be my grandmother, and she looked it. Her mulish light brown face contained more lines than a steno pad. She had been married twice, had two sons and a daughter, and owned a mansion. It was hard to believe that a woman who always wore drab dark outfits, like the one she had on now, owned and operated four high-end women's clothing stores. But I assumed that once a woman got to a certain age and size, she didn't really pay that much attention to her appearance. Sadie's short natural hair was as white as snow and reminded me of a ball of cotton.

"I was really looking forward to today. It's nice to see you again, Mr. . . . May I call you Seth?"

"Please do," I gushed. My heart was beating about a mile a minute. I silently prayed that Rachel would not make a scene. I cringed when I thought of how she could do or say something offensive in front of Mrs. West. This woman was not one I wanted to upset in any way. Next to Mother, she was one of the most straitlaced and proper women I knew.

"And please call me Sadie. There's no need for us to be so formal at this point."

The waiter took our orders, and he couldn't bring me a glass of mineral water fast enough. My throat was so dry, I could barely move my tongue. I ignored Rachel, but I suspected she was still looking at me. Each time I glanced in her direction, she was. I had never seen such contempt in a woman's eyes before in my life. Even at her worst, my son's mother had never exhibited this level of animosity toward me.

"I'm so glad you were able to fit me into your schedule today, Sadie," I said after I'd gulped down half of the water in my glass.

"You were very persistent and persuasive, Seth. I like that. It's a sign of discipline and control. Now, tell me again why you think I should do business with your company. We've been doing quite well on our own," Sadie said. "We're one of the oldest minority-owned businesses in Northern California, and some of our customers have been with us from day one. We're in a good place."

"Yes, you are in a good place. My mother and most of her friends have been shopping in your stores as far back as I can remember. But I want to put you in a better place. There are a lot of younger women, even teenagers, who fit into the big and tall category."

"Tell me about it. My granddaughter Marie is only fourteen, and she wears a size twenty-eight. The sad thing about it is, the girl refuses to go on a diet, and most of her girlfriends are just as big as she is. They don't even come into my stores. They would rather spend their allowances in stores that have to order certain items for them because they carry only smaller sizes."

"Well, I'm sure your granddaughter and her friends would like to give you some business. However, almost every young girl I know would rather shop at the malls and those dollar stores."

"Our prices are comparable."

"But a lot of young females don't know that. I am sure your granddaughter does not share that information with her friends. You know how kids are. When I was a kid, I assumed only women with money could afford your prices. I never saw any information regarding sales or anything else—not that I went around looking for it." I chuckled. I cleared my throat, which still felt parched, and continued. "At the same time, everywhere I looked, there were ads, flyers, and in some cases, radio and TV commercials promoting the cheaper stores. My staff and I, we are a hands-on company when it comes to advertising."

"Exactly what does that mean?"

Just as I was about to answer, Rachel pranced over and stopped in front of me. As much as I didn't want to admit it, she was absolutely stunning. As a matter of fact, she was even more beautiful than she was when I first met her. One thing I knew for sure was that she would never walk around the house in a bathrobe, with her hair in curlers, in the middle of the day, the way Darla did.

"Hello, Seth," Rachel said, looking from me to Sadie.

"Uh . . . uh, Sadie, this is an old friend," I stuttered. "Rachel, this is Sadie West. I hope to do business with her." I didn't know what else to say or think. After all this time I hadn't seen Rachel, and now I was seeing her twice in the same day—and *she had followed me.* This was not a good sign.

"Hello, Rachel." Sadie offered a faint smile and a quick nod. "It's nice to meet one of Seth's friends."

"Oh, I don't know about me being one of Seth's friends, ma'am." Rachel snickered. "But it's nice to meet you, too." Then she turned to me and looked at me like she was about to bite my head off. "Seth, I don't mean to be rude, but I'd like to know when you're going to pay me back some of the money you owe me."

Sadie gasped. My jaw dropped.

"I beg your pardon?" I said. "What money would that be?"

"All the money you used to pay your bills with when we were together." Rachel sniffed and looked directly into Sadie's horrified eyes. "He was going to marry me until he found out there are a bunch of crazy folks in my family. But he didn't dump me until I had helped him pay off his bills and get his business off the ground." She narrowed her eyes and folded her arms. "If he's trying to do business with you, lady, I advise you to run like hell. Not only is he a lying, cheating con man, but he's also an ass-hole who cares only about himself. You wouldn't believe some of the mean and nasty things he's said about large women like you. He knows more fat jokes than anybody I know."

I stood up immediately and grabbed Rachel by her arm. "What the hell do you think you're doing?" I snapped. I had never been provoked enough to hit a woman before in my life. I didn't even realize that I had balled my fist and was about to lunge at her. I would have if I had not looked around the restaurant and seen all the people staring at us.

As cool as a winter breeze, Rachel turned to Sadie and said, "Ma'am, I hope you don't have any mentally challenged family members like I do. That's the only reason Seth and I are no longer together. He can't cope with mentally challenged people. If you don't take my advice, you are *crazy* if you do business with him now! Especially now that you know he hates great big fat people like you."

Two waiters rushed over. "Is there a problem, sir?"

one asked, glaring at me, then at Rachel. "Is this woman bothering you?"

"No, there's no problem!" I insisted, pulling Rachel toward the exit. "Sadie, excuse me for a few moments, please," I said before I escorted Rachel out the door.

When we made it to the sidewalk, I led her down the block, cussing under my breath all the way. She was laughing and walking along with me, not even trying to pry my hand from around her arm. We stopped a few doors down from the restaurant. I released her and began to stab at her chest with my finger. "Bitch, if you ever come near me again, you are going to regret the day you ever laid eyes on me!" I warned.

"I already regret ever laying eyes on you, Seth," she shot back.

"What the fuck do you want from me? Tell me how much money I owe you, and I will pay you if it'll get you off my back!"

"I'll tell you what. You keep the money you owe me. You're going to need it." She turned away and casually walked in the opposite direction. I stood in the same spot, watching until she turned the corner.

When I returned to the restaurant, Sadie West was gone. I called her office several times that afternoon, and each time her secretary told me she was not available.

Two days later, I finally received a call from Sadie. Unlike the other times we had talked by telephone, there was no warm greeting today. Her voice was very hard and abrupt. "Mr. Garrett, I've decided to decline your proposal. Thank you for your time. Good-bye and have a blessed day," was all she said. She didn't even give me a chance to explain things to her, but I had a feeling it would not have made any difference, anyway. I stared at the telephone in my hand for several minutes before I placed it back in its cradle.

Rachel had cost me the biggest account of my career, and there was nothing I could do about it.

"Rachel, you are a bitch from hell," I said, trying to imagine what I'd do to her if I could get close enough. "You better hope I never see you again."

Chapter 54

Rachel

I WISH I COULD HAVE TAKEN A PICTURE OF THE LOOK ON Seth's face back at that restaurant. I would have framed it. Once I got back to my car, I sat there and laughed for five minutes. I couldn't imagine what that Sadie woman said to him after I left. She looked like a smart woman to me, and I hoped she was smart enough to take my advice.

I got back to my office an hour later than usual, but nobody noticed. I was in such a frisky mood, I went shopping after work. Because of the weight I had lost since Seth's departure, I had purchased a lot of new clothes in a smaller size. I didn't go out as much as I used to, so some of my new outfits were still hanging in my closet, with the price tags attached. Instead of buying more new clothes this time, I decided to get a few new things for my apartment.

After purchasing some new draperies, a new Crock-Pot, and new bed linens, I decided to treat myself to a kick-back dinner at Dino's. I rarely went out to dinner alone, but I was not in the mood to deal with any of my friends. I felt like being alone today.

After my light spaghetti dinner and two glasses of wine, I went home. I had messages from Mama and Patrice. Mama, as usual, was calling to see how I was and to tell me the same mundane things about funerals and everything else going on back home.

Patrice told me in her message that she had picked up some barbecue sauce available only in Georgia that I had asked her to purchase for me during her stopover in Atlanta. She said she'd deliver it in a couple of hours.

I had no desire to talk to my mother, and since Patrice was coming over, I didn't call her back, either. I decided to call up Uncle Albert. I hadn't spoken to him in a few days, and I liked to keep him in the loop about what I was up to.

It was Kingston who answered the telephone. "Hello, Rachel. Al and I had begun to worry about you. We haven't seen you in a while, and you haven't called. Are you all right, honey?"

"I'm doing just fine, Kingston. Is my uncle home?"

"Yes, he is. But before I hand the phone to him, tell me what you've been up to lately."

"I confronted Seth today," I said proudly.

"You did what?" Kingston hollered.

"I told him what I thought about him."

"Did you do it over the phone, or did you corner him somewhere?"

"I got in his face in a restaurant while he was having lunch with a potential client."

"How did he take it?"

Right after I told Kingston everything that had transpired, he put Uncle Albert on the telephone.

"Girl, what did you say to Seth?" Uncle Albert asked

in a loud, high-pitched voice. "I hope you didn't do anything crazy enough for him to sic the cops on you."

"I didn't. I just told that punk what I thought of him, and I told that woman he was with what a crook and a con man he is. And I told her the real reason he broke off our engagement. I don't think she'll be doing business with him anytime soon."

"My goodness! Baby, I know you're still angry with him, and I don't blame you one bit. But what you did today was a bold thing for you to do. Don't you think that was a little too harsh?"

"Whose side are you on?"

"You know I'm in your corner, sweetie. I just don't want you to do something that you'll regret someday."

"The only thing I'll ever regret is getting involved with Seth Garrett. I wasn't going to rest until I'd given him a piece of my mind!"

"It sounds like you gave him several pieces of your mind today. Oh well. He did ask for it, I guess. Straight men are such idiots! You would think that a man Seth's age would know how to treat a woman by now. Maybe he'll think twice before he hurts another woman the way he hurt you. Why don't you come by the pad so Kingston can roll you a joint? I'm sure you could probably use one. His brother in Hawaii sent us some of that Maui Wowie weed."

"You know I've never done drugs, and I don't plan on starting now," I said with a heavy sigh.

"Weed is not drugs, baby girl." Uncle Albert laughed. "Well, come over and have a drink with us. I'll cook you some collard greens, some corn bread, and deep-fried pork chops. Hold on a second. Kingston is saying something." Uncle Albert mumbled something to his boyfriend, and when he came back on the line, he told me, "Kingston asked if you changed your mind about arranging for Seth to get a good ass whupping? It could be done tonight."

"That's tempting, but I'll have to take a rain check. I'm tired, so I just want to relax tonight."

"All right then. Call if you need us."

All I could think about was my next move against Seth. I had no idea what I was going to do to him next. It had to be something that would spook the hell out of him, cause him a lot of misery, and maybe even send him to jail. . . .

Patrice didn't show up until almost 10:00 p.m. I had taken my bath and had slid into my nightgown by then. I was relaxing on the couch with a glass of wine when she knocked.

"I won't come in," she told me when I opened the door. "I'm tired, and I want to go straight home and unwind." She was still in her flight attendant uniform.

"Thanks for picking up the sauce for me," I told her as she handed me a huge bottle of mustard-based barbecue sauce.

"I would have bought more than one bottle, but this was the last one they had in stock. I'll get you some more on my next stop in Atlanta." Patrice gave me a concerned look. "Anything exciting happen while I was gone?"

"A little."

"Well, if it has anything to do with Seth, I hope it's something bad."

"I ran into him and some woman today."

"Oh? What did you say to him?"

I repeated everything I had told Uncle Albert and Kingston.

"Harrumph! If that had been me, I would have done a

lot more than that. By the time I got through blessing him
out, he would never smile again, unless he was smiling at
me." Patrice laughed. "Anyway, I'm glad you got that out
of your system."

"Now you can go after him. . . ."

"What?" Patrice shook her head and gave me a stunned
look.

"Lucy told me you used to have the hots for Seth. And
I know that's why you've always resented me."

"Look, I am not going to stand here and listen to this
shit! I don't want Seth, and I don't like to hear that you
and Lucy have been talking about me behind my back."

"Forget it, Patrice. We're done," I said tiredly. "Now,
if you don't mind, I'd like to go to bed."

"I want to get home and do the same thing. Just give
me my twelve dollars, and I'll be on my way."

"What twelve dollars?" I gulped.

"For the barbecue sauce," she replied.

"No problem." I rushed into the bedroom and returned
with my wallet. I couldn't count out twelve dollars fast
enough and hand it to her. "Do I owe you for the other
bottles you brought me those other times?"

"No." Without another word, Patrice rushed back out
the door to her Volvo.

Just as I was about to put my bottle of sauce on the
kitchen shelf, I realized the seal had already been broken.
My paranoia was in full-blown mode. I wondered if
Patrice had put boogers or spit in the bottle. Nothing surprised me after what Seth had done to me. I emptied the
bottle in my kitchen sink and then threw it into the trash-
bin under the sink that contained a few other recyclable
items. It was at that moment that I decided to sever my relationship with Patrice the next time I saw or heard from
her. And because Lucy had told me that Patrice had always been jealous of me, I realized she had never been

my friend in the first place. I couldn't believe some of the things she had said to me in the past, but her asking me to pay her for some barbecue sauce that she had volunteered to pick up for me was the last straw. As far as I was concerned, she had betrayed me. Just like Seth had . . .

After I finished my wine and checked my e-mail, I printed out an article about a recent local murder that I wanted to read later. The victim's daughter was a former neighbor of mine. Just as I was about to slide it into the manila file folder with other articles I had printed, a folder in the same drawer caught my eye. It was the one that contained the copies of Seth's 1999 tax documents. The same ones that he had made me tell all those lies on . . .

It felt like a very bright light clicked on in my head, and a brilliant idea came with it. Seth had committed income tax fraud! Why hadn't I thought about getting some mileage out of that before? I asked myself. A person could even go to jail for committing such a crime. That was the main reason I always told the truth every year, when I filled out my own forms. For a smart man, Seth was as stupid and naive as hell! Obviously, he had not given much thought to his actions during the years he'd spent with me. In that folder I had enough incriminating evidence against him that I could fuck up his life as much as I wanted to.

I took my time composing a carefully worded letter to the IRS, and I left no stone unturned. I explained in great detail how Seth had written off thousands of dollars' worth of expenses that he had not incurred for office supplies, long distance phone calls, and FedEx, and had taken numerous other itemized deductions to which he hadn't been entitled. He had even claimed lavish meals that his clients had paid for. There were even a few that I had paid for! I included information about the bogus donations to various charities that he had claimed, and about his gambling wins and losses. I didn't sign the letter, and I was not even sure it would get to the right person and be taken seriously. Normally, I would never have turned somebody in for a crime they'd committed unless it was particularly heinous, such as murder or child abuse. But there were exceptions to every rule, and this was one of them. I knew it was a sneaky and mean thing to do, but that was what revenge was all about. However, I didn't want any of my friends to know, because I didn't want them to know just how obsessed I had become with torturing Seth.

I had no idea how the IRS handled cases that involved fraud. Even if they investigated Seth, I would have no way of knowing. But that didn't matter to me.

I made a copy of the letter to keep in my file, and I put the original in my purse so I could mail it on my way to work the next morning.

Chapter 55

Seth

DARLA AND I OCCUPIED THE COUCH IN OUR COZY LIVing room, but the same room would feel more like a tomb in a few moments. We were watching an old Denzel Washington movie on Channel Two. During a commercial break, I turned to her and casually dropped a major bombshell. "Baby, um, my son is coming to live with us."

They said that the Devil came in many forms. One was the form of an angry black woman. Darla immediately got so enraged, her eyes looked like two black rocks that somebody had glued to her face. "What the hell do you mean, your son is coming to live with us?" she shrieked, with hot spit shooting out of her mouth onto my face. "Negro, have you lost your fucking mind? That boy belongs in a jungle!"

I didn't know how I was able to keep my voice calm without the aid of a stiff drink, which I wished I had had before I'd said anything about Darnell. I wiped my face with the back of my hand. "Baby, the boy's mama can't control him. He's involved with gangs, he's not going to school, and he's running wild in every other way."

"And what are you supposed to do?"

"I have to at least try to turn him around. He's my son, and I love him. I've always wanted to have him with me more, anyway. I told you that from the get-go."

"What about Gayle? She's just a toddler, and having a bad influence like Darnell in her life is not what she needs."

"So what do you want me to do? Ignore my child when I might be the only hope he has?"

"All right! You do what you have to do!" Darla threw her arms up in the air, jumped up off the couch, and stormed out of the room, cussing.

I shuffled into the kitchen and called Caroline. "I want you to pack up Darnell's things. I'll drive down tomorrow to pick him up."

No matter how pleasantly I spoke to Caroline, I couldn't remember the last time she had spoken to me in a civil tone of voice. Her voice had become deep, dark, and menacing over the years. Today she sounded almost like Darth Vader. "Why can't you send him a plane ticket?"

"I'd rather drive down there. I . . . I need the time alone to clear my head."

"What about Miss Thang? If she's coming with you, you'd better leave her uppity ass in the car, because I do not want to look at her butt face."

"She's not coming with me."

"And I'm telling you here and now, the first time my son calls me and tells me she's mistreating him, I'm coming up there to bitch slap her—and you, too, if you fuck with me while I'm doing it. Shit."

"Now, you look, Caroline. If you feel that way, we can leave him with you."

"No. I can't deal with this boy another day. If you don't come get him, I'm turning him over to the state. Let his ass rot in a foster home!"

"Caroline, I'll be there tomorrow evening. Please have him ready." It took all the strength in my body for me to remain composed. "Now, good-bye, and you have a blessed evening."

It was a six-hour drive to L.A. I cried and cussed and slapped the steering wheel off and on the whole time. I couldn't believe the mess my personal life had become. My marriage was less than ideal, my business was shaky, and to bring a troubled teenager into the equation could only make matters worse. There was not a day that went by that I didn't think about how different things might have been if I had married Rachel. I was convinced that had I done so, my son would have benefited tremendously. And maybe I would have, too. . . .

I had eaten a light breakfast—toast, one egg, and a cup of coffee. When I arrived in L.A. around 2:00 p.m., my belly was growling. I decided to get something to eat, because I was going to need all my strength to deal with Caroline in person. She had recently moved into an apartment on some backstreet in Inglewood. To get there, I had to pass Roscoe's House of Chicken and Waffles, one of the most popular restaurants in the area, because so many stars patronized it. I ordered a couple of pieces of fried chicken, some greens, and a soda. But as hungry as I was, I barely touched the food on my plate.

It was just as well. When I got to Caroline's gloomy street, what I saw was so disturbing, I would have puked, had there been enough food in my stomach. The parking lot of the four-story building she lived in looked like a three-ring circus. Drug dealers were openly selling drugs, whores were prancing around, advertising their wares, and young kids were smack-dab in the middle of this mess. A naked toddler darted out in front of my car, and if I had not noticed him in time, I probably would not have lived to talk about it. Everybody was looking at me like they wanted to skin me alive. My BMW was not that conspicuous. There were two others parked in front of the building, right next to hoopties and burned-out vehicles that looked like they had been sitting in the same spot for years. I got out of my car and spoke very cordially to a couple of scary-looking young men. Even though we all spoke the same language, my accent, which was cultured and refined compared to theirs, was a dead giveaway that I did not belong in this neighborhood.

"Can you tell me what side of the building Caroline Mitchell lives on?" I asked a dreadlocked young brother who was blocking the building's front entrance.

"You her caseworker or a bill collector?" he asked.

"You a cop?" asked the hooker standing next to him. She had a huge red Afro wig and wore a blue leather skirt and thigh-high boots.

"No, I'm a friend of hers. I'm her son Darnell's father," I said, speaking as pleasantly as I possibly could.

"She on the other side." The hooker pointed. "Uh, you want some company later on?"

I smiled. "Not today, but thank you, anyway."

Caroline lived in the first apartment on the second floor. The elevator was out of order, so I took the stairs up, huffing and puffing like a man twice my age. I was surprised to find the front door open when I got to her unit. The first person I saw was a pitch-black dude with an angry look on his face. He was stretched out on the living room couch, with a greasy gray do-rag wrapped around his head.

"Is Caroline home? I'm Darnell's father, and I'm here

to pick him up," I said. I stood in the doorway with my car key still in my hand.

Instead of responding, the dude sat up and looked toward a back room. "Wooman, get your bum out here straight-away, wooman! Somebody here to see at you! And hurry it up so you can get in de kitchen and fix me a something to eat!" He had a foreign accent, and because his skin was so dark, I assumed he had come either from the dark side of one of the Caribbean islands or straight out of Africa.

Caroline came flying into the room like a bat out of hell, and she looked like one, too. The cute girl I had known in high school now resembled an old hag. Dark circles surrounded her eyes like moats. Her lips were dry and chapped, and her skin looked like sandpaper. She wore a faded blue denim dress with stains in various colors on the front and sides, flip-flops that looked big enough for Hulk Hogan, and a blond wig that was so askew, it looked like she had been flying.

She looked at me with a scowl on her face, of course, but she turned to the man on the couch and addressed him first. "You ain't paralyzed, Oyey. If you want something to eat, you better take your black ass in the kitchen and fix it yourself. If you want a woman to slave for you, you better go on back to that village in Nigeria where you came from. Shit." She turned back to me, with the scowl on her face that was even more severe. "It's about time you got your ass down here, Seth. That boy is about to drive me crazy!" she yelled, waving her arms as she strode over to me.

It was obvious that I was not going to receive an invitation to stay around long enough to do any type of so-cializing. And based upon all the empty beer cans strewn about the room, I had a feeling a whole lot of "socializ-ing" went on in this place.

"Is Darnell ready to go?"

"You damn right he ready to go! And not soon enough!" Caroline hollered. She took a few steps back in the direction she had just come from. "Darnell! Get your black ass out here, boy! And be quick about it! I ain't playing with you!"

A few moments later, Darnell slunk into the room. It was hard to believe that this brooding young man was the same son I had cuddled when he was a toddler. This boy looked like he wanted to cuss out the world. Menacing tattoos decorated his arms and neck. His baggy clothes looked as if he had slept in them.

"Son, are you ready to go?" I asked, placing my hand on his shoulder.

"Yeah, I guess," he growled, rolling his eyes. "I ain't got no choice."

"I kept telling your ass that if you didn't straighten up and fly right, I was going to send you to live with your daddy!" Caroline barked, hands on her hips. "Maybe he can beat some sense into your hard head."

I was so sick of people telling me to beat my child that my jaw started twitching. I looked at Caroline, and I did not like the smug look on her face. "Caroline, you know I don't believe in beating children. I told you that years ago. There are more effective ways to discipline a young person these days."

"It don't matter to me what you do to get this fool to behave! He ain't my problem no more!"

From the corner of my eye, I noticed a sad look cross my son's face, and it made my chest ache. With mothers like Caroline, it was no wonder inner-city black boys were in such a sad state.

After a few more minutes of small talk on my part, I excused myself and escorted Darnell to my car. And not a minute too soon. Three boys around my son's age had already surrounded my vehicle, looking at it like it was something good to eat.

It was a tense drive back to the Bay Area. We stopped only for gas and snacks, and Darnell kept his headphones on most of the time. During the last twenty miles to our destination, he decided to talk.

"You going to hook me up with a car of my own?"

"A car? Don't you think that's a little premature?"

"*Premature.* What that mean?"

"There are other things we need to focus on before we talk about you getting a car. How are your grades?"

"All right, I guess. They been passing me on to the next grade every year," he said with a shrug. Then he looked at me with a strange expression on his face. "You still with that same woman?"

"If you mean Darla, the answer is yes."

"I was hoping you'd tell me you and Rachel got back together. She was the coolest grown woman I ever met. She still in Berkeley?"

"Uh, I think so. Why?"

"Can I hook up with her some time?"

"Absolutely not! That woman has caused me a lot of misery since we broke up, and I will not allow you to communicate with her at all. Is that clear?"

"Yeah. Why? What did she do to you for you to be sounding so mad?"

"That's not important! The important thing is I don't want you to have a damn thing to do with Rachel. Now you forget about her. She's out of our lives. I'm through with her!"

It would not be long before I found out that Rachel was *not* through with me. . . .

Chapter 56

Rachel

*I*T HAD BEEN THREE MONTHS SINCE I'D SENT THAT ANONY-mous letter to the IRS. From what I had seen on Seth's calendar, his life still appeared to be peachy keen. He had lunch and dinner dates with everybody from his parents to more potential clients. One weekend he had the nerve to take his wife and her mother to Vegas. There had been no mention of the IRS, so I assumed they had not con-fronted him yet. Since I didn't even know if they would, I had to go on to plan B. I wanted to torment him in a more personal way. That meant I had to get into his house and either trash it or take something that meant a lot to him.

I had no trouble getting the address of the fancy new house Seth had purchased. He was listed in the telephone book, so that information was public. Had it not been, I could have easily gotten it from public records at the court-house.

I checked his e-mail on a daily basis. I knew his, Darla's, and his son's schedules for the next two weeks, so my checking out his place was not going to be a problem. But since I had never broken into somebody's house, I needed some "professional" assistance. I knew not to ask Lucy or Paulette to help me. I had not seen or heard from Patrice since she'd dropped off that barbecue sauce. Surprisingly, Lucy and Paulette had not heard from her since that night, either. I certainly wouldn't have asked Patrice to help me do anything, especially since I had decided to tell her not to call me or come to my apartment anymore. I still didn't want any of my friends to know what I was up to, and for more than one reason. For one thing, if I got caught, I didn't want to take any of my friends down with me.

I knew I could not ask Uncle Albert to help me, for the same reason. Just the sight of a cop made him tremble. His boyfriend, Kingston, had offered to kick Seth's ass more than once, so I knew he was the type who wouldn't think twice about helping me with my plan. I didn't consider that possibility, though. Kingston drank a lot of that rice sake and smoked a lot of weed, so his brain was probably mush by now. It would just be a matter of time before he blabbed my business to my uncle. I had convinced Uncle Albert that I had gotten Seth out of my system and had moved on with my life. Well, I had moved on with my life, but it included getting more revenge against Seth.

As far as I knew, Seth had no idea that I was the cause of some of his problems since our breakup. Other than that day in the restaurant, when I had embarrassed him in front of his lunch companion, he had nothing on me. I would let him know eventually, because I wanted him to know that I had gotten my revenge. In the meantime, I wanted to keep my actions on the down low. I had a lot more in store for that man.

I had not seen Skirt since I'd run into him at a club a couple of months ago. He had arrived with one of his many women on his arm, and I'd been with a date, but that hadn't stopped Skirt from showing me some affection. He had strutted up to me and kissed me passionately on the lips. His sister Paulette had told me that he was still in and out of trouble with the law. That didn't surprise me. He had confessed to me one night that his criminal activity had begun with a few armed robberies while he was still in junior high school. Of all his crimes, the only one he had never been apprehended for was breaking and entering. Alarm systems and even guard dogs didn't faze Skirt. He had tools that he used to disable alarm systems. He'd laughed when he told me about the time he had burglarized a doctor's house while the doctor was asleep in bed. He had sprayed the doctor, his wife, their live-in house-keeper, and their two huge German shepherds with some kind of concoction that worked like the tranquilizers animal handlers used.

Skirt was currently between prison stints, so I knew that if I wanted to recruit him before he got locked up again, I had to act fast. I didn't act fast enough. He had changed his cellular phone number. And because he always lived with one of his lady friends, I couldn't call him on his home phone or go to his residence.

I waited a few days before I contacted Paulette and asked her if she'd give me her brother's new cell phone number.

"Yeah. Why?" she asked. "I thought you were done with that jackass years ago."

"I just wanted to say hello to him," I replied. "I know his birthday is coming up soon. I'd like to wish him a happy birthday."

"Well, don't bother. He'll probably spend his birthday in jail. The cops picked him up at my house last night for beating up his girlfriend's husband."

"Oh. Well, when he gets out, tell him I asked about him."

"Here's his number. You can call him and tell him yourself."

I wrote Skirt's new phone number on a notepad, but I was not sure if I'd use it.

A week later I ran into him at Whole Foods Market. He noticed me first. I was in the checkout line, with a basket full of fruit and veggies, when somebody blew air on the back of my neck and then squeezed my behind. I whirled around, prepared to slap whoever it was.

"Skirt! I thought you were in jail for beating up some woman's husband," I wailed.

"Girl, that was another bum rap. When I told dude how his bitch had been chasing after me, he dropped the charges. Then I heard he kicked her ass!" Skirt laughed and clapped his hands. "Listen, my sister told me you asked about me last week and wanted my new phone number. What's up?"

"I just wanted to say hello and wish you a happy birthday," I told him.

"Is that all?"

"Yep."

"That's a goddamned lie!"

"Huh?"

"I ain't playing with you, girl! You know I ain't stupid. What did you really want to talk to me about?"

I turned around briefly to make sure the people in front of me were not listening before I answered Skirt's question. I gave him a guarded look before I continued. "Well, I had a project I was trying to put together, and I thought you could help me with it."

"Uh-huh." Skirt's eyes got big. He leaned back and

looked me up and down for a few seconds, licking his lips the whole time. He straightened up and tilted his head to the side and gave me a look that made me tingle. "Baby, you look sexier than ever. Look at them titties," he said in a low voice. The last thing I wanted to do was hop back into bed with Skirt, but I was prepared to do whatever it took to get him to help me.

"Let me pay for my groceries, and I'll meet you outside," I told him.

"That's cool. I didn't see nothing I wanted to buy, so I'm out of here now. I'll wait for you out in the parking lot."

I had parked right in front of the store. When I got outside ten minutes later, Skirt was standing in front of the building, smoking a cigarette. He glanced at his watch. "It's about damn time. I thought maybe you was up in that damn store, trying to hatch an egg," he complained.

I stopped in front of him and gave him an exasperated look. "You saw how many folks were ahead of me in that line, Skirt."

"Whatever." He dropped his cigarette on the ground. "You still live in the same place? I been toting around a world-beating hard-on for you since the last time we hooked up. If I don't do something about it soon, my dick might freeze up on me or fall off."

I rolled my eyes. "Yes, I still live in the same place, but I am not interested in having sex with you again."

"What else would you want with me?" he asked with an incredulous look on his face. "Shit! A few minutes ago you said something about a project you wanted me to help you with."

I glanced around first to make sure nobody was close enough to hear what I had to say. "Uh, I thought we could do some business together."

This was the first time I had seen Skirt's jaw drop. "Business? Me and you? What the hell kind of business could me and you have other than sex?" He guffawed long and loud, and that made me angry.

"Never mind!" I snapped. I stormed off to my car, which was a few feet away, and he followed me.

"Aw, girl. Don't be like that. You can at least tell me what it is you really do want from me—if it ain't some dick. And you can have that anytime, any day, any way you want it. I ain't stingy."

"As tempting as that sounds, I'll pass. I . . . I . . . Will you help me break into my ex's house?" I said quickly.

Skirt looked at me like I was speaking in tongues. "*Say what?*" he said with his head cocked to the side and both of his eyebrows furrowed.

"You heard me."

"You full of surprises, ain't you? You was too much of a Goody Two-shoes to continue being seen in public with me back when we first hooked up, and now you want me to help you commit a crime." Skirt laughed some more.

"Never mind," I snapped. "Have a nice day." I didn't even bother to put my groceries in the trunk or on the backseat of my car. As soon as I got my driver door open, I flung the bag into the front passenger seat, and then I got in and slammed the door. Skirt remained in the same spot, shaking his head and laughing as I drove away.

When I got home, I sat down and thought about what I needed to do next. Since it didn't look like I was going to be able to break into Seth's house, I had to revise my plans and do a few other things to keep him frazzled.

Since the letter I had sent to the IRS had done no good, as far as I knew, I wondered if a phone call would be more effective. The letter could have gotten lost in the mail, for all I knew, or had not been taken seriously. Whatever the reason was, I had become impatient. The next Monday, on my lunch hour, I went to a pay phone a few blocks from my office. After being prompted to press one button after another, and after listening to automated messages for eight minutes, I finally got a live person on the line. She immediately put me on hold.

Fifteen minutes later the representative came back on the line. She sounded impatient, so I spoke fast.

"I want to report a person who committed tax fraud a few years ago. This man lied on his tax returns so he wouldn't have to pay any taxes. And he got a big refund back. . . ."

"May I have your name and address please?"

"I'd rather not say. This person has a history of violence."

"What is your relationship to this individual?"

"He's just somebody I used to know."

For the next twenty minutes I sang like a canary. I gave the agent the same information that I had included in the letter I had sent. She listened with great interest, saying "Uh-huh" and "Hmmm" at intervals. She didn't even ask for my name again or inquire why I was turning Seth in. And since I had called from a pay phone, I was not worried about her tracing the call back to me.

The agent had written down the most critical parts of what I'd told her. She read her information back to me to make sure she'd written it down accurately. Before she hung up, she thanked me for my assistance and told me to have a nice day. I placed the telephone back in its cradle. Then I pranced to the deli next door and treated myself to a nice turkey sandwich, a Chinese chicken salad, and a cup of green tea for lunch.

It was two weeks before I saw an entry on Seth's calendar that made me ecstatic. He had posted an appointment for the following Thursday with the IRS. On the subject line he had typed "AUDIT!!!!" in bold caps, followed by several exclamation points. I stared at the word, with a huge smile on my face.

Chapter 57

Seth

*O*F ALL THE PEOPLE I KNEW WHO FILED INCOME TAXES, none of them had ever been audited. I knew for a fact that my brother Damon, most of my friends, and even my own father had not always been totally honest when they filed their taxes. They had been cheating for years! The year 1999 was the first year that I had ever "juggled" the numbers on my tax returns, and it was the year I was being audited for. And it was bad.

I had no receipts for the numerous deductions I had claimed. Rather than make a fuss and possibly have them charge me with income tax evasion and God knows what else, I took the easy way out. I claimed I'd lost my files for that year, which included all my receipts.

"If you can't provide receipts, you can't claim those deductions, you know," the agent told me, looking at me like I was just another common cheat. Not only was the chair I occupied across from his desk in his drab office hard, but it also felt hot against my trembling ass. It might as well have been the electric chair. That was how nervous and frightened I was.

"Uh, I can't any provide receipts," I muttered, swallowing hard as I shifted in my seat and crossed my legs. I was sweating like a pig, from my face all the way down to the soles of my feet. I could even feel the perspiration saturating my socks.

"What about the person who prepared your taxes?"

"Huh?"

"Most tax preparers retain copies for their records. Have you contacted your preparer regarding this audit?"

"I filled out the paperwork myself," I lied. I was not about to make matters worse by dragging Rachel into this mess. Lord knows she would have helped them cook my goose.

"I see. What about the state?"

"The state?"

"If you posted the same information on your five-oh-four forms for your state income taxes, the same penalties and interest charges will apply." The tax man blinked at me and pressed his lips together. He was a brother, and I had expected him to show a little compassion toward another brother. There was such a smug look on his shit-colored face, I wanted to slap it off! I probably would have been better off if they'd assigned a Klansman to my case.

"Uh, the same information is on my state tax forms, too," I admitted. I could feel the noose tightening around my neck. I had to cough to clear my throat. "I wanted to be consistent. . . ."

"I'm sure you did," he said with a smirk. "Had you told me otherwise . . . well, never mind. I'm sure you know that we work very closely with the folks at the Franchise Tax Board to ensure that their records match ours."

"Uh . . . huh," I mumbled.

"Very well. They will be notified regarding this audit."

I was in one hell of a mess! As it turned out, not only did I have to pay all the taxes on the claims I'd lied about, but also the penalties and interest charges that had accrued almost *tripled* the amount I would have owed if I had been truthful in the first place. The generous refunds I had received from the IRS and the state would have to be paid back, as well, and that amount would also include penalties and interest.

The day after I had received the notice about the audit, I had thought about moving most of my money from my personal and business accounts. My plan had been to transfer my assets to a bank in the Caribbean islands. I'd considered putting my house in my brother Josh's name. But something had told me that I should place a call to my accountant first. And it was a good thing I had. Mark Bennett had told me things that scared the hell out of me.

"Seth, I advise you not to move your money or put your real estate in someone else's name. Uncle Sam is no fool," Mark had told me, speaking in a firm tone of voice. "They've probably already assigned a Big Brother to keep an eye on your financial movements. I'm sure they've already contacted your bank and alerted them that they may be considering a freeze. It happens to a lot of drug dealers who come to me for assistance regarding their . . . uh . . . income. You wouldn't believe how many of them are so damn stupid that they put their money in American banks before they wise up and wire it to either the islands or Switzerland. But some of those idiots wait too long, and the Man seizes every dime of it."

I could not believe the two ears attached to my aching head. Could things get any worse? My accountant had lumped me in the same boat with drug dealers!

"Then tell me what I should do, Mark," I'd whimpered.

"It's simple. I strongly advise you to pay those damn people and stay as far under the radar as possible in the future. Save every single receipt for anything you plan to list as a deduction in the future. If you're going to claim a Big Mac as a business-related meal expense, you'd better have a receipt for it. Don't think that because they've audited you once, they're not going to do it again. I have a few clients who have been audited several times."

One of the bad things about this latest mess was that I was too ashamed to tell any of my family or friends. But the only way I was going to be able to remain afloat was to hit somebody up for a major loan.

After my telephone conversation with my accountant, I paced the floor in my office for a few minutes. When I calmed down, I poured myself a shot of the vodka that I kept hidden in my desk drawer, in a Sprite bottle. As soon as the buzz hit me and calmed my nerves, I called Josh and requested another sizable loan.

"Baby brother, I won't even ask why you need to borrow money again. I was under the impression that your business was doing quite well," he said. I was glad he didn't sound annoyed or frustrated. That would have made me feel even worse. "But as long as your credit is good with me, I'll always help you out, if I can. Just don't tell anybody. Mother scolded me big-time the last time I bailed you out. She thinks we're all still spoiling you."

"I'm sorry to hear that Mother feels that way, but I've come a long way in the past few years," I said with a pout. "It's just that running a business and supporting a wife with expensive tastes, a baby, and a teenager is not easy." I had told Josh some things that I had not shared with anyone else, but I saw no reason to tell him that I had been audited. That would open up another can of worms, because he would probably want to know why I had no receipts to confirm all the expenses I had claimed. Josh was the kind of man who wouldn't even cheat on a board game, so I knew he would not condone my cheating on my taxes.

"By the way, how are things on the home front these days, Seth?"

"Are you sure you want to know?"

"That's why I asked."

"Hellish," I said, my voice cracking. "That's the best way to describe it." I had to stop talking for a few moments and take a few deep breaths and rub my chest and stomach. If an ulcer had not already begun to form in my tortured belly, I was certain that eventually a few would.

"Do you want to talk about it?"

I took another deep breath and composed myself as best I could before I spoke again. "Darla and Darnell locked horns again this morning. That's the second time in two days. Darnell doesn't like to be told to do anything, not by Darla or by me. He's skipping school, mouthing off to me and Darla, and violating his curfew, and his room looks like a landfill. I don't know, Josh. Darnell is my son, and I love him to death, but in some ways he's like a stranger with a very dark side. Darla is afraid to even leave her purse out in the open. And the other day Mother told me some convoluted story about how Darnell makes her feel nervous when he comes around. She's afraid of him. She said she doesn't want him in the house unless there are other people on the premises."

"Well, it could be a lot worse. At least he's not out robbing folks or getting violent with you or Darla."

"He hasn't robbed anybody that I know of, but last night, when I got on his case about calling Darla a bitch, he raised his hand to hit me."

"Oh my God! Did you call the police?"

"No, I didn't. He didn't hit me, and when he calmed down, I made it clear to him that if he ever hits me or Darla, it would be the biggest mistake he ever made. Violence is one thing I will not tolerate. If he ever does that, I will not hesitate to turn him over to juvenile law enforcement or the foster care system."

"Since we're on the subject, I need to tell you something."

"What is it?"

"Last week, when Darnell was at the house alone with Mother, he . . . he threatened to slap her because she refused to give him any money."

"What? How come nobody told me?"

"Mother made me promise not to tell you. Even Father doesn't know. But that's the reason she doesn't want him to come around anymore unless you come with him. Anyway, she gave him a hundred bucks, and that calmed him down this time. Now, there will be a next time, and I don't think Mother is going to give in so easily."

"Thanks for telling me. I'll have to monitor him a little more closely, I guess."

"You're going to have to do more than that. The boy is out of control, and it's up to you and Darla to turn him around."

"Sometimes it feels like I'm losing the battle," I admitted. "I will sit Darnell down and have a long talk with him. Does Damon know that Darnell threatened to slap Mother?"

"Puh-leeze! Are you kidding? Our big brother would have kicked Darnell's ass to kingdom come by now if he knew."

My life was spinning out of control, but things were going to get a lot worse for me.

Chapter 58

Rachel

NOW THAT I KNEW THE IRS HAD DECIDED TO AUDIT Seth, I decided I didn't need to break into his house. If they did a thorough job, they'd cook his goose to a crisp. I had heard plenty of horror stories about how the IRS handled people who cheated or didn't pay their taxes. I figured they would do enough damage to him to satisfy me—at least for a while.

When Skirt called me up on Saturday night to "discuss business," I played dumb.

"What business are you talking about?" I asked.

"That's what I want to know. That day I bumped into you at the market, you said something about me and you doing some business together."

"Well, I don't need you now."

"Rachel, I want you to know I still care about you. If you got a problem, I want to help you. It's the least I can do for all the fun times we had together. Now, I know you been going through some changes on account of that asshole you dropped me for. If he's fucking with you in any way, all you got to do is let me know and I will straighten him out real good."

"I . . . I don't talk to him anymore. I, uh, I did have a little job I wanted you to help me do. But I worked things out with him."

"Uh-huh. Well, I'm curious, so if you don't mind me asking, exactly what was it you wanted me to help you do? You mentioned me helping you break into your ex-asshole's house."

"My ex owed me some money and had refused to pay me. He owns all kinds of electronics and other expensive items, so I thought I'd, uh, go into his house when nobody was home and borrow a few of his things until he paid me back. But like I said, we worked things out."

"What if your used-to-be honey pisses you off again? Would you still want to get into his house? I will go up in that motherfucker and shit in his kitchen sink if you want me to." Skirt laughed. "I done did worse. . . ."

"I don't think so."

"If you change your mind, just let me know. See, breaking and entering ain't no big deal. I been doing it most of my life. That's one thing I'm real good at."

"Everybody knows that. That's why I contacted you to help me. I would have made it worth your while."

"Oh, you got that right. I don't do business with nobody if there ain't nothing real sweet in it for me."

"I'm glad I won't have to go through with it now, though."

"Well, if you need me for anything else, you got my number."

"Thanks, Skirt. I'll call you if I need you."

*   *   *

I let another two months go by, and I didn't give Seth much thought. And that was only because I wasn't sure what I wanted to do to him next. Before I could come up with another plan, Matthew Bruner reentered my life.

I hadn't been back to church in so long, I had begun to feel guilty. I had told Mama that I was going to join Trinity Baptist, a church in my neighborhood that Lucy, Paulette, and Patrice often attended, because Paulette's uncle was the new pastor. Then I wouldn't have to worry about running into Seth or his family at Second Baptist. That Sunday, I put on one of my most conservative outfits, a pink dress with a matching jacket, and drove the six blocks to the church. I was late, and there was not a single parking spot available, not even on the street. I remained in my car and just drove around, looking for something else to occupy my time. I didn't like to gamble, but when I drove by the Lytton Casino in nearby San Pablo, I parked and went in.

In less than an hour, I lost forty dollars on a penny slot machine, playing forty cents a game. That was enough for me. Just as I was about to stand up and leave, somebody flopped down onto the stool at the machine to my left.

"I thought that was you." It was Matthew Bruner, the man who had so abruptly dropped out of my life before I met Seth. "How have you been, Rachel?" There was a smile on his face that reached from one ear to the other.

I refused to give him a smile. I narrowed my eyes and pressed my lips together. I looked him up and down before I said anything. "Why should you care?" I hissed.

"I do care." There was a stern look on his face. "I spend a lot of time thinking about you."

"Well, I don't spend *any* time thinking about you," I

said with a smirk. He looked disappointed and hurt. "I was just about to leave."

"Can we go into the restaurant area, where it's not so hectic and smoky, and have a seat? We can have some wine. I'd really like to talk to you."

"About what? How you were supposed to show up for our out-of-town date that time and didn't? And how you didn't even call to tell me why? Is that what you want to talk to me about after all this time?"

"Yes. But I don't want to do it sitting on a stool in front of a slot machine."

"Well, I don't want to do it sitting in a restaurant, with a glass of wine. If you have something to say to me, say it here or not at all. And you'd better be quick about it. I was just about to leave."

"I did come to your apartment that evening."

"Oh? I didn't hear you knock. If you did and I didn't answer the door, why didn't you call me on the phone?"

"I was too angry."

"Angry? What the hell were you angry about?"

"I saw you with someone."

"Huh?"

"You kissed him."

I thought back to that evening, and I remembered it in great detail. Skirt had come to my apartment unannounced. To get rid of him in a hurry, I had given him a farewell kiss as we stood in my doorway. "Shit!" I gasped. "Look, that was not what it appeared to be!"

"Rachel, you had your arms around him, and it was not a quick kiss. When I saw that, I left. I thought about coming back later that night to confront you, but I decided I didn't want to get any more involved with you than I already was. It didn't take long for me to convince myself that you were not the kind of woman I wanted to get seriously involved with."

"Shit," I muttered, looking around. "Let's go get a table in the restaurant. I think I would like some wine, after all."

We walked in silence to the restaurant, located in the middle of the casino. We sat down at a table close to the entrance. We each ordered a glass of white wine. I had no appetite, so I didn't order anything to eat, but Matthew ordered a cheeseburger.

"Rachel, I'd still like to get to know you better," he began, taking my hand in his. "Do you think you'd like to try again?"

I nodded. "When you saw me with that man in my doorway, he was an old friend. Believe it or not, I was kissing him good-bye. We had pretty much broken up already, but that was to be the last time we were together."

"I see. Are there any other old friends you want to tell me about?"

"Not long after that, I did meet someone else. We were very serious for a while. He even moved in with me."

"What is the status of your relationship with him now?"

"Do you really want to know? It's a long, ugly story."

Matthew looked at his watch, then into my eyes. "I don't have anywhere to go this evening. If you want to share that long, ugly story with me, I'd like to hear it."

I swallowed hard and began. "His name is Seth. I loved him with all my heart, and we were going to get married." I paused. The waitress delivered our wine, and after a few sips I told Matthew the rest of my story. I told him everything—except the part about my acts of revenge against Seth. I didn't think he would have much sympathy for me if he knew about that.

Matthew sat stock-still. He stared directly into my eyes, which had pooled with tears. "Rachel, I'm sorry you had to go through that. Maybe that brother didn't really love you, anyway. For him to decide not to marry you because of your family's mental issues, but to stay on with you until you'd helped him pay off his debts, was bad enough. But for him to be courting another woman at the same time, who he married shortly after he broke up with you, that's unforgivable! You must have been so hurt."

"I was for a while. But I got over him. So now that you know about my family, you need to make up your mind now if you want to get involved with me, if that's going to be a problem in the future," I said. I knew that it was presumptuous to think that far ahead, but I had nothing to lose by telling him now.

"I have some family issues, too. If I tell you about them, you might decide you don't want to get to know me."

"Why don't you tell me and let me decide?"

"My only brother, Ralph, who is two years older than me, has been in the state mental hospital for two years. I'll bet that if you could see inside his head, you wouldn't be able to tell his brain from a scrambled egg. That's what crack did to him. My middle sister, Lila, also has a history of drug abuse. She's doing five to ten, without the possibility of parole for three years, for trying to sell her teenage daughter to a dealer to settle a debt. Her fifteen-year-old son, Jerome, doesn't do drugs, but he's currently on probation for trying to rape a neighbor's four-year-old daughter."

"Whew. That's deep. What about your parents?"

"My mother passed last year. She had a rare blood disorder. My father is still around, but I don't have a relationship with him."

"I'm glad to see that you turned out all right."

Matthew smiled and squeezed my hand. "I'm glad to see you turned out all right, too."

The waitress set his burger in front of him, but he ignored it.

"So, where do you want to go from here?" I asked.

"We can go to your place if you want to," he answered. "Or we can go to mine."

I chuckled. "That's not what I meant. What I meant was, do you want to start over again? I mean, that is, if you are not involved with somebody else."

"Do you still communicate with Seth?"

I drank some wine before I responded. "Not exactly."

"He's still around?"

"Uh-huh. But we go our separate ways."

"I'm glad to hear that, because I'd really like to see you again real soon. And I will tell you now, I don't care about your family's mental issues."

Chapter 59

Seth

*T*HE TENSION HAD EASED UP IN MY HOUSE BECAUSE I had decided to let Darnell do whatever he wanted to do, as long as it didn't impact the rest of us too much. It was the only way I could keep the peace. I didn't know what else to do. It was bad enough that he didn't go to school unless he felt like it. When he did go, he was as disruptive and disrespectful there as he was at home. On top of that, he was two grades behind and was threatening to drop out of school altogether because, according to him, education was for punks. I couldn't believe that in this day and age young black men in America had slid into such a warped sense of reality.

Sending Darnell back to his mother was out of the question. I couldn't do that if I wanted to, because Caroline had disappeared. Her telephone number had either been changed or been disconnected, and she had ignored the letters that Darnell and I sent to her. Her family was no help. No matter which one I called and tried to get information from regarding Caroline's location, they told me basically the same thing: "I don't know nothing." If I couldn't save Darnell, no one could. Apparently, Caroline had given up on him, but I refused to do so. Nor would I give up on my marriage and my business.

I just tried to make the best of a bad situation. Unfortunately, it seemed like the harder I tried, the more problems I encountered in everything. Things remained pretty much the same with Darnell and Darla from one day to the next. They were predictable. He acted like an idiot; she acted like a bitch. But I never knew what to expect when it came to my business and other personal aspects of my life. I was determined to live as normal a life as possible.

A couple of weeks after the audit, on a quiet, uneventful Saturday evening, I took my family to dinner and a Disney movie. Ten minutes into the movie, Darla got so bored, she fell asleep. A few minutes later, Darnell decided to leave and sneak into another movie in the same complex, saying, "Disney is for sissies!"

The restaurant and the movie theater were located in a mall that catered to the high-income community. The crime rate was fairly low, so I had never had a problem in this area. Until tonight. When we left the theater and returned to my car, it wouldn't start. It didn't take long for me to figure out why. Someone had put sugar in my gas tank! The clumsy motherfucker had spilled at least two pounds of sugar on the ground below my gas cap. I had to call a tow service again. I didn't even attempt to call anybody to come pick us up. I didn't want them to witness my agitated state, Darla's bitching and moaning, and Darnell's rotten attitude because of this inconvenience. I called for a taxi.

We waited for the taxi in a nearby pizza parlor. And

that was no picnic, not with a surly teenager, a horrified wife, and a cranky baby in tow. An hour later we were still waiting for that taxi. When I could no longer stand to listen to Darla's nonstop bitching, we boarded a city bus. That was another nightmare. The local city buses had become frequent crime scenes and, in some cases, toilets—literally. A strong-smelling puddle of urine was on the floor by the side of the seat that Darla and I eased down onto. There were two sinister-looking young characters occupying seats in the back, and Darnell recognized them, so being on a bus didn't bother him. As a matter of fact, the way he was shucking and jiving with his home-boys, you would have thought he was at a party in the hood. Darla continued to bitch and moan, and she didn't stop even after we got home.

I could understand her being frustrated, because I definitely was, too. Having my BMW keyed and the tires slashed had been bad enough, but somebody putting sugar in the gas tank was the last straw. Was this damn vehicle cursed? I wondered. Or was this another one of Rachel's pranks? This speculation chilled me to the bone. However, I still had no proof that she was the culprit who was tormenting me, and I didn't want to find out, because I didn't know how to stop her. In this case, I decided to give her the benefit of the doubt. My brother Damon had been the victim of the same prank in the same neighborhood a few months ago. Anyway, the car that I had loved for so many years was causing me to have headaches that made my head swim.

The following Wednesday I traded it in for a Range Rover.

Other "headaches" plagued me, though. Two days after I purchased my new vehicle, I left work around noon to go to my annual routine checkup. When I arrived at my doctor's office, the receptionist told me she had no record of my appointment. The doctor was so booked up, he wouldn't be able to see me for another two months. An hour after I returned to my office, I received a mysterious telephone call from a woman who disguised her voice. She told me, "Your wife is fucking my husband. . . ."

That was all I needed to hear! I had no reason to believe that Darla was having an affair, but I was going to confront her, anyway. As soon as the caller hung up, I called Darla at home and told her about the telephone call.

"You've got some damn nerve asking me if I'm having an affair!" she screamed. "No, I'm not having an affair, but I should be! For one thing, you're not taking care of business the way you're supposed to. I sit in this damn house all day, every day, with a baby that's driving me up the goddamned wall and your punk-ass son, while you're out wining and dining everybody in town!"

"Baby, what do you want me to do? I have to work, and part of my work is to socialize with my clients and potential clients."

"You might want to think about socializing more with your wife! I can't go on like this. I'm telling you now that if you want me to stay in this marriage, you'd better do something, and you'd better do it fast."

"What am I not doing now that I was doing when we first got together?"

Darla let out a disgusted sigh. "For one thing, you used to take me out to dinner more often. You ought to know by now that I don't like to cook. . . ." Darla served microwaved TV meals, hand-delivered pizzas, and sandwiches when she didn't feel like cooking, which was at least three times a week.

"I figured that out a long time ago," I said in a light-hearted manner so she wouldn't accuse me of being sarcastic. "Let's go out to dinner tonight. Just you and me. I'll get Mother to keep the baby, and we can send Darnell to stay with one of his friends. No, I have a better idea. Let's go to Reno this weekend. Would that suit you?"

"Vegas would suit me better. Reno is for rednecks, the Spanish-speaking crowd, the ghetto crowd, rude Asians, and senior citizens in polyester outfits."

I forced myself to laugh. "You've got a point there, baby. Start packing. I'll have my secretary make the arrangements first thing tomorrow morning."

I forgot all about that telephone call. I refused to believe that Darla was cheating on me. . . .

Vegas used to be one of my favorite hangouts, but it had become very expensive for me since I'd met Darla. Not only did she insist on staying in only the best rooms in the most lavish hotels on the Strip, but she also went on shopping sprees that almost reduced me to tears. When we visited Vegas last year, she ran up five thousand dollars on one of my credit cards and another two grand on another card in less than six hours! She purchased jewelry and clothing from several high-end stores. After she lost the two grand I had given to her to try her luck at blackjack, she got a cash advance on one of my cards for another five hundred and fed that into a slot machine. That trip had been very painful to me.

This visit would turn out to be just as painful. Maybe even more so. She insisted on us taking a stretch limo from the airport to our hotel, as opposed to a cab or the hotel shuttle. "Cabs and free shuttles are for cheapskates," was her reason this time. I didn't protest when she insisted on staying at the Venetian, one of the most upscale hotels/casinos on the Strip. The reason I didn't protest was that I had accrued a lot of points at the hotel over the years. They rewarded me with comps, which included lavish suites that I didn't have to pay for.

Our suite faced the Strip, so the view was spectacular.

"Darla, this is such a nice, romantic setting," I commented, looking around the elaborately decorated room and at the two huge beds. "I hope you're feeling as frisky as I am," I teased. I started unbuttoning my shirt and moving toward Darla. She stood in front of the window with her back to me. And she took her time turning around.

Darla snorted and screwed her face up into a grimace like I'd never seen before. "Seth, if you wanted to fuck, we could have stayed home."

"What? I thought we came down here to have some fun."

"We did. But if you think that includes sex, forget it." She gave me a cold look before she continued. What she said next horrified me beyond belief. "You're not that good, anyway. I do a much better job on my own. . . ."

Had she told me that she had been born a man, I would not have been more shocked. It was a struggle for me to come up with a response. "Thanks for letting me know," I mumbled. No woman had *ever* criticized my lovemaking skills before! Had I slid that deeply into the abyss, and was I no longer the passionate and well-honed lover I once was? Or *thought* I was, I should say. Could other women, Rachel especially, have been lying to me about how great I was in bed? Darla's insensitive comment was the kind that could turn a man from sex and drive him into a monastery. "I think I'll slip into some more comfortable clothes and go play a few table games."

"Go ahead. I'm going to go out and pick up a few items," Darla told me, already flipping through the six credit cards she kept in her wallet.

"You do that, honey. Just . . ."

She whirled around to face me. Another grimace, this one more severe than the previous one, was on her face now. "Just what?"

"Just don't lose control. I have to make payments on these cards every month, you know. It took me a long time to clean up my credit, and I want to keep it clean."

"Then I suggest you keep making your payments on time," she said with a smirk.

My chest tightened, and bile coated the inside of my throat. Credit cards had become a very painful subject to me. I still got angry when I recalled the two times my cards had got declined when I'd attempted to use them. Because of that, I never knew what to expect when it came time to use one now. What I couldn't figure out was how the credit card folks had screwed up and entered information into their system that indicated I had canceled three different credit cards on separate occasions. They had promptly resolved the issues to my satisfaction. Just to be on the safe side, I had canceled my fourth credit card and my debit card and had requested ones with new account numbers. However, I had decided that for all future lunch, dinner, or drink dates with clients, I would pay with cash.

I had no reasonable explanation for my ongoing string of bad luck. But the thought of Rachel being behind at least some of my misfortune was on my mind all the time, and so was her warning. *Karma is a bitch named Rachel.* If she truly was the person responsible for the mysterious mishaps that I had been experiencing since our breakup, I still thought the best thing for me to do was just ride it out. The bottom line was I still had no evidence against her and, therefore, no proof.

That was about to change.

Chapter 60

Rachel

*P*EOPLE RARELY CALLED ME AT 7:00 A.M. ON A SATURDAY morning. When Mama called, she never identified herself, and sometimes she didn't even say hello. As soon as I'd pick up the telephone, she would start talking like we were already in the middle of a conversation. This morning was no different.

I grabbed the phone on the first ring. "Hello." It sounded and felt like I had cotton balls in my mouth.

"Your sister finally got herself a boyfriend. And he ain't no rapper."

"Who is this?" I rolled over in bed and sat up. "Mama, is that you?"

"You don't know my voice by now?"

"I'm sorry, Mama. I was just waking up when the telephone rang. What's this about Janet having a boyfriend?" As far as I knew, the only sexual encounter that my sister had had with a man was the fiasco with the rapper in Miami. I didn't know how to react to this news. "I'm happy to hear that. What's his name?"

"Frank Morrison's brother just moved here with his three boys. Marvin, the oldest one, took one look at Janet in her blue sundress and fell in love."

"What's he like?"

"If you wondering if he's got mental problems, the answer is no. I have to say, this boy ain't no Mr. Universe in the looks department. He's got the face of a mule, but his mind is as sharp as a tack. He even went to college, and now he works for the city. He takes Janet out two or three times a week, and him and her just got together a couple of months ago. I didn't say nothing about it before now, because I wanted to see how it was going to go. Your sister treats him like Prince Charming, and he treats her like Cinderella. What more could we ask for?"

"Mama, there are men out there who will take advantage of girls like Janet. Like that rapper. I advise you to put her on some kind of birth control."

"Birth control? For what?"

"In case something happens."

"I didn't put you on no birth control, and nothing happened to you."

"I knew how to take care of myself, Mama."

"Janet seems to be taking pretty good care of herself."

"What do you know about this Marvin? What if he gets her pregnant and dumps her? Do you want to raise another baby at your age?"

"For your information, Dr. Phil, he asked her to marry him last night. That's what I really called to tell you. And another thing, she ain't done or said nothing . . . out of the ordinary since she took up with Marvin."

"I'm happy to hear that, Mama!" And I really was. If

there was hope for my sister, there had to be hope for me. "I've met somebody, too," I said in a tentative tone of voice. "Someone I'm sure you'll like."

"Oh? Well, if I was you, I wouldn't wait to tell him about our family. You better tell him real quick. Unless you want him to run off the way that Seth did when he found out about Janet and Ernest."

My mother rambled on for another few minutes about how cute Janet and her homely fiancé looked together. She ended the conversation by telling me, "I'm glad you done found somebody else. Matthew sounds nice. You say he's a parole officer? Well, you better not do nothing to make *him* mad. Next thing you know, he'll be working with the law to put you in jail. Your brother's on some new medication, so maybe there's hope for him to experience true love one of these days. I don't care how afflicted somebody is. They need love, too. I hope Seth will realize that someday."

Mama's words rang in my ears. The fact that Janet had found love, and Matthew had made it clear that my family situation didn't even faze him, brought tears to my eyes. Just thinking about the wounds that Seth had caused me and how they had just begun to heal, I got angry with him all over again.

I didn't know where my relationship with Matthew was going, or if it was going anywhere at all. For one thing, I had not heard from him since the night at the casino a few *weeks* ago. Had I jumped the gun? Now I regretted telling Mama about Matthew and getting my hopes up. Especially since I had no idea if I'd even hear from him again.

As I lay in my bed, staring up at the ceiling, all kinds of unpleasant thoughts ran through my head. Like maybe Matthew had just been blowing smoke when he told me that my family's mental illness issues didn't bother him. Maybe he had gone home and thought about what I'd told him and decided he didn't want to get involved with me, after all. I couldn't think of any other reason why he had not called. The more I thought about his second rejection, the angrier I got. It didn't take long for me to convince myself that Matthew was not serious about having a relationship with me. I dreaded telling Mama that I'd been wrong about a man *again*.

I went back and forth, cursing Matthew one minute and Seth the next, but my main focus was Seth. I had a few more things I wanted to do to him, just to make sure he would never forget me. But at the same time, I had to remind myself that he didn't know I was the one responsible for all the miserable things that had been happening to him. Now that I had refreshed my anger at him, I decided that the sooner he found out just how mad he had made me, the better.

I was glad that I still had Skirt's new cell phone number. Around ten I ate a ham and cheese sandwich. After I drank two glasses of wine to get up my nerve, I gave him a call.

"Hey, baby. It's good to hear your voice," he said. "I been thinking about you off and on since the last time we talked. I can still picture them juicy legs in one of them short tail dresses you wear sometime."

I rolled my eyes and shook my head. "Well, I'd like to talk business, if you have time right now," I said.

"Now is as good a time as any. Talk to me, sweet thang."

"Remember when I told you I wanted you to help me get into my ex's house and, uh, do a thing or two to get back at him for not paying me some money he owes me?"

"I thought y'all settled that."

"I thought so, too. He paid me with a check, but it bounced, and I haven't been able to catch up with him. So, I need to get into his house, after all."

"When do you want to do it?"

"Can we meet somewhere and discuss it?"

"How come I can't come to your place? I ain't going to bite you, but I will if you want me to."

"Be serious. I'd feel more comfortable if we could meet in a public place. I never know when somebody's going to knock on my door."

"I can meet you somewhere, I guess. But before we do that, I want to know what's in this deal for me. And when it comes to a job, I don't do nothing on credit, and I don't accept checks."

"I'll pay you three hundred dollars in cash."

"Is that all? I can't take none of the dude's shit out of his house and hock it? I do business with every fence in town."

"That's not a good idea. I don't think we should take anything."

"Then what the fuck do you want to get into his pad for? I thought you wanted to borrow some of his shit and hold it until he paid you the money he owes you."

"I did, but maybe taking his stuff might be too risky. But I still want to get into his place just to check it out. And you don't have to come inside with me."

"Girl, I don't know what kind of TV shows you been watching, but that ain't the way these things work. You want me to help you break into some dude's house just so you can 'check it out'? That's the stupidest shit I ever heard of!"

"All right. I just want to find a picture of him and his family."

"What the hell for?"

"Don't worry about that."

"Damn! I done heard some crazy shit in my life, but this *ridiculous* shit you cooking up takes the cake." Skirt snickered.

"Get serious and listen to me."

"Oh, I'm listening, all right. This is hella funny. Keep talking so I can laugh some more."

"I'm not sure if he's got an alarm system or not. Knowing him, he probably does have one. If so, I want you to disable it. I heard you could do that?" It was a question, not a statement.

"I know my shit, girl. There ain't no alarm system in the world I can't crack. And I ain't been caught yet."

"You'd better bring some of that tranquilizer spray, in case Seth has dogs."

"Oh, I got plenty of that. The white boy I buy my meth from, he whips up this spray shit in the lab he works for, and it's a good thing he do! Home owners done got a little too smart for me these days. Some of these paranoid motherfuckers is buying guard dogs left and right! Before I retire, I'd be happy to spray a few more dogs *and humans* that get in my way."

In the back of my mind, I was sorry I had come this far. I was no criminal, but I was committing one criminal offense after another. But it was too late to turn back now.

"I don't want this to get out of hand, you know."

"What do you mean by 'get out of hand'?"

"I don't want anybody to get hurt. Not even a dog."

"Look, woman. All is fair in love, war, and crime. When you break into somebody's house, things is already 'out of hand.' Now, do you want to do this thing or not?"

"Yes, I do. Uh, you can stay outside and be the lookout while I go inside. I'll give you three hundred bucks for doing practically nothing."

"Except fucking up a dude's alarm system and being the lookout and whatnot. In case you didn't know, I'll be what the cops call an accomplice."

"The cops? Didn't you just tell me you've never been caught breaking into a house?"

"Yeah, I did tell you that. But there is a first time for everything. Sooner or later, some smart-assed bastard will come up with some high-tech shit that'll throw a hell of a monkey wrench into my line of work."

"Skirt, if you don't want to help me, just say so and I'll get somebody else."

"You ain't got to do that. I'll help you. I'll make three hundred bucks, huh?"

"Three hundred bucks."

"Can you throw in a tip?"

"A tip? Three hundred dollars is your tip."

"I'm talking about a piece of ass, woman!"

"I don't think so, Skirt. Now, do you want to do this thing with me or not?"

"All right. Call me back when you know when and where you want to meet. Now listen up. Since we done went into so much detail, this is a done deal, so I'm counting on that money. I'm a businessman, so even if you change your mind now, I expect to get paid whether I do the job or not. You feel me?"

"That's fine. Now let me get off this phone. I'll call you when I need you."

I hung up and ran to my computer. I logged in to check Seth's schedule. He had posted his and Darla's appointments for the next two weeks. For a woman who had a baby and a big house to take care of, she sure got around. She had an appointment with her hairdresser, one with her manicurist, and one with her dentist all in the same day. But the one that jumped out at me was an appointment for Seth to take his son to talk to a therapist on Friday afternoon. Darla had another appointment at some spa during that same block of time.

That piqued my curiosity. I logged into Seth's AOL account to check his e-mails. The first message I saw stunned me. In an e-mail posted a few hours earlier, Darnell had contacted him, complaining about not being able to reach Seth or Darla by telephone to let him know that he had lost his house key. Seth had responded right away and had told him that the spare key was under a flowerpot by the side of the front porch. Like it always is, he had written. I shook my head. Anybody stupid enough to leave a spare house key under a flowerpot these days was asking for trouble.

I wouldn't need Skirt's help, after all. Seth had all but left the door open and invited me into his home. And I would take him up on it that Friday afternoon, while Seth and Darnell were with that therapist and Darla was kicking back at that spa.

Chapter 61

Seth

I WAS SO FRAZZLED, I DIDN'T KNOW WHICH WAY WAS UP anymore. I was forgetting appointments, I didn't have much of an appetite, and I was not so meticulous about my appearance anymore. My hair looked and felt like barbed wire, and I couldn't remember the last time I'd washed it. Other people had begun to notice the changes in me.

"Baby, are you coming down with something?" Mother had asked earlier tonight, when I'd arrived for a visit. She had rushed up to me as soon as I'd entered the living room and had felt my forehead.

"I've just been working real hard," I'd told her.

"You'd better stop working so hard," Father had commented, with an unlit cigar dangling from his lip. "You've got more important things you need to be paying attention to. Your family, for one. How are things between you and Darla? I hope she's still as sweet as she was when you up and decided to marry her practically right after you met her. . . ."

I went out of my way to avoid conversations with everybody about how quickly I'd left Rachel and married Darla. Especially since I had taken so much more time to get to know Rachel. It was hard, but I kept up the "happy face" front so well, nobody had a clue that my marriage was on life support.

"Darla is still a very sweet woman. If God made a sweeter woman, He kept her for himself." I was surprised that God didn't turn me into a pillar of salt for telling such a barefaced lie. "I'll tell her you asked about her."

After listening to my parents rattle on a few more minutes, I politely excused myself. The only reason I had come by in the first place was that I didn't want to go home and face Darla. I was still angry about the way she had treated me before I left for work that morning. Surprisingly, she'd allowed me to make love to her. Just as I was about to climax, she'd sneezed and shoved me to the side. Then she had laughed about it.

When I got back to my car, I called up Howard from my cell phone. "Dude, can you meet me for a drink?" I asked, struggling to keep my voice from cracking.

"This time of night? Why didn't you ask me before we left the office?"

"I didn't need a drink then."

"Seth, I wish I could meet you, but I have a date with a lady I've been trying to get next to for a long time. How about tomorrow?"

"Yeah, that'll be fine."

"You know, if you really need to talk, I can postpone my date." Apparently, Howard had detected the desperation in my voice.

"I don't want you to do that, bro."

"I've noticed for some time now that you seem distracted. If you're depressed about something, you need to do something about it before you wind up the way I did a few years ago."

"I'm okay. Thanks for your concern. I just wanted to have a drink with you. But I don't want you to break your date for me." I tried to sound cheerful, but my pain was so deep, I broke down and cried after I got off the phone. I still didn't want to go home, but I went, anyway. I was pleased to see that Darla had already turned in for the night. To make sure I wouldn't have to deal with her, I slept on the living room couch.

I got up the next morning and tiptoed into my bedroom to get a change of clothes. I took my shower in the downstairs bathroom. When I opened the door to leave, Darnell was shuffling up the porch steps. It was 8:00 a.m.

"Where the hell have you been, boy?" I demanded.

"Why?" he snarled.

"Because I want to know! I'm going to put a stop to your behavior, young man. You are not going to be coming in at all hours of the day or night!"

"I will come in whenever I feel like it. Now, get out of my face." He brushed past me, almost knocking me to the ground. I stumbled and dropped my briefcase.

"We . . . I can't go on like this," I whimpered, squatting down to retrieve my briefcase. Darnell turned around and was about to say something when he noticed the tears in my eyes.

"I know you ain't fixing to cry! My old man is a fucking crybaby!" He let out a sinister laugh, and then he entered the house like he owned it.

I stumbled to my car and headed to work.

No one had arrived at the agency yet, but I went into my office and shut the door. I placed my head on my desk and had myself a good long cry. Around nine, Howard entered without knocking.

"Dude, you look like hell with those red, puffy eyes, so don't sit there and tell me nothing is wrong. Whatever is bothering you, you need to let it all out," he said. "What's wrong?"

"Everything." My lips were trembling and my voice was so hoarse, I didn't even sound like myself.

Howard came around my desk and rubbed my shoulder. "Is it Darla?"

"Yes." I nodded. "But she's only part of it."

"Well, business is good, so I know that can't be bothering you."

"My son is about to drive me crazy."

"Is that all? What you need to do is beat the dog shit out of his young ass. That's all it took for me. You remember how I was when I was his age. When my mama got fed up with my mess, she put her foot so far up my ass, I was shitting mush for days."

Howard's comment made me laugh. He rubbed my shoulder some more. "See there. It's not so bad if you can laugh about it."

"No, I guess it's not. But I will not hit my son."

"Do you want me to talk to him? Sometimes a dude will listen to another dude who is not too close to him."

"Thanks, but I don't think so." I grabbed a few tissues from the box of Kleenex on my desk and honked into them. "Darnell is not *that* bad. . . ."

"I'm here for you, bro. If you still want to go for a drink after work today, just let me know."

"Thanks, Howard. I'll do that."

I got busy doing things I normally would ask my secretary to do. I reorganized my files, typed a few letters, and answered most of my own e-mail. That helped, because I felt a lot better. A few minutes before ten, Howard and I went to the snack shop a few doors down for coffee. We sat at a table in the back for twenty minutes, discussing sports, politics, and work, and not once did I even mention Darnell or Darla. And I was glad he didn't bring them up, either.

Less than a minute after I returned to my office, planning to water my plants, Darla called and told me that she and Darnell had just had another run-in.

"If you don't get that boy some professional help, I'm leaving," she warned. "All I asked him to do was not smoke weed in this house this morning and right in front of Gayle! I thought he was going to kill me when I got in his face!"

"Baby, I made an appointment for Darnell to talk to a therapist tomorrow afternoon."

"Darnell needs more than therapy, Seth. He needs a good old-fashioned whupping, if you ask me!"

"That's not the answer, honey. I'll come home early today, and we can talk then."

"Seth, we've talked and talked, and it's done no good. That punk is ruining our lives."

"Darla, I'm doing everything I can. And that 'punk' is my son."

"Well, you're not doing enough! I'm afraid to be in the house with Darnell now more than ever! Gayle is afraid of him, and my friends and family have stopped coming around because of him! Now, how much longer do you think I'm going to live like this?"

"Darla, don't ask me to choose between you and my son."

"I'm not asking you to do that. But I have thought about it!"

My head felt like it was in flames. And the rest of my body felt almost as hot. Dr. Spencer had told me to come in again, even though he had run a few tests previously and found nothing wrong with me physically. I didn't need a doctor or anybody else to tell me that. I knew what was wrong with me: my life was a wreck. But the pain relievers that my doctor had prescribed helped. However, he had refused to renew my prescription until I paid him another visit, which I was able to do a couple of hours later, when he called and told me another patient had canceled.

Somehow I made it to Dr. Spencer's office without wrecking my car or falling down from mental and physical exhaustion. My body felt as heavy as a dead horse as I dragged my feet into the building and shuffled toward the elevator. I was so preoccupied, I didn't even realize I had reached my destination until the two people standing next to me told me.

"You're fine, Mr. Garrett. You need to get more rest, stop worrying so much, and you need to drink less alcohol," Dr. Spencer told me. He gave me a fatherly look, even though we were about the same age.

"I've been constipated, too," I said, buttoning my shirt.

"Any over-the-counter laxative could remedy that."

"I've tried a few already, and they didn't work. As a matter of fact, they made me feel worse."

"I'll write you out a prescription for something that will work. In the meantime, I want you to reduce your alcohol intake and avoid dairy products. I'd like to see you again in two weeks. Have a nice day, Mr. Garrett."

I left feeling better, but only slightly. I feared my pain would start up again as soon as I got home and had to deal with Darla and Darnell. But I didn't have to wait that long.

I had parked my Range Rover at a meter. As I approached it, I noticed something on my dashboard. I knew it couldn't be a ticket. My meter still had fifteen minutes on it, and a ticket for a parking violation would not have been put *inside* my vehicle. I snatched open my door and leaned inside. What I saw on my dashboard almost made me faint. It was a wallet-size picture of me, Darla, and Gayle that we had taken at Magic Mountain a few weeks ago. It was the same picture that I kept in my spare wallet in a drawer in the nightstand next to my bed. What the hell was it doing on my dashboard?

I slid into my seat and grabbed the picture, wondering if I was losing my mind. I had not put the picture on my dashboard, and I knew Darnell and Darla couldn't have done it. They didn't even know where I was. I turned the picture over. The message that had been neatly printed on the back with a fine-point black Sharpie made my head swim: *I should be in this picture.*

I could not believe my eyes! There was no mistake about it. I knew immediately *who* had stolen the picture and placed it on my dashboard. But I got additional confirmation. The inside of my vehicle reeked of perfume: Poison. It was a fragrance that only one woman I knew wore. That woman was Rachel McNeal.

Chapter 62

Rachel

"Y OU SURE ARE QUIET TODAY," LUCY SAID, HOVERING over my desk. "Is anything wrong?" She looked like a pumpkin with a face, standing there in her orange dress.

"I'm fine."

I did feel fine. I had pulled off another act of revenge against Seth, and this one made me feel better than all the others. Breaking into the Range Rover that he had traded in his BMW for to leave the picture I'd stolen from his house had been a piece of cake. For the money people paid for SUVs, it was amazing how easy it was to break into them. I had locked myself out of my car one night a couple of years ago. Uncle Albert had to come rescue me. He had used a ten-inch metal file with a sharp end to unlock my car. After I'd locked myself out of my car several more times, Uncle Albert had taught me how to use a file, and from that day on, I had always carried one in a sheath in my purse.

"You were looking so deep in thought, I thought you'd sat here and fallen asleep with your eyes open."

"I was just thinking about something," I said.

"Well, with the stone-faced look you had on your face, I'm afraid to ask what it was that you were thinking about. Have you heard from your parole officer boo? Uh, what was his name?"

"Matthew. No, I have not heard from him."

"I figured that. If I had known it was going to be this hard to find another man to marry, I'd have begged Nate not to divorce me."

"Your husband left you to be with another woman, remember?"

Lucy exhaled and gave me a sympathetic look. "I guess I shouldn't feel too bad about my pitiful love life. Yours is just as bad. Matthew didn't even bother to call you, like he said he would, after you spent time with him in that casino. That should tell you all you need to know. Either he wasn't serious in the first place or he met somebody he likes better. If he calls now, I wouldn't be bothered with him if I were you."

"He's not the first man who took my telephone number and didn't call."

"And he won't be the last! If I had a dollar for every man that did that to me, I'd be able to retire. I think you should go on one of those singles' cruises, like I do when I get too far down in the dumps."

"Why? So I can screw a bunch of men I'll never see again, too?"

"Don't go there now! I have fun on my cruises, and I do more than just fuck a bunch of anonymous men. One night I went to the bar on country-western night so I could learn how to line dance. On top of that, I spent that night with a white boy from West Virginia, who gave me some of the best sex I have ever had," Lucy swooned. "Don't be such a sourpuss. I'm just trying to cheer you up."

I sighed. "Cheer me up by taking me to lunch today."

"Only if you let me pick the place."

I was sure that once Seth found the picture with my message on the dashboard of his car, he would know I'd been in his house, too. I wanted him to know that I was still in his life, anyway, and there was not a thing that he could do about it. But if he convinced me that he was truly sorry for what he'd done to me, I would feel that my mission had been accomplished.

I had put Matthew out of my mind. When he finally called me up on Sunday evening, around five, I was surprised and annoyed.

"Matthew who?" was the first thing out of my mouth when he identified himself.

"Matthew Bruner. I first met you in line at the Department of Motor Vehicles a few years ago. Then I bumped into you again at the casino a few weeks ago. You don't remember me?"

"Oh. *That* Matthew Bruner." I didn't even try to hide my sarcasm. "What do you want?"

"I wanted to talk to you."

"I can't imagine what you want to talk to me about."

"Give me a chance, Rachel." I didn't even have to see his face to know that there was a pout on it. "I would have called you a lot sooner, but I lost your telephone number."

I had heard that excuse from several other men, so hearing it from Matthew didn't surprise me.

"Oh, really?"

"I couldn't remember the name of the school you told me you worked for, so I couldn't call you at work," he went on. "I went back to that casino several times, hoping I'd run into you again."

"Did you forget where I lived, too?" I snarled.

"No, I didn't. But after that incident the last time I showed up at your place, I didn't want to show up without calling."

"You had my address. Why didn't you send me a note or a postcard?"

"Honey, I wish I had done that. But so much time had passed by the time I thought about doing that, I figured it'd do me no good."

"Well, it was nice of you to call," I said, sounding bored. Not only was I bored, but I was also indifferent. So far, this man had not lived up to my expectations. I was tired of men playing with my feelings. I made a mental note to go with Lucy the next time she went on a cruise. If she could have fun sleeping and partying with men she'd never see again, so could I.

"Rachel, I really would like to get to know you. When I realized I had left that matchbook with your phone number in my jacket pocket, I could have kicked my own ass."

"And you just found it?"

"Something like that. I eventually took the jacket to be dry-cleaned and didn't check my pockets before. When I picked it up today, the clerk handed me the matchbook, which he had removed and had kept in a drawer. He couldn't call to tell me, because he didn't have my new telephone number. It was an honest mistake."

I felt somewhat better. "Well, we all make mistakes. I'm glad you called." I didn't sound as bored now, but I didn't want to sound too anxious, either. For all I knew, Matthew was lying.

"Can you have dinner with me this week?" he asked.

"Well . . ."

"Tomorrow evening, if you're available."

"Monday evening would be better." I didn't want to give the impression that I had no plans for the weekend, which I didn't. "*Next* Monday. I'm really busy these days."

"I'm sure you are. I don't expect a fox like you to be sitting at home alone too often." He laughed.

The more we chatted, the more relaxed I felt. Now I really was glad he'd called. By the time we ended our conversation an hour later, I had almost forgotten that I had broken into Seth's house.

When Seth called me a few minutes later from his cell phone, I was caught completely off guard. As soon as I answered, he started yelling. "Rachel, I've had enough of your foolishness! This time you went too far!"

"Huh?"

"Huh, my ass! I know you broke into my house!"

"What? Seth? Is that you?"

"You know damn well it's me! And I know damn well you've been in my house!"

"Oh, really?"

"You broke into my house and stole a picture of me and my family. Then you broke into my car and left that picture on the dashboard. I know it was you!"

"Prove it!"

"I don't have to prove it! Now I *know* it was you who keyed my car and slashed my tires! And another thing, you were probably behind all the rest of that shit that happened to me after we broke up!"

"What shit are you talking about?"

"You canceled my credit cards, too! Didn't you?"

"You can't prove that, either!"

"No, I can't. But you're the only person who had a reason to fuck with me! Woman, do you know what kind of hell you've put me through?"

"You know something, Seth. An insensitive man like you probably has a whole lot of other enemies. . . ."

"What's that supposed to mean?"

"You figure it out!"

"I've already figured it out!"

"You made a fool out of me, Seth. I had every reason in the world to fuck up your life."

"That's all the admission I need. I'm going down to the police station and getting a restraining order. I don't want you to come anywhere near me or my family or my vehicle again!"

Seth hung up abruptly, and I called him right back.

"Remember what I told you?" I asked.

"What the hell are you talking about?" he growled.

"I told you that karma is a bitch named Rachel. Do you remember that?"

What I had just said must have really rattled him, because he made a noise that sounded like that of a wounded animal. "Why . . . why did you say that?"

"Because it's true!"

"You are talking straight-up gibberish! Fuck you!" he roared. He didn't sound so wounded now. He sounded like an angry bear about to attack. "You are crazier than I thought."

"Since it runs in my family, you're probably right. Maybe I *am* crazy. Let me tell you one more thing. A restraining order is just a piece of paper to me!"

I was the one who hung up abruptly this time.

Chapter 63

Seth

*I*T SEEMED LIKE BEFORE I COULD PUT OUT ONE FIRE, AN-
other one flared up in my face. The same day that I planned
to go to the police department to take out a restraining
order against Rachel, the cops came to my house to arrest
my son for armed robbery. Darla was out shopping that
Saturday evening and had been since the malls opened at
10:00 a.m. She had left Gayle with Mother. I had no idea
where Darnell was. It had been three days since we'd
seen him, and he had not called to say where he was.
With the way he had been behaving lately, and with the
thugs he associated with, he could have been dead, for all
I knew. I was so tired and broken by this time, I almost
didn't care.

When the cops banged on my front door and told me
what Darnell had been accused of doing, I didn't know
what to think.

"My son robbed a convenience store? You've got to be

kidding! The boy has had some problems, but he's not the type to go around robbing people!" I yelled at the tall black cop who was standing in my living room, looking at me like he wanted to arrest me, too.

"We have two eyewitnesses, and everything was caught on tape. The boy who was with your son is already in custody. He named your son as his accomplice," the stout white cop, who looked more like a wrestler, said with a smirk.

I couldn't argue with that. "Well, I haven't seen my son in three days," I admitted, rubbing the back of my aching neck. "He pretty much does what he wants to do."

"I figured that," the black cop said, rolling his eyes. "We will find him, and he will be arrested. When and *if* you hear from him before we find him, I advise you to have him turn himself in."

After the cops left, I sat down on my couch and cried like a baby for the next ten minutes. In the past few weeks I had cried as often and as hard as I had when I was a baby. Had I become that weak? The answer was yes. By the time Darla returned an hour later, I had composed myself.

"The cops came here today, looking for Darnell," I told her when she entered the living room, holding two large shopping bags. I groaned at the thought of how much she had charged to my credit card this time.

"You wouldn't believe the crowds I had to deal with. It was complete chaos!" she complained. She kicked off her shoes, set the shopping bags on the floor, and headed toward the liquor cabinet.

"Did you hear what I just said?" I asked.

Darla poured herself a shot of bourbon, swallowed half of it in one gulp, and took her time answering. "No. Did you say something?"

"I just told you that the cops came here, looking for Darnell. Apparently, he was involved in a robbery."

Darla let out a heavy sigh as she shook her head and sat down next to me. "I'm surprised the cops hadn't come before today," she said, still shaking her head. "The boy is beyond help, and the sooner you realize that, the better."

"So you keep telling me. And I keep telling you that he's still my son, Darla."

Darla finished her drink and set the glass on the coffee table. She turned to me with a stone face and asked, "Have you tried to find his silly ass?"

"No. I wouldn't even know where to start looking for that boy." I looked at the bags Darla had set on the floor. "You can't keep spending like this," I pointed out. "Business has slowed down a lot, and we already have a lot of outstanding debts."

"Can we change the subject, Seth?" Darla didn't give me time to answer. "I saw that woman."

I knew she was referring to Rachel. We didn't talk about her often anymore, and when we did, she was still referred to as "that woman."

"Where did you see her?" I asked, with my heart racing. "She . . . she didn't say anything to you, did she?"

"She didn't see me. I was driving past Dino's Restaurant and saw her walking in with some dude. He had his arm around her, so maybe she's somebody else's problem now. I'm so glad she's finally out of your life. I . . . Why is that strange look on your face?"

"She's not out of my life." I had to cough before I could wheeze out the rest of my response. "She's been in this house."

"What? How? What in the world was she doing in my house! When?"

"I don't know when she was here," I whimpered.

"What all did she steal?"

"As far as I know, all she took was a picture. It was one of the ones of you, me, and Gayle that we took at Magic Mountain last month. I had left it in the bedroom."

Darla's nostrils flared, and her eyes looked like they wanted to pop out of their sockets. "That woman has been in our bedroom?"

I nodded. "That was where I had left the picture . . . in the top drawer of my nightstand. I had just put it there last weekend, when I changed wallets. That means she broke in some time since then. She got into my car somehow and placed the picture on the dashboard."

Darla's mouth was hanging open. "Why in the hell would she do something like that? Are you sure she did that?"

"Who else could have done it?"

"I wouldn't put it past your son—"

"What reason would Darnell have to do something like that? How would he know where I'd parked my car?"

"Yes, but can you prove it was Rachel?"

"She scribbled some stupid message on the back of the picture. From what she wrote, apparently, she thinks she should have been the woman posing next to me. And . . ."

"And what?"

"I called her up."

"Did she admit it?"

"No. She didn't have to."

"Look, that woman has been fucking with us for too long. If you don't go to the police, I will."

"And tell them what? Everything she's done? I'm not even sure of what all that is. Even if I did know, I can't prove a damn thing. I was thinking about taking out a restraining order."

"*Thinking* about it! What's wrong with you, fool? If she's been in this house and in your car, there is no telling what else she's capable of!"

"Darla, I have reason to believe she's responsible for a lot of other things these past few years. I think she's the one who slashed my tires that night we had dinner at Bridges. And I'm almost certain she's the one who put the sugar in my gas tank, canceled my credit cards, and . . . ratted me out to the IRS."

Darla gasped. "The IRS? What do you mean?"

"I think she's the one who gave them the information that initiated that audit. They knew too much about my financial activity for nineteen ninety-nine. Um . . . some of the information on my forms was fraudulent. Rachel was the only person who had access to that information."

Darla looked at me like I had just sprouted horns. "I can't believe what I'm hearing! If you were stupid enough to cheat the IRS and let that lunatic bitch know about it, what else are you stupid enough to do? How do I even know your business is not a front for some . . . some God knows what else? Ad agency, my ass! That little one-trick, Mickey Mouse business of yours could be a front for drugs, for all I know!"

"Well, it's not, so you can get that off your mind. I'm stupid, but not *that* stupid."

"I can't believe that that crazy-ass woman has been in my house," Darla mouthed, looking around. "Did you even check to see if she took anything else? I find it hard to believe that she broke in here and all she took was a picture."

"I checked, and I didn't see anything else missing. I think that after I take out that restraining order, she'll get the message."

Chapter 64

Rachel

*T*HERE WAS NEVER A GOOD TIME OR PLACE TO HAVE someone approach you and hand you a restraining order. I was glad that the process server had not come to my job. I would have had a hell of a lot of explaining to do. But I had some explaining to do, anyway, because he came to my apartment on a Monday evening, while I was cooking dinner for Matthew.

"Rachel McNeal," the man said as soon as I opened the door just enough to see his face and the document in his hand.

"Yes," I replied.

He handed me the paper and said in a mocking tone of voice, "You've been served."

"What the . . . ? Wait a minute!" I yelled as he made a swift turn and trotted back to a Volkswagen parked in front of my building. I heard Matthew walking up behind me, so I folded the paper and closed the door.

"What's going on, Rachel?"

"Uh, nothing serious," I said as I glanced at the notice.

Before Matthew could ask me another question, somebody else banged on my door. Assuming it was the same guy who had just left, I snatched open the door again without looking through the peephole first. I was horrified when I saw Skirt standing in front of my door!

"What in the world? What are you doing here?" I asked, shaking my finger in his face.

"Since you ain't took the time to call me and let me know what was up with that business thing we discussed, I decided to come over here and find out. Where's my money?" Skirt's face was so close to mine, I could smell the weed and whiskey on his breath.

"What money?"

"Them three hundred bucks you promised me!" Skirt paused. I realized he was looking over my shoulder when I turned around and saw Matthew standing even closer to me now, with his hands on his hips. Skirt couldn't have looked more like a street thug if he had tried. His hair was in cornrows, his plaid shirt was wrinkled and dingy, his pants were two sizes too large, and he had a fresh tattoo of a cobra on the side of his neck. The only thing missing was a set of gold teeth.

"I want my money!" Skirt yelled.

"You smell like a damn liquor mill! I . . . Can we talk about this later, after you go home and sober up?" I asked, trying to shut the door. Skirt forced it to remain open by placing his foot against the doorjamb.

"Will somebody tell me what the hell is going on?" Matthew asked. He put his hand on my shoulder and shook me. "Rachel, who is this dude, and what does he want?"

"This dude wants to get paid!" Skirt hollered. "Your woman and me was supposed to do some business together, and she promised to pay me, whether we did our business or not! I been waiting a coon's age to hear from her, and I ain't heard a peep out of her. Well, today is pay-day. *Shit!* Rachel knows I ain't nobody to play with when it comes to money! I'm leaving here with my money, or somebody's butt is mine!"

I had never seen a more horrified look on a human being's face than the one on Matthew's face now. You would have thought that he was staring at Satan himself. "What is he talking about, Rachel? Who is this character?"

"Look, motherfucker, don't you be calling me no 'character,' because I will hurt you!" Skirt shook his fist in Matthew's direction. "And since this silly bitch ain't told you nothing, I'll tell you what I'm talking about! I heard through the grapevine that the suit-wearing mother-fucker she was supposed to marry cut her ass loose so he could marry another girl, and Rachel copped a serious at-titude. She wanted to bust into his house and do some crazy shit . . . steal something or break up something or whatever! She wanted me to—"

I held my hand up to Skirt's face. "Stop talking, Skirt! You don't have to go there. I'll tell Matthew everything," I whimpered.

"Fuck that shit! You can tell dude whatever the hell you want to, but I'm telling him what I know so I can get my money!" Skirt pushed past me and steamrollered into my living room. "Keep playing games! I'll find my money myself and—" He spotted my purse on the coffee table and staggered toward it. "Take what's mine, plus a tip for all the trouble you put me through!" He ended his sentence with a maniacal grin.

I sprinted across the floor, grabbed my purse, and re-moved my wallet before he could get to it. "I'll give you your money, and I want you to get the hell out of my sight for good!" I yelled. I couldn't fish three one-hundred-dollar bills out of my wallet fast enough. "Here's your money! Happy?" I handed the cash to Skirt, and he snatched it so hard, he almost took my hand with it.

Skirt grinned. "Hell, yeah, I'm happy now." He stuffed the bills into his shirt pocket and sniffed. Then he turned to Matthew and winked. "Dude, this bitch is as nutty as a fruitcake! That's why I dropped her ass!"

"You two were involved?" Matthew calmly asked, looking from me to Skirt. From the look of disgust on his face, I knew he was wondering why I'd get involved with a hood rat like Skirt. All of a sudden, Matthew's face froze, and he stumbled toward me. "Were you . . . ? Hey, wait a minute! This is the man I saw you kissing that evening."

"Kissing ain't all this bitch's mouth is good for. Man, she used to suck my dick *all night long*," Skirt said with a sigh. "And I sure do miss that. . . ."

"Get out of here!" I roared, pulling Skirt by his arm toward the door. I didn't realize just how strong I was until that moment. All it took from me was one mighty shove and he was out the door. I shut and locked it and then turned to Matthew. "I can explain everything."

"I sure as hell hope so, because I don't like what I just witnessed. Maybe you're not the woman I think you are, after all."

"Be quiet and let me talk," I said, motioning for Matthew to sit on the couch. He folded his arms and remained standing.

"I'm listening," he said in a gruff tone of voice. "And this time, tell me *everything*."

Matthew finally sat down on the couch, and I stood in front of him. I told him everything there was to tell. Even the part about me breaking into Seth's house. I even told him that the man who had come by a few moments before Skirt had served me with a restraining order that Seth had initiated.

By the time I ended my confession, Matthew's face looked as hard as stone. And there was a look in his eyes that made me shudder. He no longer looked like the same man I knew. When he spoke again, he didn't sound like him, either.

"Rachel, I've been associated with law enforcement for a lot of years, and I've seen and heard all kinds of excuses as to why people commit crimes. But what you did . . ." Matthew paused and gave me a look I could not interpret. For a split second, he looked like he wanted to cry. "You fooled me."

"I didn't fool you. I didn't see any reason to tell you all this shit before now!"

"So what you're telling me is that you've been involved in criminal activity since you split with your ex?" he asked with a dumbfounded look on his face.

"I don't know if I'd call it that."

"What would you call it, Rachel? Last time I checked, it was against the law to tamper with another person's credit cards, commit vandalism against that person, and break into his house."

"That's all behind me now," I said. "I'm through with Seth Garrett. And low-life men like Skirt. Meeting you has made such a difference in my life."

"When did you decide that? From what you've just told me, you continued to do these things even after we met."

"I know, I know. But . . . I've made the statement I wanted to make. I had made up my mind to leave Seth alone. That's why I didn't call Skirt to go with me to break into his house."

"But you hacked into his e-mail and got the information you needed so that you could break into his house on your own. That's pretty low, Rachel," Matthew said, rising. "I'm sorry about dinner. I think I should leave!"

"You don't have to go!"

"Oh, yes, I do."

"But why? I'm through with Seth!"

"That's the same thing you told me in the casino restaurant that day."

"I was through with him then. I just . . . I was just still mad enough to do a few other things to him." I swallowed hard. What I was saying was not doing me much good, but I kept talking and making excuses, anyway. "And you don't have to worry about Skirt. I gave him his money, so he has no reason to speak to me again!"

Matthew had already made it to the door.

"When will I hear from you again?" I asked, grabbing his hand.

He snatched his hand out of mine and gave me a hopeless look. "I don't know," was all he said.

He walked out the door and slammed it shut so hard, every picture on my living room walls shook.

Chapter 65

Seth

*D*ARNELL CALLED ME FROM JAIL TWO DAYS AFTER THE cops had come to the house, looking for him. It was a few minutes after 6:00 p.m.

"Hey, Pops. You need to come bail me out of jail," he said. He sounded just as arrogant as always. "These damn roaches up in here is big as shot glasses, and the food is slop that a hog wouldn't eat."

"Did you do what they say you did, son?" I asked in the gentlest voice I could manage.

"Who me?"

"Yes, you. Did you participate in a robbery?"

"I ain't did nothing wrong! I was there, but I didn't do nothing but try to buy me some nachos and a moon pie! I was set up! I didn't know Derrick was going to pull out a gun!" he boomed. "Now when you coming to get me out of this motherfucker?"

It was April Fools' Day, and I felt like the biggest fool

of all, because I had lost complete control of my life. All because of the bad choices that I had made all my life. Well, it was time for me to start making some good choices, and I was going to start with my troubled son.

I sucked in some air and closed my eyes for a moment. Then, with renewed strength, I said, "I'm sorry, son. You're right where you need to be."

"What the fuck? You just a fucking punk, like Mama always said you was!"

"Darnell, I can't get you out of this. And to be honest with you, you had it coming. They . . ." I stopped because I was about to say the last thing I ever thought I would say, and I had to think about it for a few seconds first. I could not believe the next words out of my mouth. "Son, a few years ago, I betrayed somebody. She told me that karma was going to be a bitch in my case. And she was right."

"Karma, scharma! What the fuck kind of off-the-wall crap is that? I always knew you motherfuckers up here in Berkeley could come up with all kinds of weird, new age shit! I never thought my own daddy was into that shit! You just as bad as them white motherfuckers, talking all that smack! Karma, my ass!"

"Let me use a couple of phrases I'm sure you're probably more familiar with. What goes around comes around. And you've made your bed, and now you have to lie in it."

"Why, you no-good . . . I . . . I can't believe my ears! You one poor excuse for a black man!"

"And so are you," I said.

My son slammed down the phone so hard, my ears were still ringing five minutes later.

I spent most of the night drinking and wondering how I had allowed myself to end up with such a mess on my hands.

* * *

I had no idea where my wife was. She didn't get along that well with her family, so I didn't even bother calling her mother or any of her siblings. I called my mother instead, because she was the one Darla depended on the most when she needed a free babysitter.

"Mother, I'm sorry to be calling so late, but I was worried about Darla. Do you know where she is?"

"No, but she was here earlier. She didn't stay but a few minutes, though," Mother told me, sounding stressed. "That was around six o'clock this evening." It was almost midnight now.

I had to struggle to keep the anger out of my voice. "Did she leave Gayle with you again?"

"She sure did, honey."

"Did she say where she was going?"

"She said she was going out with a friend. That's all she told me. I put Gayle to bed hours ago, so you don't have to worry about coming to get her. She's got plenty of clothes over here, so I'll get her up and off to school tomorrow. Now you go to bed and get some sleep. You sound tired. Good night, baby."

"Good night, Mother."

I was so tired mentally and physically, I couldn't keep my eyes open. I fell asleep as soon as my head hit the pillow. I got up a few minutes before 6:00 a.m. the next morning to shower and dress. Darla was not at home.

Mother called around 8:00 a.m. "What time did Darla come home last night?"

"She didn't," I muttered. I felt so defeated, I wanted to crawl back into bed and stay there until things got better.

"My Lord! I hope she's not lying in a ditch somewhere! You'd better check with the hospitals." I didn't have the nerve to tell my mother that Darla had come home after I had gone to bed last night and then had gone back out. The only way I knew this was that she had left a big mess in the bathroom.

"Um, she called, though. She's fine. She had a little too much to drink and decided to spend the night with her friend."

"Bah! You need to sit her down and tell her she needs to start behaving like a married woman! She has no business running up and down the streets, drinking with her friends, when she should be at home with you and those kids. But I know how much Darnell gets on her nerves, so maybe it helps for her to get out once in a while."

"You're right, Mother." I agreed because I didn't want to prolong this conversation.

I went to work as if everything was peachy keen.

I didn't know which problem to address first—my son's dilemma or my wife. That was enough on my plate. But I still had to stay on guard as far as Rachel was concerned. I didn't know if the restraining order was going to be enough to keep her off my back, and if that didn't work, I didn't know what else to do. I did pray about it, though, but since I had not even been to church in years or acknowledged God in any other way, I wasn't sure He wanted to hear anything I had to say.

I picked Gayle up from my parents' house after I got off work. When I got home around six thirty, Darla was taking a bubble bath.

"I'm glad to see that you're all right," I told her as I stood in the bathroom doorway.

"Why wouldn't I be?" She gave me a disgusted look.

"Who was the friend you spent the night with?"

"Who said I spent the night with a friend?"

"You told Mother you were going out with a friend,

and you didn't call me to tell me otherwise. What else would I think?"

"You can think whatever you want. Now will you please shut that goddamned door?"

I couldn't believe that Darla had not asked about Gayle. "By the way, Mother took Gayle to school this morning."

"Good."

I rubbed the back of my neck, raked my hair back with my fingers, and moved a few steps closer to the bathtub. "Darla, we need to talk."

"About what?"

"We need to talk about a few things. We can start with Darnell. He called me from jail yesterday. He wasn't too happy when I refused to bail him out."

"I'm glad to see that you do have some balls, after all."

"Meaning what?"

"It doesn't matter. What else do we need to talk about?"

"Us, I guess."

"What about that Rachel bitch? What are you going to do about her if that restraining order doesn't keep her in line?"

"Please let me worry about Rachel. I'm more interested in talking about what I need to do about you. I'm willing to talk to a marriage counselor if you are."

Darla looked at me like I was speaking a foreign language. "A marriage counselor? I don't need to talk to a marriage counselor. There's nothing wrong with me."

"Fine. But I'm telling you now, I am not going to let things go on this way. I want this marriage to work, but I can't do it on my own."

"I know you're not threatening to divorce *me*," she said. That was followed by a snicker. "Is that what you're trying to tell me? Do it, then. I dare you! I'll take your bitch ass for everything you've got."

"You can have everything I've got."

"Well, you can forget about a divorce. I like being married."

"I like being married, too, but I'm trying to tell you that I am not going to stay in a marriage that is causing me so much pain. I never thought . . ." I couldn't even finish my sentence.

"Never thought what?"

"I never thought you'd change so much after we got married."

"Duck soup! I guess the next thing you'll tell me is that you wish you had married Rachel, after all, huh? I guess you sit around every day, wondering how things would have been if you had married that woman."

I dropped my head for a few seconds. Then I looked Darla in the eye. "I do. I wonder what my life would have been like if I had married that woman."

That must have been the last thing Darla expected to hear. When she spoke again, spit oozed out of the corners of her mouth like venom. "Well, it's not too late! You don't need to divorce me so you can run back to the bitch! I can pack my shit and be up out of here within an hour!"

"Rachel is not an option. I'm sure she doesn't want to be with me any more than I want to be with her. Under the circumstances, I'd be a damn fool to even consider resuming a relationship with her."

"You're a damn fool, anyway! And I must be one, too, because I don't know what in the world made me get involved with your lame ass in the first place. I wish I had boarded a different train that day I met you!"

"I wish you had, too, Darla."

* * *

Two more months went by, and Rachel had done nothing else to torment me. I assumed that the restraining order had made a major impact on her. But I was not convinced that I was out of the woods. *That woman* had gone for longer periods of time between incidents before, so a two-month break didn't really mean much.

All I could do now was wait.

Chapter 66

Rachel

LIKE I HAD TOLD SETH, THAT RESTRAINING ORDER WAS nothing to me but a piece of paper. It didn't stop me from fucking with him, but something a lot more serious did: I was pregnant. For the first time since I had begun to torture Seth, it didn't seem so important anymore. Knowing that I would soon have to be responsible for another human being made me realize just how critical it was for me to behave appropriately for a woman in my position. However, disrupting Seth's life had given me a strong sense of empowerment, something that I had had all along but had never really appreciated until now. I didn't need him or any other man to define me. I didn't need to retaliate when somebody betrayed me.

If I continued to do so, would I ever know where to draw the line? Had I not decided to change my routine, I would have had to go after people for the rest of my life! And that was not something I wanted to do. Now that I was thinking more clearly and rationally, there was one thing that suddenly became a major concern for me: what if karma kicked *me* in the ass as payback for all the shit I had done to Seth? I hadn't given that any thought until now. And I was giving it a *lot* of thought. . . .

Despite the morning sickness and my bloated belly, I felt so blessed, I wanted to do something to make someone else feel the same way.

It had been a week since Hurricane Katrina had devastated New Orleans. I organized a collection among my coworkers and neighbors, and we donated several thousand dollars to the Red Cross to help some of the families. And even though I didn't have any loved ones in the affected area, I wanted to stay informed about what was going on and what else I could do to help. When I was not at work, I was in front of my television, watching the news.

It had been four months since the night Matthew stormed out of my apartment. He had not called me, and I certainly had not called him. As far as I was concerned, our relationship was dead in the water. But Lucy didn't feel that way.

"Girl, when are you going to let that man know you're having his baby?" she'd asked.

"I'll tell him when the time is right," I'd told her.

Paulette was at Disneyland with her husband and their kids, and Patrice was at home, recovering from dental surgery. They knew I was pregnant, and they both felt the same way as Lucy. They had told me I needed to let Matthew know right away. "If he cared about me, he would have called me by now. I don't care what I did, I think he could have at least talked things through with me," I'd told everybody. But the one person who wouldn't let up on me was my mother.

"Do you mean to tell me you ain't told that man yet

that you will be giving birth to his baby in a few months? What's wrong with you, girl?" Mama had hollered. "Who is going to help you raise that baby?"

"I can raise my baby on my own," I'd insisted.

"A baby needs a mama and a daddy!"

"I know that. But you did all right with me and Janet and Ernest," I'd reminded.

Mama had let out a loud, raspy sigh. "And I always thought Janet would be the fool when it came to men. . . ."

"What are you trying to tell me, Mama?"

"Your sister, with all her problems, she knows more about making a relationship work than you do. She and that boy she is with, they make a perfect couple! Maybe you ought to talk to her and let her give you some advice. Since you don't want to listen to none of us normal folks!"

The only people who were not on my case about Matthew were Uncle Albert and Kingston.

"Baby, you do whatever you think is right for you and your child. I've still got your back," Uncle Albert had told me. "I'm handing the phone to Kingston."

"This kid will be spoiled rotten by the time we get through with him or her," Kingston had told me when he came on the line. "If you need anything, including a place to stay after you give birth and need to recuperate, you're welcome to come here."

I was happy to know I had people in my life who really cared about me. I'd hurried off the telephone because I didn't want Kingston to hear me crying.

One thing I did know was that Uncle Albert was not the one who had ratted me out to Matthew. To this day I didn't know who had contacted him and told him I was pregnant. He showed up at my door at the end of my fifth month.

Ever since Seth had sent that process server to my apartment, I had been very cautious about opening my front door. I never opened it now without checking to see who it was. When somebody knocked that Wednesday evening, I immediately looked through the peephole. I almost swallowed my tongue when I saw Matthew standing there.

"What are you doing here?" I cracked the door open just enough for him to see part of my face. "You've got some nerve showing up after all this time."

"Rachel, I came over here to talk to you about our relationship."

"What relationship?"

"You know what I'm talking about," he whined.

"Do I? Well, it took you long enough to get here," I smirked.

"I know, and I'm sorry. I wanted to come sooner. But I didn't know how you'd react. I mean, I know I pissed you off the last time I saw you, and . . . I didn't want to risk . . ."

"You didn't want to risk going through what Seth went through with me? So you thought I might go off and come after you, too? Did you think I would slash your tires and cancel your credit cards? Well, you don't have to worry about that. I haven't bothered Seth any more, and I don't plan to. I have more important things to deal with now."

"So I've heard. And when were you going to tell me about the baby?"

I felt as if I had been backed into a corner and the only way out was for me to come clean. "Who told you?"

"That's not important. What is important is that I know."

"How do you know it's yours?"

"Is it?"

"Yes, it is. But it's my problem."

"It's my 'problem,' too, if that's what you want to call it. I don't. I consider it a blessing."

"What do you want, Matthew?"

"I want to talk to you so we can decide what we're going to do about your condition." Matthew shifted his weight from one foot to the other. "Are you going to let me come in or not?"

"There is nothing for us to talk about—"

"The hell there isn't! If you're having my baby, there is a lot for us to talk about. We don't need to have a relationship, but I am going to be in that baby's life, whether you like it or not. We can figure out something either in or out of court. You decide."

I opened the door all the way and waved Matthew into my living room. "As long as you don't start any mess, there won't be any mess up in here," I warned.

"Woman, I can assure you, I am not going to do anything to set *you* off. My mama didn't raise no fool." Matthew laughed. It had been so long since I had laughed, my jaws ached when I stretched open my mouth to laugh along with him.

I was thrilled to see Matthew. If anybody could help me sort out my life, he was the one. I hadn't told any of my friends or even Mama, but the past few months I had been concerned about my mental health. For one thing, what I had done to Seth was not normal. Did I have a mental condition, too?

"Matthew, I am not sure I'm well. . . ." I had no idea why I said that.

Matthew gave me a puzzled look. "Why would you think that?"

"Because of my family history and the things I did to Seth."

"Look, if it'll make you feel any better, I can arrange for you to talk to a professional. Otherwise, what you did to Seth was not good, but it is not a sign of mental illness. I have dozens of parolees, male and female, on my list that have done a lot worse shit than you did, and they are all as sane as I am. So you need to get the notion that *you* have a mental condition out of your head. All right?"

I nodded. "All right." He was the right man for me. I realized that now. But I was not about to take anything for granted. However, had he touched me, I would have been all over him in a flash. That was why when I joined him on the couch, I left a lot of space between us.

"Listen, I am sorry about the way I took off that last night I was here. I drove home, but I came back an hour later. I sat in my car in front of your building until the next day," he confessed.

"Why didn't you come back inside or call me?"

"Like I just said, after you told me all that shit you'd done to old boy Seth, I didn't want to experience your wrath." Matthew didn't laugh this time. "Rachel, I love you, and I want to be with you. I think for our child's sake, we at least need to be friends."

I stared at the wall for a few moments.

"I wish . . . I wish I had never messed with Seth in the first place."

"You didn't love him?"

"Yes, I did. What I mean is, I wish I had been woman enough to accept his decision not to be with me—and the reason he decided that." I looked at Matthew and blinked. "To be honest with you, I don't know if I would have married him if he had told me his family had a history of mental illness."

"Rachel, let that go. What you need to focus on now is your future. Besides, I have a few demons I'd like to let go."

"Huh?"

"After my wife died, I didn't think I'd ever want to be in another serious relationship again, especially one that involved the possibility of me having children. The pain of my loss was too deep, and I didn't think I could go through it again. I didn't want to. When I met you, my feelings began to change. Even more so when we reconnected after being apart those few years. I was going to ask you to marry me. That's what I had planned to do the same night that Skirt fool showed up again."

"I still think you could have stayed and talked to me about it. And after the way Skirt behaved, I'm sure you believe me when I say I will *never* see him again."

"I believe you. But he's not the one I'm really worried about. I'm more concerned about you and Seth. Do you want to talk about him now?"

I shook my head. "I'm over Seth completely."

"Do you want us to try again? I mean, do you want to be with me as much as I want to be with you? We can take things one day at a time."

I gave Matthew a thoughtful look. "I was scared when I found out I was pregnant. I didn't know what I was going to do. I don't believe in abortion, and raising a child without a father is not something I thought I'd ever have to deal with."

"And you won't. I can promise you that. So?"

"I just want to know who told you I was pregnant, Matthew."

"All right. I'll tell you this much. It was someone who cares about you. That's all you need to know."

"I don't want to live with a man I'm not married to. I did that once, and I promised myself I'd never do it again."

"You don't have to." Matthew shrugged.

"Is that a proposal? Are you asking me to marry you?"

"What do you think?"

"If you're asking me to marry you, the answer is yes."

Epilogue

Seth

May 2015

*I*T HAD BEEN ELEVEN YEARS SINCE I'D SPOKEN TO RACHEL McNeal. I had spotted her in various places from time to time, shopping, having lunch with a friend, and just walking down the street. Each time I had ducked out of sight before she saw me.

I had no idea what I'd say to Rachel if I found myself in a predicament where I couldn't avoid her.

It had been almost two years since I had seen or spoken to Darla. After all that bellyaching she had done about me threatening to divorce her that night, that bitch had filed for divorce a month later! She hadn't even waited for it to be finalized before she bolted and moved in with the dude she'd been seeing behind my back the last year of our marriage.

Not only had she decided that she didn't like being a

wife, but she had also decided she didn't like being a mother, either. She had left Gayle with me and had not even hesitated to sign away her parental rights. I had been awarded full custody of Gayle, and Darla had never even asked for visitation privileges. That had saddened me, but I'd got over it soon enough. I was glad I didn't have to see her lying, skanky, cheating self anymore.

I still had my business, but things had changed dramatically. Most of my clients had either moved on to bigger agencies or decided to handle their advertising in-house. With so many other things on my plate, I had not been able to maintain the level of enthusiasm and commitment that I had started out with. I was making just enough money to remain afloat. I had to lay off most of my employees, so now it was just Howard and myself. We couldn't even afford to pay a full-time secretary, so we had temps come in on an as-needed basis. We had to move back to a much cheaper location, too.

I had sold my house three years ago and had moved into a two-bedroom condo near the school my daughter attended, when she felt like going to school. She was only twelve, and so far she had been kicked out of three different schools because of her bad behavior. At the last school, she had slapped her homeroom teacher when the teacher had told her to stop texting. In the school before that, she'd stolen one of her classmate's earrings, then had had the nerve to wear them to school the very next day. When the girl confronted her, she'd punched that girl in the nose.

My son was twenty-nine and still lived with me. He hadn't worked in two years, and he continued to break the law. He had just been released from jail again a few weeks ago for attempting to rob a bank. I had just dropped him off to meet with his parole officer that Monday afternoon in May, the week before Memorial Day. I had an appointment with a therapist who'd been helping me work through a few lingering issues. His office was in the same building as my son's parole officer. I planned to swing back and pick up Darnell after my session so we could have a late lunch.

I avoided my parents and almost everybody else, including my brother Josh, who had always been in my corner. I had a hard time being around "happy" people and trying not to let them know how much pain I was in. I had convinced myself that depression had become my new BFF.

I looked at life from a much more realistic perspective now. One reason was that I truly believed in karma now. And not because of what Rachel had done to me. She had got her revenge, but she had nothing to do with the problems that I had encountered with my wife and children. That was the part of karma that hurt me the most. I prayed that my debt to fate had been paid in full. Because of all I'd been through, I had stopped lying and using people. I'd promised myself that I would go out of my way in the future not to hurt another person, especially a woman. I'd met a few fantastic women since Darla left, but so far, none of those relationships had panned out. No matter how fantastic those other women had been, not a single one had come close to being as fantastic as Rachel Mc-Neal had been to me—before I pissed her off and she tried to drive my ass crazy with her revenge tactics.

Despite all the things that Rachel had done to me, she was the one woman I would never forget. I had finally reached a point where I felt that the nightmare that had begun with that trip to Alabama was over. Had I married her, things would have turned out a lot differently for me. I believed that with Rachel's guidance, my son would not have become a criminal. And I would never have met a witch like Darla. On my more pleasant days, I wondered about the children that Rachel and I would have had. . . .

I was waiting for the elevator so I could go to my therapist's office two floors below when I felt someone walk up and stand beside me. I was so preoccupied, I didn't notice her at first. Then I saw her out of the corner of my eye. I was so taken aback that before I could stop myself, I yelled her name. "Rachel! Oh, my God!" I couldn't believe my eyes. She had been on my mind just seconds before.

She whirled around and gasped when she realized it was me. She looked as stunning as ever. Even with noticeable lines on her forehead and around her mouth, and a few strands of gray hair on her head. She wore a light blue dress and navy blue pumps. Her make-up was flawless, and her hair was in a braided style that was very becoming on her.

"Seth! It's so good to see you!" she said with not a hint of hostility in her voice.

I was glad to see her, but I didn't get too close. I had no hard feelings toward her, but I had no idea how she felt about me now. With the way I was feeling, the last thing I needed was for her to slap my face and cuss me out. I was flabbergasted when she hauled off and hugged me. She felt so good in my arms, but she didn't stay in them long. She moved back a few steps. There was a smile on her face, and that put me more at ease.

"It's been so long! How have you been?"

"I'm doing just great, Seth."

"How is your uncle Albert? Is he still with Kingston?"

"Puh-leeze! Those two are joined at the hip." She rolled her eyes in mock exasperation. "They got married last year and are in the process of adopting a little Haitian girl with HIV whose mother abandoned her."

"Is that right? I'm glad to hear that there are still some people left in the world who are willing to take on a responsibility like that."

"So am I."

I couldn't figure out why my heart was thumping so hard or why I had begun to sweat. Rachel was not behaving in a hostile manner at all. I wiped my forehead and continued. "And what about your posse? I don't remember the last time I saw Lucy or either one of the two Ps."

"Lucy married some guy she met on one of her cruises five years ago, and they live in Dallas. They have two little girls. Paulette and her husband had another little boy about three years ago, and they moved to San Diego to take care of his elderly parents. Patrice stopped speaking to me about ten years ago. Lucy and Paulette only hear from her every now and then. The last I heard, she had moved to New Jersey and had married an airline pilot. How is your family?"

"Uh, my father got involved with another woman, and when Mother found out, she promptly divorced him. She's doing as well as can be expected. Father's affair hit the family real hard. I knew he'd been having affairs for years, but he'd always been very discreet. Well, believe it or not, the other woman was my brother Damon's wife, Helene. Uh, I'm sure she went after him, though, because he was not the type to fool around with women too close to home. Especially the woman of his own son. I'm surprised Father never tried to hit on you."

Rachel's eyes got big, and her lips trembled for a few seconds, as if she was about to laugh. She didn't laugh, but she snorted, and a mysterious smile appeared on her face. "I guess I wasn't his type." She cleared her throat with a few short coughs. "How are your brothers doing?"

"Josh and his wife have four kids now. Damon immediately divorced his wife when he found out about her and Father. Damon married a girl from Jamaica six years ago. They have a son and a daughter."

"And how are *you* doing these days?"

I had to think carefully before I answered. I didn't want Rachel to know the extent of my remorse. "Well . . . I've learned from my mistakes," I admitted. "I'm still getting used to middle age." I chuckled, patting my expanding belly. "Other than that, I am doing just fine, too."

"I'm glad to hear that." I expected her to give me a smug look, but she didn't. Instead, she gave me a sympathetic look and then another smile. "Are you and your family ready for the holiday?"

"My wife divorced me years ago. I don't even know where she and the man she was having an affair with moved to." I tried to sound as composed as possible. I didn't want Rachel to know just how bitter I was. But things didn't seem as intense today. Her presence and upbeat demeanor had brightened my mood tremendously.

"Oh. I'm sorry to hear that. Then you don't get to see your daughter?"

"Darla left Gayle with me." I snorted.

"Oh," she said again. "I hope you'll enjoy the holiday, anyway."

I nodded. "I'm sure I will. My mother is going to barbecue, and some of her folks from Louisiana are in town. What about you?"

"My husband and I are leaving for Mexico on Friday. We usually spend our holidays down there in the condo we own in Puerto Vallarta."

"So you're married now?" As soon as I said that, I realized what a stupid question it was. A woman like Rachel had probably been proposed to by more than one man after I broke up with her.

"My husband works in this building, and I dropped by to see if he wanted to take me to lunch. But he was just about to talk to one of his parolees, a young man who can't stay out of trouble."

"Uh, I just dropped my son off for his regular meeting with his parole officer. Matthew Bruner seems like a caring dude, and Darnell likes him."

Rachel's eyes got as big as saucers. "Matthew Bruner is my husband!"

"What a coincidence! I guess it is a small world, after all, huh?"

"I guess it is, Seth."

The elevator stopped, but we both ignored it.

"Uh, I hope I'm not being too forward, but can we go have a cup of coffee? I am really happy to see you, and I'm really happy to see that you are doing so well."

"I'd love to," she said.

There was a coffee shop within walking distance, and that was where we went. As soon as we sat down, I started sharing my tale of woe, and I didn't want to stop. I noticed tears in Rachel's eyes when I told her how out of control my daughter was and how my son kept going to jail.

I expected her to gloat, but she didn't.

"I feel so blessed to have such a wonderful husband and a daughter who has never given us any trouble. I'm sorry to hear that your wife left you. And I'm really sorry to hear about your children." It almost sounded like she was apologizing to me because her life had turned out so well. "My daughter, Camille, is on the honor roll, and she's already talking about what college she wants to go to. She's only ten and already reads on a high school level!"

I gave Rachel a pensive look. "You know what's so ironic?"

"What?"

"I . . . I didn't want to marry you, because I thought we'd have children with some serious problems. My folks are intellectuals, so they would have had a hard time dealing with your folks down the road. Well, the class thing is what it is. But I ended up with children with serious problems, anyway. But you didn't. And neither one of mine can blame their behavior on a mental condition like your—"

"You can go ahead and say it. It doesn't bother me at all. Just to let you know, my sister, Janet, is happily married and has two sons. And neither one of them has any problems . . . so far. Mama finally put my brother in one of those board and care homes, and he's doing so much better, she's mad at herself for not putting him there sooner. But I still feel that my family is blessed. Things could have been a lot worse. My mother could have had a lot more serious problems to deal with."

"Like I have? After all the planning and scheming I did, you're the one who ended up with the perfect marriage and a perfect child. . . ."

Rachel shook her head. "My child is not perfect, and my marriage isn't, either. We have the same issues that most families have."

"Rachel, I need to ask you something. You don't have to answer me if you don't want to. Did you really love me?"

"I did. And before I leave, I want you to know that I am really sorry about what I did to you. It was wrong. I knew it was wrong when I was doing it, but all I cared about was getting back at you."

"And you sure did that! I can't tell you which one of your stunts pissed me off the most! But that time my credit card got declined while I was having lunch with a potential client was bad. That's the one thing I think about the most. I'm so paranoid now that when I pull out a credit card to pay for a purchase, I hold my breath until I know it's been approved." I laughed.

"Well, if it'll make you feel any better, last month, when I attempted to make a purchase at a Walmart, of all places, they declined my credit card."

"Oh?"

"But only because I had reached my credit limit." We both laughed.

"Rachel, I need to ask you something that's been eating at me for years."

"What's that?"

"Did you sic the IRS on me?"

She looked me in the eye and nodded with a straight face. "Did they come down hard on you?"

"Like a boulder." I sighed. "Well, that was my own fault. It took me almost eight years to pay them off in full. I haven't told even the smallest fib on my taxes since."

"I'm glad to hear that, Seth."

"Anyway, I'm glad I ran into you. I wish you nothing but the best." I held my breath and tried to come up with the right words to say next. I had to blink hard to hold back my tears. "Rachel, I should have apologized to you years ago about the reason I didn't want to marry you. I'm doing it now, and I mean it from the bottom of my heart. I was a fool, and I eventually realized that."

My belated apology surprised Rachel. She gasped and began to stutter. "Seth . . . I . . . I . . . I accept your apology. I owe you one, too."

"And I accept it. Like I just said, I wish you nothing but the best."

"I wish you the same, Seth." She looked at her watch and exhaled. She stared at me; I stared back. I didn't know what to say next, and apparently, she didn't, either. Finally, she looked at her watch and said, "I want to run over to Macy's and pick up a few items to take with me to Mexico, so I'd better get going."

With her eyes still on mine, she rose. Our table was in front of a window near the entrance. When she stood up straight, a bright ray of sunshine streamed in and illuminated her face. It gave her a glow that almost seemed like divine intervention. Maybe it was because a feeling of warmth and peace came over me and made me want to look at my situation from a different point of view.

I knew then that my outlook on life was going to improve dramatically, because I had finally made peace with the only woman I had ever truly loved.

"Good-bye, Seth. It was really nice seeing you, and . . . no hard feelings, right?"

"Right." It felt so good to tell the truth. The more I told the truth, the better I felt. I couldn't wait to see what the future held for me now that I had become the man I should have been years ago.

"Good luck, Seth."

"The same to you, Rachel."

I stood up and was about to walk off in the opposite direction. But before I could, she trotted up to me and gave me another hug and a quick kiss on the cheek. It made me feel better than I had in a long time.

DON'T MISS

ONE HOUSE OVER

by Mary Monroe

A solid marriage, a thriving business, and the esteem of their close-knit Alabama community—Joyce and Odell Watson have every reason to count their blessings. Their marriage has given well-off Joyce a chance at the family she's always wanted—and granted Odell a once-in-a-lifetime shot to escape grinding poverty. But all that respectability and status comes at a cost . . .

Enjoy the following excerpt from *One House Over* . . .

Chapter 1

Joyce

June 1934

OTHER THAN MY PARENTS, I WAS THE ONLY OTHER person at the supper table Sunday evening. But there was enough food for twice as many people. We'd spent the first five minutes raving about Mama's fried chicken, how much we had enjoyed Reverend Jessup's sermon a few hours ago, and other mundane things. When Daddy cleared his throat and looked at me with his jaw twitching, I knew the conversation was about to turn toward my spinsterhood.

"I hired a new stock boy the other day and I told him all about you. He is just itching to get acquainted. This one is a real nice, young, single man," Daddy said, looking at me from the corner of his eye.

I froze because I knew where this conversation was going: my "old maid" status. The last "real nice, young, single man" Daddy had hired to work in our store and tried to dump off on me was a fifty-five-year-old, tobacco-chewing, widowed grandfather named Buddy Armstrong. There had been several others before him. Each one had grandkids and health problems. Daddy was eighty-two, so to him anybody under sixty was "young." He and Mama had tried to have children for thirty years before she gave birth to me thirty years ago, when she was forty-eight. But I hadn't waited this long to settle for a husband who'd probably become disabled or die of old age before he could give me the children I desperately wanted.

I was tempted to stay quiet and keep my eyes on the ads for scarves in the new Sears and Roebuck catalog that I had set next to my plate. But I knew that if I didn't say something on the subject within the next few seconds, Daddy would harp on it until I did. Mama would join in, and they wouldn't stop until they'd run out of things to say. And then they would start all over again. I took a deep breath and braced myself. "Daddy, I work as a teacher's aide. What do I have in common with a *stock boy*?"

Daddy raised both of his thick gray eyebrows and looked at me like I was speaking a foreign language. "Humph! Y'all both single! That's what y'all got in common?" he growled.

"I can find somebody on my own!" I boomed. I never raised my voice unless I was really upset, like I was now.

Daddy shook his head. "Since you thirty now and still ain't got no husband—or even a boyfriend—it don't look like you having much luck finding somebody on your own, girl."

"Mac is right, Joyce. It's high time for you to start socializing again. It's a shame the way you letting life pass you by," Mama threw in. They were both looking at me so hard, it made me more uncomfortable than I already was. I squirmed in my seat and cleared my throat.

"Anyway, he said he can't wait to meet you. He is so worldly and sharp, he'll be a good person for you to conversate with."

"I hope you didn't say 'conversate' in front of this new guy. That's a word somebody made up," I scolded. "The correct word is *converse*."

Daddy gave me a pensive look and scratched his neck. "Hmmm. Well, *somebody* 'made up' all the words in every language, eh?"

"Well, yeah, but—"

"What difference do it make which one I used as long as he knew what I meant?"

"Yes, but—"

"Then I'll say conversate if I want to, and you can say converse. It's still English, and this is the only language I know—and it's too complicated for me to be trying to speak it correct this late in the game. Shoot." My Daddy. He was a real piece of work. He winked at me before he bit off a huge chunk of cornbread and started chewing so hard his ears wiggled. He swallowed and started talking again with his eyes narrowed. "I got a notion to invite him to eat supper with us one evening. He is a strapping man, so he'd appreciate a good home-cooked meal. I even told him how good you can cook, Joyce. . . ."

My parents had become obsessed with helping me find a husband. My love life—or lack of a love life—was a frequent subject in our house. One night I dreamed that they'd lined up men in our front yard and made me parade back and forth in front of them so they could inspect me. But even in a dream nobody wanted to marry me.

"What's wrong with this one? Other than him being just a stock boy?" I mumbled as I rolled my eyes.

"Why come you think something is wrong with him?" Daddy laughed but so far, nobody had said something funny enough to make me laugh. If anything, I wanted to cry.

"Because he wants to meet *me*," I said with my voice cracking. My self-esteem had sunk so low, and I felt so unworthy, I didn't know if I'd want a man who would settle for me. "He's probably homelier and sicklier than Buddy Armstrong." I did laugh this time.

"I met him and I sure didn't see nothing wrong with him," Mama piped in. She drank some lemonade and let out a mild burp before she continued. "He ain't nowhere near homely."

"Or sickly," Daddy added with a snort.

"And he's right sporty and handsome!" Mama sounded like a giddy schoolgirl. I was surprised to see such a hopeful look on her face. Despite all the wrinkles, liver spots, and about fifty pounds of extra weight, she was still attractive. She had big brown eyes and a smile that made her moon face look years younger. Unlike Daddy, who had only half of his teeth left, she still had all of hers. They were so nice and white, people often asked if they were real. She was the same pecan shade of brown as me and Daddy. But I had his small, sad black eyes and narrow face. He'd been completely bald since he was fifty and last week on my thirtieth birthday he'd predicted that if I had any hair left by the time I turned forty, it would probably all be gray. I'd found my first few strands of gray hair the next morning. "I know you'll like this one," Mama assured me with a wink. She reared back in her wobbly chair and raked her thick fingers through her thin gray hair. "You ain't getting no younger, so you ain't got much time left," she reminded.

"So you keep telling me," I snapped.

Mama sucked on her teeth and gave me a dismissive wave. "He got slaphappy when we told him about you. I bet he been beating the women off with a stick all his life."

Mama's taste in potential husbands for me was just as pathetic as Daddy's. But her last comment really got my attention because it sounded like a contradiction. "Why would a 'sporty and handsome' man get 'slaphappy' about meeting a new woman—especially if he's already beating them off with a stick?" I wanted to know.

Daddy gave me an annoyed look. "Don't worry about a little detail like that. And don't look a gift horse in the mouth. You ain't been out on a date since last year, and I know that must be painful. Shoot. When I was young, and before I married your mama, I never went longer than a week without courting somebody. At the rate you going, you ain't never going to get married."

I'd celebrated my thirtieth birthday eight days ago, but I felt more like a woman three times my age. Most of the adult females I knew were already married. My twenty-five-year-old cousin Louise had been married and divorced twice and was already engaged again. "I guess marriage wasn't meant for me," I whined. I suddenly lost my appetite, so I pushed my plate to the side.

"You ain't even touched them pinto beans on your plate, and you ate only half of your supper yesterday," Mama complained. "How do you expect to get a man if you ain't got enough meat on your bones? You already look like a lamppost, and you know colored men like thick women. Besides, a gal six feet tall like you need to eat twice as much as a shorter woman so there's enough food to fill out all your places."

"It ain't about how much I weigh," I said defensively. "Last year I weighed twenty pounds more than I do now, and it didn't make a difference. But . . . I wish I could shrink down to a normal height." I laughed, but I was serious. For a colored woman, being too tall was almost as bad as being too dark and homely. I wasn't as dark or homely as some of the women I knew, but I was the tallest and the only one my age still single.

"Well, look at it this way, baby girl. You ain't no Kewpie doll and you may be too lanky for anybody to want to marry you, but at least you got your health. A lot of women don't even have that." Daddy squeezed my hand and smiled. "And you real smart."

I was thankful that I was healthy and smart, but those things didn't do a damn thing for my overactive sex drive. If a man didn't make love to me soon, I was going to go crazy. And the way I'd been fantasizing about going up to a stranger in a beer garden or on the street and asking him to go to bed with me, maybe I had already lost my mind. "Can I be excused? I have a headache," I muttered, rubbing the back of my head.

"You said the same thing when we was having supper yesterday," Mama reminded.

"I had a headache then, too," I moaned. I rose up out of my chair so fast, I almost knocked it over. With my head hanging low, I shuffled around the corner and down the hall to my bedroom. I'd been born in the same room, and the way my life was going, I had a feeling I'd die in it too.

Branson was a typical small town in the southern part of Alabama. It was known for its cotton and sugarcane fields and beautiful scenery. Fruit and pecan trees, and flowers of every type and color decorated most of the residents' front and back yards. But things were just as gloomy here as the rest of the South.

Our little city had only about twenty thousand people and most of them were white. Two of our four banks had crashed right after the Great Depression started almost five years ago. But a few people had been smart enough to pull their money out just in time. Our post office shared the same building with the police department across the street from our segregated cemetery.

Jim Crow, the rigid system that the white folks had created to establish a different set of rules for them and us, was strictly enforced. Basically, what it meant was that white people could do whatever they wanted, and we couldn't eat where they ate, sleep or socialize with them, or even sass them. Anybody crazy enough to violate the rules could expect anything from a severe beating to dying at the hands of a lynch mob. A lot of our neighbors and friends worked for wealthy white folks in the best neighborhoods, but all of the colored residents lived on the south side. And it was segregated too. The poor people lived in the lower section near the swamps and the dirt roads. The ones with decent incomes, like my family, lived in the upper section.

The quiet, well-tended street we lived on was lined with magnolia and dogwood trees on both sides. Each house had a neat lawn, and some had picket fences. The brown-shingled house with tar paper roofing and a wrap-around front porch we owned had three bedrooms. The walls were thin, so when Mama and Daddy started talking again after I'd bolted from the supper table, I could hear them. And, I didn't like what they were saying.

"Poor Joyce. I just ball up inside when I think about how fast our baby is going to waste. I'm going to keep praying for her to find somebody before it's too late," Mama grumbled. "With her strong back she'd be a good workhorse and keep a clean house and do whatever else she'll need to do to keep a husband happy. And I'd hate to see them breeding hips she got on her never turn out no babies." Mama let out a loud, painful-sounding groan.

"What's even worse is, I would hate to leave this world knowing she was going to grow old alone."

"I'm going to keep praying for her to get married too. But that might be asking for too much. I done almost put a notion like that out of my mind. This late in the game, the most we can expect is to fix her up with somebody who'll court her for a while, so she can have a little fun before she get too much older," Daddy grunted. "Maybe we ain't been praying hard enough, huh?"

"We been praying hard enough, but that ain't the problem," Mama snapped.

"Oh? Then what is it?"

"The problem is this girl is too doggone picky!" Mama shouted.

"Sure enough," Daddy agreed.

I couldn't believe my ears! My parents were trying to fix me up with a stock boy, not a businessman, and they thought I was being too picky. I wanted to laugh and cry at the same time. A lot of ridiculous things had been said to and about me. Being "too picky" was one of the worst because it couldn't have been further from the truth.

I had no idea how my folks had come to such an off-the-wall conclusion. I couldn't imagine what made them think I was too picky. I'd given up my virginity when I was fourteen to Marvin Galardy, the homeliest boy in the neighborhood. And that was only because he was the only one interested in having sex with me at the time.

I was so deep in thought, I didn't hear Daddy knocking on my door, so he let himself in. "You done gone deaf, too?" he grumbled.

"I didn't hear you," I mumbled, sitting up on my bed.

"You going to the evening church service with us? We'll be leaving in a few minutes."

"Not this time, Daddy. My head is still aching, so I

think I just need to lie here and take it easy." I rubbed the side of my head.

"And it's going to keep on hurting if you don't take some pills."

"I'll take some before I go to sleep."

Daddy turned to leave, and then he snapped his fingers. "I forgot the real reason I came in here. Mother's going to Mobile tomorrow morning with Maxine Fisher to do some shopping and she'll be gone most of the day. If you ain't got no plans for lunch tomorrow and that headache is gone, I'll swing by the school around noon to pick you up and we can go to Mosella's. Monday is the only day peach cobbler is on the menu, and I been dying for some."

"You don't have to drive all the way from the store to pick me up. That's out of your way. One of the other aides has an appointment with her doctor in the same block, so I can ride with her and have her drop me off at the store. I need to pick up a few items anyway."

"That'll work," Daddy said, rubbing his chest. "I'll see you around noon then?"

"Okay, Daddy."

It was still light outside, but I went to bed anyway. Each day I slept more than I needed and wished I could sleep even more. At least then I wouldn't have to talk to people, walk around with a fake smile on my face.

Chapter 2

Odell

I WAS SO ANXIOUS TO GET BACK TO WORK, I COULDN'T WAIT for tomorrow to come. I'd only been on my new job at MacPherson's since for a week. It was a dyed-in-the wool country convenience store with benches inside for people to sit on when they needed to take a break from their shopping. Regular customers could expect a complimentary pig foot or some lip-smacking pork rinds on certain days. I could already tell that this was the best job I ever had. It was a nice family-friendly business, and I was really looking forward to the experience, especially since I'd be working for colored folks. Mr. MacPherson didn't pay me that much to start, but as long as it covered my rent I didn't care. I was a born hustler, so I knew I'd find ways to cover my other expenses once I got a toehold on my new situation. Stocking shelves was much better than dragging along on farms and other odd jobs I'd done all my life. The small building where MacPherson's was located sat on a corner next to a bait shop. There was a sign printed in all capital letters in the front window that said: WE SELL EVERYTHING FROM APRONS TO MENS' PINSTRIPE SUITS. But they never had more than six or seven of each item in stock at a time. When inventory got low, the MacPhersons immediately replenished everything and gave their customers discounts when they had to wait on a certain item. The customers were happy because this kind of service kept them from having to make the eight-mile trip to nearby Butler where there was a Piggly Wiggly and much bigger department stores.

People kept complaining about the Great Depression we was going through, but it didn't even faze me. Like almost every other colored person, I couldn't tell the difference because we'd been going through a "depression" all our lives. Some of the white folks who used to have enough money to shop at the better stores started shopping at MacPherson's. On my first day, me and Mr. MacPherson had to help a nervous blond woman haul a box of canned goods, some cleaning products, produce, toys, and even a few clothes to her car. The whole time she'd belly-ached to him about what a disgrace it was to her family that they had to shop where all the colored people shopped, something she'd never done before. In the next breath, she complimented him on how "happy-go-lucky" he was for a colored man, and because of that he was "a credit to his race."

One of the things I noticed right away was how loosey-goosey the MacPhersons ran their business. Like a lot of folks, they didn't trust banks, especially since so many people had lost every cent and all the property they owned when the banks failed. One of the richest white families I used to pick cotton for had ended up flat broke and had to move to a tent city campground with other displaced families.

Preston "Mac" MacPherson and his wife, Millie, only kept enough in their checking account to cover their employees' checks and to pay their business expenses. I'd found that out from Buddy Armstrong, the tubby, fish-eyed head cashier and the nosiest, grumpiest, and biggest blabbermouth elderly man I'd ever met. The other cashier, a pint-sized, plain-featured, widowed great-grandmother named Sadie Mae Glutz was almost as bad as Buddy.

On my first day, they'd started running off at the mouth before the first morning break, telling me all kinds of personal things about people I had never met. Buddy and Sadie was good entertainment, so I pretended to be interested in their gossip and even egged them on. The MacPhersons was their favorite target. Even though it was supposed to be a company "secret," they wasted no time telling me that Mr. MacPherson kept most of his money locked up in his house. At the end of each day he'd plucked all the cash out of the two cash registers and stuff it into a brown paper bag.

"I hope that information don't get to the wrong person. I'd hate to hear about some joker busting into that house robbing such a nice elderly couple," I said.

"You ain't got to worry about nothing like that. Mac keeps a shotgun in the house," Buddy assured me.

"I hope he never has to use it," I chuckled.

"He done already done that," Sadie added. Before I could ask when and why, she continued. "A couple of years ago, some fool tried to steal Mac's car out of his driveway. Mac ran out just in time to stop that jackass."

"Did he kill him?" I asked, looking from Sadie to Buddy.

"Naw. He shot at him, but he missed," Buddy answered. "And that sucker took off in such a hurry, he ran clean out of his shoes. Then he had the nerve to try and steal another man's car in the same neighborhood. He wasn't so lucky that time. I was one of the pallbearers at his funeral."

"I'm glad Mr. MacPherson didn't kill that thief. He is such a nice man, I'd hate for him to get involved with the law," I stated.

"Thank you. Him and Millie got enough problems already. Especially trying to marry off that gal of theirs." Sadie shook her head and clucked her thick tongue. "She grown and still living at home. And she look like the kind of woman no man in his right mind would tangle with. She a whole head taller than me and probably twice as strong. If I seen her fighting a bear, I'd help the bear. Wouldn't you do the same thing, Buddy?"

"Sure enough." Buddy chuckled for a few seconds, and then he started yip-yapping about Joyce some more. "And she got the nerve to flirt with me almost every time I see her, with her *mugly* self."

"'Mugly'? What's that?" I asked.

"Oh, that's just a nicer way of calling somebody ugly. Anyway, she been messing with me ever since I started working here last September, grinning and sashaying in front of me like a shake dancer. But I would never get involved with a woman with feet bigger than mine. First time I make her mad, she'd stomp a hole in me."

This was the first time I'd heard about Joyce, and it wouldn't be the last. Every time things got slow on my first day, Buddy and Sadie would wander over to where I was stacking or reorganizing merchandise and start conversating and laughing about the MacPhersons' pitiful daughter.

"Y'all got me so curious now, I can't wait to meet this beast," I admitted, laughing along with them.

"You'll see exactly what we mean when you do meet her," Sadie told me.

"Why don't y'all like her? Is she mean-spirited, too?"

Buddy and Sadie gasped at the same time. "No, she ain't no mean person at all, and we do like her," Sadie claimed. "We talk about all the folks we know like this. But Joyce is such an oddball; we talk about her a little more than we do everybody else."

"I hope you'll like her too," Buddy threw in. "She ain't got many friends, so she need all the ones she can get."

By the end of the day, I had heard so many unflattering things about the MacPhersons' big-boned "old maid" daughter, it seemed like I'd known her for years. I felt so sorry for her. The next day when Mr. MacPherson bragged about how smart and nice and caring his only child was and how much he loved her, I told him I couldn't wait to meet her. I'd only said it to make him feel good, because I wanted to make sure I did everything possible for him to keep me on the payroll. I had heard that the stock boys before me had never lasted more than a few weeks. A couple had just up and quit, but the MacPhersons had fired all the others. I hoped that I'd get to stay a lot longer, or at least until I found a better job.

I had just enough money to last until I got my first paycheck. Mr. MacPherson had promised that if he was pleased with my work and I got to work on time, he'd eventually give me more responsibilities and more money. He really liked me and even told me I reminded him of himself when he was my age. I told him that if I looked half as good as he did when I got to be his age, I'd be happy. That made him blush and grin, and it made me realize that complimenting a man like him could win me a lot of points. It was true that I had a lot going for me in the looks department. But I never took it for granted. People had been telling me I was cute since I was a baby. My curly black hair, smooth Brazil nut brown skin, slanted black eyes, and juicy lips got me a lot of attention. One of the main things the women liked about me and complimented me on all the time was my height, which was six feet four.

Some women believed that old wives' tale that tall men had long sticks between their legs. I couldn't speak for other tall men, but I had enough manly meat between my thighs to keep the women I went to bed with sure enough happy. I wasn't just tall; I had a body like a prize-fighter. Years of backbreaking farm labor had rewarded me with some muscles that wouldn't quit. Women couldn't keep their hands off me. When I was younger, I used to have to sneak out back doors in bars just to throw them off my trail. I was thirty-one now, so I still had a few good years left to find a wife and have children before my jism got too weak. I was between ladies now, and because my last two breakups had been so bad, I was in no hurry to get involved with another woman anytime soon. I changed my tune Monday afternoon when I met Mr. MacPherson's daughter.